The Way Back
To Florence

Glenn Haybittle

Published by Cheyne Walk

www.cheynewalk.com

ISBN-13: 978-0-9932863-0-8

Photo by: www.lospecosmutantes.com

Acknowledgements

For inspiration, sustenance and feedback, thanks to:

Charles Cecil, Freddie de Rougemont, Georgiana Anstruther, Emily Pennock, VJ Keegan, Cayetana Soto de Garcillàn, Hugo Wilson, Rupert Alexander, Eloise Anson, Alex Tobey, Jessica St. James, Robert Indge, Charlie Warde, Mary Killen, Paola Rosà, Tim Binding, Alex Preston, Mark Jackson, Annabel Merullo, Charlie Campbell, Justin Sparrow, Anna von Kanitz, Christabel Brudnell-Bruce, Marc Dalessio, Vanessa Garwood, Antonia Barclay, Cristina Zamagni, Paolo Cristellotti, Talitha Stevenson, Hamid Khanbhai, Mark Roberts, Freya Wood, Richard Burton, Katie St. George, Charlotte Raymond, Josephine Rea, Caroline Scott, Ebba Heuman, Marco at Osteria dei Benci, Stefano at Tarocchi.

Author's Note:

For purposes of heightening drama, I've taken one or two mischievous liberties with historical fact in this novel, most notably my RAF raid on Florence in 1943. This never happened. It was the USAAF who carried out this particular raid.

Poor ghost, old love, speak
with your old voice
of flaming insight
that kept us awake all night.
In one bed and apart...

~ Robert Lowell, *The Old Flame*

Part One

1 - September 1943

SHE DIPS THE BRUSH into the copper pot of balsam. She is still, at twenty-six, experimenting with mediums, with glazes, with all her manifold materials. She has learned how untrustworthy the chemicals she needs for her art are. The primers, the pigments, the sun-thickened oils. They betray her constantly, like unfaithful lovers.

I paint from nature; I paint what I see.

She adds medium to the colour she has mixed on her palette. Her palette with its pageantry of firebrand earth colours. She squints at the flow of light on the boy's face. The choreography of shadow shapes and submerged half tones. She adds another touch of cadmium red to the colour she has made on her palette. The oily colour glistens pink like the flesh of a newly spliced watermelon. She holds out her sable brush as she strides forward. Her narrowed blue eyes move back and forth between the image on the canvas and the face of the boy by its side. Seeking out the essence of his form, the lights and shadows of his personality. There is a rhythm in the act, as if a pendulum swings back and forth in her mind. She strokes down lines on the air as she walks, quick corkscrewing flourishes of the brush, rehearsing her intention, marshalling her forces, whipping up her blood. She stops at her easel. Stands forward on her toes. Makes a new mark on the canvas. In her idle left hand she holds a dozen brushes, splayed out like a fan.

Today is a good day. Today she feels she is the master of her craft. Today she is free of the grinding tyranny of doubt. The voice that mocks her ambition. The voice that bites and slanders and causes her more heartache than any other voice. Today she is focused, she is exultant. Her every brushstroke like a wake of radiance. Today she can move the paint around the canvas at will. If only painting were like this every day. Without the sudden extinguishing of light, the collapsing of belief, the cursing and flailing, the knots and clenched fists in a world gone suddenly dark.

Sharp lines draw too much attention to themselves, like vanity. What's vanity but a series of sharp lines which have yet to be softened?

Maestro's teachings are often in her head. She hears him deliver them in his clipped fey voice. His critiques. Like psalms. Psalms they, his students, were expected to learn by heart.

She picks up another, smaller brush. Weighs it in her hand. Chews the end while staring at her picture.

The boy, Leo, blinks when she studies him. She senses he has to steel himself against the audacity of her exacting eye. He sits with the sleeves of his jersey pulled down over his hands.

There is a physical intimacy when she is up at her canvas, when they are side by side. His body heat, his heartbeat, some essence of his being is part of her mood as she lays down paint. She breathes him in, breathes him out, onto the canvas. Sometimes she feels an impulse to touch his face, to trace the contours of his skull with her hand.

She lays down a brushstroke, smudges it delicately with her finger. There is paint beneath her nails, ingrained in the lines on her palms. Her smock is a grubby rainbow of fused colours. She wipes her brushes on the blue fabric. Everything in the studio is peppered with pigment, smeared with oil paint, sticky with resins. The coins and banknotes in her purse often have alizarin crimson or raw umber fingerprints on them. Her ration coupons are crisp with sun-thickened oil stains or blackened with charcoal dust.

While she follows the stroke of the brush over the canvas her eyes narrow to thin slits, her brows wrinkle up, her tongue darts out frequently and licks at her upper lip or she pulls faces she would be horrified by if she saw herself in a mirror.

Up at her canvas she gets a whiff of rabbit skin glue. A rotting kind of smell that catches at the back of her throat, that makes her feel queasy. A smell of death among earthroots. There is a blackened pot of the fudge-coloured solution that she has recently heated on the stove in the small kitchen.

She looks at her image in a small mirror where it seems distant and separate from her, the umbilical cord cut, the intimate connection severed.

She frowns. She curses aloud, forgetting she is not alone. Scrapes away some of the paint she has laid down with a palette knife. Every decision is measured, is intricate, is fatal.

But this is pretence on her part, another trick one part of herself plays on another part. A brushstroke is never fatal. But it is a vital element of the painting process to pretend this is not the case. To pretend there is no room for error. She plays countless tricks on the artist in her. Holds back knowledge from her as though the artist in her is a child and she the mother, filtering through intelligence only when she is sure it won't do any harm. A brushstroke can be erased as though it never existed. She erases many of the strokes she puts down.

The air raid siren begins shrieking and before long she hears the now familiar low drone of planes in the sky. The grumbling noise gains in intensity. It becomes a sensation in the body, an irritation on the skin, like a feeding insect. The window frames rattle. All the jars of primers and pigments and sun-thickened oils on the tables and shelves jingle. Circles shiver on the surface of the balsam in the pot on her palette. She goes to the window. Lifts the black drape that keeps out the reflected glare of sunlight. She tilts up her head as if to receive the gentle splash of rain on her face. Never have the planes been this low in the sky before. The metallic insect drone becomes a skip in her heartbeat. The remorseless roar grows more encompassing. Everything she thought of as solid vibrates with its own vulnerability.

2 - September 1943

FREDDIE SETTLES down in his chair. Notebook, charts and maps spread before him on the long desk. Next to him is his navigator Cyril Harris. A former wallpaper salesman from Croydon with a cheeky forelock of crinkled blonde hair. There's usually a blob of spittle on his tongue when Cyril speaks. Freddie didn't choose Cyril. Cyril chose him. As if Cyril saw something lucky in him.

Sometimes Freddie remembers the men no one perceived as lucky. The day in the hangar at the Operational Training Unit when, after being given a mug of tea and a large sticky bun, they were told to crew up among themselves. The surprised look on everyone's face at this news. Because they all thought crews would be allocated by some higher command. The hangar became like a hall at the beginning of a dance. The pilots huddled in a group, casting glances over at the other groups. The bomb-aimers, the wireless operators, the gunners, the flight engineers. Everyone fearing to be a wallflower. Everyone fearing to be the little boy no one wanted in their team. Each and every pair of eyes roving for attractive partners. For men who exuded confidence. For men who inspired a feeling of safety. That was when Cyril appeared. To Cyril he exuded confidence. It was possibly the most important compliment he had ever been paid. After an hour or so he had his crew and there were about thirty men no one had chosen. Who had to crew up among themselves. Two of those crews, he knows, failed to return from their first sortie.

"I've got ten bob on today's target being an outing back to the Happy Valley. What do you reckon, Freddie?"

He shrugs his shoulders. His smile there but in hiding. "I'd like to say The Fox and Crown but it looks like the weather's clearing up. What a topsy turvy life, eh? Waking up depressed because the sun's shining; rubbing your hands with glee because it's chucking down with rain."

"Did I tell you I saw a barn owl last night?" says Cyril. "Flew right across my path when I was cycling back from the pub. Do you think that's a bad sign?"

"No. I think that's a very good sign."

Station Commander Alan Hythe and his briefing officers enter the room. Chairs scrape as everyone stands to attention.

"At ease, men. First off, well done for the other night. Jolly good effort. Intelligence reports a substantial amount of damage inflicted on the heavy engineering and tank factories in Magdeburg."

Roll is called. Freddie answers for his crew. Then Station Commander Hythe steps up onto the dais. Draws back the curtain.

Freddie recognises the enlarged aerial photograph beside the large map of Europe without need of being told where it is. The route to be flown indicated by a red tape stretched across the map with each turning point indicated by a drawing pin.

"The target tonight, chaps, is Florence."

"There goes another ten bob," says Cyril under his breath.

"This thin strip here." Hythe jabs at it with his stick. "The marshalling yards of the station at Campo di Marte. A vital artery of the Hun's supply line. Today is a day when precision bombing has to be just that. Got that you bomb-aimers? Precision. This here," he says with another tap of his stick, "is the English cemetery. Elizabeth Barrett Browning is buried there. Anyone here know Elizabeth Barrett Browning?"

"I do, sir. Better poet than her husband."

"That, Sergeant Park, is a matter of opinion. But whether she was or was not a better poet than her husband we don't want to disturb her rest."

A short burst of eager laughter. Nothing eases tension like laughter. Freddie Hartson is a man who inspires smiles rather than laughter. He is not a showman. But his favourite companions are the ones he is eager to make laugh.

"The white areas and, as you can see, there are a jolly lot of white areas, are sites of artistic or historical importance. To be avoided at all costs. You're to go in low. Met Office confirms weather conditions are ideal."

There is a low grumble of scepticism. The Met Office is renowned for spectacular errors in its forecasts.

"You'll hear more about these conditions in due course. So no excuses. Anyone who drops his bomb load on one of those white areas don't bother coming home because there will be hell to pay."

"Can we expect much flak, sir?"

There are men who want to know what will happen before it happens and there are men who are willing to trust themselves to the unknown. Freddie is the former but he aspires to be the latter.

In the locker room, Reg, his flight engineer, is sitting on his parachute while pulling on his silk socks. Freddie chose Reg. Not because he looked lucky or had the reputation as an accomplished engineer but because he liked the look of him. His longish dark hair, his elegant eloquent hands, his witty mouth. Reg was someone he immediately wanted to make laugh.

"How are you feeling about this?"

Freddie wriggles into his lifejacket. "You're in for a treat, Reg. Florence is beautiful." He is in skipper mode. Cheerful, confident, a little louder than comes naturally to him. It is second nature now to slip into skipper mode. Like storing all personal effects in a locker and emerging into an empty room. Reminds him of being a little boy. This business of outward pretence. Pretend you're a pirate or a Red Indian and before long your absorption into the game whittles you down into pirate or Red Indian.

"Do they know your wife lives there?"

"Does who know?"

"Good point."

"It's not just my wife who lives there, Reg. I live there. That's where my home is. Most of the things I own in this life are there. Here, look at the target map."

"Your house isn't on there, is it?"

"No. Not that far off though. And given the accuracy of some of our crews...But this building here by the cemetery is where I met Isabella. It's an art studio. I was taught there. I can picture what my old teacher is probably doing at this very moment. He's got another eight or so oblivious hours before there's a distinct possibility that his life's work will be obliterated. That building there is the bar where we used to go during breaks for our morning coffee. It's owned by a man called Claudio. Both within half a mile of the target area. In other words just as likely to take a hit as the target itself."

"Why are we smashing up Florence anyway? Why are we smashing up Italy? I don't mind so much dishing it out to German cities. They had it coming to them. But Italy...The Italians, spiritually at least, are on our bloody side now."

"How was your date with the parachute packer?"

"Becky? All right. Though to be honest I prefer her friend."

"Why doesn't that surprise me?"

Outside Freddie lights a cigarette. Waiting for the truck that will ferry him and his crew to V Victor. The slow taunting no-man's land between briefing and take-off. The mud suck of the dragging minutes. The strain of keeping the etchings of fear from prising through onto his face.

He has handed in the letter that will be forwarded to his wife if he doesn't return.

Today I was out cycling in the countryside. The green and gold land sweeping out to the horizon. Breathing out peace as if everything was in its rightful place. Whenever life is beautiful you become part of the moment. It's as if for a moment a wind makes your skirt rustle and lifts up into the air a ghost of your presence. It's then I always find myself wishing that you could see me for a moment. Just long enough for me to give you back the smile I never quite had until I met you.

Look after the painting you did of me in my fisherman's jersey. I think that's how I would like to be remembered.

Everywhere the glimpsed faces of women who, for a hallucinatory moment, look like her.

He thinks about his wife whenever he is alone. He most often pictures her wearing his clothes. One of his white shirts. Nothing else. Or else a jacket of his draped over her shoulders. It always gave him pleasure when she appeared wearing some article of his clothing. As if she wanted to feel him on her skin even when he wasn't there. When he thinks of his wife now it is like walking barefoot down steps to the sea at night. A secretive act. A moment of wonder he treats with caution as though shielding a buffeted flame.

Like everyone else he has his superstitious rituals before climbing into the cockpit. He has his photograph of his wife in his top pocket. He doesn't look at it. He doesn't need to. He knows it off by heart. He touches it. To make sure it's there. And by touching it he brings her closer. Until he can see her and her expression fountains into a wide smile. He will not leave the corrugated iron hut with its twelve beds until he has seen her smile. It is another part of his superstitious ritual before flying to cast a glance at his kitbag with his name and service number painted on the side, at his five or six books, at the gramophone and at his stripy pyjamas on the bed. As if by establishing a connection with these details he will be more likely to return to them. Leaving the hut is like the childhood feeling of leaving the house before a dentist appointment. The leg-sagging disbelief that there is now anything beyond the dentist chair. In the back of the lorry he puts his wedding ring in his mouth. His mouth that is always bone dry before he climbs into the cockpit. This too is a ritual. Woodsy, the mid-upper gunner, has a different ritual. He always urinates over the rudder of the aircraft before he is willing to climb aboard. Everyone else urinates over the rear wheel.

"Sixth run. Six is my unlucky number," says Woodsy. To no one in particular. To himself. This is his other superstitious ritual. To always declare his pessimism before taking his place in the mid-upper turret. To make a point of releasing his doubts into the atmosphere, like a message in a bottle. He wants to be proved wrong. This is what he wants from life. There is a joke among the crew that he probably told his wife-to-be he was an inept lover. In the hope of being proved wrong.

"Come on Woodsy! You can dampen our bloody spirits better than that," says Cyril. Cyril's superstitious rite is to wear the same unwashed shirt he wore on their first sortie. He is convinced that if he ever washes this shirt it'll be curtains for him. "Tell everyone your theory. Woodsy's worked out the casualty rate here."

"Thirty-eight per cent. A higher casualty rate than in the trenches on the Somme. And the life expectancy of a Lanc is about forty hours flying time."

"By my maths we should already be dead then." Spike is the bomb-aimer. His pencil thin black moustache is like a permanent bristle of irritation. He is neat and tidy. A stickler for accuracy. In civilian life he is an optician. He frowns on those of the crew who drink. His superstitious ritual is to refuse to hand in his locker key before every op.

Spencer, the rear gunner, always brings with him the piece of flak that ripped through the perspex of his turret and missed his eye by a whisker on their second operation.

Davy, the young good looking wireless op, is the last one to climb into the aircraft. This is his superstitious ritual. Last one in, last one out. Always.

The act of stepping up on to the ladder, of climbing in through the hatch is always a floodtide moment. A moment of dying. Freddie feels the presence of time in the beating of his heart. He wonders what might be added or subtracted were he able to spend one more day with Isabella in his life, which is what he often finds himself most wishing for. Given another day, might he make himself less of a disappointment to her? He follows Reg down the length of the cluttered and clattering fuselage. Ducking underneath bits of equipment and hanging wires, clambering over the main spar. In the cockpit he puts his parachute on the seat and sits down on it. Reg helps him into his harness. He and Reg run through the list of checks before the engines can be started up. They make sure the oxygen and intercom system are working. Freddie sets the first course on the compass. Runs up the engines to full power. Signals to the ground crew to pull away the chocks from the main wheels. Then he closes the side window. And begins to ease V Victor out onto the perimeter track where she joins the queue of growling Lancasters. He opens the throttle on all four engines. His gloved hand fitting snugly over the four levers. The balls of his feet on the rudder panels. Gradually he slides the throttle levers up the quadrant. Running the engines against the brakes. There is a thundering noise in the cockpit, the swelling from beneath of an enormous exhilarating power.

Reg cranks the engines to full revs. The green flare is dispatched from the black and white chequered control caravan near which a cluster of WAAFs, the cookhouse staff, the chaplain and ground crew wave farewell to all the departing aircraft. He releases the brakes. Flames stream out of the exhaust, licking at the wings. Reg calls out the air speeds.

"Ninety-five."

V Victor feeds its roaring shuddering power into his bloodstream.

"One hundred."

For a moment V Victor with her heavy cargo of bombs and fuel seems to lack force to clear the ground. Freddie finds himself thrusting up his hips and shoulders in an effort to help will the shuddering machine off the ground. The roar of the slipstream increases a notch. Then this act of hubris is accomplished and the runway begins to reel away beneath the wings.

"Undercarriage up."

Reg places his gloved hand over Freddie's on the column control, like an act of betrothal, and between them they ease the lever of V Victor through the gates for maximum thrust. He has to circle the aerodrome for fifteen minutes before levelling off at 2,000 feet and setting course for the first rendezvous point over the south coast of England.

Freddie's hand goes to the microphone switch on his mask. The static in his headphones like the gibbering of ghosts. "Ten thousand. Put on oxygen."

Fifteen thousand feet over the Channel he gives the okay for rear gunner Spencer and mid-upper gunner Woodsy to test their guns. Reg stops writing in his logbook. Looks across at him with the expression that best suits him. A kind of bemused scepticism. Reg, the affinity he feels with him, is a vital part of his courage. The recoil of the inadequate Browning guns reverberates along the length of the fuselage, travels up his legs to his heart.

V Victor crosses the invisible line of enemy radar. Fate too is a cat's cradle of invisible lines. The coast of France appears below and then its fields and farms and grid of roads.

Up ahead there are some threaded arcs of unravelling light down below. Puffs of black smoke appear in the sky. The aircraft is jolted upwards. Jarred and rattled like a car going too fast along a pitted dirt track. All around, among the wisps of cloud, shells are bursting into shrapnel. Dirtying the clouds. A noise like someone shaking stones in a tin bucket every time flak hits the undercarriage or wings. A noise that makes everything in the world seem hollow. The smell of cordite thickens in Freddie's nostrils. He begins throwing V Victor to left and right. Weaving her through an imaginary thicket. He has to knuckle down to hold onto his sense of mastery over her. It feels like someone is doggedly trying to snatch away something he holds in his hand.

Then the sky is clear again. He takes V Victor up to 20,000 feet. Mountain peaks of dazzling white cumulus below. Snowdrifts of tumbling cloud higher up. Every ten minutes or so he tips V Victor sixty degrees to port. Waits to be told by his crew that there are no enemy fighters beneath them. No Messerschmitts. That remind him of mosquitoes. The way they dive down from nowhere, skid past and then disappear into the light like a magician's trick. Then he tips her sixty degrees to starboard.

The sight of Florence below, the cluster of churches and towers and palaces tiered up on either side of the river, as familiar as his own hand, as surreal as any nightmare. The setting of many of the most intimate and heartening moments of his life. Taunting him now with a spell of inaccessibility. He remembers Maestro once said that Florence exists to educate our memory. He throttles back the four engines. Brings V

Victor down. Since the advent of war many things have happened to him that he could not possibly have imagined. He wonders if this is one of the subliminal reasons men wage war. To increase the daily frequency of surprise and shock. The forerunners of revelation.

He thinks he can identify her studio. There, by the side of the ribbon of river. Extraordinary that she's down there. Oblivious to his presence up in the sky. Or perhaps she looks up at the sky every time she hears the sound of approaching planes. Wondering if he is piloting one of them. From down there the released bombs will look like a broken rosary of black beads parting with reluctance from their string. He looks down at the arches of Ponte Santa Trinita. Palazzo Vecchio and Giotto's tower and the Loggia dei Lanzi. His skin prickles beneath his RAF issue clothes. He looks over at the black and white marble church of San Miniato – so tiny he could cup it in the palm of his hand. Traces a line across to where his house should be, on the steep slope between Ponte Vecchio and Fort Belvedere.

When he has set V Victor's nose on the target he lightens his hold on the control wheel as if to make a visual show of his relinquishing of all responsibility for what happens now.

"All yours, Spike," he says without any of the disgust he feels evident in the tone of his voice.

Spike always double coughs into the microphone before answering any question. Even in moments of high stress. It is a source of amusement to the entire crew. "Tracking in nicely," Spike says. "Steady. Bomb doors open."

3 - September 1943

ISABELLA PULLS down the black piece of cloth from its nails above the window frame. The shock of the river so close is always like the gentlest brush of fingers at the base of her spine. Its arresting glitter, its teetering laughter of light, reflected as a pale gold glow up onto the high windows of the riverside palaces.

Down below the usual group of boys stripped down to their shorts on the Santa Rosa weir. Opposite the chalky white façade of the church of Ognisanti. Ribcages etched on their nut-coloured torsos. The prolonged food shortage has left its mark.

She often watches these boys during her breaks from painting. They always jump into the water from the platform of the weir. Taking a long run up and leaping as high as they can, cartwheeling arms, scissorkicking legs, before splashing down into the river with a joyful shout. Today all the boys are statues. Heads tilted up at the sky.

She and Leo watch through the shuddering glass. A formation of bombers, arriving from the north, much lower than usual, thundering over the river. Some guns begin popping off to the right. The bombs, like black beads glinting silver in the sunlight, fall down from the sky. They tumble earthwards in a mesmerising almost playful fashion. For a while they look as though they are swishing down towards her roof. The whistling as they pierce the air and the convulsing series of explosions make her feel the ground is as soft and slippery as snow. A cloud of billowing white dust appears behind Giotto's tower, over the burnt ochre rooftops towards Campo di Marte on the far side of the river and then a ghoulish fog of black smoke begins rising up towards the sky. It seems as though the smoke will eclipse the sun itself. There are more explosions. More white dust, more black smoke. Colour begins to disappear from the world. The hills cradling the city lose their emerald lustre and then vanish behind the smog of dust.

"They're bombing Florence," she says, her voice sounding small.

She joins her neighbours out on the street. There is a compulsion to draw physically together. People have an air of being more vivid to themselves. As if they are standing on the top rung of a ladder. A woman she doesn't know clutches Isabella's arm by the river wall where they stand staring at an event that has an apparitional quality. Staring across the placid water at the cloud of filthy smoke filling the sky. Staring at a moment of history. Her right hand, her painting hand, is clenched into a fist.

Later she cycles on her green bicycle along the river. Towards the area where the bombs have fallen. Towards the English cemetery and Maestro's studio. The forbidden zone. She has a nervous feeling in her stomach as she gets closer. She understands this as a sign that Maestro is unharmed. That nothing has changed and his curse on her is still active.

There is a powdered smell of burning chemicals and charred brick dust. The dust settles in her hair and on her clothes. It prickles her nose and throat. She is overtaken by fire trucks and ambulances and military vehicles. They shrink her. Frighten her with their urgency and noise.

She passes two little boys pretending to be planes. Running and swooping at each other with arms outstretched. The splinters of glass from the many empty windows threaten to puncture the tyres of her bike. She gets off and wheels it. Wheels it towards what looks like the smoking ruins of an excavated city. Skeletons of houses with collapsed floors looking like jagged precipices beside craters in the road. Dazed people sitting on the rubble. Scavenging among the fallen stones and wooden beams and scorched broken tiles. She walks past a building missing its outer wall. All its rooms exposed. A dress draped over a chair in one room. There is another building where only the façade is standing like some kind of meaningless magic trick. The ripped open houses with their exposed arrangements, their laid bare secrets, are like portraits. Each one has its own individual facial expression. More identity is on display in the midst of the destruction. More intimacy. It makes her realise how vulnerable these achievements are. Identity. Intimacy.

Water flows out from under the doors of some of the houses. Oddly gentle as a spectacle, almost prankish, in the midst of such sepulchral dereliction. Smell of gas and sewage and plaster and burnt petrol and a fizzling noise and sparks from the crumpled cables of the tramlines. Ambulances and fire engine crews. Men in a dozen different uniforms blowing whistles and shouting. A section of another wall tumbles down as she walks past. She sees an umbrella, a woman's hat and negligee, a frying pan, a cabbage. She makes a painting of some of these deracinated items. It is her way of defending herself from this harrowing collapse of structure. Her eye has been trained to find composition in the juxtaposition of objects. There is an armchair stripped down to its springs sitting by the side of the road. Everything is layered with ash and dust. An elegant notebook lays splayed open in the vicinity of a small fire. The light from the flames flickers over the exposed pages, gives the handwritten ink script a glow of solemnity as if it is the expression of an inspiration. Then the flames creep over the pages and the ink begins to blur as the paper curls up at the edges and crisps and crumbles into black flecks which fly up into the air of cinders and smoke.

In the midst of all the running and shouting, the whistles and sirens, the labyrinth of rubble, the dust of ages, she stops in front of a little boy holding an older girl by the hand. The girl's eyes are closed. Her face and clothes shrouded in blackened dust.

Isabella takes the little girl's hand. "Are you all right?"

"My eyes hurt," says the girl.

"Where's your mother?"

The little boy points with the solemnity of a grown man. She looks over at the woman spread out on the pavement. Someone has thrown a sheet over her but it no longer covers her face that is caked in white powder and makes her look like a plaster cast with smears of red blood. Her eyes are open. A haunting expression of bewilderment around the white crust of her mouth. When the horror passes Isabella bows her head with respect. It is the first time she has laid eyes on death.

She takes both children by the hand. The warm pressure of their small fingers on her skin has more heartbreak in it than any previous moment of her life. Her instinct is to take the two children home and look after them herself. Instead, feeling inadequate, out of her depth, she hands them over to two nuns. Two quiet nuns amongst the shouting and bluster of uniformed men.

Afterwards she realises she never asked the children their names.

On her way home she stops off at the English cemetery. Some of the names on the headstones among the lemon trees and azaleas are hidden behind the rising tide of wild grass and weeds. She sits down on a stone bench by three cypress trees. Wipes the shroud of dust from her clothes. Catches a hint of her own scent as she pulls up her knees and hugs them. She remembers sitting here with Freddie before they were lovers. The surprising catechism of intimacy with her own body when their hips touched while sitting side by side on the stone bench. She still now sometimes searches for his hand in the dark.

She sits within sight of Maestro's studio. The building is unscathed. The sight of it makes her feel like a nervous twenty-year-old girl again.

4 - May 1937

HER HEART is thumping nakedly. She is stripped down to what is primitive in her. What is drummed out in the blood. Her resolve crumbling at the edges like footprints in wet sand.

She walks past the English cemetery. The maze of blackening white headstones and carvings among the cypresses. With her portfolio of drawings and painted sketches under her arm. Wearing lipstick the colour of ripe raspberries. Feigning self-possession. Wishing it was an ordinary day. That little was at stake. As seems to be the case for the people she passes on the street. The people sitting in the tram that clanks and jolts by. Sparks jumping up from its wheels.

She reaches the door before she is ready. The myrtle green door with its blistered paint. She needs to slow down her intake of breath. She looks up at the large arched window. To make sure no one is up there spying on her. Then she walks off. Practising what she might say. She walks in a circle. Is soon back at the green door. This time she rings the bell.

On the stairs the smell of sun-thickened oils. The smell of turpentine. She enters a large darkened room. The clerestory windows almost entirely covered in black drapes. Motes dancing in the upper air where a sheen of reflected light enters the high-ceilinged studio. Five boys standing at easels. They all look over at her. Seeming glad of the distraction. This break in concentration. But a bit hostile too. As if she is intruding into a private realm. A temple precinct.

"Is Maestro around?" she asks the boy with the kindest face. She has been told to call him Maestro.

"Through that door there."

She walks into an almost identical room. This too with its large arched windows draped except for the highest pane of leaded glass. Her footfalls on the terracotta tiles announce her presence. Two men are over in the corner. The younger man is fitting two stretcher bars together. The older man is holding a glass jar up to the light. He is the man she wants to teach her how to paint. How to paint like the old masters. He looks around. Still holding the glass jar up to the light.

"Maestro? I'd like to study with you," she says. Coughing the words out too abruptly. The sound of her voice exposes her. As if she has shed a layer of clothing. She sounds arrogant, she thinks. Not nervous, not scared half to death which is how she feels. Maestro is a small brittle man with pronounced bones and a perfectly shaved head. He is wearing a silver waistcoat, a bow tie and a monocle in his right eye. She walks over to him. Offers him her hand. There is something fastidious about the way he takes her hand. Gives it the limpest of shakes. He is shy of her. She detects it immediately. His shyness feeds more shyness into her.

"You want to study with me? Did you hear that, Fosco? She wants to study with me. This is Fosco Scarafuggi. My assistant."

Fosco doesn't offer his hand. He gives her a curt nod of acknowledgement. He has dark black curly hair, a thick beard and watchful dark eyes.

"That's what I'd like, yes. My name is Isabella."

"And why do you want to study with me? Haven't you heard, I'm out of vogue? Why not go to Rosai. Why not go to one of the futurists? They're the future. Not me. I'm the past. The obsolete. The denigrated. Isn't that so, Fosco?"

He says this with a fiery pride. As if beckoning a charging bull with a red cloth.

"I don't like their work," she says. "I want to paint like the old masters."

"Did you hear that, Fosco? She doesn't like Rosai. This girl has taste at least. The trouble with painting though, with all art, is you can't *prove* you're better. Isn't that the case, Fosco? It's not like a hundred-yard sprint where there's a piece of technology to indisputably grade the contestants. Artists, like criminals, are dependent on a jury. And the jury says Rosai is a better artist than I am. What's your name?"

"Isabella," she says again.

"And how old are you, Isabella?"

"Twenty."

"I've never had a girl as a student before. Not in all my twenty years of teaching. Fosco here maintains women can't paint. That they're not capable. That they lack the necessary intellectual discipline. I can only teach you if you're capable of thought. If you're able and willing to think through what you're doing. Let me tell you, learning the art of oil painting is a purgatory. Are you sure you want to enter purgatory?"

She follows what he says word for word. As if he is a fortune teller. But she has no answer to these things he is saying. She waits for him to say something else.

"Let me see your work. I take it that's your work you're holding?"

"Yes." She hands him the folder. Her heart a thumping drum. She can hardly bear to look at her work while he is leafing through it. Never has it looked so inept, so unaccomplished. She screws her hands together. Rubs at her knuckles. Waiting to be told she has no future.

"Your work isn't bad," he says.

She can't help it. The grin that wants to part her lips. She clamps it down. Pushes it away. This grin. This sudden burst of happiness.

"It isn't great but neither is it bad. What do you think, Fosco? Does she have potential."

"Everyone has potential," Fosco says.

She doesn't like this Fosco Scarafuggi. His cold calculating watchful eyes. And she senses this dislike is already mutual.

"Can you show me your profile a moment?"

She shows him her perplexity but doesn't voice it.

"Your profile. Can I see it."

He moves to one side of her. She turns her head away from him.

"Now look down. Chin a bit lower."

He takes hold of her jaw. Pulls it down.

"Don't you think she's just what we're looking for?"

"Eve?"

"Yes. There's an element of detachment about her beauty, just as I always picture Eve. Look at the line of that jaw. That refined nose. Those young sensual lips. I see temptation when I look at her. Are you a temptress, Isabella? Could you be a temptress?"

She blushes. She can't help herself. He keeps making her body do things she can't prevent.

"I'm going to offer you a deal. I'll teach you. I'll even teach you for free. But there's one condition."

"One condition?"

He turns to Fosco. She senses a new pulse in the older man's being. An excitement that is both youthful and fastidious. "You primed the canvases, didn't you?"

Fosco nods.

"And they're dry?"

Fosco nods again.

"Here's the deal. You pose naked for me. And Fosco will be working alongside me. You pose as Eve. As the temptress. Starting today."

She frowns. Looks to him for confirmation that he is being serious. She tries to imagine taking her clothes off for these two men. Standing in front of them naked. Her breasts bared. Her buttocks. Her pubic hair on display. Their eyes on her. Studying every detail of her anatomy.

"I can't do that," she says.

"Then you don't have enough passion, enough commitment for me to teach you how to paint," he says. He is angry. She feels his anger as a kind of static on his clothes. Like the anger of a cat bristling over its fur.

She looks at him with fierce defiance. Wanting him to know she is not intimidated. She is not humiliated. Even though she is. Then she leans down to take off her shoes. Looks at him again with the same flash of defiance. The arousal of blood. Swivels round her skirt. Unfastens it. Steps out of it. Pushes it away with her foot. She stands for a moment looking down at her bare feet on the terracotta tiles. Then she looks him in the eye again.

"I want to paint you as Eve, not Medea or Lady Macbeth," says Maestro with an uncertain smile. "And however small you feel now I can guarantee you that my teacher made me feel smaller. You'll never achieve anything until you stop feeling pleased with yourself."

"I too have one condition," she says.

"And what's that?"

"I'll pose for you but I won't pose for him," she says, nodding at Fosco.

This makes Maestro laugh. "So be it," he says. "Fosco, looks like you'll be working in the other room."

5 - June 1937

"ISABELLA," HE SAYS. He has a lingering secretive way of pronouncing her name that makes it seem part of her nakedness.

They are walking up the path of the English cemetery. She and Freddie, the English boy studying at Maestro's atelier. He is pale with thick dishevelled dark hair and an air of having dressed in a hurry. He is taking a break from painting the life model. She is taking a break from posing for Maestro. The gravel rasps and scatters underfoot as though they are an incoming wave. On either side greying headstones. A weeping women in stone. An angel with clasped hands.

"If looks could kill," she says.

"Okay, Fosco doesn't like you. But I wouldn't take it personally. He doesn't like anyone."

"He seems to not mind you."

"That's because I have no talent. Because I'm inept. He likes me for that. It's his favourite trait of mine. Not very complimentary. Or very charitable."

They sit down on a marble bench in front of a large stone urn. In the midst of a circle of cypresses with lavender coming into flower near their feet. The scent of newly aroused pollen.

"You do have talent," she says. She likes Freddie. His company. He makes her feel she is standing barefooted in the world. Sometimes on warm springy grass; sometimes on sharp stones.

"I don't. You're just being kind. If I did I might not drink a demijohn of wine every night. I don't have the secret, like you do. The natural gift. I wish I did. Nothing I'd love more than to be a painter. Now I've got to imagine a different future. I've applied for a job in the old masters department at Christie's. If I can't produce good paintings myself at least I'll be able to look at those done by others every day."

She feels a contraction inside at the thought of him no longer being around. A chill of apprehension.

"I wish you weren't going. Leaving me at the mercy of Fosco," she says, trying to make a joke of it.

The shadow of a bird flits over a blackened white marble headstone. She sees one stencilled movement of its wings on the stone.

"You'll have forgotten my existence within a month."

"No I won't."

"I'm already beginning to miss it here. Florence feels like home. Feels like fate."

"Is that why Maestro's being a bit offhand in his behaviour towards you, because he knows you're leaving? He doesn't like change, does he?"

"Can't blame him for that. I don't like change either. Sometimes I think my idea of happiness would be to do exactly the same set of things every day. Which, of course, is exactly what Maestro does. But I suppose he feels I've let him down. I've rendered his will impotent. He couldn't help me despite all the time and energy he spent trying. I've become a traitor. Someone outside his jurisdiction. Maestro has divided the world up very simply but effectively into allies and enemies. All his allies are under his command. Anyone not under his command is his enemy. Enemies though are just as important to him as allies. Without enemies I think he'd lose a lot of his drive. His raison d'être. He likes to feel he's an endangered species."

"God, it's all so political."

"All so fascist."

She inhales the peppery warm breath of the cypresses. She loves their scent. It's a scent that seems to make moments memories even before they've stopped happening.

She returns to Maestro's private studio. The filtered smoking daylight high up in the room of echoes looks more like moonlight.

She always turns her back to Maestro when she unfastens her bra. The act of undressing is more intimate than the posing naked. More likely to arouse shyness in her. She lays it down on top of her skirt and blouse. She still has her back to him when she steps out of her knickers. Her knickers are always the last thing she takes off. She has bought herself several new pairs. Pretty things with lace. Her underclothes have become an emblem, an extension of her nakedness since she has had to take them off in front of him. So she wants them to be pleasing to the eye. She tells herself this is only natural. Her knickers are always on top of the soft heap of her clothes when she turns round to face Maestro naked. She looks over at them sometimes while she is on the model stand. When Maestro is up at his easel. Her discarded clothes. They give her the thrill of adventure. She is doing something her mother could never have done. She has already ventured beyond her mother's boundaries. She is staking out new territory.

Maestro has transformed her with his pigments and his sun-thickened oil into a beautiful desirable woman.

She gets into pose on the model stand. Becomes Eve. The temptress.

"So, you and Freddie," he says, wiping a brush on an old piece of rag.

"What do you mean?"

"Are you going to have babies together? Perhaps it's better that you give up painting and have babies. Keep Mussolini happy. We all have to keep Mussolini happy."

"I don't want to have babies. At least not for a while."

"But sooner or later you'll want babies. All women want babies."

The contempt with which he says "babies".

"Freddie and I have become good friends. That's it. We're not going to have babies."

"Not what Fosco said. He thinks you'll be making babies before the year's out." He holds up his paintbrush to the light. Squints at the dab of colour on the tips of the bristles.

"And of course Fosco always knows best."

A fugitive smile. He likes it when she's disdainful about Fosco. In this way he betrays Fosco. She thinks of what Freddie said. How he sees a potential enemy in every ally.

"Freddie's got no talent, you know," he says. He walks up to the canvas. His elbow almost brushing her naked hip as he lays down a brushstroke. "It's for the best that he leaves. There's no point in me wasting any more of my time on him. I've done my best. I can't train his eye. He refuses to see. And if you can't see you'll never be able to paint."

He is defying her to disagree with him. He is giving her a choice – betray Freddie or betray me. This is one of his tricks. His constant demand of loyalty always at the expense of someone else. Because you're not allowed to disagree with him. Just as you're not allowed to disagree with the fascists.

"He's very appreciative of your efforts to help him," she says. "He thinks he just doesn't have the necessary natural talent."

"He doesn't have the necessary natural talent. I'm glad he appreciates my effort at least." He relaxes. The anger ebbs out of him. "But Freddie does have a genuine love of art. A real passion for it. And for that I like him. He knows beauty when he sees it. You'd think everyone would know beauty when they see it but they don't. That's why we've got these monstrously ugly buildings going up everywhere."

Maestro never stops talking. His shyness makes him talk. Makes him keep up a running commentary. As if not to hear the sound of his own voice is to be consigned to some private oblivion.

Fosco walks in noisily. His heavy shuffling cynical walk. Wearing his fascist pin on the lapel of his jacket. Holding a pair of rusty pliers. Even though he has been told not to enter when she is naked on the model platform. He does it out of spite. To let her know he is higher up in the hierarchy than she is. She bristles when he is in the room. Fidgets. Loses her sense of the pose.

"Come here and take a look, Fosco. Stand back against the wall. What do you think of the hand? Should I drop it down a bit? Do I want it casting a shadow over the private part? What do you think?"

She feels Fosco's eyes on her "private part".

6 - October 1937

ISABELLA HAS the attention of everyone in the room. Because she has broken a sacred law in what suddenly seems a temple. The other five students gather around her. Eyes fixed with wonder at the swirl of ultramarine blue on her palette. They speak in hushed voices. Marvelling at her act. Not sure if she is being courageous or foolhardy. Distancing themselves from her. But at the same time edging closer with secret pleasure and fascination at this breaking of a taboo. The room pulses with the excitement of impending drama.

Maestro only permits his students to use four colours on their palettes. Black, lead white, cadmium yellow and red ochre. Maintains these are the only colours required to paint human flesh. Unless one is going to falsify the colour values of human skin tones.

Maestro is out at lunch with Fosco. Expected back at any moment.

"Oh dear, Isabella. Are you wanting to bring down the thunder on us?" Oskar is German. A German Jew. Oskar wants to be a dancer rather than an oil painter. He dances all the time. Turns the most basic human actions into dance steps. Turns daily life into choreography. She likes Oskar. Everything he says in Italian sounds like text from an instruction manual. Because his accent has a harsh officious quality. She tells him she can hear the grinding of cogs in his voice.

"Like a clock with a cuckoo?"

Now he sometimes makes cuckoo noises after saying something to her. Sending himself up to make her laugh. But not now. Not after telling her she is going to bring the thunder down on them.

"Oskar's right," says Roberto. "Maestro will go mad. Why make him angry simply for the sake of a bit of extra colour?"

"What's wrong with extra colour? I wish I had a bit of extra colour in my life. But because I don't I'm going to have a bit of extra colour in my painting."

Oskar imitates Maestro in a cold rage. Bites the colour out of his lips. Paces back and forth with his hands curled up into fists. His shoulders thrown back. Twitching with withheld fury. "Do you listen to anything I say?" he says. He doesn't sound like Maestro. He sounds like an angry German official. "Are you even capable of rational thought? Why must you falsify nature? We are given eyes to see with. Why pervert what you see with gratuitous acts of imagination?"

She smiles at his performance. "What's wrong with experimenting a bit?" She lets some sun-thickened oil drip down onto the blue pigment on her palette. Stirs it in with her brush. "I can see blue in the flesh tones. Carmelo, can you get into the pose?"

The naked boy steps up onto the platform. Places his feet on the charcoal marks on the wooden box by the far wall. Settles down on his hips in front of the pale silver background drape. Holds out his hands. As if in supplication.

"Look at the splash of light on his pelvic region," she says, pointing with her brush. "Now tell me you don't see blue there. Look how cold that value is."

"There's maybe a hint of blue if you squint," says Roberto.

"And that hint of blue adds expression. It adds a new dimension to how we see the familiar," she says, sounding a bit pompous to herself but unable to stop and, anyway, she is only twenty-one years old and surely should be allowed a little idealism, a small margin for extravagant claims. "Maybe it's even an optical illusion. But illusions too are part of our reality. Why just paint what is plain to see?"

"Because," says Roberto, "we're being taught a specific technique with specific rules. And we should respect those rules. This is a school..."

"An atelier," she corrects him. She strides up to her canvas. Lays down a stroke of blue paint.

Everyone stares at it. This act of blasphemy. And at the same time listens out for the tell-tale footsteps on the stairs.

"And by definition a school has to impose guidelines. Do away with those and you are sowing the seeds for anarchy."

"I thought you were a communist, Roberto. You sound much more like a fascist to me." She lays down another stroke of ultramarine blue pigment. Walks backwards away from her canvas. Tilting her head at an angle to appraise the effect.

"Are you sure you're not doing this on purpose? It's as if you deliberately want to get a rise out of Maestro. If you don't mind me saying so."

But it isn't Maestro she wants to get a rise out of. This gesture of defiance is aimed at Fosco. She is making a statement. Proving to Fosco she is not afraid of Maestro. Is not slavishly servile like he is. That she will not be denied to think aloud her own thoughts. Put them into practice. She has already been on the receiving end of one of Maestro's tirades. For experimenting with impasto. Laying down thick chunks of lead white paint to dramatise the blast of reflected light on a model's forehead. Maestro told her to remove it. That she would not receive another critique from him until she removed the impasto. She told Freddie about this in a letter. She also told Freddie about the debate that went on about the ethics of allowing her to join a figure class with a naked male as a model. ("Though it's true this was the first time I had ever seen the anatomy of a fully naked man.")

She is looking forward to telling Freddie about the ultramarine blue on her palette too. She and Freddie write to each other at least three times a week. His letters are what she most looks forward to. The sight of an envelope addressed to her in his handwriting gives her the feeling of spinning in a circle. Her skirt lifting up in a fan around her waist.

The tension when Maestro enters the room makes him look around with a puzzled expression. No one offers an explanation. She watches the bemusement on his face give way to the first stirrings of a defensive anger. She has a moment of doubt. She brings some saliva up into her mouth because it is so dry. Suddenly wishes she could make the blue paint on her canvas and on her palette disappear. She loves her life at this studio. It so structures her days that she sees only a vacuum if she imagines her life without it. It suddenly seems absurd to put it in jeopardy. And all for three strokes of ultramarine blue paint.

"Can you get a bit of colour in that lower lip, Roberto?" says Maestro, peering through his monocle at Roberto's canvas. "Or are you afraid of colour? What about you, Oskar? Are you afraid of colour?"

"I live in terror of colour."

Everyone laughs. The tension eases. Until Maestro looks at her painting. The three ultramarine blue strokes. He takes them as a personal affront. Which everyone knew he would. He takes most things that happen in the world personally. The colour drains from his lips. His eyebrows bristle up.

"I'm not going to give you another critique until you remove that pornographic blue stain on your painting. Are we painting corpses here? If you want to paint corpses go to the morgue. But don't do it in my studio."

He marches out of the room. Fosco follows him.

She is ten minutes late the next morning. When she enters the figure room everyone looks at her with disbelief. As if she has returned from the dead. It frightens her. This disbelief with which her presence is greeted.

"What's wrong?"

Roberto sidles up to her. Says in a whisper, "Somebody has turpsed all the paint off Maestro's Last Supper. You, apparently."

"Me?"

"I'd collect your things and leave if I were you."

"Oskar, what's going on?"

Oskar leads her out of the room. Onto the stairs. "It's true. Someone has sabotaged his painting. It's devastated him."

"And he thinks it was me?"

Oskar performs his impersonation of Maestro. "A year of my life. I had to quarry that picture out of the depths of my soul. I painted that picture with my life's blood."

"That's what he said? Okay, this is ridiculous. I'm going to speak to him."

"Fosco's in there with him."

She knocks on the door. Pushes it open without waiting for a reply. Maestro turns his back to her as soon as he sees her. She stares at the ruined painting. All its harmonies and meaning gone. All its beautifully fused colour and highlights. The poignant living expressions on the faces of the disciples. All gone. The figures are grey ghosts now. Dimly remembered grey ghosts. Barely holding their shape.

"It wasn't me," she says.

"Maestro wants you to pack up your things and leave," says Fosco.

"Maestro?" she pleads, ignoring Fosco. "It wasn't me who did that. I would never do such a thing."

Fosco pushes her out of the room and closes the door.

7 - June 1938

FULLY DRESSED, Freddie walks into the sea. Far out on its dark expanse the moon trembles. He takes a bow. "She said yes," he says up to the night sky. He holds aloft a bottle of red wine. Over his shoulder waves dribble ribbons of foam across the hissing shingle. "But if she knew the truth about me she would probably say no."

"What are you mumbling about?" Isabella calls out. From her vantage point on the rocks at the side of the small cove where she sits with Oskar's pregnant French wife Fanny.

"I'm engaged to be married," he says, louder. In clarion tones.

"I thought you'd never ask," she calls out again.

"Yes. I know. What a coward I've been. But that time is past. Here's to the new enterprising and heroic me."

She watches as he is struck at the back of the knees by the surging tide. He sways and extends out his arms as if balancing on a tightrope.

"And I'm with child," says Oskar. He too wades into the Mediterranean. Up to his knees. He too fully dressed. He turns round to face the two women sitting on the rocks.

"What are you two going to do next?" Isabella calls out.

Beneath her, chasms in the rocks suck in the advancing waves and spit them out with a low elegiac sigh.

"Let that be decided by higher powers," says Freddie with an uncertain smile. He sits down in the sea. All but his head and shoulders vanishing beneath the black and silver water. The beam of the lighthouse catches him fishing up a tendril of seaweed. He examines it briefly. Flings it away.

"Freddie is drunker than I am. The first time this week. I take off my hat to you, Freddie."

"Not wearing a hat."

"Then I take off my shirt to you, Freddie." Oskar does as he says. Whirls it around his head by the sleeve. "See. Here is my shirt. A nice German shirt. But white. Not brown."

"I take off my shirt to you, Oskar." Freddie climbs up to his feet. Falls back down. He holds in his hand a soggy wad of banknotes he has extracted from his trouser pockets. "All my money," he says. "All my credentials."

"Now I take off my trousers to you, Freddie."

"Where is this going to end?" Isabella calls out.

"I take off my trousers and my shorts for you, Oskar."

They both stand naked in the sea. With their backs to the shore. Holding their clothes in a bundle. Another withdrawing wave rakes through the shoals of shell fragment and pebbles on the beach.

"The first time I've seen my husband-to-be naked," Isabella says.

"They look nice in the moonlight, don't they? Like ideals of themselves. Without all their flaws. Their annoying habits."

"I haven't learned yet what Freddie's flaws or annoying habits are."

"You're still living in a state of grace. His habits simply haven't started annoying you yet."

"But they will?"

"Unless you're a saint."

"I'm not a saint. My old art teacher always maintained the male body is more aesthetically evolved than the female."

"Because women are more primitive," says Fanny and laughs. "So, tonight?"

"Tonight?"

"Are you two still going to sleep in separate rooms. Now that your union has become official?"

"I don't know. You'll have to ask him."

"That's not the impression I get."

"What do you mean?"

"You'll be the one who makes most of the decisions in your relationship. I think that's what you like."

"You make me sound like a Mother Superior."

Fanny has a nasal whinnying laugh.

"Did you and Oskar never have something going on?"

"We sometimes had races on our bikes. He always won."

"He likes you. I can see that. But he would be too wilful for you. Too dangerous."

"You think Freddie's a pushover?"

"No. But he'll be more easily trained. Perhaps it's his English education. He'll let you have the final say. Oskar wouldn't. Oskar wants attention all the time. He wants everyone to be watching him. Perhaps that is a necessary trait for a dancer. I don't mind being his audience to some extent. You'd hate it."

Isabella wonders for a moment if she should feel offended. If she is being goaded into some sort of fight. She looks out at the two men swimming. Leaving a trail of phosphorescence in their wake on the black water.

"Nothing whatsoever happened between Oskar and me," she says.

"It wouldn't upset me too much even if it did. But don't mind me. I always say what I think. I can't help it."

"That's an admirable quality in this day and age. I'm not used to people saying what they really think. We're not allowed to in Italy. We live in an atmosphere of wariness. Of mutual suspicion. We don't finish our sentences. Or even our thoughts. It doesn't seem worth the trouble. That's Mussolini's Italy. Everyone everywhere is suspicious of their neighbours. At dinner parties, in restaurants, on trams you make polite conversation. You dare not go any further. If you can avoid talking to strangers then you do just that. In case they're party members. You get to the point of treating everyone as if they are a party member."

"I didn't realise you had any political axes to grind."

"Neither did I."

She accepts the cigarette Fanny offers her. She can smell her perfume. A hint of sweet seduction among the pungent odour of salt and seaweed.

"So we have two more days here. And then?"

Isabella sits hugging her knees. The taste of brine on her skin. Sometimes she feels the future coiled up inside her like a sleeping serpent.

"Freddie goes back to London for six months and I return to Florence."

"It must be hard living apart."

"It is and it isn't. It isn't because I love getting his letters so much. I'm not sure I like the thought of mornings without the anticipation of one of his envelopes waiting for me. He's more handwriting and ink to me than flesh and blood."

"But next year he will come and live in Italy and you will get married?"

"Yes. He's inherited some money and is thinking of opening up an art gallery in Florence."

"Perfect for you."

"I suppose so. But that's not why I'm marrying him."

"Why are you marrying him?"

"Because he knows how to create intimacy. And that's what I most love in life. Intimacy. Good painting has that quality. Makes you feel intimate with it. What about you and Oskar? Will you have this child in England?"

"Yes. Oskar is going to continue studying with his dance teacher for another year. Kurt. He's a very noble soul. He left Germany when the Nazis tried to force him to expel all the Jewish dancers from his company. Moved the school to Devon. So our child will be born in Devon. I didn't even know Devon existed until last year. Funny, isn't it, how things work out?"

"Do you miss Paris?"

"Yes. I was born there and have lived there all my life. But we will live in Paris eventually. When we leave Devon. We can't go to Germany. Not until Hitler and the Nazis have gone anyway."

"Oskar was telling me about Germany. When you were in Hanover. It sounds horrid."

"Yes. That vile flag draped over every other building. All the girls have plaits and all the boys wear shorts that are too tight."

"Are you Jewish too?"

"Yes. And I thank God Hitler and the Nazis have no power in my country."

8 - April 1939

THEY ARE SITTING side by side in a moored gondola. She and her new husband. Facing the black and gold sweep of the Grand Canal. The boat sways gently with the current. The bells from a nearby church have just tolled midnight.

"What did you mean once when you said if I knew the truth about you I wouldn't have accepted your hand in marriage?"

"Did I say that?" Freddie fiddles with the cap of his flask. She expects him to take another deep swig of whatever it contains but he doesn't. He fiddles with the cap.

"Yes. You were drunk but even so."

"Just drunken nonsense then."

But he doesn't convince her. She senses him retreat, stealthy and embarrassed, into some crucible of his being where she can't find him.

"It was the night you proposed to me."

"When Oskar and I swam naked in the sea."

"Yes." She leans over the side of the boat and trails her hand in the dark water.

"Well I was very very drunk that night."

"You were very very drunk last night."

It is the third day of their honeymoon. But they have still not consummated their marriage. Nor have they discussed why they have not consummated their marriage. This failure, this bewildering abeyance, has wedged a barrier between them. She feels now as though they are talking through a hole in a wall that separates them.

Their first night in Venice there was a thunderstorm. White flares of lightning brought the distance closer as they walked across Piazza San Marco. The storm transfixed them. They made no move to seek shelter. Finally all the roaming electricity in the sky gathered directly above them. Produced a sundering crack. Then the rain came down. Quietly at first, then with a kind of evangelical hysteria. They were already quite drunk and the rain made them drunker still. It fell in torrents as they ran laughing through the narrow alleyways. Soaking through her clothes. Her skirt clinging to her thighs. Drops sliding down between her breasts. The intoxicating effect of the rain undressing her. They stood by the open window of their hotel room with the rain sweeping into their faces. A bolt of lightning lit up the Grand Canal. Struck it out of the darkness in a searing eloquent flash. The expectation was that the night to come would be no less bracing, no less eloquent.

But after they had disrobed and climbed into bed something went wrong. Something embarrassing and alienating. Something which nothing had prepared her for. There was to be no blood on the sheets. He muttered an apology. Said he had drunk too much. She felt rejected by his subsequent behaviour. His retreating far back into himself. His moody silence.

The same thing happened the second night. After a day trooping round Venice's churches, marvelling at the Titians and the Tintorettos during which he often had an absent strained look on his face. The same thing happened the second night. Except this time he offered no apology.

She doesn't understand what is wrong. Is it her fault? Is she doing something wrong? She is more physically shy than she expected to be. As shy with him as he seems to be with her. They don't seem able to be natural or bold with each other. Can't make the act of love a natural extension of the heartening intimate talks they have together. She hasn't found the courage to ask why. And so this failure to mate has exacerbated her feeling that she can't be reached. That in her depths she is untouchable. Neither can she find an appropriate language to talk about it. The language, when she thinks the problem through, is too ugly, too matter-of-fact, too brutal. To bring the subject up seems an act of heresy. *Why is it hard when we kiss but then all of a sudden becomes soft at the moment of entry?* How horrid it sounds. How humiliating for him.

She wishes he was wearing his fisherman jersey. Instead of a shirt and tie. He is more transparently himself in his fishing jersey. More prone to relaxed spontaneous tactile gestures. More porous.

"Beautiful, isn't it?" he says. Nods towards the streaks of light on the black water. "But in a wistful kind of way. As if one is already remembering it."

"I keep thinking, when is all this going to happen to me?" she says. She holds out her palms. A residue of Venice's brine and dust on her skin.

"Is that what you're thinking?"

"Why don't you take your tie off?"

"You don't like my tie?"

"Do you know you're different depending on what clothes you wear?"

"How do you mean?"

"I don't know. Am I like that too? Different depending on what clothes I wear?"

"I hadn't really thought about it."

The tide lapping against the nearby wooden landing stage makes a plaintive noise. He unscrews the cap of his flask. Takes a deep needy draught. Offers it across to her.

"We can't be drunk all the time," she says.

9 - June 1940

HE IS WITH ISABELLA in Piazza della Signoria the day war is declared. The strident voice of Mussolini crackling over the loudspeakers in the crowded piazza. *An hour appointed by destiny has struck in the heavens of our fatherland.* They are standing by the Loggia dei Lanzi. Imprisoned in the sweaty clamp of the crowd. If he turns he can see bronze Perseus holding the head of Medusa. Predator and prey. *The declaration of war has already been delivered to the ambassadors of Great Britain and France. We go to battle against the plutocratic and reactionary.* The cheer is exultant and insolent and frightens some birds up into the higher air. He and Isabella look at each other with raised eyebrows. A show of solidarity. A renewal of the marriage vow. Letting each other know how divorced from the proceedings they are. As if they are watching another bad film together.

"What's there to cheer about?"

"What? I can't hear you."

He shouts. "Why are all these people acting as though there's some kind of personal blessing or windfall in this news? Some of these idiots are cheering the abrupt shortening of their own lives."

She shouts back. "People like cheering though, don't they? Any excuse will do. Don't be too harsh on them."

"I hate them for the fact that they're making me feel I know better. That they're making me cynical. I want my innocence back. What the hell does plutocratic mean anyway?"

"We'll have to look it up in the dictionary when we get home."

When one has a friend, one marches with him to the end.

"I'll have to go back to England."

And we salute with our voices the Führer, the head of great ally Germany.

"What? I can't hear you."

"I'll have to go back to England."

She shouts back. "I know."

"You won't come with me, will you?"

Afterwards there are raucous processions through the centre of Florence with standards and flags and singing. He and Isabella tag along for a bit. Out of curiosity. He still has the song going through his head when they return home.

E per Benito Mussolini,

Eja, eja, alalà

Freddie is now officially the enemy. His unauthorised presence in the city a tightrope along which he has to walk back and forth every day. The streets bristle with black shirted men carrying guns who believe themselves taller than they are. Everything he carries within himself becomes secret, something that gives off illegal light and heat inside him. Sometimes he feels like a shadow that glows with this light, this heat.

The city undergoes a bleak cosmetic transformation. Crude asbestos sheds hide the Gates of Paradise of the Baptistery and the sculptures in Piazza della Signoria vanish behind ugly industrial casing. The stained glass windows of Orsanmichele are boarded up and sandbags and protective barricades are placed around the statues of the saints.

His eye is drawn to the grotesque stone carvings ornamenting many of the old palaces - nightmare images, underworld threshold guardians, here a Cyclops, there a mutant serpent with bat's wings. Had they even existed yesterday? The city seems to have unleashed ghouls as if to commemorate his own exile from his home.

The aspect of himself he least likes is his distance from things, an unwilled diffidence in his nature that exiles him from the thrust and interaction of life. Inwardly he edges away from contact. He sees this diffidence reflected in the forbidding facades of the palazzos, the protective casings built around the statues. It's as if he has been waiting for a wave to wash over him. Leave him glistening and exposed and primed for a more full-blooded communion with life. He expected Isabella to provide the wave. He now wonders if war is to be the wave.

His last breakfast in Florence. The play of light on the old medieval wall opposite. Making him think of the history of the stones, the struggles of blood and line they have witnessed. There is a campanile nearby and as he sits at the table reading a newspaper the bells chime. Bold timeless strokes which, like light after rain, give to the moment an undertow. The sun is warm on the back of his neck. Above, a woman throws open green shutters. Hangs a dripping sheet on the line. Then the waiter arrives. "Cappuccino," he says and when the cappuccino arrives he is shaken by the realisation of how much happiness there is in habit.

Later he and Isabella return home from a trattoria. His last supper.

"I still can't imagine you as the pilot of a plane."

"You think I'll fail at that too?"

"What else have you failed at?"

"Painting. Husbandry."

"I could never imagine being married to anyone else."

"Is that a compliment or a failure of imagination on your part?"

She throws a fork at him. Just like that. It flashes through the air. Strikes his cheekbone. Leaves a razor cut on his cheek.

He touches his cheek, looks at the smudge of blood on his fingertips.

"What was that for?"

"Because I hate men and you're a man. Because I'll miss you horribly. Why can't things just carry on as they were?"

He walks over to the window. Looks down at the candlelit Madonna in the tabernacle on the corner where the street divides into two roads. "As they were?"

"Yes. As they were. Who cares if you can't love me."

Being with her is as natural as pulling water up from a well.

"Probably I should have seen a doctor. I'm sorry I didn't see a doctor. Can doctors help with this kind of thing? I thought about it. Had imaginary conversations with imaginary doctors in my head. But I could never find the right words. Could never overcome my embarrassment. I even thought of confessing to a priest. Could it be classed as a sin? It often felt like one. A sin against the truth of who I am, what I feel. But it's not something one wants to admit. Especially at a time like this."

"At a time like what?"

"Fascism is like some giant national parade in honour of the male erection. Isn't it?"

"So all along this has been a political statement? The manifestation of your anti-fascist sentiment?"

"Well, Mussolini would hardly be proud of me, would he?"

She swivels her chair round at the table to face him. There is paint on her wedding ring, lead white and alizarin red. She hitches up her skirt, opens her legs. Shows him the inside of her thighs, her prettiest white knickers. She opens wide and closes her legs several times in succession. Uses her skirt as a fan, looking down between her thighs and then at him.

He watches her. The expression on her face. An expression she might have were she crawling about on all fours.

She stands up. Pulls down her knickers from beneath her skirt, with a shimmy of her hips, holds them in her hand.

"Perhaps if you believed I was someone else?"

She covers his eyes with the warm white undergarment. Knots it behind his head.

"I must look ridiculous."

"Then stop looking at yourself."

She bites his neck and pops open two of the buttons of the fly of his trousers. She slips her hand inside the gash. Her fingers and his naked flesh are separated by the cloth of his shorts. She fumbles about for the opening. Slides her whole hand inside and takes the tip of his stirring manhood between thumb and forefinger and tickles it with her nails.

She straddles him. Grips his erection firmly as she lowers herself down onto him. There is no smooth unguided entry. Like animals achieve. There is a little essential sharp male thrust, the thrust of possessive pride, which he seems to lack. She fumbles around a bit. Like she's trying to open a door with the wrong key. He loses connection with the part of him she grips in her hand. She repositions her hips. Shifts her centre of gravity. Then he is inside her. He has been inside her before but never for very long. The expectation of failure is already like a mosquito buzzing in his ear. Luring him away from the moment. He concentrates on keeping his body and mind in the present tense. On avoiding all shifts into past or future tenses. He screws up his face. Grits his teeth. As if in the midst of a struggle. As if someone is doggedly trying to snatch away something frail he holds in his hand.

She settles into a slow rocking rhythm. He listens to her breathing. Concentrates on that. The dragged out sea notes from deep places inside her. A connection is made. A new level of arousal is achieved. A circuitry of pulses tingle and ache just beneath the surface of his skin. He screws shut his eyes more tightly. Centering himself in the rhythm their bodies have made. The precarious equilibrium that hangs together like a piece of music. His hands stretched wide over her flanks. Still fearing the intrusion of anything coming between him and this rhythm they are making. But a gasp from him causes a rhythmic skip in her movement, like a scratch on a gramophone record. And the tingling is snuffed out. He no longer feels the connection. He comes adrift from the moment. His mind active again. The expectation of failure like a mosquito buzzing in his ear.

She stops moving on top of him. A breath of cold air enters the place where formerly they were joined. He peels off the blindfold.

"Sorry," he says.

10 - September 1943

"NO ONE SALUTES anyone here, do they? I like that."

The gap between her front teeth and the faint smudge of blueberry lipstick on the enamel. It's the only chink in her armour. The only place he can detect any doubt in her. She stands by his side in her red cardigan, grey skirt, silk stockings with a pencil and notebook. Her eyebrows plucked to a thin commanding line.

"Is everything I say going to be taken down and used as evidence against me?"

"I don't have to use your name," she says. Kate, this attractive young woman who works for the magazine *Collier's*. She and Freddie have come to the end of their stroll around the perimeter track. They are standing near the red telephone kiosk. A locked chain circling it now that tonight's target is known. ("In case we have spies in our midst," he tells her). The runways taper over the green grass of the airfield towards the distant lines of yellowing chestnut trees. The windsocks all hang limp. She runs her hand down his arm. "And everyone dresses a bit differently. Everyone has their little quirk of clothing. You can see some individuality in the way you all dress. In the army you only have hair to go by. Are there no rules here?"

"Get out of PT and parades by hook or by crook. That's one of my rules."

There it is again. The gap between her front teeth. He watches her touch her earring. He is reminded of Isabella. Sitting at her mirror. *When a woman tilts her head to fasten an earring she so often becomes for the moment a quintessence of herself,* he thinks. *She becomes a thrilling foreign language.*

"Why did you go to see the CO earlier? After the briefing."

"Because we were assigned a different aircraft for tonight's op and the crew kicked up a stink. We're all attached to our kite.

Vicky, we call her. Every Lancaster has its own personality. Flies differently. Has what you called its own quirks. And we none of us care for N Nan. The kite we were originally assigned. N Nans are jinxed. N Nans have a habit of not making it back."

"You're very attached to your crew, aren't you?"

"You say that in a faintly slighting way, as though it's unnatural."

"War is unnatural, isn't it? Modern warfare. It's our machines against their machines. Isn't it bound to create unnatural emotional attachments?"

"How can an emotion be unnatural? Reg would call that an oxymoron."

"You see! You talk about Reg as though he's your wife."

He looks down at her feet in the dainty grey lizard skin shoes. *When I listen to you I feel I'm listening to the future*, he thinks.

"Our lives depends on our crews. We do our best to keep each other happy just as the mechanics do their best to keep the aircraft happy. Simple as that."

"It's a shame you're going out on an op tonight. I would have liked to talk more. Perhaps tomorrow night we could have dinner?"

He doesn't like her taking tomorrow for granted on his behalf. It feels like the rasp of a cat's tongue on his flesh.

"To think you'll be flying over Berlin while I'm listening to wretched jokes in the Fox and Garter or whatever that pub's called."

"The Fox and Crown," he says. "No garters."

The empty gnawing sick feeling in his stomach tightens its grip. The absence of saliva in his mouth.

"Time for me to get kitted up."

"Good luck." She leans forward. Slides a hand over his hip and kisses him lightly on his lips.

There is little conversation in the locker room. It's the moment when the coward in him is most vociferous, most demanding of attention. Like the others he has to denude himself of his identity before take-off. Must carry on his person nothing that gives any clues to his squadron or location. He is given his thermos flask of coffee, boiled sweets, chewing gum and bar of chocolate.

"Thanks for getting us Victor back," says Davy. The shy beautiful boy with green eyes, long lashes and hair as black as a crow's wings. Davy usually only speaks when spoken to. It gives him a thrill of privilege every time Davy begins a conversation with him. He wants others to notice when he is sharing a moment of confidence or laughter with Davy. Feels more protective of Davy than of anyone else. The awkwardness between them dispelled a little by the bicycle race they had to the pub the other night. They laughed into each other's eyes afterwards. And then the shyness returned. But he knows now that Davy likes him.

"The Wingco thought he was doing us a favour by giving us N Nan. Reckons she's in better nick than Vicky."

Spencer, the rear gunner, mutters something by way of a comment. He always talks quietly and quickly. Almost under his breath. But a current hums and crackles through Spencer's short stocky frame even when he sits still. As if he is wired up to a generator.

The knots of tension unravel the minute Freddie gets the green light. When V Victor picks up speed down the runway she feeds all her power into his blood. It's like the feeling he had when racing his whippet over the sands as a boy. The affection he feels for this aircraft is like the affection he felt for his dog too. As if she is a living thing.

Soon he is looking down at the shadows lengthening over the fields and roads of England. The taste of malt vinegar returns to his mouth. He shook out too much of the stuff on his bacon, eggs and chips. It is not an auspicious taste.

He has tacked the photograph of Isabella onto the control panel. She looks up at him from the dials, the needles, the rudders, the throttles, the levers. The controls that obey his commands, as his body doesn't. But it is the woman Kate he can't get out of his head. And every time he pictures her he gets an erection. He has an erection when they leave the English coastline behind and the sea far below is a puzzle of chalked doodles. Another erection when they fly over the Dutch coast near Alkmaar. Until the sky around them begins winking with comets of red fire as the coastal flak batteries open up and all of a sudden V Victor seems to grow in size around him. Become an enormous target for the gunners below. He changes course every fifteen seconds to confuse the men down there who want to kill him and his crew. Twitching the rudders. He is attentive again to the rhythm of V Victor's engines. Not his body's. But this infidelity to his wife worries him. In a superstitious way.

I haven't done anything wrong, he inwardly complains.

"So. You going to accept Kiss-Me-Kate's overtures?" Reg wags a gauntleted playful finger at him.

The question startles him. As if Reg was listening to this thoughts.

"You want me to join your club?"

Reg is betraying his young fiancé with a WAAF teleprinter operator called Madge. The friend of the parachute packer. He is wearing one of her perfumed silk stockings around his neck. Now and again the scent of it slinks its way into Freddie's oxygen mask through the stink of rubber and oil.

"I can't say no if it's handed on a platter," says Reg through the intercom.

"I've noticed."

"It's like saying no to life. I'm always left with such a barren idea of myself if I let an opportunity pass. I get home and I feel like yesterday's dirty plates, smeared in dried sauce and grease. I have this idea that it's the women we don't sleep with who haunt us. They become like a missing page in our book. The part of the story we'll never know. That we have to skip. That's why faithful married men have such thin books."

"Nav here. Just to say you two crack me up."

"Thanks Cyril," says Freddie. "That's what we're here for. To keep you chaps entertained."

The nose of the aircraft burrows into another thick reef of cloud. Darkening the cockpit. Muffling the noise of the engines. Freddie watches the clouds shroud the length of the port wing. Then tear free. The moon is huge. Like a hooded face staring in through a window. A daunting fortune-telling presence in the darkening sky.

Cruising at 25,000 feet. Where they can't be seen by the human eye from the ground. Holding the air speed steady. The tips of the wings swaying with mesmerising poise. Lending a touch of grace to the grinding engine noise. The ghosted glaze of moonlight on the layers of cloud below. Of the formation of about five hundred aircraft he can see no more than three. There is a feeling of peace and liberation. A feeling that comes and goes. That lasts no more than a moment. He listens to the increased volume of his breath in the oxygen mask. Reg chewing gum beside him. His tension a current in the cockpit. The Third Reich below. A grid of indistinct outlines appearing and disappearing through streamers of vapour and banks of cloud. Condensation sketching cryptic reflections on the perspex. Darkness thickening to a black vacuum through which the aircraft noses its path onward. Illuminated every now and again by the yellow marker flares laid down by the Pathfinders.

Five or six miles away in the distance he sees thin methodical moving pencil strokes of silver. Probing the night sky like scissors.

"Nav here. That's it. Berlin. Hitler's down there somewhere, chaps."

"Don't forget we're looking for red target indicators with green stars."

The pressure in his eardrums as he brings her down. He yawns. To make his ears pop. Reg shouts to make his ears pop. To relieve some tension. V Victor, as if in the midst of a coughing fit, bumps along in the slipstream of the bombers up ahead. The world below is a madcap firework display. Red and green globes melting living colour over the horizon. Fountains of tracer shooting up in dying arcs. An incandescent gold, red and white stitching embroidering the black canvas of sky. The foraging fingers of the searchlights moving and crossing in slow deliberate arcs. An army of them. Like sentient beings from another galaxy. Burning holes in the sky. The smoky scarlet light from German fighter flares hanging eerily above. Freddie can see all the noise but can't hear it. Because of the mighty hum of the aircraft's engines.

A searchlight catches the plane for an instant. Freddie's body goes icy cold and his heart is jolted as though a current feeds electricity into his veins. The cockpit is awash with searing bluish brightness. As if a revelation is about to take place. As if an angel is about to appear. He can't see the instrument panel. The finger of light has the aircraft in its grip. Holding her suspended above the city. As if she is perched on a tightrope. Visible to the whole of Berlin down below. The glare bites into his eyes, sucks strength from his legs. He kicks the rudders to the right. The starboard wing tilts down. He pulls the wheel back. Below, a shifting tableau of coloured globes slide over the tilting smoking surface of the earth. Some roads and buildings made visible by fires and incendiaries.

The beams are now off their line. They settle on another Lancaster just above. Pinioning her to the sky. He has never seen anything so nakedly exposed. But he doesn't look for long. He struggles to get his night vision back. More streaks of crackling light come yearning up from below. The aircraft rocks and shudders. Shrapnel drums against the fuselage.

The radar directed flak intensifies. Like swarms of angry red-and-yellow-eyed snakes slithering up invisible ropes in the sky. The sky around them is a glittering maelstrom of light. The stars pale into insignificance. Down below the city is lit up in sections as shockwaves fan out in kaleidoscopic bursts. Shell smoke rising up from the ground. On his right a burst of flame and a thick guttering of black smoke lit up by the geometry of the searchlights.

"I think that's N Nan that's been hit."

"Where are you, Davy?"

"In the astrodome, sir."

I wish you wouldn't call me sir.

The aircraft over to port explodes in a mushrooming orange fireball. The noise penetrates the cockpit. Jolts the aircraft into a skittish leap. Spatters her with flaming debris. Freddie instinctively ducks in his seat.

"If that is Nan, could it have been us?" says Reg. "Makes you wonder, doesn't it?"

Freddie sees briefly the recently arrived aircrew of N Nan as he remembers them. He didn't know any of them except as faces at briefings and in the mess. Their faces are already pallid, spectral.

"Bomb-aimer here, skipper. Bomb doors open."

"Got you, Spike. Turning on radio."

The oxygen mask chafes the skin on his face.

"Bomb on the red flares with the green stars, please," says the Master Bomber over the intercom. His casual voice, as if he is giving advice to his tailor.

"Left, skip."

Far below a grid sheeted in quicksilver and every bomb sends a mist of ripples through it like heavy rain splashing down on a puddle.

"Straighten up. Steady. Steady. Nearly there."

A more violent wave of turbulence shakes the fuselage. Freddie senses the close presence of another kite before Woodsy warns him.

"Skipper, there's a Lanc swinging across almost directly above us."

Aircraft crowd the smoke-strewn sky. He can see at least a dozen silhouetted against the smoking flares. The Lancaster above to port has its bomb doors open.

"Left a little."

"I can't. Unless we want a cookie dropping down on us."

He gives the wheel a nudge and twitches the rudders. Keeping a watchful eye on the bulk of the looming Lancaster. Cursing her pilot under his breath.

"Then we'll have to go around again."

"Just drop the fucking bombs, Spike," says Reg.

"Negative. Target is to the left a little."

The massive outline of the Lancaster above veers away just as he is about to take further evasive action.

"Okay, Spike. Let's get rid of these damn bombs."

"Steady now. Steady."

The flak is a meteor storm now. It is better not to look. He fixes his eyes on the control panel.

A string of bombs, lit by chandelier flares, somersault lazily down past the cockpit from another aircraft above. He looks back at Reg. His eyes saying, bugger this for a lark.

"Bombs gone."

He knows this from the quickfire medley of thumps beneath his seat and the sudden jubilant leap into the air of V Victor.

He doesn't allow himself to think about the people below.

He keeps V Victor level and steady for another thirty seconds. So they can get the photographs they need for this to count as another of the thirty ops they must tally up before being granted six months leave.

"Skip. Two fighters. None o'clock. Corkscrew! Port!"

He shoves the screaming aircraft into a steep downward turn. Trying to elude the searchlights. The shrapnel. The fighters. Then jerks it upwards in the opposite direction. The ground, lit up by all the blast rings of the bombs, tilting from side to side and at times appearing almost upside down. His wrists and arms beginning to ache with the physical effort and tension. Beads of sweat gluing fabric to the back of his neck. Harness straps sore on his shoulders.

"Woodsy! Fighter coming down towards you."

"Time to lose your virginity, Woodsy. Shoot the bastard down," says Reg. His throat sounds dry.

He hears the clatter of Woodsy's guns in the headphones. The recoil sends shudders through the fuselage. He checks he's wearing his parachute harness. Word is you get lynched or burnt alive by the civilians if you float down into one of these German cities you're bombing.

11 - October, 1943

"ARE YOU Jewish?"

The SS officer in the grey-green field uniform hides his smile but she registers the highlight of amusement in his eyes. His mouth is small and thin lipped. She would aim for the petulance in its line were she to paint it. There is a punctiliousness about his gestures, like a code of chivalry he prides himself on possessing. He has black greased hair that is shaved above his ears. Like his Führer.

"No. Why do you ask?"

"Because I'd like to be in a position to do you a favour."

Isabella is standing by a chipped snowy goddess amongst the box hedges and potted citrus trees on either side of a gravel path. The fourteenth century Palazzo Pellegrino, up in the hills above Florence, still retains a ghost of the sunset's glow on its honeyed stones, its terraced façade.

"Even if it meant betraying your Führer?"

"It would be our secret. I think I would like us to share a secret."

She turns to look down at the tiered vineyards and, beyond, the vignette of Florence in the valley as if scooped up on a spoon. Its domes and spires and rooftops appearing to float on a tide of unearthly mist as inviolate and inaccessible as a private longing.

"I would very much like to see your studio. Maybe I could even commission you to paint my portrait?"

"How do you know I paint?"

"It's my job to find out what people do."

The silver sequins of her dress catch and relinquish light every time she moves. She moves now and fiddles with the pearls around her neck. She catches him looking down at her hand. His alert chilling eyes. There is a fleck of paint on her wedding ring. Rose madder.

"My task at the moment is to track down two paintings that have both gone missing. There. I've told you a secret."

"Which paintings?"

"Pontormo's Saint Anthony and Ghirlandaio's Annunciation. Do you know them?"

"I've never seen the Ghirlandaio. I've heard it's very beautiful."

"It is very beautiful. It was owned by a Jew. You haven't got them, I suppose?"

She doesn't return his smile. Max, the man who brought her to this concert of Bach cello sonatas, becomes visible amongst all the swimming figures on the candlelit lawn. He walks with a limp. The legacy of a shrapnel wound in his right thigh while fighting in Greece.

"Here comes your husband."

"How do you know he's my husband?"

"I always begin with the most logical assumption."

"Actually, we only met two days ago."

Damn, she thinks. *Why did I tell him that?*

She knows though why she told him. It is another attempt at assuring herself she is not betraying Freddie, not even in the eyes of strangers.

"So you know very little about each other? Not much more than we know about each other. Where, if I may ask, is your husband?"

"I don't know. He's one of the missing. Welcome back," she says, accepting the glass of wine Max hands her. "I would introduce you except I don't know your name."

"Captain Erich Heinkel."

A shrill scream makes her turn round. A little boy is chasing two girls in print dresses across the lawn towards the limoniaia. It's like one of her own memories. For a moment she is wearing the same floral dress, damp with grass stains, she made into a fan by twirling round in circles.

"We were just discussing secrets. Secrets are now our sanctity, wouldn't you agree, Max? Perhaps they always have been. There are people out there who will torture you for your secrets. One side tries to keep secrets; the other side tries to extract them. That's the game we're playing now. But excuse me. There's someone I need to talk to."

She watches Captain Erich Heinkel stride off. The someone he needs to talk to is a very good looking young man with a buoyant mass of dark hair and hungry pouting lips.

"A friend of yours?" Max says.

"Hardly. If he was wouldn't I know his name?"

"You might have been bluffing."

"Was it you who told him I paint?"

"I've never seen the man before in my life."

He presses his hand to his forehead, as if he has a headache. She succumbs to a moment of doubt about Max. She and Max have still not discussed politics. She knows very little about him but her instinct is that Max is no fascist. The question now is whether or not she can trust her instincts.

"And you're not bluffing either?" she says.

"No. I've stopped bluffing now."

"What does that mean?"

"This isn't the time or place for revelations."

"I don't know. Florence crouched down there like some fairy story kingdom waiting to happen."

She smiles and he smiles back, smiles up into her eyes and there is a faint weakening in her legs that she resists by sliding her wedding ring in a half circle on her finger.

Before they take their seats on the candlelit lawn she scans the faces of the audience again. *Who told him I paint?* It unnerves her that there is someone here who possesses knowledge of her, knowledge he must have stolen and have no right to possess.

The seat next to Isabella is empty. She has been waiting for someone to appear, to take this seat next to her. She looks around for other gaps in the rows of seated people on the lawn but there are none. She tells herself it is ridiculous to feel the empty seat has been claimed by Freddie's ghost.

The woman in the spotlight positions the cello between her legs. A hush descends. An intermittent smell of laurel leaves, of flattened herbs spices the early evening air. Isabella looks up at the night sky. The sickle moon high over Brunelleschi's dome. The yearning notes succeed each other as inevitably as ink forming letters into words on paper. The music sweeps the world clean. As if a sunken order of reality is about to rise up. She is aware of the map the stars make overhead and there seems to be a glistening dew on everything, as if she will pass into the next moment through a secret opening. The music and the timeless quality of the night make her miss Freddie. She feels curled up in his smell.

The last time Max asked about her husband she told him she would rather not speak of him. You don't want people knowing you have an English husband. Now that the Gestapo are here. So she was told. But Max asks again while driving her home through the blackout.

"I haven't heard from him in almost three years. I write him letters. I don't know if he reads them. I never get one back. No doubt that's not his fault."

"Was he on the Russian front?"

The headlights of the car tear a tabernacle out of the darkness and then fling it aside as they swing to the left, following the twist in the road. She has to decide how much she can trust him, this man called Max who walks with a limp she has once or twice found herself deeming an act.

"No. He's English. The last I knew he was training to be a pilot."

Max changes gear. He performs the act with an absence of grace. The car complains. The wrenching noise shudders up along her thighs.

"So that's the mystery?" he says.

"No mystery. It just isn't wise in these times to let too many people know you have an English husband."

"No. I understand."

He stops the car outside her home.

"Thanks for tonight," she says.

"You're not going to invite me in?"

"No," she says.

"But you'll see me again?"

She leans across and kisses him on the cheek.

"You know when you're on a train at a station and there's another train opposite and the other train starts moving and there's that utterly convincing illusion that it's your train that is moving and you feel a bit disorientated when you realise you're still standing still. That's what my life has been like since Freddie left." She says these words quietly to the mirror in her bedroom. Sitting in front of the bottles and pots and tiny caskets, the strewed jewellery, the smudges of coloured dust on the wooden surface, the one or two fingerprints and misted patches on the glass.

She lights a candle and stands in front of the full-length mirror. She takes the pins out of her blonde hair and watches it fall down on either side of her bared collarbone. There is a moving ache in her body. A sense of waves plunging in and out of hidden crevices, rasping and sighing.

She gathers up the hem of her white cotton nightgown and lifts it so as to see her bare thighs; twists around and peers over her raised shoulder to see herself from behind. She feels estranged from the body in the mirror. As if it is something already in the past tense, like a photograph. She looks down at her tanned feet and their red toenails. It strikes her as waste that no one is in the room to see what she sees in the glass.

12 - November 1943

FREDDIE STANDS on parade with the rest of the unit. The cold drizzle of early morning soaking into his battledress. He, like most of the men and women lined up, knows the disgraced man. The disgraced man with head bowed. A lesson to them all. They are all being treated as potential deserters by the new CO, Wing Commander Archibald Ramshaw, a middle-aged man of the old school with a rainbow dazzle of decorations on his tunic and a permanent sneer behind his moustache. Since his arrival everyone has had to smarten up. Everyone has had to submit to his slingshot diction, his regime of morning parades and inspections and drills. On days when operations have been scrapped due to bad weather Ramshaw sends them out on cross-country runs or orders comprehensive PT sessions. One day they were made to watch a film which showed in graphic detail the results of VD on the male and female genitalia. Just before lunch. This public humiliation of a man who has flown nineteen operations is the last straw. Ted Greenwood is about to be stripped of his wings and his rank badges. Freddie has never seen a man look so alone, so utterly humiliated. He knows Ted as the rear gunner who always gives his chocolate ration to a girl confined to a wheelchair who lives in the cottage next to the village pub. Ted's best friend, another rear gunner, bled to death after his legs were severed above the knees by a cannon shell during a sortie over Mannheim. Ted saw his friend's body when the badly shot up Lancaster arrived back at base. Ted's own electrically heated suit failed on his next operation and he spent four days in hospital with frostbite. Enough was clearly enough. Ted climbed out of his turret while his Lancaster was about to taxi and point blank refused to climb back in.

Ted Greenwood is made to stay on the parade ground after everyone is dismissed. Freddie looks back at him. He is picking at the strands of thread where his NCO stripes had been.

"Just when you thought Ramsore couldn't become any bigger a bastard..." says Cyril.

"Can you believe he's making us do a training flight today? I can't even see my boots."

"Let it be made clear. I will suffer no yellow bellies in my squadrons," says Cyril, imitating the CO.

At three o' clock Freddie walks towards V Victor with the rest of his crew. In the sleet and rain and thick swirling mist. The ground crew in their oilskin coats offer condolences with sympathetic shrugs of shoulders. Woodsy carries the cage with the homing pigeon inside. They call the bird Percy. Though it is probably always a different bird. Woodsy talks tenderly to it through the wire of the cage.

After half an hour in the air Freddie says into the intercom, "Sod this for a lark. Cyril, what's the nearest airfield?"

"Wickenby."

Freddie puts V Victor down at Wickenby. He delays any return to base because of the poor visibility. While he and his crew are chatting with some WAAFs a message arrives for him over the tannoy to report to the station warrant officer. The station warrant officer, clutching his swagger stick but with a faint smile of apology, tells him he has been ordered to fly back to base immediately or face court martial. Freddie rounds up his crew and, against his better judgement, takes off through a wall of fog.

The eerie muffling effect of the swamp of black cloud creates an uneasiness in the cockpit. Reg, he knows, thinks the worst just before setting foot on the aircraft. "Over imagine something beforehand and you take the pulse out of it when it happens. I've learned that to my disadvantage in the past. With women. Now it's a trait of mine that's finally become useful."

Freddie rolls back his head. All his neck muscles are tight with tension. It is cold too. And the oxygen tastes stale. V Victor bumps along like a toboggan. During training he had to fly a Lancaster with the windscreen blacked out. It isn't much different now. The markings and needles on the instrument panel, painted with radium, the only glow in the dark.

"I wish someone would tell me what the point of this is. Aren't we short of crews? Aren't we short of petrol?"

Then a startling flash tears apart the darkness. Lights up the clouds. As if God has taken a photograph. Then another. Suddenly blue flames are dancing in a madcap circuit over the framework of the windscreen. Freddie looks to starboard to see the propellers are two cartwheels of flame, like the preparation for a circus trick.

"Bloody hell. My gun barrels and the trailing aerial are covered in flames. And I'm being attacked by hailstones."

It is Spencer in the rear turret.

"I'm losing radio reception," says Davy.

Snakes of electricity are performing a kind of mating dance with V Victor, wreathing her in blue flames. Leaping up from the guns to the window rivets and then shooting along the fuselage by Freddie's side.

"Anyone else expect to see a giant wizard with a wand at any moment?" he says into the intercom. He reaches out his hand and the blue light jumps from the metal framework of the canopy to his gloved hand.

For a while he can get no response from Flight Control. Then there is a beautiful female voice in his ear. "V Victor, you are clear to land, over," says the voice over the r/t.

When Cyril tells him he should be approaching base he strains his eyes through the murk for the white marker lights on either side of the runway or the glide path indicator lights. The altimeter shows 1000ft. Down below he can make out only the ghostly blur of V Victor's red navigation lights, which he flashes, reflected on the murk.

"Anyone see anything?"

"I can see a pinprick of light to port."

When he unstraps his harness and rises up from his seat he can just make out specks of light flickering like ashes in what looks like a billowing infinity of grey smoke.

He makes the approach, throttles back and some of the mist peels away from the squat square watchtower at the edge of the perimeter track. It is a relief to know the world down below still exists. He points the nose at the pathway of flares and down they go at 100mph. The fog swirling below and all around. When the wheels screech down on the concrete and V Victor comes to a halt with a hissing of brakes he is exhausted. He can feel a small pulse throbbing beneath his left eye and wonders if it is visible.

Spencer appears from the rear turret coated in frost and has a six-inch long icicle hanging from the valve at the bottom of his mask.

"Who do you think you are?" says Cyril "The abominable bloody snowman."

Freddie catches Davy's eye when he laughs.

Then he is told the CO wants to see him.

"What now?"

Wing Commander Archibald Ramshaw sits behind his desk wearing his best imperious expression. Freddie salutes.

"Do you know what you are, Hartson?"

Freddie can feel one of his eyebrows twitch up. He likes to think of himself as someone who can give quick clever answers to awkward questions. It is an important part of his self-esteem. Can lower his spirits when he finds himself slower than another man. But this, of course, is a trick question. "I like to think so, sir," he says.

Shouldn't have said that.

A kind of static bristles over the Wing Commander that seems to lift his hair. He sucks in this thin bottom lip before the bellowing voice bursts forth.

"You're a bloody disgrace. I don't like you. I don't like you at all. Do you know why I don't like you?"

"No, Sir."

"Because I don't like you."

He is imagining recounting all this to Reg.

"When I set a crew under my command a task I expect them to finish it. Who the blazes gave you permission to swan off to Wickenby?"

"The kite was struck by lightning, sir."

This answer seems to interrupt his line of thought. His freckled hand swivels the inkwell on his desk and then picks up a sharpened pencil which he points at Freddie. "When was the last time you had a haircut, Hartson? And when was the last time you polished the brass button on your cap? Look at the state of you. You look like a desert rat. How old are you?"

"Twenty-six, sir."

"And you wonder why you're still a non-commissioned officer?"

He has never once wondered this. He is happy with his bunk in the hut with the rest of his crew. Only Reg is restless. Because of the attractive batwoman who attends on some of the officers. Officers who pretend they don't hear her throaty good morning sir and so have to be shaken awake by her manicured hands with her breath closer to their necks.

"You know what I ought to do, Hartson?"

You ought to have me court martialled.

"I ought to have you court martialled."

The next day, on stand down, he, Reg and a bomb aimer from a new crew called Ivor catch the train to London. It turns out Ivor was on the same ocean liner as Freddie when he sailed into the harbour at New York and climbed up the rigging to get a better view of the Statue of Liberty. Then they were sent to different RAF training bases in Canada. Except Ivor broke his leg in a flying accident and has only recently arrived at the squadron. Usually it is general policy not to befriend new crew members because so few of them survive more than a month but Freddie felt drawn to the shy solitary Ivor and invited him on a whim. Reg was annoyed.

"Do you know how much chance he and that awful bloody crew of his stand of returning from even two ops?"

"Have a heart, Reg."

"It's precisely because I do have a heart. Why do I want to get to like someone who will probably be dead this time next week?"

In the carriage Ivor opens up a bit and shows them the ivory swan he wears under his lapel that his fiancé gave to him for luck. Then he shows them a photograph of his fiancé.

"Bloody hell! She's beautiful," says Reg. He slips the photograph in his breast pocket and then turns to look out of the window.

"Give Ivor back his fiancé, Reg."

The train shuttles past the slums outside London, row upon row of ugly terraced houses. Then they begin to see the bomb damage. The ghost structures. Whole streets of flattened debris. Jagged standing walls like ruined citadels. Dozens of barrage balloons are floating on their wires high above the rooftops and rubble.

There are no free tickets for any classical concerts. Only for a revue show.

"Why not?" says Reg. "Dancing girls is just what I feel like. What about you, Ivor?"

Ivor smiles, his hands buried deep in his trouser pockets.

After tea in Lyons at Marble Arch they are escorted to the manager's private box when they arrive at the theatre. The show is appalling. So appalling it becomes enjoyable. They are given free drinks during the intermission. The manager then appears on stage among the scantily clad chorus girls. He takes a microphone and begins delivering a speech about the bravery of the armed forces. When a spotlight shines up into his face Freddie's heart begins racing and he feels the possibility of panic in all his body's pulses. For a moment he is over Germany, coned by searchlights with guns flashing below and the muscles in his body poised for the exertion of throwing the aircraft into a steep lurching dive.

"Come and join us on the stage, gentlemen."

He, Reg and Ivor are led down onto the stage and greeted with thunderous applause. The manager hands the microphone to Freddie.

"Thank you very much," Freddie says. He can't think of anything else to say.

Then the band starts up and he finds himself between two chorus girls who are inciting him to dance. With each hand pressed to the bare midriff of a perfumed and painted chorus girl he performs a few dance steps to more thunderous applause.

He only begins to enjoy what happened when he steps off the tube at Liverpool Street station, when it becomes a story he can tell. He imagines telling it to Isabella. They have to step over all the mattresses and bodies under blankets on the platform and push past men and women undressing for bed. This is what he doesn't see and rarely imagines when he is piloting V Victor over German cities.

Freddie wakes up with a start on the train. His head on Ivor's shoulder. The world outside is gleaming with a fresh covering of snow. The first snowfall of the year. A wondrous silence has settled over the landscape.

"Isn't it a bit early for snow?"

"Who's complaining? With any luck we'll be grounded for the whole winter."

They get back to base just before curfew. There is a snowman on the bonnet of Wing Commander Archibald Ramshaw's two-seater green Bentley. And written beneath, I ought to have you court martialled.

"Thank God, I have a watertight alibi," Freddie says.

13 - October 1943

IN PIAZZA D'AZEGLIO, Isabella kicks through the fallen ankle-deep leaves of the high sycamore trees. Children used to play here before the war. Now the large square is used to grow corn and cabbages. A fascist militia with a light machine gun hanging from his shoulder stands guard over the cabbages. He looks at her with stern defiance, as though daring her to ridicule the role he has been assigned in the war. Corn and cabbages. It is another example of the comic ineptness of the measures taken by the fascists to prepare for war. She remembers in 1940 when the city's population had been called upon to donate all the metal objects they could spare. Married women were asked for their wedding rings. Florence's piazzas were thus heaped with enormous piles of tarnished rusting metal objects. She had thought that if her country was in need of this heap of junk to fight a war then it was a war it would surely lose. There was something almost touching about the slapdash poverty of the contribution. Candelabras, door handles, pipes, bits of engines, tools – how much rubbish there was in the world! It later occurred to her that these bits of waste metal would in all probability be melted down and fashioned into weapons, ammunition maybe. That the candelabra she was looking at might end up lodged in someone's chest in the form of a bullet, someone who would never know that a household ornament of mysterious provenance would cause his death.

Later the government called upon the populace to donate all their copper to the war effort. She was out walking one day not long after this decree was issued when two planes appeared in the sky. A man looked around, assuring himself he had an audience, then pointed up at the planes. "Look," he said in a very loud voice, "There go my saucepans."

As she gets closer to Maestro's studio memories seem to settle on her skin like pollen dust. She remembers how beautifully Maestro painted her as Eve, right down to her pubic hair. She often thinks of that painting. Wishing it safe.

The green door is open. She climbs the familiar chipped marble stairs that turn off at a sharp angle near the top. She enters the corridor, where some of Maestro's landscapes and portraits hang. The paintings greet her like mildly oppressive friends. This is where she learned discipline. This is where she began to hew her life of ascetic routine. Fosco, her old nemesis comes to meet her. Like a threshold guardian. His curly black hair is swept back from his forehead but thick at the back of his ears, like a beret.

He says nothing. Has nothing to offer her. No greeting, no show of surprise, no hostility even.

"Who is it?"

Maestro's voice, still forbidding with its hair-triggered irritability, comes from behind the black drape that seals him in his inner sanctuary.

"It's Isabella, Maestro. I came to say hello."

"Come in."

She sweeps aside the curtain. Maestro is sitting in a chair, beneath the high draped north window. He holds an old sable brush. Still wearing clothes she recognises, still smelling sharply of himself, an insidious medicinal smell. A boy with tousled dark hair is getting dressed over in the corner. He has his naked back to her. Isabella looks at the picture Maestro is painting. A dashing young man with a bare torso which Maestro has painted with pulsing sensuality. She recognises the painted model at the same time he turns round to face her. It is the young man she saw whispering with the German SS officer at the Bach concert. There is recognition in the look he gives her too. She is aware of a sudden flare in her body, a flush of blood though she does not know what its message is.

"Saint Sebastian. Tomorrow I will start painting the arrows and the wounds. Perhaps I will ruin it. What do you think?"

"It's beautiful."

"I've been told the Third Reich would approve of my paintings. Is that a compliment, do you think?"

She kisses Maestro on either cheek, something she has never done before. Such gestures were frivolous. Women were frivolous. That was what he always made her feel.

"Thank you, Ascanio. See you at the same time tomorrow."

The boy in his tight clothes and rakish hat slings a rucksack over his shoulder and gives her a knowing smile before he leaves. Fosco accompanies him.

"Fosco found him. Perfect Saint Sebastian, don't you think?"

"You've lost weight."

"The black market isn't what it was now the Nazis are here. Most of all I miss my morning coffee. That always took me back to square one, which when you're a serious painter is where every day should begin."

Is he implying I'm not a serious painter? Reading layers of meaning into his comments about her art was her homework as a student. She sat in squares at lunchtime, replaying his critiques in her mind, studying his words as though they were primitive cave paintings with concealed depths of meaning.

"I'll try to get hold of some real coffee," she says.

"I heard you married Freddie."

"Yes, I married Freddie."

Fosco returns to the studio. There's a new brightness in his eyes, as if his face is lit by a flame.

She looks around, primarily for his painting of her. She can't see it.

"So Fosco was right. He said the two of you would make babies."

He still talks about people as if they're not in the room with him.

"We haven't made any babies."

"Did you hear that, Fosco? Isabella and Freddie got married."

"Congratulations," says Fosco. He gives off a chill and it is as if she can see the breath accompanying his words on air.

"Fosco thinks the English no longer have any initiative as a nation."

"You're still a fascist then, Fosco?" she says.

Fosco cracks his knuckles. Makes it plain her question doesn't warrant an answer.

"Fosco's taken up billiards. And cards. He says he only enjoys pursuits whose rules he can understand."

"I'm still painting," she says.

She realises that the expectation, the desire that Maestro will cast his eye over her work is still an important part of her aspiration at the beginning of every new picture she paints. That she still craves his approval. Even now. Nearly seven years on.

"Have you still got your painting of me?"

"Yes. It's here somewhere. I've left it to you in my will."

She begins to cry. It's the natural response to everything she has learned about life but she hates it that Fosco sees her cry.

14 - November 1943

FREDDIE and Reg don't attend Ramshaw's early morning parade. They stay in bed. Luckily there is no roll call.

The battle order for tonight is posted on the notice board outside the mess.

After breakfast Freddie and his crew are ordered to help shovel away the snow on the runways. Word is Wing Commander Archibald Ramshaw is furious. The paintwork on his Bentley was scratched during the construction of the snowman.

It isn't until half an hour before briefing that Freddie sees him. He is walking past the ops room with Ivor when the CO emerges at the door. Freddie is immediately aware of the mud on his boots and his loosely knotted tie after toiling with a shovel for three hours. He and Ivor stop in their tracks and salute.

"It was you, wasn't it, Hartson?"

"Sir?"

"You might want to pray you don't return from the sortie tonight."

"Yes, sir."

Tonight V Victor will be going to Düsseldorf. The big surprise is that the CO is coming along.

Please god, not on V Victor.

"I will be accompanying Flight Lieutenant Trevor Hanway's crew in W Willie as an observer."

Freddie tips back on his chair and twists his head towards Ivor sitting at the bench behind. Ivor is Trevor Hanway's bomb aimer.

Ramshaw points out all the known German anti-aircraft batteries along the route, the fighter bases likely to be activated.

Jabbing at the red hatched areas on the map with his swagger stick.

"And no more of this damn cowardly weaving to avoid enemy fighters. I want this to stop. If I see any of this squadron weaving tonight I'll court martial the whole crew. You're to fly straight and level so as to provide a stable platform for the gunners to fire from."

"With our bloody pea shooter guns against their cannons," someone behind says beneath his breath.

Briefing over, Freddie hands out the escape kits to his crew – maps of the target area printed on rice paper, needle and cotton, razor and a tiny stick of soap, hard tack rations, in the form of chocolates, nuts, vitamin tablets, water purifying tablets, Benzedrine tablets, a tiny compass disguised as a fountain pen, German currency. All in a little cellophane packet. They also have a collapsible rubber water bottle and a passport photograph of themselves.

Then it is sausages, chips and eggs in the mess. They have twenty minutes before they are expected in the locker room.

"As if your crew wasn't ghoulish enough already," Reg says to Ivor.

"They're not so bad. Simon the wireless operator is a good chap."

"Ramsore will probably inspect your buttons during the bomb run. We expect a full debriefing tomorrow morning. I want to know everything he says and does."

There is an argument in the locker room. Someone has stolen a ragdoll, the lucky mascot of a Rhodesian wireless operator who is famous for starting soda siphon fights in the mess. Eventually it is restored to him with nervous laughter. Freddie has the feeling of having smoked one too many cigarettes. Doesn't stop him from smoking another. There is the smell of vomit on someone's breath. Once again he has handed in his farewell letter to Isabella. Haunts him now with its inadequacies. He wishes he had written a new one. He is about to make a note to do so tomorrow when a shiver of superstition forbids him to take tomorrow for granted so casually.

Standing together on the grass by the dispersal pan with their parachutes and flight bags they see the Wing Commander and his crew exit from a truck. The Wing Commander stands his crew to attention. Then his voice bellows over the darkening flat fields – "By the left, quick march, left right, left right" - and he marches his crew to W Willie.

"I've seen everything now," says Cyril when he stops laughing. "Can you believe that pompous old git? If ever I've willed anyone to get the chop…"

Freddie might be willing it too if it wasn't for Ivor.

The knowledge that Ramshaw is in the Lancaster that will follow V Victor onto the perimeter track makes Freddie nervous. The memory of his apprehension, his fear of failure, the first time he ever piloted a Lancaster on an operation has returned to his muscles and reflexes. The perimeter track is narrow and winds in places like a race circuit. V Victor is bloated with twelve tons of bombs and fuel. He has to deftly guide her with brakes, rudders and timely bursts of power from the outer engines while at the same time running through the checks with Reg. If he miscalculates she will crab off into the grass and get stuck there, holding up the entire operation. He imagines this happening and can't help smiling when he pictures Ramshaw's expression in the Lancaster behind.

"Trim?"

"What you grinning about?" says Reg swivelling round on his collapsible canvas seat.

"Trim?"

"Ready for take-off. What are you grinning about?"

"Private joke. Flaps?"

He sees a Lancaster climbing slowly upwards, silhouetted against the light in the sky above. Then another following in its wake.

He waits for the green light. Opens the throttles. The power of the four engines thundering up through the seat of his pants. Then they are airborne. Beginning their eighth operation. Eight, it has been established, is no one's unlucky number. He circuits around the base three times to gain altitude.

The smell of hydraulic fluid, petrol and oil is replaced by the pungent stink of rubber as he puts on his oxygen mask. As they approach the first rendezvous point over the English coast he begins to make out other bombers in front, behind, to the left and right. Somewhere over the North Sea they all disappear again.

It takes about an hour to climb to today's operational height of 20,000ft. Moonlight is dancing on the airscrews.

"Navigator here. You know we were told there would be fairly light winds coming from the east?"

"Yes Cyril."

"Well, in actual fact, they are blowing at about 90mph from the west."

"In life, there's pukka gen and there's duff gen," says Reg. Then he pinches his nose and blows out his cheeks, presumably to relieve the pressure on his eardrums.

"Enemy coast ahead," says Cyril.

Even through the headset he can sense the heightened tension and alertness that suddenly invades the aircraft. He now begins to drop V Victor's wings, first to starboard, then to port, then back to starboard to give the gunners an opportunity to spot any stalking night fighters below.

"Tinsel time," says Reg.

Reg is soon crouched down by the chute. Throwing out into the night sky the aluminium strips of foil that will appear on German radar as aircraft.

Now and again Freddie tries to imagine the German direction finding stations down below, all those busy men and women whose task it is to send his death up to him.

"Wonder how Ramshaw is getting on?" says Woodsy.

"If we spot him at any point you have my permission to open up your guns on him," says Reg.

V Victor passes through streamers of moonlit cloud.

Freddie needs to urinate. He uses an empty syrup jar. It isn't easy to pop open the tiny buttons of his fly when wearing zippered flying gauntlets and, beneath, silk flying gloves. When finally he manages to fish it out he sits there with the jar in his lap trying not to splash any urine on his trousers. Always wondering if Reg is looking.

Over Holland the constant glints of water fatten into one wide river, the Rhine. Ice begins flying off the propeller and hitting the fuselage, like a pack of gremlins trying to gain entrance to the aircraft.

Reg is down on his knees balancing the flow of fuel from the various tanks and jotting down his actions in his logbook.

"You okay, Spencer? Must be damn cold back there."

"Don't worry about me, skipper."

"That's right. Don't worry about him. Just keep on weaving, skipper."

Up ahead the latticework of searchlights is turning the cloud into a froth of light against which some bombers are silhouetted at varying heights. The beams flick back and forth in V Victor's flight path.

"Cyril, we've got searchlights about five miles to port. Should they be there?"

"No. Must be mobile flak units."

A white flash on the ground then red, green and white squirts of light hosing up into the ghost haze of the searchlights. V Victor, escaping attention, flies overhead. Then only moonlight for a while picking out hills and valleys in heavy shadow and twisting ribbons of water and the occasional cluster of buildings. Poignant in the spell of peace they evoke.

"How's our wireless operator?" asks Freddie, still more shy with Davy than any other member of the crew. Davy told him the other day that he passed his exams to go to grammar school but his parents couldn't afford the uniform so, at fourteen, he went to work as an apprentice electrician.

"In the astrodome with my eyes peeled, sir."

Why does he still call me sir?

V Victor reaches the last turning point over the Rhine. Cyril gives him the new course. Cloud has formed and there is now a vast white moonlit canopy below the wings.

"Who did build the snowman on Ramsore's Bentley? Anyone know?"

"You did, skipper. That's the word."

"That's what he thinks. Said he's going to have my guts for garters tomorrow."

"Another month of him and his bloody lectures on indiscipline, untidiness and inefficiency and I reckon the whole squadron will be giving themselves up to the Germans," says Woodsy.

"Better idea would be faking a crash landing in Sweden."

"Good idea. Give me a course for Stockholm, Cyril."

If you're bantering and joking, if you're finding humour in the situation are you less likely to die? Sometimes it seems so. Sometimes it seems it is the bond of laughter and camaraderie more than his crew's technical skills that will stop any cannon shells from piercing the skin of V Victor.

"Nav here. Estimate one five minutes to target."

Through gaps in the cloud the city is canopied by the thickets of groping searchlights and lit up by the incendiaries and the continuous flashing of bombs. Red and yellow tracer shells crisscrossing in parallel lines from the flak batteries.

"They're firing at us now."

V Victor enters a hailstorm of flak. Yellowy red bursts and heavy smoke from previous shell explosions. Tracers drifting up lazily and then zipping past at high speed. Freddie steels himself to guide V Victor through this dazzling panorama of terrors, this unceasing barrage of hot exploding metal.

And he has to play the guessing game with the flak gunners. No doubt they are predicting him to take evasive action. But are they predicting him to lose height or gain it? Swing over to the left or swing over to the right?

Up ahead red flares with green stars cascade down like melting wax. Everyone is talking at once on the intercom. Spencer reports a bomber shot down by fighters. Then the dry laissez faire voice of the master bomber,

"Don't bomb the greens. Bomb the reds. Bomb the reds."

So as not to impair his night vision Freddie struggles not to look at the fires, the otherworldly reds and greens of the target marker flares, the fireworks of flak. He can't though help looking at a small orange ball that rapidly expands and flares up with bright white light. He watches the port wing fall off the flailing Halifax. Fluttering down through the coloured smoke like a wafer. A tiny man appears beneath the tail, clasping his knees to his head, performing a triple somersault with the moon low behind him. The aircraft begins twisting and dropping towards the ground. Then it explodes and disintegrates. Freddie eases to starboard to avoid the debris.

"Anyone see what happened to that chap?"

"No. He just vanished."

V Victor begins rattling, her engines no longer fusing smoothly into one central pulse.

"Look out, skipper!"

The windscreen is suddenly filled with the lumbering shape of another Lancaster swinging into V Victor's flight path. It is huge, lit by the flashes of flak and the light of the fires below. He throws the stick forward. Then ducks instinctively. As they go down he sees the belly pass over his head through the perspex. So close he can see splashes of mud on its bomb doors.

"There's another bugger directly overhead with its bomb doors open."

He looks up in time to see the ugly canisters tumble down in slow motion towards the cockpit. They pass by within a whisker of V Victor's starboard wing.

Searchlights splay out, then stop, then come together again. Another waterfall of red flares. Red blobs that change shape as they fall slowly out of the sky, like bubbles of blood seen under a microscope.

Another Lancaster slides across V Victor's flight path with a JU 88 just behind it as if attached by an invisible thread.

"Bomb doors open."

Spike begins giving him instructions in his flat nasal voice. Then the exuberant lift into the air when he says, after clearing his throat, "Bombs gone."

The photo flare drops and explodes while the camera underneath takes the photograph of the target. Freddie puts the nose down to gain speed. Dives down to about 16000ft. Higher to port the bright blue smoke of fighter flares shows up the silhouettes of dozens of Lancasters.

Soon they have cleared the defended area. Cyril gives him the course that takes them thirty miles south and then on a westerly run home across the Rhineland and the Ardennes south of Belgium.

V Victor is now the only thing moving in the sky except for the odd shooting star.

The first traces of a new day brighten the sky when they cross the Dutch coast.

Freddie drops down below 10,000ft.

"Everyone can take his mask off."

Reg pours him a coffee from the flask. It's one of the best things he has ever tasted. He already wants another cup before has barely started his first cup.

Cyril gives the estimated time of arrival for the English coast.

Over the North Sea Davy tunes in to some dance music and they all sing along over the intercom.

The outline of Lincoln Cathedral seemingly afloat on the skyline heralds another successful homecoming. Always he wonders while looking down at it on its hill if he will ever see it again on an outgoing flight. Always it is a benediction when it comes into view on their return.

They are greeted by the duty ground crew on landing. Slapped on the shoulders and asked the usual barrage of questions. The frosted white grass sways beneath his feet as he urinates. He sees his breath on the air as a kind of marvel. Reg and Davy and Cyril are all urinating nearby. Everyone's hair flattened by the helmets they wore. They all piss while the young attractive WAAF driver waits. No one can muster a blush out of her but not from want of trying. Freddie can still feel the pressure of the oxygen mask on his face and taste the oxygen in his mouth. The WAAF drives them in the flight truck to the Ops Room for debriefing.

At debriefing Reg shows off for the WAAF intelligence officer. Freddie sips his tea laced with rum while his crew refer to their logbooks to answer the endless questions. He exchanges a few words with the Anglican padre. Nice of him to always stay up so late to welcome them back. On the blackboard W Willie still hasn't been chalked in as returned. The room is thick with smoke. There is still no sign of Ivor or Ramshaw when they leave debriefing and head to the mess for more eggs and bacon.

Before Freddie falls asleep the searchlight beams and gun flashes flicker behind his eyes. His ears still ringing. The image of the rearing bomber filling the windscreen is printed vividly on his mind every time he closes his eyes.

There are two empty bunks in the hut. A clock still ticking by one of the beds.

15 - October, 1943

BY THE OLD city wall, Isabella startles a cat that is nudging a maimed lizard with its paws. Dashes of red, like pigment, offset the luminous green scales. She knows a moment of shame for finding the contrast of colour beautiful. There is still a faint pulse in the neck of the reptile. It and Isabella look at each other. For a moment the world is all heartbreak and sadistic malice. She shoos away the cat.

Max is arranging a blanket over something in the wooden boat when she arrives down on the bank of the river. The grass is overgrown and strewn with litter. Here and there anthers are bright with uncollected pollen. She treads a piece of glass underfoot and the crack of it makes Max turn round swiftly. She catches the expression of alarm on his face before he masks it.

"Well this is something I've never done before," she says.

"I thought it would be nice to row you down the river at sunset."

She is struck again by how enlivening Max's appearance is to her. The pleasure she takes in it spreads like sunlight over the surface of her skin.

"Are you sure this is appropriate? I mean, you don't think it might be a bit decadent?"

"No, I don't think that at all," says Max. "What happened? The bruise under your eye."

"Oh. I upset a fascist brute at the cinema yesterday. He slapped me because I didn't join in in the singing."

Last night she had gone to the cinema. After the film there was newsreel of the progress of the war. Footage from the air of the German bombing of London was greeted with raucous cheering. Whole streets gouged out, flattened wastelands of smoking rubble. The snarling Italian commentator gloated over the destruction of "the heartland of the Imperialistic Terrorists".

She felt disgust. When the film finished the fascists all stood up, made the stiff-armed salute and began chanting Duce, Duce, Duce. The purpose of this saluting and chanting was to identify any detractors in the audience. She hadn't stood up, she hadn't chanted, so, against the backdrop of the glowing blank screen, a man in uniform slapped her.

Max flicks his head, settling his springy hair back into place. "God, these new Republican Fascists are nothing but street criminals and thugs."

"I had to get slapped to find out what your political views are," she says with a broad smile.

"If you're truly interested, and I can trust you not to be in the pay of Carità's secret police, I'll tell you what my political views are. But let's get this boat on the water first."

The old bells of the church of San Frediano toll with bold resounding strokes. In their wake broadening rings of silence seem to echo up over the rooftops. The setting sun rakes incandescent highlights over the water. A group of waterfowl on an island of grass half way across the river appear made of silver light. Two or three young boys are swimming in the water, breaststroking towards the church of Ognisanti and the Grand Hotel with its Nazi banners and staff cars parked outside.

She settles herself on the cross-slats in the stern of the boat and Max pushes it out onto the tide. He jumps in and the boat rocks and for a moment she feels she is about to be tipped over into the river. She screams and then laughs but Max seems oblivious. His boyish face looks strained, tense around the mouth, as if he has a toothache. He appears in a distant cemented kind of mood. She already misses his smile today. It was his smile that drew her to him. The frequency and generosity of it, its dance of ease and reassurance.

Max rows the boat towards the arches of Ponte alla Carraia. The rhythm of his oar strokes is a little ragged. There is a sheen of sweat on his brow. He rests the oars for a moment to take off his tie. Stuffs it into the pocket of his olive green corduroy jacket.

"Don't know what's the matter with me. I guess I'm not as young as I thought I was."

"Why don't you stop rowing for a bit? Let's just bask in all this beauty."

"I'd rather not."

"Stop rowing or bask in all this beauty?"

He resumes rowing, avoiding eye contact with her across the bow of the boat. Isabella begins to feel a bit uneasy. Realises how little she knows about this man. Her knowledge little more than a thin sheen of brightness, like reflected sunlight on an opaque pond. When she looks over at the rippling reflection of a Nazi banner on the water she is thinking of Freddie and berating herself.

"There's something I need to tell you," he says.

"I thought so."

"Why do you say that?"

"Because you seem like someone I don't know today."

"That doesn't augur well. I prided myself on being a good actor."

"Actor?"

"I do have something to tell you but it might be better if I wait until we've got past the German sentries on Ponte Santa Trinita before I tell you."

She frowns. Losing her patience with him for the first time.

"It's to do with politics," he says.

The shadow of a whirling gull passes over his face. There are half a dozen soaring in half circles and diving down in formation over the water. The riverside palaces are reflected in the water on either side of the river as rippling golden wafers. There is a pink underglow on the marble façade of San Miniato on the hill. The mosaic of Christ reflecting the benediction of the sun's dying rays over the city.

Max rows the boat with the tide towards the centre arch of Ponte Santa Trinita. She catches the eye of a German sentry in khaki uniform looking down at her from the parapet of the bridge. When the boat emerges on the other side she looks across at Max expectantly and impatiently. He continues rowing, glancing up at the parapet of the bridge.

"Well, we haven't been shot," she says.

"I'm working for the Partita d'Azione, Isabella."

"So you're against the Germans and you're against the fascists. I don't think I would have felt any desire to know you otherwise."

"Yes, I am against the Nazis and the fascists. Which means I'm putting you in danger every time I see you. I don't need to tell you what a wasp's nest of informers and spies this city is now."

"The odd thing is you make me feel a bit safer. Or you did before now."

"I'm happy to hear that. But you won't like what I'm going to say now."

There is a smell of river slime as they pass beneath Ponte Vecchio. Reflected watermarks ripple over the underside of the arches. A chill at the back of her neck makes her press her hand there.

"What?" she asks when the boat emerges back into clear air.

"Inside the suitcase under that blanket is an English radio transmitter. It was dropped by the Allies the other night along with a cache of weapons. I have to move it. Yesterday one of my companions was arrested by Carità's secret police. I have no idea how they got onto him but a whole group of us are in danger now. Carità and his thugs will torture him. I don't have much faith he will be able to hold out."

She knows he has used her tonight. A couple in a boat would arouse less suspicion than a lone man.

16 - November 1943

THE DEATH BEAMS slide around the sky like dancers on ice. As if exchanging partners in this vaulted ballroom of coloured smoke. He imagines a Strauss waltz accompanying the dance of the Nazi searchlights.

"Isn't it as if those searchlights are moving in time to a Strauss waltz?" he says into his microphone and hums a few bars of a Strauss waltz. He isn't sure which Strauss waltz it is he is humming. The most famous one.

No one replies to his humming.

He looks down through the swirling cloud smoke. The clouds look like kicked up sheets. He sees globes of molten red paint melting over the surface of the earth. Waterfalls of luminous colour. The medleyed pulsing of silver surf. He can't remember which city it is down there. He feels a bit drunk.

"Is that Florence down there?"

"Corkscrew. Starboard. Go."

His body primes itself for the operation in a flash. But he can't corkscrew to starboard because the formatted Lancasters to starboard and astern are too close. There is another Lancaster directly above. Her bomb doors open like a leering toothless mouth. The pilot in the aircraft to starboard is gesticulating madly at him. He can see the man's eyes above his oxygen mask. What does he want? He has to peel off to port. Into the night fighter's sights. He stamps on the port rudder. Expecting to be thrown forward inside his harness like a rag doll. But nothing happens.

"Reg?"

Reg isn't there. *Where the fuck did he go?* He decides Reg must have gone to the Elsen toilet. *Damn stupid time to go to the toilet.* He realises he too needs to urinate.

Flak. Shooting up in straight lines of illuminated dots. Each flash lights up the tiny German gunners down in the concrete bunkers. *Surely we're flying way too low?* He sees a group of little boys in the middle of a road, pointing excitedly up at him. *We're definitely flying way too low.* The bursting red-hearted shells. The grotesque masks of black smoke. *The tenth shell is for us.* He counts to seven. He checks all the dials on the instrument panel. All the needles are whirling round in a drunken dance. Not a single one of the aircraft's functions responds to his command. It's as if the aircraft is opposing his will. Arm wrestling with him. He looks out along the wing for signs of fire. Then the cockpit is flooded with blue light. The light burns into his eyes. It floods his whole being. He looks down into his naked lap. *Why aren't I wearing any clothes?* The perspex windscreen shatters. A lump of burning metal appears before his eyes. Spinning and smouldering.

Freddie wakes up sweating. His mouth tastes of stale crackers. His head is all pulsating sensitive tissue. A cymbal crash between his eyes. His body groans like mooring lines at high tide. He is curled up naked in an unfamiliar bed. In the half-light he can make out three other beds. There are photographs curling at the edges stuck to the walls above each of the beds. A smell of perfume. He can see a woman's underclothes strewn on top of a kitbag on the lino floor.

He went to see *For Whom the Bell Tolls*. With Reg and his teleprinter operator Madge. And Cyril was there too. Afterwards they met a rowdy group of American crewmen. Reg disappeared with Madge. To a bed and breakfast that cost five shillings. He knows this because Reg asked him for the five shillings. Reg disappeared with Madge and he got very drunk with Cyril and the Americans. They did shots together at the bar. Toasting the dead and those soon to die. He doesn't remember what happened to the Americans. He remembers stopping off at the bakery with Cyril. *Didn't we buy some jam tarts?*

Cyril made a bet with him as they were walking past the WAAF shower hut. Freddie kept looking up at the stars as he took off his clothes. In the movies two naked women in shower cubicles without doors or curtains would have screamed if a naked man walked in on them. But these two girls didn't scream. They froze with astonished expressions etched on their dripping faces. Then one of them said, "Well?"

"What beautiful legs you have," he said.

And that's the last thing he can remember.

He can hear an aircraft circling overhead. The drone of its engines dragged about by the wind. He remembers Davy is out on an op tonight as a replacement wireless operator for a scratch crew. The target was Berlin. You don't want to go to Berlin with a scratch crew. That's the last thing you want. The squadron notice board lists new arrivals. And underneath, on the Missing in Action list, the same seven names often appear. The wire bases of another seven stripped beds waiting to be made up again. Was that why he got so drunk? Fear for Davy's safety.

He swings his legs out of the bed. Arches his back.

"You're alive then?"

The whispering voice startles him in his nudity. He is not sure which of the three beds it comes from.

"Over here. I always wake up when the kites arrive home."

He sees a curved naked foot at the foot of the bed opposite. Toes curling up.

"Any idea where my clothes are?"

She lifts her head from the pillow. Tousled blonde hair frames a small pretty face with something pixie-like about it. "Hanging up beside my bed," she says.

"Sorry about last night. Were you..."

"One of the girls you ogled naked in the shower? I was the one you said had beautiful legs."

"Yes. I remember that." She had small breasts almost entirely covered by nipples like saucers.

"I'm glad to hear it."

"You might want to avert your eyes."

"You weren't so shy last night."

"I think it was a bet."

"Joan over there, the one with the two sanitary towels over her eyes, wanted to report you but I talked her round."

"Thanks. Did I ogle her too?"

"No. No one ogles Joan. She undresses behind a towel she holds up. And she kneels down by her bed to say her prayers at night."

"I can be a bit old fashioned at times too."

"You could have fooled me."

He smiles. She smiles. He looks at the photographs on the shelf above her bed where there is also a gas mask. "Was I wearing a gas mask at some point or did I dream that?"

"Can't say I remember that bit of the show."

He smiles again. Then feels awkward. "One of my crew is on ops tonight. Bit worried about him. Going to make sure he gets back okay."

She makes a show of covering her eyes with her hands. He walks naked across the icy brown lino. He imagines her peeking through her fingers. He finds he likes the idea. He finds himself looking at his naked body through a chink in her fingers. "What's your name?"

"Poppy."

"I'm Freddie."

"I know."

He pulls on his trousers. "You can uncover your eyes now."

"I hope your friend is all right," she says.

He looks for signs of luck in everyone he meets. Especially the women. As if every woman is an omen. As if every woman has the power to transfer to him some good or bad fortune. He is unsure about the pixie girl. Whether she has rubbed off onto him some dust of good or bad luck.

He walks out into the early morning air. The ground mist and the last of the night's darkness making everything look like a sketched idea for a painting. It has been raining. The smell of wet grass. Of newly aroused seeded life. The sun has not yet risen. He follows the paths past the mess and recreation sites towards the operations block and control tower. Towards the lights.

"Looks like you need a cup of tea," says a WAAF when he enters the Operations Room. The fluorescent lights hurt his eyes. He looks over at the large blackboard. Most of the crews are chalked in as returned. But not E Easy.

The WAAF brings him a cup of tea. A straightforward energetic kindly woman. No fear of her tea bringing about a jinx of any kind.

"Any news of E Easy?"

"She's been badly shot up. Rear gunner is dead and upper gunner is hurt. She's coming back on two engines. She's still carrying incendiaries too. The pilot advised the crew to bail out but they're all sticking it out with him. And the pilot's wife is expecting a baby any day now. He's only twenty-one."

He pictures Davy inside his curtained alcove, twirling his pencil over the radio log sheet, listening through the static of his headphones for signals, clicking the switch from C to A, radioing in the SOS call.

He goes outside. Hugging his mug of tea. The three searchlight beams form a ghost canopy over the aerodrome. The blue taxiway lights blinking like a string of glass beads in the grass. The runway is lit by long necked cans of paraffin with a rag wick poking out. A tapering avenue of flames extending out towards the distant line of trees. It's like a stage on which some magical event is about to take place.

Two fire engines, trucks and an ambulance are on standby. The green Very light puffs up from the caravan. He watches E Easy come swinging down very low over the trees to face the flarepath. Her undercarriage is down. The pilot is applying hard left rudder. Throttling back the port outer engine. He watches her wings tilt uneasily from side to side. The dead engines sucking at her centre of gravity like a malevolent current.

She's going to overshoot, he thinks.

The starboard wheel hits the runway with a squeal. E Easy performs a moment of ballet for a split second. Then the port wheel bumps down too. The pilot pulls back the throttles. All effort now a strain to strangle life from the two engines. The aircraft careers down the runway, skewing off to the left. Freddie can feel the pilot's effort to keep command of her in his own muscles. She knocks over some paraffin cans as she skits off the concrete onto the grass. Bumps over the wet uneven ground. Undignified now like a man trying to run with his trousers down around his ankles. All Freddie's will is straining to bring the aircraft to a halt. He is a child saying a prayer. E Easy veers slantwise towards a hedge. Crashes through it. The starboard engine is torn away. She totters down into a ditch. He waits for the explosion. But there is no explosion. Applause rings out from the group of people watching. He sees Davy jump down onto the grass. Shyness prevents Freddie from running over to shake his hand.

17 - November 1943

MARINA STANDS naked on a wooden box. Isabella feels as she lays down brushstrokes that she is exploring Marina's body with her hands, memorising the map of her nakedness with her fingertips. Her eye traces the curve of the gentle swell of her left breast. She steps up to her canvas and replicates the line in pigment. The act of painting like channelling clairvoyance down into her fingers.

She works quickly. Her blood is pumping. There is the glow of elation. As if she is being lifted off the ground by a lover. She skips back and forth over the boards. Her limbs are light with love. She is returned to herself as if newly anointed. As if glistening with dew. She takes twelve steps forward. Puts down with the utmost accuracy a new mark. Walks backwards twelve steps. Her head tilting at a variety of birdlike angles as she studies what she has done. It is an exhilarating dance.

She mixes another spiral slither of lead white into the colour on her palette.

"So the university has more or less shut down?"

"Not officially, "says Marina. Marina's face has an elegant high bone structure. Her wide thin lips find severity more easily than mirth and sometimes suggest the icy self-regarding stasis of winter. She has almond shaped dark eyes that are shy on your behalf. Her hair is a coal black tumble of medusa curls. "But half of the professors have gone into hiding. Because of their political views."

Isabella fans out the collection of brushes in her left hand. Selects one.

"Isn't your father a fascist? He used to go to all the district gatherings and assemblies, didn't he?"

Marina nods. "But he doesn't like the new Republican Fascist Party. He says they're all crooks now."

"I never liked the fascists. Not then, not now. I don't like their art," she says and laughs.

"No news of Freddie?"

"No."

"He once gave me a ride on the handlebars of his bicycle."

"Did he now?"

Isabella walks home alongside the river. She feels suddenly lonely. A bit envious of Marina. It is almost four years since she stood naked in front of anyone. She senses Marina feels emboldened by the ease with which she is able to display her nakedness. It's like a mysterious gift. A new chemical in her blood. Marina is six years younger than she is. Isabella doesn't feel she has the experience to warrant these extra years of hers. Feels like these extra years are blank walls, empty drawers.

Two militiamen are inspecting the papers of a frightened boy near the San Frediano church. For the life of her she does not understand this avidity on the part of so many men to bully other people. *Leave him alone*, she feels like shouting. The world shakes as a German tank with the menacing black insignia rumbles towards her. She has the sensation of the ground no longer being solid beneath her feet, as though she is walking on shingle. She watches the two fascists in their tasselled berets turn and click their heels and salute the bemused German soldier in the turret.

She is still thinking of the frightened young boy when she sees Max waiting for her outside her building.

"Is this a coincidence?" she says, biting off her pleasure at seeing him.

"Can we call it fate?"

"So you weren't arrested?"

"No. I'm still at large. But I've been living a state of absolute dread for the past few days. Do you know it's often only our memories that stand between us and a complete moral collapse?"

"I sometimes feel I've come adrift from my memories. They seem so remote and ghostly."

"Stand by for a moral collapse then."

"You've got your smile back."

"I wanted to ask you if I can cook you dinner?"

"Now?"

"Yes."

She quickly calculates the effect of her clothes. And, surprising herself, reminds herself what underwear she is wearing. "I've got paint on my hands. Probably on my face too."

"I can wait while you get ready."

Max lives close to the San Frediano gate and the medieval city wall, not far from her studio. He leads her up a lot of stairs to a small apartment with a roof terrace overlooking the river. She watches him rinse the earth from some leeks under the tap with his sleeves rolled up; chop garlic with lightning fast precision; skip from the cutting board to the stove and stir things in pans and remove them from the flame with a cloth. He brings her dinner on the roof terrace. As the sun becomes a red rim sinking into the hills the clouds over Giotto's tower and Brunelleschi's dome are flooded with a crimson dye until they come to resemble to Isabella a huge cluster of proffered red roses.

For a while, while they eat, there is too much privacy on the terrace and she is made to feel how little hoarded intimacy she and Max have to draw on.

When darkness settles over the city two prongs of light suddenly reach high up into the night sky. The searchlights remain fixed, two bright smoking fingers lighting up the underside of clouds and providing a canopy of light over the city. She feels enchantment forging a ring around the moment.

"Do you know there's a loneliness in you, as if you're watching rain from behind a window," he says.

She smiles. "Isn't there the same kind of loneliness in everyone?"

She realises he is both little boy and father. That there is something both playful and strict about him. His deep voice carries authority; his eyes hint at mischief. Sometimes, when his guard drops, she sees the depths of shyness and uncertainty in him, like the shimmer of something on an ocean bed seen through clear water.

She returns the plates to the kitchen. There are remnants of disembowelled red peppers on the chopping board by the sink, a scattering of seeds stained red by the juice.

When she returns to the terrace she takes her glass of wine and stands by an urn of bright red geraniums, leaning over the parapet. The cold stone of the balustrade startles her into realising how hot her body is. Scuttling wisps of cloud are blown across the moon that is bright above the outlines of the hills of Fiesole, visible beyond the domes and towers of Florence. The moon seems to shine back at her the increased need of intimacy, of secrecy and seclusion the war has made everyone feel.

"The moon is like the keeper of the peace," she says, without turning round. She pushes at her wedding ring with her thumb. She knows his hands are going to encircle her waist before she feels his breath on the back of her neck. They have been kissing for a few minutes when his body goes rigid in her arms. Two cars have pulled up directly outside. He is leaning over the parapet.

"It's the Gestapo," he says. "Or Carità and his thugs."

"Don't let them in."

"My father will open the door. He's downstairs. With his new mistress. Listen, they won't keep you. I'll make sure of that."

18 - November 1943

MARINA WALKS towards a knot of fascist guards in their rakish tasselled berets. They look her up and down as if her clothes are transparent. They are only boys but the uniform they wear gives their interest in her a menacing current. She walks along the river. All the shuttered palaces are reflected in the grey-green water at high tide. She watches a procession of children in starched black uniforms, black tasselled fezzes and black cloaks cross Ponte Santa Trinita. They are singing a fascist song and marching in orderly formation with banners and pennants.

In Piazza della Signoria she sits down by the Neptune fountain. The sculptures in the Loggia dei Lanzi are hidden inside corrugated iron and wooden sheds. There are sandbags heaped around these sheds. She watches a little boy stand in the spray from the fountain. He shuffles about finding the spot where he will get most wet.

Two women in fur stroll across the square with parasols unfurled. Their chatter is pitched on high notes, like birdsong. Now and again the smell of a steaming mound of horse manure nearby reaches her. She watches a pigeon land on the green awning of a café on the other side of the square. There are German soldiers and officers sitting at many of the outdoor tables.

Before long she sees Francesco walking towards her, alongside the arches of the Uffizi. He has his two lurchers on a lead. She hasn't seen the dogs for some while. Because Francesco's mother doesn't find her suitable as a girlfriend for her son. She is socially too far below him. Francesco's family live in a 17th century villa near San Miniato with a tennis court and a drive longer than most of Florence's streets. She lives in an apartment with damp patches on the walls and warped cupboards. So Francesco broke off the relationship. Since then

Francesco's family have become social pariahs. Because of the legislation forbidding Jews all kinds of legal rights. Francesco is no longer allowed to study at the university. His mother, her enemy, has been excluded from all her clubs, has been turned into a social outcast – exactly what she tried to make Marina feel. Francesco's family are now socially below hers. In her meanest moments Marina thinks of Francesco's mother's new plight with a bitter twist of satisfaction.

It used to be as if sparkling waves slopped around her bare ankles whenever she saw Francesco. It isn't like that anymore. That feeling has been stolen from her. She stands and lets herself be kissed on either cheek. A ceremony performed with mutual shy stiffness.

"Big news. Not good," he says.

She is pleased the dogs remember her. Envies them a little the ease with which they can wear their mood.

"What's the big news?"

He sits down beside her on the steps. "We are sailing for America. Or that's the plan." His hands are knotted around the leather lead in his lap. "Nothing has been finalised yet but my father is making arrangements. There is a boat from Genoa next month. My mother, of course, does not want to leave our home and there are arguments every night. But I've never seen my father so firm. He says we will end up in a work camp if we stay in Italy."

She looks over at two fascist militia walking towards the wizened little man selling hot chestnuts. "Some people think the war will be over in six months. The BBC says the British and Americans forces are already moving towards Rome now that they've liberated Naples."

"The Germans probably won't yield Rome so easily though. But even if it were over in six months my father thinks that is too long. That we'll be arrested before then. It's even dangerous for us to stay another month. Some friends of ours have already been arrested. They tried to escape to Switzerland. Paid a guide to lead them across the border. But the guide didn't show up after getting his money. So, idiotically, the father denounced him to the police. The head of the police told him he was under orders to arrest all Jews and that he would have to arrest him but advised the man to send his family away. That he would overlook them. The father refused. Saying he would not be parted from his family. So they were all arrested. Father, mother and three sons. My sister gave violin lessons to one of the sons. Their house has been requisitioned by the Nazis."

"Probably your father is right," she says.

She feels him go tense beside her. His radius of awareness shrink. As if the piazza and all its chatter and bustle has ceased to exist for him. As if he is alone, talking to her on the telephone. He looks at her for a moment. It is as if his face is buffeted by a wild mountain gale. "I was an idiot, Marina. I've realised that now. Letting my mother influence me."

She fastens a button on her coat.

"You're my best friend, Marina," he says. "You always have been."

"Will you write to me when you're in America?"

"Of course I will."

Before returning home she does some shopping for her mother. Always the same two or three shops where the shopkeepers know her name. Tearing off the ration coupons like in a children's game. There is nothing sweet on the shelves. Sugar and jam have vanished from the world. She buys some flour, some goat's cheese, some mushrooms, some potatoes, some bread, a bottle of milk. The bread is grey and tastes bitter nowadays and contains little hard pellets that get stuck between your teeth.

When she gets home everyone is in the kitchen. The blistered green shutters are fastened and it is gloomy inside. Her mother and father have gaunt expressions like strained haulage ropes. It's clear they have been waiting anxiously for her, that there is news. There is a pause, a kind of vacuum, like the moment when a flock of birds settle again after being startled into flight by a loud noise.

"Is he dead?" she asks, turning her back on the room. She feels sure a telegram has arrived announcing her older brother's death. She notices her father seems ill at ease in his body as though he has just got back on his feet after being knocked to the ground. He is still wearing his apron smeared with grease and lacquer and his lustreless hair needs washing. He smells of tobacco and varnish and beeswax.

"No, we've still not heard anything about Marco." Her mother's chaffed red fingers grope for her rosary and she says a Hail Mary. She is pale, harried. Wrinkling up like a disturbed pool of water.

"Sit down, Marina," says her father. "I need to talk to you."

She looks over at her mother standing by the sink. She always gravitates there in times of strain. Her faith in the revitalising powers of cleanliness is the fulcrum of her nature.

"Signor Becchi came to see me today."

Her father can't look her in the eye. He looks like a smaller scale likeness of himself. He is polishing an apple on his trouser leg.

"That old slimeball," she says with a contorted ugly face.

"He's not my favourite person in the world either," he says, still polishing the apple. "But I owe him rather a lot of money. That's the problem."

"How can he think about money at a time like this?"

"He's got loads of money anyway," says her brother Leo. "Have you seen his new car?"

"No one asked for your opinion, Leo. He told me he could now requisition my property, as is his right by law. But that there are always loopholes to be found in the law. Especially if you know the right people. And he's made it one of his goals in life to know the right people. Knowing the right people, he said, is what some people call fate."

Marina knows how to decipher all her father's small gestures, fleeting expressions. They are like sealed letters she has secretly opened and read. Today he is ashamed of himself on her behalf and it makes him avoid eye contact with her and reluctant to come to the point.

"He said he's doing some war work for a bureau dealing with requisitioned objects. Valuables taken from criminal elements in our society. And that he and his fellow bureau members are keen to make sure some of these requisitioned heirlooms stay in our country, rather than get carted off to

Germany. I have to sign for them on the pretext that they have been damaged in transit and have arrived at my workshop for restoration. And by this means they hope to delay their transportation to Germany. He also wants you to go and work for him, Marina."

Marina stares, makes a feeding fish mouth.

"As a housekeeper and maid. His mother is unwell. You will be given your own room and your wages will be subtracted from my debt. I had to say yes. He's got my hands tied. He's offering generous terms."

"That man hates you, dad. And he'll take out his hate on me."

"You start on Monday week," he says. He puts the apple on the table without taking a bite.

19 - November 1943

"DARLING MARINA…. I have wasted a year of my life. That is my feeling today. At a time when one can't even be certain of remaining alive for another year…"

Francesco stands by the open window of the lodge by the tennis court. He stands in the dark. An outline of himself. He has no pencil, no paper. He is not writing his letter to Marina. He is reciting it aloud to shadows.

"Tonight I have argued with my mother. It is the first time I have ever shouted at my mother. You didn't know she was a member of the Fascist Party. I was too ashamed to tell you."

He marches across the stone floor, picks up a tennis racket and thwacks it against his thigh.

"You seemed cold yesterday. I don't blame you for viewing me with mistrust now…"

He paces back and forth, hitting himself with the tennis racket. Every sentence he composes sounds trite, mocks him with its inadequacy. Yet there must be a combination of words that will revive Marina's former feeling for him if only he can dredge them up out of the mud and slime into which he has fallen.

He notices now a blurry icon of light appear between the trees outside. It disappears and then returns. It is floating towards him. He presses his face to the glass and sees the ghost of his mother, dressed in her nightclothes and slippers. He reels back in horror.

She's died and is coming to me as her ghost.

But he can hear footsteps on the gravel. Like the sighing of a sea over shingle.

"Francesco?"

"Mother?"

"What are you doing? It's two o'clock in the morning."

The light from the candle shows all the strain in her face.

"Put that candle down," he says. He takes it from her. He carries it over to the windowsill. During his passage its flame throws light on an old armchair, its springs showing through the torn upholstery. On the chair is a deflated beach ball, a folio of sheet music and a doll missing one of her glass eyes.

"I can't bear it when we argue. Did you really expect me to sleep after the things you said to me tonight?"

"I didn't say them to stop you sleeping."

"You know I've always had your best interests at heart, Francesco? In everything I've done. My overriding motive has always been your happiness."

"You didn't like Marina because she's the daughter of a furniture restorer."

They both stiffen as they hear the hum of engines outside and then the crackle of gravel increasing in volume. The lawn is suddenly ablaze. Wobbling beams of light lick away the darkness. The topiary shapes in the cypress hedge along the drive take on a startling lucidity. The shadows of monsters flit over the yellow ochre stone façade of the villa. He counts three vehicles.

"They've come for us."

"Who has come for us?"

"Your fascist friends. We need to get out of here."

"We can't just leave your father and your sister."

"We don't have any choice. We'll have to go down into the tunnel." He picks up the candle, places it down on the stone floor by the wooden hatch that leads to the cellar. The light, a beautiful delicate thing, becomes their enemy, becomes an informer.

"I can't go down there. I'm not even dressed. There will be rats and all kinds of filth."

"The alternative is probably a German labour camp."

No one goes down into the cellar any more though it was one of Francesco's favourite places in the world as a boy. He lifts the hatch, drops down rung by rung into the damp odorous underworld realm. The candle flame startles the bricked vault. For a moment something down there seems to move back in alarm. The shadow of his hand and the candle it holds is enormous on the brick and mortar. He helps his mother clamber down the wooden ladder. Bites off his impatience with her slow fussy progress down the rungs.

"Let's just hide here, Francesco. They won't find us here. Do we even know where the tunnel comes out?"

"The crypt of the chapel. I went in a few times as a boy."

"I can't do this, Francesco."

"We have to. They might have seen the light of your candle. Anyway they'll have the names of everyone they want to arrest and our names will be on the list. When they don't find us in our beds, they'll search everywhere. They've got dogs."

The trapdoor has an ancient iron ring. He tugs at it until the rusted metal draws blood from his hand. It becomes a recognisable challenge. A challenge to demonstrate his autonomy from his mother. And she, he knows, is willing him to fail. Not only because she fears the tunnel. But also because she wants him to remain a boy, her boy. The iron ring becomes her will that he's tugging at with all his strength. It flies open with a dramatic suddenness that knocks him back on his heels. He upsets the candle in his fall and the flame fades to a tiny dying star and then absolute darkness smothers him like a summons.

He feels inside. Presses his palms to the surface of cold clay and stone. Like a blind man. He has to kneel and bow his head as if in prayer to get inside. The temperature drops. The air has a raw bitter taste.

They hear dogs barking.

"I'll go first. You follow."

"Please let's not close ourselves in, Francesco. I don't think I can bear it."

"We have to."

He has crawled inside. He can hear his heart pumping in his ears.

He thinks of Marina. Tries to make of her his incentive, his courage in this moment of fear.

The barking of the dogs seems closer.

"I can't shut the door."

"Make yourself as small as possible and I'll try to squeeze past you."

His hand touches an unknown part of his mother's body in the dark. There is a repulsive jolt of intimacy in the contact which makes him recoil from his own physicality. Forced to touch her again, he reaches past her and pulls the door shut.

He edges forward, on his hands and knees, crawling and wriggling beneath the earth's surface like a reptilian thing. Behind him his mother makes little gasps and groans. She sounds like a much older woman than she was at breakfast. She has always hated dirt. Even a newspaper she holds with fastidiousness, fearing the print might come off on her hands. She refuses to be seen in public with him if he goes a day without shaving. All kinds of things to her are dirt that to other people are just nature.

The ground sandpapers the skin from his knees, feeds its chill through his palms. His lungs ache as if the darkness is swelling up inside his body. His longing for light is soon a hysteria he has to fight down. His voice doesn't sound like his own. And every time he speaks to his mother he is jostled by this stranger inside his body.

On and on it goes. The oblivion. The primeval sorcery of darkness. His mother is whimpering. Twice now he has known the bottomless panic of believing there is no longer any way forward. Both times the tunnel curves on at a sharp angle.

Then his hand touches splintered wood. He fumbles for some kind of handle. He pushes against the wood. He slides his legs out from under him and uses them to kick at it. Again he feels on trial before his mother. The need to prove he is a man and not a little boy. He keeps kicking at the door until his thighs and testicles ache. He is sweating and his heart is pounding. His mother moans out fatalistic noises into the darkness. Then the door bursts open onto a lighter shade of darkness. For a moment he can see clearly as though he himself is the source of light. Wooden coffins stacked one upon another. Those at the bottom have been crushed by those on top. Bones have spilled out onto the stone floor.

20 - November 1943

"ATTILA?" SAYS THE MAN with the face of a hog, with chicken liver and garlic on his breath. He is the man in charge. Captain Mario Carità. The most hated and feared man in Florence.

"This bracelet I took from the Jewish bitch in via Maggio says four inches."

"I was going to say four inches. All right, two hundred lire that he can't even get it up."

"Vincenzo?"

"Five inches. Two hundred lire."

"I take it I'm not required to be typing this?" The stenographer is a woman with pinched features, squinting eyes and frizzy hair. She sits behind a typewriter. Also on the desk is a half-eaten sandwich, a bronze bust of Mussolini, a pair of boxing gloves, a rusted pair of pliers, sheaves of paper, a cascade of photographs and a rusted blowtorch.

"Luigi?"

"He looks like a big dick to me so two hundred lire says ten inches."

Isabella has been made to stand on tiptoes with her hands on her head. Every time she rests her weight down on her heels a man with a puckered scar beneath his left eye calls her a whore and slaps her face.

The room is large and high, painted an industrial shade of grey. Sounds leave a spectral memory of themselves on the air. A heavily made-up young woman clutching a tiny groomed dog to her breast now enters. She is wearing an extravagant feathered hat with a black lace veil and a fur coat. Sticky lavishly applied red lipstick. She puts the dog down and it begins running around the room, sliding on the parquet floor, barking at everyone. The men incite it to paroxysms of impotent rage.

"So what have we here?" says the woman, looking at Isabella with theatrical distaste and then settling herself down on the green sofa and lighting a cigarette. She calls her dog to her. Fufu.

"Another two filthy communists," says a man in a wide collared white satin shirt with staring seagull eyes. His name is Luigi. He is holding a chewed chicken wing. Grease glistens on his top lip. Isabella has taken note of the names of these men. Made a point of memorising every detail of their physiognomies. It is the only means of appeasing her disgust and horror. As if one day she might be given the chance to testify against them in a court of law.

Max has his hands cuffed behind his back. He is wearing only shorts. There is blood on his face and on his torso. He has been hit with pistols, a poker and the metal buckle of a belt. At one point Max wet himself. All the men laughed at the darkening stain running down his trouser leg. Isabella knows Max has discovered himself to be less brave than he hoped. To begin with he tried to charm his captors. Responding to questions with his shy boyish smile as if he found it hard to believe anyone might dislike him. But they shouted abuse at him with malevolent disgust, which, she saw, disturbed him. He no longer looks over at her. Now his gaze is riveted to his bare feet.

"Let's begin the show," says the young man with the gold tooth. Attila. He yanks down Max's shorts. "Bloody hell! It's tiny."

"That's because he's shitting himself."

The man with the face of a hog, with chicken liver and garlic on his breath walks over to Isabella. He is capable of speaking in a reasonable, almost friendly way and then, without warning, exploding into a homicidal fury. He pulls her by the hand over to Max at the centre of the room. There are bloodstained footprints on the floor by Max's bare feet. She looks into Max's eyes. She feels they are like two animals looking at each other. Carità forces her hand down to make contact with Max's shrivelled manhood.

She pulls away her hand. "No," she says.

"She says no," Carità says to the room, standing with his hands on his hips. "Piccolo, she says no."

Piccolo is a huge, apparently dull-witted man who never speaks and whose features never change expression. His hands are clenched into fists as though holding captive something precious he is fearful of losing before he can show it to someone. He strikes Max with a ferocious punch to the jaw, knocking Max to the floor. Piccolo and Luigi pick Max up by the feet and hands and hurl him against a wall. There is more blood coming from Max's nose and ears and mouth. Max is pulled to his feet and dragged over to where Isabella stands.

"Get him hard or we'll cause him even more pain."

"Do what Capitano Carità says," barks the man with blank staring seagull eyes and creaking boots. He strikes Max in the face with the butt of his pistol. Opening another gash on Max's face.

"Just fucking do it," says Max.

She recoils from this betrayal, from the snarl of his mouth, the terrorised stare of scorn in his eyes directed at her. She grabs hold of his penis as if it is something she is about to gut and fillet on a chopping board. It shocks her that it is warm. That anything could give off warmth in this room. With reluctance, with repulsion, she begins to yank it back and forth. She doesn't hear all the joking and cheering around her. Is aware only that all moral restraint has gone from the world.

She fails to coax Max's manhood into an erection, just as she failed with Freddie. Except this time it is a relief. As if they have both been spared a further humiliation.

"I win," says Angelo. The least pitiless and boastful of the men in the room. A younger male with dark curls and a sad slant to his mouth whose eyes every now and again betray a veiled hint of compassion. He scoops up all the money and jewellery on the table and stuffs it into his trouser pocket.

Carità pushes her away. "Who is Corvo?" he yells at Max.

"I swear I don't know anyone called Corvo," says Max.

Isabella collapses down onto her haunches by the window. The man with the scar pulls her to her feet by her hair. He slaps her face. The clotted surge of contempt for him again. It rises up in her like heated mercury in a thermometer.

Carità punches Max in the groin. He motions towards the pliers on the desk. Turns to Seagull Eyes. "You know what to do. Let's see if he has any balls."

Seagull Eyes brandishes the rusty pliers under Max's nose. "I'm going to pretend your balls are a nail I need to pull out of a piece of wood," he says. He grimaces with an imaginary effort. The man with the face of a hog, with chicken liver and garlic on his breath grins.

Max's legs are shaking and more urine escapes from his bladder as Seagull Eyes kneels down in front of him with the pliers poised. Isabella closes her eyes. Her eyes are forced open by the bellowing scream that sets the dog barking more hysterically than ever. Fufu. Max has passed out on the floor.

"Take her downstairs," says the man with the face of a hog, with chicken liver and garlic on his breath. Mario Carità. Head of the Republican Fascist secret police in Florence.

She is taken down lots of stairs by a guard with a torch. Her hands are now cuffed behind her back. The metal gouging into her wrists. It is damp. Different laws seem to be in place here. Like in dreams. There is a smell of coal. Smell of urine. She is pushed along a narrow corridor. She passes small closed doors on either side. The guard stops and opens one of these doors with a large rusted key. He directs the beam of the torch inside. Inside is a feral creature. A thing that looks to have mutated out of slime and darkness. Prone and brittle. A naked boy, his hands cuffed behind his back. Foetal. Blackened skin hanging from his back in strips. His face swollen with cuts and bruises. There is a cockroach scuttling over the stone floor. There is a dented tin bucket scabbed with rust. The cell is without windows. She is shoved inside and the door closes behind her.

She has difficulty sitting down on the stone floor without the use of her hands.

"Can you hear me?" she asks.

No reply. Cold rises up through the stone floor. She shivers. She wants to wrap her arms around herself. But she can't. Every time she drops off to sleep she is awoken by a still more piercing and horrifying cry and there is the shock of not being able to free her hands from behind her back.

She is so thirsty she can no longer produce spittle to swallow.

Later they bring someone else into her cell. A young man with a disfigured face. One of his eyes has closed up behind a swollen lump. There is clotted blood in his ears, in his nose, in his mouth. His hands are not recognisable as hands.

"Was there a girl in here pretending to be blind?" he asks.

"No."

"She's a spy. She works for Carità. They send her down here in the hope of learning secrets. She always puts her hands on the men and of course this is nice after the beating you've just had. Did they make you talk?"

"I don't know anything to tell."

They listen to a muffled distant voice pleading. And then shrieking out in pain.

"All walls become thinner in the dark," says her companion. "What's your name?"

"Isabella."

"Okay, Isabella. I'm going to trust you. This is very important. The man you were arrested with. Max. Did he mention any meetings he has in the next week or so?"

Is he trying to trick me?

"No," she says.

"I'm not a plant, Isabella. Look at the state of my face. Max was supposed to tell a contact about an informer. There's a man called Branimir out there who tells Jews he can get false identity papers for them. Except he leads them to their doom. If they let you go will you tell our contact about this man Branimir? Our contact will be in the church of Santa Trinita next Friday at five in the evening. A lot of lives depend on this information being passed on."

She is taken back upstairs. To a different room. Max is hanging by his wrists from a wooden beam. His features have disappeared behind more cuts, bruises, swellings and dried blood. There is a smell of charred flesh, singed hair. She sees all

Max's pubic hair has been burned off. It is the man with the scar who holds the blowtorch. She has still not learned his name.

"Your yellow-bellied boyfriend has squealed. He has betrayed all his comrades. Except he says you know nothing."

"I can vouch for that."

She turns to see the German SS captain she met at the concert. He bows to her with a grave expression of humility.

"She is a painter, not a terrorist."

"She has an English husband," says Carità.

"I didn't know that but I do know she's doesn't play any part in whatever it is this man is plotting."

"She's all yours then. We've got work to do."

Captain Erich Heinkel holds out his gloved hand to her. "It appears I am now in a position to do you a favour. Will you allow me to drive you home?"

21 - November 1943

DOWN BELOW to starboard are fields the size of napkins, farm buildings the size of matchboxes, a stream like a spill of blue ink. Beyond is the village where Freddie's parents live. A huddle of stone cottages around the church by the village green. Close to the coastline. He banks V Victor and rolls down steeply with her. She clears the roof of his house at an altitude of 400 feet. He pictures the effect of her thunder inside the house. All the familiar framed photographs jumping up and down as if suddenly animated, toppling over.

Reg has a grin on his face. It's hidden by his mask which he holds to his face to speak into the microphone but Freddie can see it in his eyes. "You're getting a right rollicking from someone in the village. Look."

A tiny figure outside the toy post office is waving his fist in the air.

"That, if my eyes don't deceive me, is Edward Cronk. Haven't seen him since I was a kid. We used to break his greenhouse windows with cricket balls. Not on purpose. If Hitler were English he'd be as happy as Larry. He'd probably volunteer to set up the local Gestapo branch."

"You'd better hope he doesn't have good eyesight or it could mean the mop and bucket for you. For me too if it comes to that."

"I'm going in lower next time. Give him another chance to jot down our serial number."

"And if he reports us?"

"I'll take full responsibility. My dad's dying, Reg. This might be the only chance I get to say goodbye to him."

He brings V Victor around again. This time flying a little lower. Now his parents are out in the garden. Two figures no bigger than his thumb. He waves down at them. But they don't wave back. His father has always kept his hands close to his body. He is dressed in stripy blue pyjamas. Even from up here he can sense the new frailty in his body, the disease. He wobbles the wings of V Victor as a parting wave and turns her through ninety degrees and lifts her nose back up towards the clouds.

The image of his father stays with him. His weakened father. He can't recall ever seeing his father in pyjamas before. There is an air of finality about the picture. As if the next frame will be credits and stirring elegiac music.

Father love is ancient and austere, like mountains. It is difficult to accept the collapsing of a mountain.

Later that day he is brought before the new CO. A kindly softly spoken man called Hugh Barrington who loves fishing and flowers.

"We've had a complaint. Any idea what that might be?"

"It was foolhardy of me, sir."

"You don't need me to tell you that as skipper of your crew you're supposed to set a good example."

The CO is doing a good job of making him feel like a truant schoolboy.

"What were you doing so far from your scheduled flight path?"

"I found out my father is dying, sir."

"Do you want to apply for compassionate leave?"

"No sir. I have four more ops until I'm due some leave. I can wait until then."

The thought they both share that the odds of making it through four more ops are about even is not spoken. Compassionate leave though might look like he's succumbed to a dose of LMF. He does not want any stain on his integrity. Any whispers going around that he is lacking in moral fibre. It's important to him how he is seen by the other men. That he is respected is a big part of his courage and resolve. If there's even a suspicion that he has lost his nerve he fears it will enter his bloodstream and begin remoulding him to this idea. Men return from leave softened. Especially married men. They return with a revitalised desire to carry on living.

"However you've solved me a problem for which I'm grateful. I'm in need of a relief pilot for a scratch crew that need to be broken in. Their pilot has been taken ill."

Please let it not be that crew of hapless Australians, he thinks.

"It's the new crew of Australians. In all likelihood you'll be on the battle order for tomorrow night. Might be a good idea for you to get to know them a bit."

Reg is waiting for him in the mess anteroom. Burrowed down in a leather armchair by the log fire. Flicking restlessly through the *Illustrated London News*.

"Well?"

"Going up with a sprog crew."

"Not those Australians?"

"Yep. Are they really that bad?"

"Worse. There's a rumour that their navigator got lost coming back from the pub the other night. And their rear gunner was so hungover he fell asleep when they were doing fighter affiliation exercises. They're runaway favourites to be the next crew that gets the chop. We won by the way."

A log on the fire splinters and hisses out sparks.

"What?"

"Our photograph has pride of place on the intelligence library notice board. No one got their bombs closer to the target at Düsseldorf than Spike."

He revisits the scene last night over the burning German city. The interminable few minutes of the bomb run. All that twilight debris jumping up, raining down in front of the perspex. When the bomb doors are open and you're flying straight and steady over battery upon battery of radar guided guns with ten thousand pounds of explosives and two thousand gallons of high octane petrol exposed under your seat it feels like you're dangling a piece of raw red meat to a great white shark. That's how he once described the bomb run in a letter to his father.

"I suppose that's some consolation for this nerve-shredding fixation of his for pinpoint accuracy. I thought he was never going to let those bombs go."

"You've got to admire his cool nerve."

"Or his lack of imagination."

"He's a perfectionist. Perhaps though it's his conscience? Wants to be as careful as possible not to hit innocent civilians?"

"Do you believe that?"

"No. I believe Spike's a competitive son of a bitch who's probably going to get us all killed."

"That's pretty much what I believe."

"Didn't you at least get a pat on the back from the CO?"

"Didn't mention it. But I like him. He always makes a point of learning all the names of the new boys. It's a nice gesture, calling them by their names. Makes them feel better."

Spike enters the mess eating a doughnut. Grains of sugar twinkling on his severe moustache. He is eating a doughnut but his breath smells of spam.

"Well done, Spike."

"Thanks. Team effort though," he says picking up a newspaper. Shaking the crease out of its pages with gusto.

"I'm on a different team tomorrow. Team B. Team Z."

22 - November 1943

FOR THE THIRD TIME she douses the pair of Freddie's shorts in turpentine and wipes off the brushstrokes she has recently put down.

"Are some people harder to paint than others?"

Captain Erich Heinkel in full uniform, peaked cap, medalled chest thrown forward, sits in a thin-legged chair adorned with arabesques and whorls. The chair is perched on the wooden model box made of old packing crates. Isabella fashioned it herself with hammer and nails.

She wipes her brush on the sleeve of her blue smock.

"Sometimes I think you have to be able to see something of yourself in a face to paint it well," she says.

"And you can see nothing of yourself in me?"

Her painting of him is ugly. It leers back at her. Leeching away her self-esteem. A caricature. She has channelled no pulse of life into her brushstrokes. She is embarrassed by it and does not want him to see it. It further irritates her that she cares for his good opinion. She wants to believe he is not a bad man. Today he brought her flowers, cigarettes and real coffee. She is trying hard to see him as he might be with his children, as he might be when imparting knowledge or inspiring laughter. Even though she can't find it within herself to like him.

"Your mind is elsewhere today?" he says.

She watches him remove his cap. His hair flattened and dampened. He draws his hand over his forehead as if to erase some perceived stain there.

"I wouldn't say that."

But she is lying. Her mind is elsewhere. She is still debating whether or not to fulfil the request made to her by the man in the cell. The church of Santa Trinita at five o'clock. *Branimir is an informer. Lives depend on you carrying out this task.*

"Just not in the mood?"

"Surely that happens to you? With your job, I mean."

"All the time. Actually I'm curious about what you think my job entails."

"I have no idea. Paperwork? Giving orders? Delegating responsibility?"

"Yes, I suppose that is the gist of it. I have an office in Palazzo Vecchio. I sometimes work in a room designed by Vasari. There are beautiful things wherever I look. I spend most of my time feeling unworthy. Do you mind if I stretch my legs?"

She knows, as he knows, that it is a charade of formality for him to ask any concession of her. His boots creak when he steps down stiffly from the model chair. Reminding her of the man with the scar who repeatedly slapped her during Max's interrogation. She has dreamed about this man. He has become more, instead of less, vivid to her.

"Have you found those two paintings you were looking for?" she says, accepting the cigarette he offers.

"No. Why do you ask?"

"Just making conversation," she says.

"If you don't mind my saying perhaps you are in too much of a hurry to finish this painting? I suspect my presence in your studio is awkward for you."

That an official of the Third Reich drove her home at eight in the morning and is now frequenting her studio has not gone unnoticed. There is a bakery next door to her building and often the smell of warm pastries drifted in through the window when she and Freddie were talking in bed together. Signor Marcusi, the baker, always put his hand on her shoulder when asking how she was. His hair and cheeks dusted in flour. Now and again he whispered complaints about the fascist regime. "Now they want the tyres of my bicycle and my wife's wedding ring. What next? My teeth?" Today he greeted her with a perfunctory nod and wrapped her bread with what she felt was abrupt disdain. The cobbler whose workshop is two doors away and used to repair Freddie's shoes glared at her and spat this morning when she went to join the queue outside the grocery store. The women silently queuing, staring into private voids, pinched expressions around their mouths, like scars.

Captain Heinkel has picked up a copy of yesterday's *La Nazione*. He shows her the headline, Terror Raiders Destroy a Children's Orphanage in Pisa. Twenty-three Children Killed.

"Your husband is a pilot," he says.

"I haven't heard anything from him since 1941."

"Does he pilot fighters or bombers?"

"I don't know. If he writes me letters I never receive them. Why do you ask?"

"Because I can feel you disapprove of me. Supposing I told you my home in Hamburg was destroyed by British bombs. The bodies of my wife and two children never found."

"I'm sorry."

"What is happening in the world is not of your husband's choosing, nor is it of mine."

He looks down at the floorboards, frowning, as if he sees the trail of his wife and children's blood and ashes there. Instinct tells her he has never cried over the loss of his family. That all the stoppered stale emotion she has sensed in him is caused by his inability to shed tears. Perhaps he thinks she can bring them forth for him. Perhaps this is the real reason for his visits.

"I'm afraid I have some bad news for you. I didn't want to tell you until we finished our session today."

Her mind races. She can't for the life of her imagine what this bad news might be. *Surely it can't be anything about Freddie?* She feels as though a spotlight is suddenly trained on her face and has to struggle to keep her composure.

"You heard about the assassination of Lieutenant-Colonel Gobbi?"

"Yes."

"The Italians are not happy. They want revenge. Therefore as a reprisal five Italian prisoners are to be shot tomorrow morning. Your friend Max, I'm afraid, is one of the condemned men."

"Can't you do something?"

"It is nothing to do with us Germans."

23 - November 1943

"WOOHOOO. That's what the rear gunner Bluey shouted into my headset when we took off. He has a yellow brassiere as his good luck charm. Before that Mac, the mid upper gunner, accidentally fired off some rounds before we had even taken off. The Wingco, the Padre and the groundcrew of B Beer all threw themselves to the ground while the bullets whistled over their heads. Then the navigator Ned forgot his charts. Had to be ferried back to the operations block so we had to wait and were last leaving. His grandparents are German. Still speak German. Emigrated to Australia thirty years ago. Tonight is the first time he will visit the country of his ancestors. The bomb aimer Lofty is English. His lucky charm is a teddy bear that looks like it was sicked up by a whale. His parents were killed by German bombs and so he doesn't much care for the Germans. As I speak he's feeding the aluminium strips out of the chute with relish. Euphoric that he's buggering up the German radar system. Until he realised he had also thrown the flight engineer's logbook down the chute. I feel like dad with a car full of unruly children..."

Freddie thinks it will be a shame if he never gets to recount this sortie in B Beer to Reg. Already he has enough material to keep Reg amused for half an hour and they haven't even reached the enemy coast yet.

Reg and Davy and the rest of his crew were by the side of the runway to wave him off. The sight of them shivered the back of his neck, like a ghost story. He belonged by their side. That was his feeling. He imagined they were all wondering if they would ever see him again. For a moment he saw his name on the green sheet of paper pinned to the notice board in the squadron office. The list of men who hadn't made it home the previous evening. The stillness of the trees beyond the airfield boundary seemed to hold this secret. The secret of whether or not he would return. He felt a pang of deep affection for his crew. He felt resentment towards this new crew of brash uncultured colonial boys among whom he felt like an outcast. It seemed an injustice that he might die with strangers.

He pushed the two port throttles forward. Swallowing the vomit in his throat. It was more of an effort for him today to keep the aircraft straight on the runway. She pulled to starboard like a dog straining on a leash that has scented blood. He thought maybe he was more frightened than usual and fear had drained some strength from his arms.

The sick feeling was still there when he eased off the brakes, pushed forward the throttles and pedalled the rudder controls. At 110mph the tail lifted and the surge of power from the engines entered his blood, throbbed in all his muscles. The undercarriage thudded up into its housing. The sick feeling was gone.

He climbs up to 12,000 feet. Still there is no sign of a single other aircraft in the sky.

"Skipper to navigator. Are you sure we're on the correct course? And at the briefed airspeed?"

"As sure as eggs are white, skip."

"What part of Australia you from, Ned? Cos where I come from eggs are bloody yellow, mate."

"You're the one who's bloody yellow, mate."

"Skipper here. Can we stop the chatter. And rear gunner, keep your eyes peeled, will you."

He feels like a nagging old maid. It's the second time he's queried the navigator's course. The third time he has told the rear gunner to keep his eyes peeled. And the fourth time he's had to put an end to ebullient intercom chatter.

"Navigator. Take another fix, will you. There are four hundred and fifty kites taking part in this raid and it's frankly more than a bit strange that we haven't seen a single one."

"We were late out, skipper. That might explain it."

"Okay I'm going to increase airspeed. Increase the revs to twenty four."

Curly, the flight engineer, does as he's told.

They still have the sky to themselves half an hour later. He flies her up to 15,000 feet through the rolling layers of starlit clouds. He struggles to feel intimate with B Beer. To refer to it as she in his thoughts. To think of it as more than a factory assembled machine. V Victor becomes an extension of his body, an agent of his will when he flies her. He shares with her a physical understanding. Knows her moods, her idiosyncrasies, her signals. This is not the case with B Beer.

"Nav to skipper. We should be about fifty miles north of Paris. ETA is 1.10."

"Hey skip, can I bale out when we're over Paris? They tell me Parisian women are bloody beauts and have no morals."

"Might not have morals but they do have eyes, sport."

"Yeah, one look at your ugly mug, Bluey, and they'll soon get their morals back."

"Go and drink with the flies, Mac."

"Okay. Enough chatter."

He imagines the wireless op and the navigator pulling faces behind the curtain. Mocking him. His carping ministrations.

The only thing they see of Paris are gun flashes beneath the cloud and flak bursts in the sky.

In the distance he finally sees a few other Lancasters. Black silhouettes against a deep red glow. The searchlights, a lane of a hundred or so, lance the canyons of cloud below. The clouds froth up a lustrous white. Turn pink and golden. Then the 88 mm guns begin their barrage. Black balls with a fiery red heart pop up into B Beer's flight path. Dispersing grotesque masks of smoke. Lit up by the drift of eerie lustre. Soon there is a thicket of bursting shells with no apparent way through.

"Holy shit! Don't tell me we're going through that."

B Beer is knocked back and forth, bumped up and down. Globes of vivid red flare smoke stick to the sky and then drip down like splashes of thick paint. Flashing with added brilliance every time another curving line of silver tracer rips up into the sky.

When the cockpit is flooded with the otherworldly blue light of the master beam he shields his eyes and recalls childhood prayers. Kneeling by the side of his bed in pyjamas and bare feet with his palms pressed together and his mother providing guidance. Mentally he touches all his lucky charms. Isabella's letters. His wedding ring. A dozen searchlights are now sweeping across the darkness towards B Beer. He opens the throttles, throws the column forward, stamps down on the left rudder. Only his harness, burning into his shoulders, keeps him from being thrown against the roof of the cockpit. B Beer's starboard wing tilts towards the ground and she swings down with a screaming roar of distress. Then, wrenching reserves of strength from the muscles in his arms and shoulders, he heaves back the column, hits the right rudder and aileron. B Beer, tipped on her side, ceases to plunge earthwards. She swings suddenly up in a 180-degree turn with a racking shudder. Tips over onto her other side. Curly, by his side, lifts his oxygen mask and is sick. Yellow bile spatters against the perspex. A thermos flask goes flying. Gives him a start when it strikes his knee.

B Beer is the last aircraft in the stream to fly over Stuttgart. She flies through a ghost gallery of yellow flare smoke. A maelstrom of bursting shells. The gunners down below using radar to predict her course. How she is not hit is a wonder to him.

"Bomb doors open."

He flicks open the bomb doors. All around are light storms, streamers of incandescence, followed by billowing black cloud smoke.

"All right, you Nazi bastards. As Butcher Harris said, reap the fucking whirlwind of the wind you sowed."

"He didn't say fucking, Lofty."

"Stick it in your kick, Ned, and mind your own bizzo."

"You call that an Aussie accent?"

"Skipper here. For fuck's sake shut up."

"Okay, skip. Nearly there. Steady."

"Come on Lofty. Let them have their bloody prezzies and then we can get out of this bloody hellhole."

"Steady."

He peers down at a grid of black and grey squares, wrinkling up like a newspaper crossword puzzle succumbing to flames.

"Bombs gone."

He waits for the camera control to click over. Constant exploding flashes making a ghoulish red transparency of the cockpit.

"Fighter. Eight o'clock."

He sees a tiny black-on-black smudge out of the corner of his eye.

"Flash bastard is doing a loop and a roll over."

"Get the bastard, Bluey."

There's the rattle of gunfire in his headset. Heavy breathing and muttering. A faint stink of cordite snakes into the cockpit.

"I got the bastard. I got him. Take that you sticky beat bastard. Fuck me. Look at that. His engine's on fire."

"Well done, Bluey. First time any kite I've piloted has shot down a fighter."

"Thanks skipper."

"Your blood's worth bottling too, skip."

When the sky is blue-black and empty again he lights a cigarette.

Fuck the rules, he thinks.

That he's earned the respect of these swaggering bantering Australians is a source of pride to him.

The sky is seeping up a glimmer of light on the western horizon when he brings B Beer down towards the twinkling perimeter lights. Not his best landing. He bounces her down from three or so feet and she skids into the runway. An airman he doesn't recognise guides him to the concrete apron.

Outside, he stretches up his arms beneath the brightening sky. His breath and heartbeat like a gift newly restored to him. The airbase settles into its familiar configuration before his tired eyes. It welcomes him back as home.

His crew are waiting for him outside the briefing hut.

"Good to have you back, skipper," says Spike. Spike shakes his hand with unusual vigour. His eyes shining with heartfelt emotion.

He feels chastised for every ungenerous remark he has ever made about Spike.

Reg too shakes his hand and offers him a wry smile. Davy puts an arm around his shoulder. Cyril and Woodsy crack jokes he is too elated and exhausted to register. Spencer, wearing pyjamas under his greatcoat, mumbles something with an odd lopsided grin.

He is a bit embarrassed by all this affection. Feels his response is inadequate. Because he loves these men but can't show it.

"So how were the Aussies?"

"They're actually a great bunch of lads..."

"Hear that?" says Woodsy. "He's bored with us. He's happier with the Aussies now."

"I'll tell you what. They seem to live a charmed life. We were the last kite over Stuttgart. We even got coned and still came out without a scratch. Then we were attacked by a night fighter and Bluey only went and shot the thing down."

"Next you'll be telling us you want to swap Victor for B Beer."

"No. I didn't much care for B Beer. She doesn't have the easy handling of Vicky. Learnt some more Aussie slang. Liquid laugh. Vomit. Flight engineer threw up when I corkscrewed."

"My favourite is, have a naughty."

Cyril slaps Reg on the back. "No surprises there, Reg."

"So did you lose any money on me making it back, Cyril?"

"What kind of heartless bastard do you take me for, skipper? I wouldn't bet on your safety. One goes, we all go. That's how I see it. I was terrified you wouldn't make it back. If we get the chop let's all get it together."

24 - November 1943

MARINA STANDS naked on a wooden box. Keeping her shape against a host of niggling temptations to fidget.

The smell of turpentine and the smell of the sun-thickened oils seem to seclude the studio in a safer time. It is like a childhood world. The bright colours. The quiet pulse of concentration. The learning of new smells. The feeling of being enclosed from the world outside.

"And now because of him everyone around here thinks I'm working for the Germans," says Isabella.

"You know what people are like in San Frediano. Always gossiping."

"He brought me flowers yesterday. They're still there. Look. I haven't put them in water. Can you do me a favour? Just let it be known locally that I'm not colluding with the Germans in any way?"

"Of course."

When Marina returns to her home downstairs there is the shock of finding Francesco sitting at the kitchen table. Unshaven, in a crumpled and filthy white shirt and black tie. He is moving crumbs about with his forefinger. There is little assurance in the act. Her mother voices silent words at her from the kitchen sink where she is filling the coffee pot. Marina can't decipher them.

"I'll be back in a second. I just need to go to my room for a second," she says.

"Best not to, Marina. Francesco's mother is lying down on your bed. The poor woman is shattered."

She looks quizzically at Francesco but can't help feeling aggrieved. The mere mention of his mother turns a dial in her, moves her into that scratchy hissing hinterland between two radio stations. She throws her bag down on the kitchen table.

"As I've just explained to your mother, Marina, the Germans came to our home the other night and arrested my father and sister. My mother and I managed to escape but we've got nowhere to stay. We've become too dangerous to know for my mother's so-called friends."

"That's terrible," she says. And does her best to sound and look like she means it. But her body beneath her dress still glows with the memory of its recent nakedness.

"I've said we can put them up, at least for tonight," says her mother. "We'll have to talk to your father first but I don't see any problem. They can sleep in your room and you can sleep in Marco's bed."

"We don't want to put you to any trouble."

"It won't be any trouble at all."

But it will be trouble, Marina thinks. *Dad will be terrified of sheltering Jews in his house.*

"I'll leave you two alone for a while. There are things I have to do in the other room."

"What's that you're reading?" asks Francesco, nodding down at the red leather book partly visible in the cleft of her bag.

She snatches up the bag. Puts it down on the floor. "That's my diary."

"I didn't know you wrote a diary."

"Well, now you do," she says and smiles.

She becomes aware they are no longer alone. She tips back in the chair and swivels round. Francesco's mother stands in the doorway. Like a ghost of herself. As if today is some kind of unhappy anniversary and she has returned in spirit form to haunt the spot.

"Hello Marina. I hope you're well."

Signora Conte does not hold out her hand or offer her cheek to be kissed. And there is a struggle in her voice. As if she is playing the part of a character in a drama and is yet undecided what kind of voice to adopt for the role.

Surely she's not going to continue with her snobbish attitude towards me, she thinks.

"Hello Signora Conte. I'm sorry to hear of your troubles. I can't begin to imagine what it must be like to be turned out of one's home."

"Your mother has been very kind."

Francesco ushers his mother to a chair at the table. Both Francesco's mother and the chair groan when she sits down. Marina looks round at the kitchen. Giving it a stealthy fearful inspection. Seeing it as if for the first time. Seeing it as it might appear to Francesco's mother. She recoils in embarrassment from her inspection. The spick and span poverty. The chipped tiles blanched of their original colour. The blackened saucepans hanging from hooks by the sink. The rusty old bicycle propped against the wall that belongs to her older brother. The tawdry flower design on the frayed dishcloth. The clouded glasses. The crack in the china milk jug.

"I could cycle to your house and pick up anything you need," she says.

"Oh no. That might be dangerous for you. Supposing those men are still there?"

"We'll both go," says Francesco eagerly. "In fact I have to go. We need some money. We've got to have some money, mother. And I'd like to make sure the dogs are all right too."

25 - November 1943

FRANCESCO and Marina are climbing the steep steps sprinkled with pine needles up to the church of San Miniato. He can't stop looking at her. Any excuse to turn his neck and look at her mouth again. Her hair brushing her collarbone. The buttons down the front of her dress. His arms ache with tenderness for her.

She is like the rain that loosens the scent from things.

Kiss her now; you might never have the chance again.

He doesn't kiss her. He feels it would be an act of violence, like climbing in through the window of a locked building.

The front gate of his family's home is wide open. They proceed with caution. Talking in whispers. He feels like an intruder in the grounds of his own home. Fearful that they are being watched, of there being unseen enemies in the clotted darkness among the trees. It's like a childhood game.

The two lurchers come bounding up the gravel path to meet him. Giving the game away. He kneels down to greet them.

When he enters his home the three servants are sitting in the drawing room. Drinking wine and smoking in the firelight as if it is their home now. They are embarrassed when he appears at the threshold, and then, an instant later, resentful that they have been made to feel in the wrong. Carla the maid twitters with apologies but Valentino the gardener and driver has a steely sly look about him. He sits back down in Francesco's father's armchair by the fire. There is a note of hostile condescension in this man's greeting of him. It pains Francesco to feel himself disliked. Angers him a bit too that Valentino flaunts his new lack of respect for him in front of Marina.

"Don't mind us," he says. "We've just come to pick up some things."

He leads Marina up into his mother's dressing room. He has to walk over the carnage of her clothes strewn over the floor. He is surprised Carla hasn't tidied up. Makes him realise how little we know people, even the people we have spent our entire lives with. Shards of broken porcelain and glass crunch underfoot. It is horrible to see his mother's intimate undergarments exposed. She who hates disorder, who likes to keep hidden as much as possible.

Her jewellery box is empty. He can't find her identity papers either.

"This is the moment of truth," he says. "If the money's gone I don't know what we're going to do."

He kneels down by the fireplace and reaches up inside the chimney. He removes a loose brick. His hand reappears holding a brown package. He counts out six hundred lire, two hundred each for the members of the household staff, stuffs these notes into his trouser pockets. The rest, a thick wad of crisp banknotes, he conceals in his inside jacket pocket.

He pulls out a suitcase and throws in a selection of his mother's clothes, shoes and bags.

His room too is a litter of devastation, of overturned and scattered and broken things. His possessions all turned into debris.

"The end of my childhood," he says. "Perhaps it's time it ended."

She picks up a photograph of him. There is a crack across the glass frame that makes the face in the photo look scarred.

Then they hear the sound of a car, the cunning quiet crunch of its tyres over the gravel.

"Shit."

"What shall we do?"

"Upstairs. Carla's room. They're less likely to go up there. Unless Valentino gives us away."

"I'm not sure I liked him."

"He's not so bad."

Car doors slam. Male voices. Italian. One of them singing. Flustered activity downstairs echoes up the staircase.

He stuffs the suitcase in the wardrobe and leads Marina down the hallway and up a narrow twist of stairs.

Carla's small room is a hushed enigma of tidiness, like a crossword puzzle. There's a smell of harsh soap and weathered leather. Crochet work on a chair by the bed. They hide under the small bed. Lying on their backs, as if on a lawn staring up at the stars. Their bodies touch at the hips. He is aware of the points where their bodies make contact.

For a while they listen in silence.

He imagines the moment when the men enter the room. Their boots will be visible.

Don't cough; don't fart.

It is still eerily quiet down in the house. Marina has taken his hand. He strokes her finger with his thumb. He swims into her bloodstream, she pulses in his heartbeat.

The voices of men. Three. Perhaps four. In turn, blunt, self-pleasuring and aggressive.

"Attila? Where are you?"

"Here. Looks like the bastards beat us to it."

Question and answer come from different parts of the house. Creating a circuitry of sound from one room to another. He doesn't move. Hardly dares blink his eyes. For fear of transmitting his presence onto this circuitry. Footsteps mount the main stairway. The menacing ascent of steel-shod military boots.

She takes his hand again. A mosquito buzzes in his ear. Taunting him. Tagging him. Before moving away. It returns for another quick game of taunting and tagging.

A man begins shouting. Downstairs. The ugliest voice he has ever heard in his family home. It seems to be coming from immediately below, from his mother's dressing room.

There is more shouting. It makes his heart beat faster. Brings out a dampness of fear on his skin. He lets go of Marina's hand. Not wanting to communicate to her his fear. Not wanting her to know he is frightened.

There is an interminable period in which nothing can be heard.

Eventually there are voices outside. Boots crunching gravel. Doors slamming with a dull thud. Two cars drive off.

The staff are all in the kitchen.

"They brought your father here."

"My father was here? Was he all right?"

Carla nods.

"But they were shouting at him?"

"Yes. They wanted money. I think he had arranged some kind of deal with them. Money in exchange for letting him go. Except the money wasn't where he had hidden it. And that's when they got angry."

I've screwed everything up, he thinks.

"They said if we see you to tell you that they will let your father and sister go in exchange for money. They want you to go and see them. At the bureau for Jewish affairs. Here's the address. You have to ask for Giuseppe. You've got five days. After that your father and sister will be taken to a transit camp. They said they doubt if you'll ever see them again after that."

"Thank you," he says.

Thank you for not betraying us, he means.

He gives each of the members of staff the lire. Despite everything, he takes a flutter of pleasure from the generosity of his gesture. The true motive of the gesture, he realises, is not quite as altruistic as he believed. He wants to win approval from Marina.

They each wheel out a bicycle onto the gravel drive.

He is chastened, distraught.

"It's not your fault. You weren't to know," she says.

"But if I hadn't come here my father and sister might be free now."

"It was my idea. Remember?"

"Should I go to this bureau of Jewish affairs, do you think?"

"It might be a trap."

"I know. I won't tell my mother what happened tonight. It'll only upset her. At least I've got some of her things."

He kneels down on the gravel with the lurchers.

"We should go. There's only fifteen minutes until curfew," she says.

They cycle back to Marina's house with the suitcase. It breaks his heart to abandon the dogs.

26 - November 1943

ISABELLA WEARS a headscarf and dark glasses. She wants to feel she has drawn a mantle of invisibility around her. The stench from a drain, like the brown water in which flowers have died, is like the smell of her own apprehension. She walks past the armed German sentry on Ponte Santa Trinita. Recalls how she used to hoist herself up onto its wall and lower herself down the other side onto the jutting triangular platform above the bridge's middle pillar; that tiny precarious precinct of her own above the moving water. That was where she often sat to read or sketch the church of San Miniato on the hill.

She becomes more nervous the moment the river's choreography of light is doused by the tall buildings on either side of via Tornabuoni. She studies every face she sees in the vicinity of the church. She is accustomed to studying faces. Usually what she seeks in them is inspiration. Today she looks for signs of malice and treachery. She arrives at the wooden door of the church of Santa Trinita five minutes early. It is like night inside. She moistens her fingertips in the holy water. Makes the sign of the cross. There is a smell of damp stone, camphor and incense. Smells that bring death closer. Two women in black are kneeling before an icon of the Holy Virgin. There is another shadowy figure with his back turned to her at the far end of the apse. Where, behind black iron gates, several suspended censers in the chapel beside the sacristy burn a red glow in the gloom. *That must be him.* Her heartbeat skips a beat. Her heels echo her steps down the right transept. Make them sound decisive. Only she and God know what a sham this miming of assured self-possession is. The figure in the red glow of the censers turns round as she passes an altarpiece with scenes from the life of the Virgin, including the miracle of the snow. But it is only an altar boy.

She kneels down in one of the front pews before the altar. The virginal chill of the marble rises up through her knees when she says a prayer for the safekeeping of Freddie. She sees an image of Freddie standing in front of the Ghirlandiao fresco of St Francis in this church. Freddie's features blurred as though reflected in a disturbed pool of water. She worries about the difficulty she now has of summoning up his features clearly. As if he is slipping away from her and her protection.

Ghirlandaio's frescoes of St Francis in the Sassetti Chapel are boarded up behind bricks and sandbags. It is a shock not to see them in their accustomed place, like looking in a mirror that reflects nothing back.

She sits down in a pew near the altar. *A lot of lives depend on this information being passed on.* She decides she will wait another five minutes. She keeps looking at her watch. Then the door opens behind her and a thin spray of light momentarily flickers overhead. Footsteps drum down on the marble floor, their echo creating a vacuum of suspense in the high air overhead. She gets to her feet and risks a quick glance in the direction of the door. It is Fosco, thickly bearded, with a hat pulled down low over his brow. As if intent on showing the world as little of his face as possible. It would be perfectly fitting were he an agent of the secret police. Come to arrest her.

"What are you doing here?"

"Last I heard churches were public places," he says with a faint smirk in which she can detect no trace of duplicity.

The inward struggle to keep the suspicion she feels from her features, to appear innocent and poised.

"I came to see the Ghirlandaio frescoes," she says.

"No one's seen them since 1940."

They are standing by the Spini chapel with its wooden sculpture of Mary Magdalene. Flat-chested, wizened, Magdalene holds her vessel of consecrated oil. Still possesses, despite her drained features and brittle body, the female's power to heal.

"So now we know what I was doing here, what are you doing?" She attempts a playful smile.

"I just came to collect my thoughts. How about we go for an aperitif?"

She walks with him past Palazzo Strozzi. War has made her realise how many of Florence's palaces look more like fortresses than homes. The sun is setting. There are some pink twists of cloud over the Baptistery and Duomo.

They go to a café, Giubbe Rosse in Piazza Vittorio. Thread their way through all the tables outside. Most of them empty because it is cold. They take a seat inside.

She finishes her first drink quickly. The alcohol makes her feel less accountable. Turns her mind into a medium she swims through. Her tolerance today seems to be low.

"It's strange how differently the same things can affect us from one day to the next. I feel a little drunk after just one glass."

"Let me get you another then."

She frames his face with her eyes. Makes a portrait of him. "Did anyone ever tell you you have Machiavellian eyebrows?"

"No. I don't believe they have."

"Well you do. The one on the right is perpetually arching up with mischievous glee."

"Mischievous glee?"

"You were full of mischievous glee when you were plotting my downfall. At least I hope so. Don't tell me you were acting on any kind of principle. That would make you horrendous."

"Perhaps I am horrendous?"

"I used to think so. You barely said a word to me for two years. In fact it's rather a shock to discover you can talk. You always used to communicate in conspiratorial whispers."

"I'm going to get you another drink."

She watches him at the bar. Talking to the painter Ottone Rosai whose work she knows he disapproves of. Then the man standing with Rosai turns round to look at her and it is the man with the puckered scar under his eye who slapped her. And the man with a gold tooth is there too. Who flashes his gold tooth as if it is some kind of princely signet ring.

"Are you still a fascist?" she asks him bluntly when he returns with her negroni.

"Not so loud," he says.

"Are you?"

"If I were I could have you arrested for the contempt with which you say the word fascist."

"I've already been arrested."

"You're looking at me as if you think it was my fault."

"Who were those men you were talking to?"

"Surely you know Rosai? Florence's most famous living painter. The bane of Maestro's life."

"The other two men."

"A couple of thugs who work for Carità."

"Friends of yours?"

"My work throws me into the path of some unpleasant individuals."

"What work?"

"I'm on the committee of the Soprintendenza delle Belle Arti. Once upon a time I felt I was doing noble work. Ensuring the city's works of art were kept safe. But word is we'll soon be valuing heirlooms stolen from requisitioned Jewish homes. The confiscated treasure is to be collected in a warehouse and it will be my job to sort through it, identifying what's of monetary value."

She isn't convinced. It's unlike him to supply so many details. Defensiveness has made him garrulous.

"Why did you hate me so much?"

"I don't hate anyone."

"Dislike then. Why did you dislike me so much?"

"The studio to me, its political side, was like a game of chess. You were an opponent. You were trying to outplay me too. Don't deny it."

"I do deny it. I was terrified to begin with. Afraid to open my mouth. Make a sound. Draw any attention to myself. All you males. And so conspiratorial. So implicitly condescending about the idea of a woman painting."

"You had your clique. Freddie and Oskar. You spoke in conspiratorial whispers too. Quickly erased guilty expressions from your faces when I entered the room."

"I married Freddie and you married Maestro."

She watches this remark pierce his stiff formality and make him wince. A flicker of dislike appears in his guarded nutbrown eyes.

"What I mean is, when I was at the studio I believed it was just an isolated phase of my life. Whereas it turns out to have been an embryo. The centre of all gravity. For you too."

She watches him settle back into his habitual manner again. The stiff coiled formality that is him at his most relaxed.

It's as if he is relentlessly standing guard over some dark shaming secret, she thinks.

"Were you really so scornful of the notion that a woman might be able to paint?"

"Maestro was always putting his words into my mouth."

"Sometimes I used to think you secretly hated him."

"Because I was financially dependent on him?"

"Maybe. You're not anymore?"

"No, now I'm his lackey out of charity."

"Did he agree to teach me to put his theory to the test? I felt that. Like it was the Inquisition. And I was on trial. Everyone wanted me to fail. To buckle under interrogation."

"But you didn't fail. You won him over. And he did want to paint you."

"Did he? Or was that another way of humbling me. Getting me to strip naked in front of you all."

"That is still my favourite painting of his."

"I was so angry when he allowed you to paint me too. That was a serious breach of contract on his part. What happened to yours?"

"I painted over it. Nothing personal. Perhaps that was another reason I didn't like you. You eluded me."

She points her finger at him. Her eyes bright with laughter. "You've admitted you didn't like me." She feels a handclap of triumph that she has managed to prise a grain of truth out of him at last. The glow of satisfaction an interrogator might feel who finally induces his victim to speak. "I elude everyone. It's my party trick," she says, elbows on the table, hands joined beneath her chin. Then she throws herself back in the chair. "But what a pair of fascists you two were!"

"Not so loud please. The walls have ears. Can't we go back to the mischievous glee?"

"Do you know why I hate fascism? It's a male cult. It's all about exalting the male. Believe, obey, fight. Men are here to maintain order and women to bear children. Unbelievable really that we've agreed to go along with such simplistic suffocating nonsense for so long. Where are the women in the history of art? Wasn't that one of Maestro's favourite lines? He often asked me why I thought women couldn't paint. We are an inferior species to him."

"And yet you adore him."

"I do adore him. As many women are said to adore Hitler. We women are suckers for men who bring their fists down hard on tables. But it was you who vandalised his painting, wasn't it? His Last Supper. What on earth possessed you? What did it feel like? Turpsing off all that endeavour and inspiration. I've often pictured you doing it. But I can't quite imagine your emotional state."

"Did I do it with mischievous glee, you mean?"

"How could you do it at all? That's what I mean. Has he ever confronted you about it? Asked you why you did it?"

"We don't know who did it."

She shakes her head. "How little you're willing to give away."

"I can't help my nature."

"No. And nature is the great teacher," she says, quoting Maestro.

"I'd like to visit your studio one day."

"Would you? Do. I don't have a card. Or a piece of paper."

"Here. Write the address on this."

He hands her a twenty lire note.

27 - November 1943

HIS MOTHER is beneath the covers in Marina's bed. Francesco is jealous of his mother's privilege. She becomes a kind of rival for the first time in his life. He wants to sleep in Marina's bed. It seems to him a tawdry joke on the part of fate that his indifferent mother has been granted his most sprawling wish. He will sleep on the floor where some cushions have been arranged. He unbuttons his white shirt by the light of a candle. He does not enjoy this ceremony of undressing in front of his mother. It is another tawdry joke on the part of fate.

She tells him off for not folding up his clothes.

"Good to see you've got your priorities straightened out again," he smiles.

"Chide me all you want but never have appearances been more important."

He blows out the candle. Light slowly drains away into the darkness like the weaker of two mixed solutions.

He is pleased she has made some effort with Marina. That she talked to her over supper. But there is still an uneasiness between them, a film of frost.

"The irony is, if it wasn't for Marina you would have been arrested as well. Me too," he says in the dark. He keeps his voice low.

"What do you mean?"

"I saw Marina the day the fascists came and as a result I couldn't sleep. That's why I went out into the garden. That's why I wasn't in my room when dad and Ivana were taken."

"We won't be able to stay here another night. The father doesn't want us here. And I don't want you to go to that office. I couldn't bear it if you were taken away as well. I won't survive on my own, Francesco."

"Okay, I won't go. I'll send someone else. A non-Jew. Perhaps my friend Paolo."

He and his mother whispering to each other in the dark. Their emotional history a heavy presence in the darkness, like the smell of washed clothes that have taken too long to dry. It's as if he and his mother are prising out secrets from each other that neither of them want.

He is waiting for his mother to go to sleep. Waiting for the whole house to go to sleep. Marina, he saw, left her bag in the kitchen. Her diary is still inside the bag. He has convinced himself she is seeing someone else. This is why there is a new reserve in her.

He pictures her in her bed on the other side of the thin wall. Her bare feet beneath the covers. Her hands clasped perhaps between her thighs. The sheets fragrant with the scent of her hair and neck. He strains his ears for some sound of her in the dark next door. But it is always his mother's nasal intake and release of breath he hears.

Now and again he knows guilt for not giving more thought to his father and sister. Who knows where they are sleeping tonight.

He rests his hand on the door handle. Tugs it down and pulls. The door scrapes against the stone floor. Barefooted, he pads into the kitchen. As quietly as his ghost might perform the act. Her bag is still on the kitchen table. The tips of his fingers prickle with the guilty anticipation of his next move. He slips his hand into the bag and extracts the book. Feeling he is standing on the tips of his toes. He holds it in his hand. Opens it. The loose-jointed pages, stained with mulberry smudges, curled up at the edges, are swollen with their secret script. There are small deposits of candle wax on some pages, like braille, and on another page there is an inked fingerprint. The writing though is blurred. Something in him refuses to bring the script into focus. A pang of conscience. This act makes him feel grubby. He recognises it as a treacherous violation.

You're an idiot, doing this, says a voice inside. *There isn't anyone else.*

He goes out onto the balcony to smoke a cigarette. To celebrate and prolong his new feeling of optimism. He sits down on a groaning cheap chair. Rests the diary down on the stone balustrade of the balcony. Next to a dead plant in a pot. Searchlights criss cross the sky over the cathedral dome. Three prongs of light. Swinging back and forth in a mimicry of entwining limbs. He pivots back on the chair. Thinking it closer to the wall than it is. The chair tips back and carries on tipping back. His arms fly out in a pantomime effort to save himself from the fall. His flailing hand knocks Marina's diary off its perch. He doesn't hear the thud it makes on the pavement below because simultaneously he has landed in a heap among pots of basil and rosemary.

He has just got back to his feet, smiling to himself, when Marina's mother appears in her nightdress. Looking alarmed.

"Are you all right?"

"Fine. I couldn't sleep so came out for a quick cigarette."

"As long as you're all right."

"Fine. I'm going back to bed now."

When he returns to the kitchen Marina's bag is no longer on the table. For the first time it occurs to him that a catastrophe may have taken place. The need to go downstairs and retrieve her diary becomes a dizzying tidal surge.

Go back to bed, he silently pleads with Marina's mother.

But she remains in the kitchen. Irritating him with her idle refusal to do as he wishes. He is forced to return to his makeshift bed.

The enforced curfew outside appeases his fears to some extent.

At least there's no one out there to pick it up, he thinks.

He strains his ears for sounds of activity in the apartment. He has to wait a good half hour before he can get up again. Wait for the apartment to settle back into slumber. He goes down the stairs in his bare feet. Dressed only in shorts and an undershirt. He has brought a magazine with him. To act as a wedge for the front door.

That would cap everything if I was locked out during curfew in my underwear, he thinks.

There is no sign of Marina's diary on the pavement. He puts more effort into his gaze, trying to summon up the book by force of will. Panic finally arrives. Self-pity too. Anger at himself and at God, the stars, the mathematics of chance.

Then, two hundred yards away along the river, he sees two figures. They look like fascist militia. He feels sure they have picked up Marina's journal. What other explanation is there for its disappearance?

He sets off in pursuit.

Are you mad?

I'd rather be arrested than have to explain to Marina that I got up in the middle of the night to read her diary.

The two fascist officials vanish down a side road. Towards Santo Spirito. He is getting perilously close to the bridge, to Ponte alla Carraia where there will be German sentries who are under orders to shoot anyone who breaks the curfew.

Why did I take Marina's diary? Why?

He wonders if Marina has incriminated any of her university friends in her diary, some of whom he knows are opposed to the fascists.

She could even be arrested now, he thinks.

He increases his pace. Winces in pain every time he stamps his bare feet down on a splinter of glass, a sharp stone. He goes down a darker side street, off the river, to avoid the German sentries on the bridge.

28 - November 1943

FOUR OF THE Australian crew are engaged in a wheelbarrow race on the uncut grass between two runways. Cheered on by a group of ground crew and a blonde WAAF dressed up as an airman. Freddie is sitting on the grass near J Jig with Reg, Davy, Woodsy and Jack. Jack tries to smile. But he appears discomforted by this hullabaloo of frivolity. Jack is nineteen. Fresh out of training school. Freddie now knows it is an embarrassment of shyness and fear rather than some private form of conceit that is responsible for the stiffness of his manner. Earlier Jack confided that he has never kissed a girl. His face went bright red.

"They're just shooting a line for the WAAFs up in the control tower." Reg nods up towards the three smiling girls peering out of the window.

"Is it allowed to take a WAAF up in a kite?" asks Jack.

"No. That's why they've dressed her up as a man."

"And if they got caught?"

"The pilot would get a stiff talking to, probably lose any chance he might have of a commission. What else can they do? Send him to the front? Most chaps would consider the front a holiday compared to what we go through here."

"I wouldn't consider the front a holiday," says Freddie.

"Where is the front anyway?"

"Last time I heard, about four hundred miles from your house."

They have just landed after the air test in J Jig, the bomber he will be piloting later. The Wingco has appropriated V Victor for tonight's sortie on Berlin. J Jig is a new Lancaster. Barely off the assembly line. Only has a solitary bomb symbol painted below the pilot's window. Jack will come along for the ride as a dickie pilot. Jack keeps asking questions of a perfunctory nature.

At every opportunity he lights someone's cigarette as if to prove his hands aren't shaking.

Cyril walks over. With his ever-present satchel slung over his shoulder.

"How about we all go for a bike ride before ops?"

"We'll have to find Jack a bicycle."

"We can borrow Taffy's before it's auctioned off."

Freddie wonders if it's a good idea to give Jack the bicycle of a dead pilot. Already he and the crew found themselves having to fend off the rising damp of superstition when Jack climbed aboard J Jig with them earlier. They were, and still are, worried about the nature of the energy Jack is bringing on board the aircraft. It has been discussed. The karma he has left behind and will bring back later.

"I wish we didn't have to take him along. I think he's got that jinxed look in his eye," said Woodsy.

"He's fine," Freddie said. "He's just shy and nervous how he'll respond to being shot at. Remember? You don't really know until it happens."

"You know you've still got traces of make-up on your face?"

Freddie does know. He saw it in the washroom mirror and was careful not to wash it away. The faint smudge of black pencil beneath both his eyes. Last night there was a fancy dress party in the mess. He went as Cleopatra. Two WAAFs painted his face and lent him some clothes. Davy went as a Roman Centurion. Jokes were cracked about Marc Anthony and Cleopatra. He and Davy danced together until Poppy the pixie girl with the clairvoyant blue eyes forcibly prised them apart and demanded Freddie jitterbugged with her.

After briefing the Wingco apologises for appropriating V Victor and then comments on his appearance.

"Are you planning on becoming the first member of the Allied forces to go into battle wearing mascara?"

"Yes sir," he says.

"You could get away with murder with that smile, Hartson."

"Thank you, sir."

Spike and Spencer return from the chapel. The only two members of his crew who go to prayer service. A solemn private look about them. Spike with his pipe.

At Oxford Freddie mocked the idea of a personal god. Of any kind of benevolent deity. He doesn't mock this idea any more. Wishes he never had. He is willing to believe in any and every god now. For fear of getting on the wrong side of one of them.

Outside the locker room he greets the Australians. They have a new pilot. They are going to Berlin in unlucky N Nan.

"Hope you've got your lucky charm," he says to Bluey, the rear gunner.

Bluey pulls out the yellow brassiere from inside his flying jacket and waves it in a loop over his head. "See you at breakfast," he says.

"Hello J Jig. Hello J Jig. Yes you may take off. Off you go. Off you go. Over."

The airspeed indicator shows 110mph when he lifts J Jig off the shining wet runway. The huddle of onlookers, blowing on their hands and stamping their feet, look too forlorn to convey any good wishes. Freddie pulls her into a steep climbing turn to port. The force pushing his weight down into his seat carries a slightly disarming charge, like being touched by an unfamiliar hand. His body knows this is not V Victor.

The pale sun on the horizon throws long shadows over the fields surrounding the shrinking aerodrome as J Jig climbs up towards the cloud smoke to join the circuit. He casts a glance down at the building where he sleeps. Pictures his clothes and books and his bed waiting inside for him to return. Lincoln Cathedral disappears beneath the nose. At ten thousand feet J Jig joins the first stream of thirty or so heavy bombers. Jack sits just behind Reg. The presence of the young pupil makes Freddie more conscientious but also more in a mood for showing off.

At twelve thousand feet J Jig breaks through canyons of cloud into a clear stretch of brighter sky. To left and right one four-engine bomber after another noses up through the bumpy cumulus. They are flying now above a dreamscape of rollercoasting white cloud crests. It feels sometimes like a premonition of death. Being so high up in the sky where no other living creature can survive. Where there is nothing solid. Just shifting transparency, luminous endless space.

He spoke to his mother earlier. His father is not expected to live more than another week.

"Okay. I'll be down the day after tomorrow," he said into the mouthpiece. Inside the painted red box. Just before the chain was looped round it and locked. In case there is a German spy on the base.

The oxygen mask is irritating his face more than usual. Too much alcohol last night, not enough sleep has made his skin prickly.

He lets Jack fly the plane over the North Sea. Starry darkness begins pressing in through the perspex. Distance gains in depth what it loses in visibility. It can be felt beneath the skin, welling up inside, prising open reserves of wonder. The lights on the instrument panel are now the brightest things in the world. He wants Jack to know he trusts him. So he leaves the cockpit. Pushes the blackout curtain aside and steps into Cyril and Davy's secret alcove. The orange light startles his eyes for a moment. The temperature rises. The engines and the echoing rattle of the fuselage is louder, more jarring. Cyril, strapped to his desk, is hunched over his maps, logs and instruments on the green table. Davy, pressing both palms to the headphones clamped to his ears, showing a moment's surprise to see him.

"Just taking a leisurely stroll," he says. Always he comes out with idiotic things when talking to Davy. Davy lowers his mask and mouths the words, Can't hear you, and Freddie is glad. He silently mouths an entire sonnet of disconnected words and grins to let Davy know this is a joke.

It is forty degrees below zero outside. The wings are glazed with rime. The propellers spit away the ice that makes a continuous clattering noise against the fuselage.

He takes over the controls again as they near the Dutch coast. Jack has his first experience of flak. Splashes of dull orange light beneath the clouds. Freddie weaves J Jig from left to right, up and down. Having to concentrate hard to average out all the twists and turns so as to keep on the scheduled course. Not a shard pierces J Jig's skin.

Over Germany J Jig becomes sluggish. Peevish. Her controls less responsive. Because of the ice. He now regrets climbing so high to avoid the main force of the stream. It annoys him because it makes him look incompetent in front of the boy.

"Met man was looking on the bright side as usual. I think we're pretty badly iced up."

Clouds begin converging on J Jig again. Rolling towards the perspex like an alpine avalanche in slow motion. He sees faces in them. These faces are not kind. J Jig begins bumping. The engine noise is muffled into a soporific drone.

"I sift the snow on the mountains below..."

Reg looks across at him, his left eyebrow arched above his oxygen mask. "You still drunk?" he asks.

"Shelley," Freddie says.

"Shelley's dead."

"So would you be if you were born in 1792."

It's Davy he imagines listening, who he wants to make smile when he banters over the intercom.

Spike clears his throat into the microphone. "There's the target. Looks like 10/10ths flak awaits us. Prepare yourselves for a rocky ride."

Up ahead the shells burst in clusters of thirty or so. He can feel Jack's fear and, surprising himself, enjoys it a bit. Realising that it is an accolade that he faces this danger week in, week out. He wants to tell Jack not to worry too much. That he too felt terrified when he had to go through all this in the company of strangers. But that everything changes when you have nested into the companionship of your own crew. How much additional courage you derive from your companions. That he won't be as frightened when he faces these dangers as part of a brotherhood.

The silent puffs of black smoke get larger. Shaped like maps of non-existent countries. Evil kingdoms in a fairy story. He watches the searchlights lancing the clouds. These turrets of light that can reach 20,000 feet up into the night sky. Swinging after a plane in front. She banks off to port. But the beam follows her. Like something supernatural in a nightmare. The beam sticks to her now and a dozen others converge on her. She is like a startled naked thing in the sky. As helpless as a tortoise lying on its back. There is some relief in the knowledge that the lights now have prey. That he can slip J Jig through while the guns are occupied on the captive Lancaster.

He counts to himself. Making sure he does not fly the same course or height for more than twenty-one seconds. Offers this ploy as advice over the intercom to young Jack.

"No more of this damn cowardly weaving to avoid enemy fighters. If I see any of this squadron weaving tonight I'll court martial the whole crew," says Cyril, imitating poor old Archibald Ramshaw.

"How many searchlights do you think are down there?"

"About five hundred."

"Another kite has been hit. To starboard."

He looks across at the sheet of flame burning off the port rudder of the wounded bomber.

"And I think that's Doug's kite that is now being coned."

Doug was dressed as a Zulu warrior at the fancy dress party. He drives a battered old Austin 12. Now and again gives Freddie a lift back to base from the pub.

"She's had it. Bail out lads."

"Rear gunner here. Are we getting the order to bail out?"

"No, Spencer. Keep your hat on."

"I see two chutes. What are the others waiting for?"

"Frying pan into the fire. Can you imagine jumping out into that inferno?"

Spike clears his throat twice. "Tracking in nicely, skipper. Open bomb doors."

His gloved hand reaches for the bomb door lever on the left side of his seat. Berlin, the government quarter near the Branderburger Tor, including, it is hoped, the Gestapo headquarters, is burning in filigrees of fire down below. The bright red target indicator flares continually vanishing behind rippling silver explosions and mushrooming black smoke.

"Keep her straight and level, skipper. No more weaving now."

Spike clears his throat twice before saying "steady". He says steady about fifteen times and every time he does the double cough routine first.

Spike lets the bombs go.

"Okay, nav. Give me the course out of here."

"Nav to skipper. Might be best to press on east until we're out of this shooting gallery."

"I was thinking the same."

There are combats all around. His eyes are pulled this way and that by all the trails and flashes of light, the looming and vanishing smudges of shadow. He rarely sees any of the German night fighters swooping in among the stream. Performing acrobatics. Blazing their cannons. But he can hear Woodsy and Spencer's guns.

"Either of you two lost your virginity yet?"

"Nearly. Just then. Frightened the blighter off."

"Flak directly beneath us."

"Streuth! That was awful close."

There is a huge explosion in front. A bright orange flash that spits bits of flaming debris at the perspex and bellows out a cave of black smoke. For thirty seconds they are rocked about inside this black maelstrom. The control column jumps forward. The starboard wing rocks. J Jig feels like a hooked fish being tugged at from another element.

"What's going on? Have we been hit?"

"I think we've been hit."

"Rear gunner to navigator. The coned kite has gone down. I saw three chutes."

Cyril will write all this down in his logbook. In his looping drunken handwriting. Recount it to the intelligence officer at debriefing when they will all huddle around the table with a mug of coffee laced with rum and their affection for each other is at its height. If they get back.

Orange smoke from fighter flares lights up the cockpit. As bright as a circus clown's clothes. Down below the green globes of the target indicators and the red flashes of the 88 mm guns. The night is all the colours of children's sweets.

"Skipper from navigator. There was a fire but we've put it out. Ruddy big hole in the fuselage though. I think another Lanc dropped an incendiary on us. My equipment is all over the floor. And it's bloody freezing."

"Okay. When we get out of this hell-hole take it in turns to come up for stints into the cockpit when you get too cold."

"Also we've lost a parachute. It got burnt. Let's hope we don't have to bail out."

He has often imagined baling out. It terrifies him. To picture himself outside the aircraft, in the midst of all that scything light and screaming metal, makes him realise how relatively safe he feels inside. The thought of losing forever all the daily details of his life at the station. Especially the homecomings. The moment of stepping down onto the ground again into a world silvered with the first tremors of dawn. The sense of elation and thanksgiving while eating bacon and fried bread in the mess at four or five in the morning amidst the animated chatter and the echo of cutlery. Going to bed exhausted at dawn.

"I can't get nothing on the set, sir. It's dead."

He wishes Davy wouldn't call him sir.

"You can't get anything on the set, Davy. Not nothing," says Reg.

"Pompous oaf," says Freddie.

He imagines the concern in the control tower. They will think J Jig has gone down when they hear nothing. People will think of him in the past tense.

The gyrocompass reads 081 degrees. He pushes the column forward.

Then the world is dark again. The sky empty. No bright flashes or flares erupt from the enveloping blackness. J Jig is devoured by relentless encompassing cloud and fog. One of her engines is dead. The wireless set is dead, as is Gee, the radar navigational system. There is no longer a pulse in the invisible artery between the aircraft and the ground station. Cyril clearly has little idea where they are. J Jig has become a desert island.

They have no contact with the outside world. They have to guess what is down below.

Three hours pass. Visibility is no more than a hundred yards. Davy and Cyril take it in turns to warm themselves up in the cockpit.

"Skipper to nav. Are you sure we're not heading for China?"

"I'm afraid I wouldn't bet my life on it, skip."

"Where *should* we be?"

"Half way across the North Sea?"

He takes J Jig down to 1,000 feet. In the hope of being able to spot some landmark. Something they can correlate to a map. But it is as if they no longer belong to the world. As if they have flown behind the surface of things.

Whenever he looks at the fuel gauges he thinks of the missing parachute. As the likelihood of having to bail out becomes more and more probable.

An hour later the barest slither of coast is sighted. There are pale blue lights down there through the mist. Ghost lights.

"Looks like we've made it back to England, skipper."

He circles the avenue of lights.

"It's definitely an aerodrome."

He decides to go in. A green light briefly flicks on through the gloom. He brings J Jig down in a tight left spiral. As he eases down the air speed and straightens her out over the flarepath at about fifty feet he is seized by doubt.

Spike clears his throat into the microphone. "I can see a Nazi flag down there."

"Okay. Overshooting. Full throttle, flaps, undercarriage up." Freddie heaves back the stick. J Jig's frame shudders. Orange sparks streaming off into the slipstream. He just manages to clear the boundary trees. Expects at any moment to hear the ack ack of guns.

"Bloody hell. We almost put down at a Luftwaffe base."

He swivels round in his seat and smiles for Jack.

But J Jig is losing airspeed. Losing height. Running out of fuel.

"Skipper here. We need to start chucking things out. Everything we don't need."

Down in the nose Spike is wrestling with the cumbersome bomb aimer. A blast of freezing air gusts into the cockpit when he kicks open the emergency hatch. Reg unfastens the armour plating behind Freddie's seat and out the hatch that goes too.

"Tanks are more or less empty. You're going to have to ditch her in the next five minutes."

He fights to keep J Jig straight, trimmed and nose up. She is retching and spluttering, bumping him about inside his harness as if he is a dice in a clenched shaking fist. He still can't see the sea even when he knows it must be just beneath them. When the grey swell finally appears it is terrifying, the most elemental sight he has ever seen, like the open mouth of death.

"I'll never again complain about stewed prunes and semolina pudding."

"Yes you will, Woodsy. And probably tomorrow."

"Open the hatch and get the dinghy ready. Crash positions everyone."

Probably I'm going to beat my father to it.

Spray spatters the perspex. He turns off all four engines. Pulls the control column back against his stomach. Braces himself for the impact. For the North Sea to come flooding into the cockpit.

"The Lord is my shepherd..."

It is Spencer mumbling the Lord's Prayer.

J Jig bumps down with a lot of crunching and grinding noises but little violence. Miraculously she doesn't break up. There is something unnatural and bewildering about the experience. As if he had let a Ming Dynasty vase slip through his hands onto a stone floor and it didn't break. His eyes stare with astonishment at what has happened. J Jig is riding the waves. Icy water slops in through the nose into the cockpit. He disconnects the intercom and the oxygen jacks. Clambers out after Reg onto the starboard wing. Beneath the thick fog the heaving sea is a sight he barely has the courage to acknowledge. The yellow dinghy slowly opens and inflates. One by one they help each other climb in. Woodsy carrying Percy, the homing pigeon, inside its cage.

29 - November 1943

FRANCESCO BLINKS himself awake. Pushes back the blanket that was covering most of his face. Marina stands smiling down at him. Her hair is piled up in a beehive. She is wearing only a red towel knotted under her armpits. There is a darker damp patch on the part of the towel that covers her naval. She stands smiling down at him, holding pretty female underwear.

"Sorry to wake you up. I needed some new clothes," she says, holding out the folded soft fabrics as if offering them to him as a gift.

"What time is it?"

"Nine something."

He sees she has left wet footprints on the floor. She smells of the essence of some wildflower. The smell of her is like fingertips caressing the back of his neck, the inside of his thigh. Then the memory filters through. The memory of the two fascist militia. How they vanished. And with them all hope of retrieving her diary. The walk back along the river in his bare feet. Walking all the way with his eyes riveted to the ground. In the desperate hope that her secret book would suddenly materialise. He remembers he is now a condemned man. There is a snake in his stomach.

"Good news. I've persuaded my dad to let you and your mother stay another night."

"Thanks."

"Are you all right?"

"Haven't quite woken up yet."

"See you at breakfast," she says and skips out of the room.

He goes into the bathroom. There is a mist on the mirror. The glass erases most of the detail from his face. He splashes some cold water up into his eyes. He sees there is still cloudy bathwater in the tub. He pictures Marina's naked body in this same water. He tests it with his hand. It is still warm. He pulls his undershirt up over his head. Steps out of his shorts. As he is about to climb into the tub, submerge himself in her dirty bathwater, he notices the wicker basket.

He presses the soft twisted material to his lips. Inhales the smell of her secretions. Like seaweed and brine. Like the inside of a seashell. He looks down at his erection. At his bare feet on the speckled brown tiles.

If these belonged to her mother this smell would repulse me, he thinks.

How do you know for sure they don't belong to her mother?

He removes the panties from his mouth. Restores them to the wicker basket. Arranging them into the precise form he recalls finding them.

He gets into the water. Her water. He never wants to come out.

"I admit I was going to read it but I didn't. Not a word. I absolutely swear."

Her anger does not abate one iota.

"I even risked arrest to get it back. I chased after two fascists. In just my shorts. But I lost them."

Still her anger does not abate one iota.

He is imagining this conversation. Still lying back in her dirty bathwater. Still reluctant to ever leave it though the water is cold now. Wrinkling up his penis and reducing it to the size of his thumb.

Everyone except Marina and her father are sitting at the table when he enters the kitchen.

"We were just saying how much we miss real coffee," Marina's mother tells him.

Marina's mother has given his own mother a large dollop of cherry jam to spread on her bread. He suspects this is the family's entire ration of jam for the week.

When Marina enters the kitchen she is frowning.

"All right, Leo. Very funny. Now give it back."

Leo dunks a chunk of bread in his mug of hot milk. There is a white stain on his upper lip. "What are you talking about?" he asks, chewing.

"You've hidden my diary."

"I haven't touched your diary."

"Mum?"

Her mother wipes imaginary crumbs from her lips with a napkin. "Don't look at me."

"It was in my bag last night."

"I hung your bag up in the hallway during the night but I didn't touch anything inside."

Francesco feels Marina's mother's eyes on him for a moment.

He rubs his palms along his thighs under the table. "I've made up my mind to go and see this Giuseppe at the bureau for Jewish affairs today," he says.

"I won't allow it."

"But we can't just leave dad and Ivana. If there's a chance of getting them out we have to risk it. And lots of these new fascist officials are just petty criminals. They'll turn a blind eye for reimbursement. Anyway, I won't take the money with me. I'll try to negotiate a deal. But I'll make it clear they have to release dad and Ivana first."

"You said you'd get your friend to go."

"What if they took him hostage though or something? I can't risk getting a friend into trouble. It's best if I go."

30 - November 1943

WHEN ISABELLA arrives at Maestro's studio she is relieved there is no sign of Fosco. She has given a lot of thought to Fosco's fortuitous appearance in the church. It surely could not have been a coincidence. *But which side is he working for?* Every night in bed she thinks of the possible repercussions of not passing on the warning about the man Branimir. She has to keep telling herself she was right not to trust Fosco.

Maestro's painting of Saint Sebastian is on an easel. She goes up close and studies the brushstrokes, the consistency of the paintwork.

"Beginning a painting," he says. He is wearing a tight, buttoned waistcoat and a bright blue and yellow striped tie beneath his grey painting smock. "What a marvellous and terrifying moment that always is. The promise of happiness. The fear of failure. And always the same outcome."

"What outcome?"

"Disappointment. The painting you saw in your mind was beautiful when it was your secret. Once it's on the canvas it's as if someone else has got hold of your secret and sullied it, distorted it."

She steels herself, musters up all her effrontery. "It wasn't me who destroyed your Last Supper. I would never do a thing like that. It hurt me that you thought I did."

There is no struggle of surprise in him. She realises how rarely Maestro seems unprepared for what he's told. "I never believed it was you," he says.

"But you had Fosco throw me out of your studio."

"Perhaps, every now and again, we are granted a prophetic insight into the future. I don't think I could manage without Fosco now. He takes care of all the chores that demoralise me."

"What's he doing? Where does he stand, in this war?"

"He works for the Ministry of Education. He's trying to prevent the Germans from stealing our art treasures. Though I'm not sure this is his official task. He oversaw the building of the protective wall in the Bargello. He's proud of that. I nearly threw Fosco out of my studio not long after you left. We locked horns. He was fornicating with the models. The sly old goat. He was abusing his position of power in my studio to seduce nineteen-year-old girls. Is that why I set up an atelier? To provide whores for my assistant?"

"I always felt he hated women."

"He does. He hates them for the power they have over him. The power to arouse him against his will."

"I once saw your Saint Sebastian chatting with an SS officer."

"Highly unlikely. Ascanio is Jewish. He's staying in my apartment until we can find him a safer hiding place."

"We?"

"Fosco is trying to arrange it."

"So Fosco has changed sides?"

"Fosco does what I tell him. I've supported him his whole adult life, you know that, don't you? Without me he'd be on the Russian front now."

"And you trust him?"

"Of course I don't trust him. Now, I summoned you here for a purpose. Let's see how well I managed to train your eye."

He turns round two canvases that were facing the wall. Her jaw drops.

"I don't understand," she says.

"Which is the Ghirlandaio and which is the forgery?"

She stares at two identical beautiful paintings of the Annunciation.

"This is what I meant when I said Fosco is intent on saving Florence's works of arts from the Nazis. It wore me out copying the damn thing. That's why you're going to copy the Pontormo."

Maestro holds up a gilt framed picture. 78x66 cm. A plump coarse-faced woman and a swan in a murky pastoral setting. The picture is muddy and fussy. Any liveliness of gesture and poise it once possessed dulled by years of candle smoke and grease.

"That surely isn't a Pontormo. It's the most unlikely Leda I ever saw," she says. "She looks like she's having a break from gutting fish."

"Precisely why you're going to paint over it. No one is quite sure who painted it. What we do know is that it was painted roughly at the same time Pontormo was alive. And it's the same size canvas. Look at it. It reeks of the days of plagues and witch hunts. You paint Pontormo's saint on top of Leda."

Maestro fishes out another painting hidden behind a stack of canvasses. He has a twinkle in his eye. "Saint Anthony, patron saint of lost things." She stares at the four hundred year old portrait, mesmerised. The beautifully controlled swirling rhythm of its lines becoming a beat in her blood.

"Think you can copy this? Well enough to fool a member of the German secret police," he says.

"No. Firstly where would I find the impetus to create something that's already been created? It goes against the grain," she says.

The act of creation, the impetus to undertake it, is always some kind of feeble attempt to understand one's own creation, the nature of creation itself. Didn't Maestro once say that?

"Secondly?" he asks.

"Well, even if I could replicate Pontormo's brushstrokes, get an exact likeness in the face, the precise tone of every shade of colour in this canvas, there's no possibility whatsoever that I could give it the look, the sheen of a sixteenth century painting."

"That's where you're wrong," he says. He produces two vials of a murky brown resin from a shelf. "How do you think I got my Annunciation to look so venerably ancient? Phenol formaldehyde," he says.

"What's that?" she says fascinated by the slightly sinister compound in the tubes.

"Mix it in with all your colours. The solution in these two vials is the secret to eternal antiquity. After it's been baked a bit in an oven. We've only got to fool a couple of Gestapo buffoons. Think of it as your contribution to the war effort. In a few weeks Fosco says the inventory will be checked before St Anthony and all the rest of the Uffizi booty is being moved to various villas in Tuscany for safekeeping."

Isabella walks back to her studio with the two paintings wrapped in brown paper under her arm. Her heart pounding every time she encounters a man in uniform. She is furious with herself, furious with Maestro, furious at her inability to ever say no to him.

She sets up the Pontormo painting on an easel. Sits down in front of it. Her body aglow with reverence. It is a marvel to her that they are alone together in her studio. A marvel that the same materials on her palette have preserved the living face of this man and conveyed it through four centuries. This living male face pretending to be Saint Anthony in his brown Franciscan robes, with a stave, with a scroll. He refuses eye contact and yet she feels they are exchanging secrets. The severity of his expression, the high tide intensity in his eyes reminds her of Maestro.

She sets to work. She wipes the dust off the Leda painting. She uses the old pair of Freddie's shorts doused in turpentine to remove the outer layer of grease. It is satisfying to see the residue of time transferred from one surface to another.

She prepares the lead white base with which she will whitewash poor Leda. Down on her knees, down on the bare boards, she stirs the creamy primer with an old piece of wood. She gives some thought to the unknown artist who painted the picture, a picture that has somehow survived four hundred years but that she is now going to erase. It is an act of vandalism she is about to perform. Who can guess the impetus and toil that went into the execution of this painting? She feels a chill of superstition, as if she is being watched from a realm she can't see. Appeases some of her guilt with the thought that the painting will still be there, still layered into the strata of paint and oil but it will be hidden, like something lodged in the earth, waiting to be rediscovered.

Captain Heinkel arrives wearing a raincoat over his uniform. Insists once again that she calls him Erich. It causes her an almost physical pain to call him Erich, like when, as a little girl, some neighbouring boys had pinned her arms to a wall and forced her to say aloud the most vulgar and offensive words in the Italian language. He looks her full in the face as he always does. Making her feel she is being studied under a magnifying glass. She takes his crisp raincoat. He stands in the spheres of reflected light slanting in through a gap in the black window drapes. She has to steel herself to avoid looking at the place beneath the pile of folded drapes where Pontormo's Saint Anthony is hidden. The whitewashed Leda sits drying against a wall, its secrets immune even to his relentlessly prying eye.

"You might be interested to hear we finally have one or two leads regarding the missing paintings," he says.

Surely the flush of emotion is visible on her face. She carries on mixing a flesh colour on her palette without looking up.

"Oh?"

"Yes."

"I don't understand what right you have to take these paintings. Surely they belong to the Italian government."

"Mussolini himself promised them to the *Führer* for his new museum in Linz. It's therefore causing a good deal of embarrassment to your Duce that they can't be located."

She remembers what Maestro said about only having to trick a couple of Gestapo buffoons. Turns out, she imagines saying to Freddie, we've got to trick Adolf Hitler himself.

31 - November 1943

FREDDIE SITS between Reg and Davy in the dinghy. When Reg cut the umbilical cord that attached the dinghy to J Jig he also mistakenly cut the cord that attached the emergency survival pack to the dinghy. Freddie had to dissuade Reg from swimming over to it in the freezing cold sea.

It is two hours since they all watched J Jig roll over on her side and sink down beneath the surface of the North Sea in a great froth and swirl of water. For a while Freddie couldn't stop looking at the spot she had been so conclusively erased from. Then he couldn't help picturing the ocean bed, as if he was down there, of his bones corals made.

The muffling eerie fog is lifting but each new wave seems to lift the dinghy a little higher.

"This is beginning to make me feel like I've got a hangover," says Reg.

Freddie looks at his watch. 6.15 am. Another wave lifts them up, drops them down. There are now about three inches of water in the dinghy. It soaks up into the seat of his trousers. He uses his empty thermos flask to scoop some out. The others follow his example. Then another wave chucks more water in. The dinghy is buffeted forward, turns a few circles, then edges forward again, like a fairground ride. Cyril reckons they are about ten miles from the English coast. That's what he wrote on the note he attached to Percy, the homing pigeon. They all envied it as they watched it fly off.

"Isn't that France it's heading towards?"

"Probably, if it had the same navigations officer as I had at OTU," says Reg.

"Do you think anyone's looking for us yet?" asks Jack.

"We'll be chalked in as missing by now. Failed to return. In about four hours friends and family will be getting their telegrams," says Woodsy.

Freddie thinks of his mother and father reading the telegram. And then of the impossibility of Isabella being able to imagine what he is going through at this moment in time.

"I'm trying to think of anything that might be worse than this," says Reg. "We've got thirty horlicks tablets, a tube of condensed milk and two tins of water but then, on the bright side, enough German currency to buy a hotel."

Spike blows on his whistle again.

"You might want to take a look around before driving us all mad with your bloody whistle," says Reg.

"You never know."

The dinghy is lifted up, dropped down. Every time the dinghy is lifted up Freddie scans the horizon through the mist.

"Aren't we supposed to do exercises? To keep the circulation going," says Spike.

"What do you suggest, Spike? Forward rolls?"

"No. We take the hands of the man opposite and take it in turns to tug each other first by one arm and then the other."

"I must have missed that part of dinghy training."

Jack's teeth are chattering. As soon as Freddie notices his own teeth begin chattering.

"Exercises might not be a bad idea," he says.

"And singing."

Spike takes hold of Davy's hands across the dinghy and begins tugging him this way and that. Reg laughs. Then Spike begins singing Jerusalem.

"Bring me my bow of burning gold!

Bring me my arrows of desire…"

"What happened to the first verse, Spike?"

"I've forgotten the words."

"The only line I know is the bit about England's green and pleasant lands," says Woodsy who is holding Freddie's gloved hands. "I often have it in my head when we're flying over Lincoln Cathedral on our way to Naziland."

Woodsy, it occurs to Freddie now, looks more quintessentially like England than any of them. His springy blonde hair, his blue eyes, ruddy cheeks, his eagerness to both complain and laugh. But he is also the one who could most easily pass as a German.

"Bring me my spear. Oh clouds unfold."

Spencer vomits over the side of the dinghy.

"That's what Spencer thinks of your singing, Spike," says Reg.

Then Jack vomits too. The wind blows some of it back into the dinghy and Freddie too retches. The dinghy rises up on another swell. Drops down. More spray is flung up into Freddie's face. Making his cheeks sting where the oxygen mask has chaffed his skin. The seat of his trousers is soaked through. Reg, waving away Cyril's attempt to start tugging his arm, tries to light a cigarette. Shielding the lighted match under his flying jacket but it goes out again.

"For fuck's sake," Reg says, frowning at the weather or the sea.

Freddie notices how violently Reg's hands are trembling.

"Might not be a bad idea to think of pretty young WAAFs. To get some hot blood into the body," says Woodsy.

"I was thinking earlier of the day I lost my virginity."

"No wonder we got lost, Cyril," says Woodsy.

"A boy at school told me a woman had two entrances – a right one and a wrong one. He told me that when the big moment finally arrived to make sure I didn't poke it in the wrong hole. This was my principal fear, growing up. Of making a clot of myself by getting my holes mixed up."

"Do you think women know how terrified we all are of proving ourselves inept?"

"Shame women aren't more like Tiger Moths, so forgiving of a beginner's mistakes," says Freddie.

"I hope we're not talking about Italian women here," says Reg. "The first time I realised the girl I was kissing was prepared to go upstairs to the bedroom I excused myself for a few minutes and made straight for her parents' drinks cabinet. I was as naïve in those days about alcohol as I was about a female's sexual anatomy. I gulped down the contents of the first bottle that came to hand. The only thing I therefore learnt from my first sexual experience was that it is a very big blunder to frantically drink large quantities of sherry."

"You're upsetting Spike, Reg."

"Sorry Spike."

"Don't mind me."

"What about you, Davy? What was your first time like?"

"Still hasn't been a first time, sir."

"Now I feel bad for pulling you away from Eileen, the Grim Reaper."

"I was only chatting with her."

"Anyone else still a virgin, besides Spike and Davy?"

Jack is sitting with his head bowed down between his knees.

Freddie supposes that technically he is still a virgin. But he can't admit this.

1.30 pm. Freddie can no longer feel his hands or feet. With every new swell of the tide he feels the increased weakness of his body. It is difficult to smoke a cigarette. When it falls from his fingers and lands in his lap he almost topples out of the dinghy in his effort to stop it burning through his trousers and then burning through the rubber of the dinghy. The dinghy feels limper beneath the seat of his pants, as if it is very slowly deflating. He wonders if it has a small puncture but does not voice the fear aloud.

"Wonder how Percy is enjoying himself in France? Useless fucking bird," says Reg.

"Don't underestimate Percy," says Woodsy.

"I don't. I can picture him mounting a French woman pigeon as we speak."

"Quiet. Did you hear that?"

"Hear what?"

"I thought I heard an engine."

"You sure it wasn't Spike?"

Spike is asleep with his mouth wide open. Snoring. His officious moustache gently rising and falling on his upper lip.

"How does he do that?"

Spencer twists round and vomits over the side of the dinghy. Jack follows suit. Again the wind blows some of it back into the dinghy and again Freddie too retches. The dinghy spins in a few circles then drifts on. The sea quietly writhing and surging beneath it. Jack slides down off the edge of the dinghy. Lies now in the six or so inches of water inside. His white lips smeared with vomit and drool.

"There, look!"

There's a dark smudge quite low in the sky, half a mile or so away. It appears and disappears among the dark rushing storm clouds.

Freddie leans forward to pick up the flare gun. He can't move his legs. He has to lift them with his hands. His feet swollen inside his tightening boots. His frozen fingers too refuse to obey his commands. He tries to take off his gauntlets. Using his chattering teeth. He can't move either of his thumbs. He attempts to hand the gun to Reg. The gun feels like the heaviest thing he has ever held in his hand. Reg can't get a grip on it either.

"Davy?"

Davy manages to get some kind of grip on the gun but he can't get his finger round the trigger. The engine noise grows fainter. The dark smudge in the sky vanishes.

"Stupid bastard. Is he blind?" says Woodsy.

Freddie tries to warm his hands by clapping them. He senses his laboured stiff clapping has the look of someone clapping sarcastically. As if he is applauding an act of unusual idiocy. Reg laughs and then Freddie laughs too because Reg's laugh is infectious. Soon everyone is laughing. Even Spencer. In fact Spencer is laughing more hysterically than anyone. Freddie continues to clap his hands and everyone continues to laugh.

Then the engine noise returns.

"Are we sure it's not a Jerry? Sounds a bit like a Heinkel."

"Can't you try out some bloody optimism for once in your life, Woodsy. You never know, you might find you quite like it."

"Just saying."

The black smudge reappears, zigzagging below the black clouds. Sniffing at the sky. Or that's how it looks.

Everyone begins shouting. Freddie, like everyone else, tries to lift his arms to signal to it. But it is a comic performance of ineptitude. As if his arms are strapped to his sides and he is desperately trying to release them. The aircraft, a Hudson, gets a little larger, still weaving this way and that, still sniffing, and then becomes smaller again.

"I've got a flask of brandy in my pocket. If you get it out that might warm your fingers up."

"If I can't squeeze a trigger how am I going to unscrew a cap?"

"I'll try," says Spike.

"You don't drink. It's against your religion."

Spike manages to get the flask out. He unscrews the cap with his teeth. They all watch as Spike, spluttering and pulling grotesque faces, gulps down huge quantities of brandy. Then Spike grins. Freddie has never seen Spike grin before. Spike has to use both thumbs but with a superhuman effort fires off a cartridge. The recoil knocks him back and he topples over into the sea. Red stars shoot up into the sky in an arcing line. Bathing the dinghy in a beautiful canopy of red smoke. Spike is in the pinkish water. His Mae West holding him up in the swell. He is still grinning. Glittering red sparks cascade down around him into the water.

"Jolly good show, Spike."

"I've just remembered the first verse," Spike says, still grinning. He begins singing.

"And did those feet in ancient time
Walk upon England's mountain green?
And was the holy lamb of God
On England's pleasant pastures seen?"

"Okay Spike. You've proved your point. Now get back in the bloody dinghy."

Spike attempts a reply but his teeth are chattering so much no one can understand what he says. He is drifting further away from the dinghy. Slopped up and down by the swell and probably swallowing too much seawater. The aircraft becomes more distinct. The growing engine noise a tickle of immense thanksgiving at the base of Freddie's spine. For the first time he is able to look forward to telling this story to all the boys in the mess. The aircraft comes down lower. He can make out the pilot who is waving. He feels a bit ungrateful for not waving back but his arms are still as if stitched to his sides. The aircraft circles above them. Fires off a flare. The faces opposite him in the dinghy are sheened in an otherworldly green light when they start cheering.

Spike, his head looking tiny above the yellow rubber of his Mae West, seems to finally sober up and starts swimming towards the dinghy. It is another comedy of errors trying to pull him in.

When the launch arrives they are all sitting with their arms around each other singing Jerusalem. All except poor Jack who is still green.

And when they are undressed by members of the launch crew and stand naked together in front of the stove they begin singing Jerusalem again until the sailors put lighted cigarettes in their mouths to shut them up.

32 - November 1943

FRANCESCO CLOSES the door behind him and steps out onto the street with his bicycle. He has left his father's savings with his mother. The imploring weight of her gaze still dragging at his limbs. He doesn't allow himself to finish any of his thoughts. Because they all lead down to the sick feeling in his stomach. He decides to cycle out into the country before going to the bureau of Jewish affairs. Perhaps he will just keep cycling. Never to return.

The countryside depresses him. Because of all the lies it tells. Its lies of freedom and peace. He climbs over a high wall and enters an untended olive grove. A breeze blows chaff into his hair. The sun has little warmth in it. He walks past the carcass of a dog in the long grass. Spilled entrails fusing into the soil.

He stops on noting a flicker of movement in the parched grass up ahead. A black snake seems to be having an epileptic fit. On closer inspection he realises it is two black snakes, entwined, and moving slowly, sometimes in unison, sometimes in conflict, undulating together with sudden whiplash jerkings and leaps off the ground. The bared fangs of the snake that seems to be the aggressor. It makes several attempts to bite into its adversary's sleek black skin just beneath the head. Then he understands that they aren't fighting; they are copulating. He watches spellbound, following them at a distance. Coiled and lashing together in a fluid double spiral, they slither and gyrate over the bracken and crisp dry grass. There are quiet moments when they are aligned into an almost inseparable writhing unity of wave motion, as if swimming together with their tails gently touching. Then there is another sudden thrashing of violent outcry when an electrical charge seems to bolt through the length of them and toss them up into air, like a rope trick.

This is what I'll never do with Marina, he thinks.

He cycles down the hill towards the gate in the old city wall at Porta Romana. The friendly whip of breeze on his face wants him to exult in his youth as he has done so many times in the past while free-wheeling down this road.

He feels sick when he enters the building in via Cavour. He is directed up a marble staircase. There is a punctilious watchful atmosphere inside the building. He is allowed so little of his identity here, pared down to a poverty of circumstantial details – that is his feeling. He looks up at the high ceiling where there is a tawdry fresco of cherubs and clouds.

He enters an office. A woman behind a desk, typing. The quickfire clatter of struck keys in the high vacuum of the office creates an atmosphere of efficient aggression. The clak clak of the typewriter sounds like a weapon, warding off danger. The woman keeps him waiting. There's a framed photograph of Mussolini above her head. He lights a cigarette.

When he tells the woman he wants to see Giuseppe there is an unpleasant curl to her lip when she looks at him. She straightens some papers on the polished desk.

"Name?" she says.

He doesn't want her to know his name. He doesn't want anyone in this building to know his name.

"Just tell him I've come to see him about Signor Conte," he says. He has never disliked the sound of his own voice so much. It has no authority in it. She sends him back to the chairs at the far side of the room. He watches her make a telephone call. He can't hear what she is saying. She is speaking in a watchful secretive way. He lights another cigarette.

Two militiamen enter the office. Daggers in their belts. Tasselled berets perched jauntily on the back of their heads. Trousers tucked inside percussive black boots. One of them snaps his fingers at Francesco. The man, all in black, has a skeletal face, so lean of flesh that his cheekbones shine as if polished.

"What?"

"Papers."

"I don't have them with me."

"That's a crime in itself. But you're Francesco Conte?"

It is terrifying to hear his name spoken aloud by this man in this place.

"Yes?"

The guard grabs his hands and cuffs them behind his back.

"What are you doing?"

"We're taking you in for questioning."

"I've come to negotiate the release of my father and sister. I've got money."

The man grins. "All you Jews have got money," he says and winks at the woman behind the typewriter.

33 - November 1943

WHEN MARINA steps off the tram with her bag heavy on her arm and she walks towards the tall grey shuttered house in the road near the railway line the air raid siren is shrieking. The siren whines out its warning every day now.

There is a long delay after she rings the bell, during which she refrains from ringing again. Perhaps no one will come to the door and she can go home. She watches a man in dirty clothes push a handcart heaped with bundles tied with string. A pigeon flaps up into the air in front of an arriving car. Then Signor Becchi himself opens the door. Muttering a complaint that he has to open his own front door. He looks her up and down with his shrewd eyes before letting her in. He doesn't offer to carry her bag.

She is made to wear a uniform. It is much too big for her. It makes her feel brittle, like an ornament.

The cook is a short severe woman from Calabria. Her dress is stained under the arms with sweat marks. She speaks in dialect, often to herself, oblivious to whether or not Marina understands, as though Marina is of no more consequence than a cat or a piece of furniture.

The large bedroom on the second floor where the old woman lies on a huge high bed smells of disinfectant and lavender or lilies. But there are no flowers in the room. Marina enters with a tray.

"*Buongiorno*," she says. "Lunch."

"Who are you?"

The woman's voice is drawn out thinner than the thread of a cobweb. Mutual dislike is immediate. Another disappointment. Another hardship to be born. She had hoped to like this woman. To have one friendly presence in this cold house.

She has never seen anyone who looks so old, so finished with life. Her mottled wrinkled face is blue with transparency. The ring with the bright stone on her finger looks too heavy for her wizened hand.

"I'm not hungry. Take it away."

Later a nurse arrives. Marina is relieved her duties won't include the toiletries of the old woman.

The cook leaves her some bread soup for supper. She eats it alone in the cavernous kitchen. She watches herself spoon up the soup in the glass of a cabinet opposite. She looks like a ghost in the glass. After washing her bowl she breaks a water jug. She is furious with it. She picks up the pieces with a sense of childhood guilt and carries them up to her room. She will not, she decides, admit to her crime. She steps as lightly as possible on the stairs, especially on the first floor where the old woman lurks. Her guilty secret is hot and prickly on her skin. She is child again, fearful of discovery and punishment. In her tiny room at the top of the house she hides the shards and splinters of the jug in a drawer beneath her undergarments.

Her room has a skylight of begrimed glass. There is a washstand, an austere chair, a portable yellow stained bidet, a narrow hard iron bed. There are streaks of dried brown blood and the spindly legs of squashed mosquitoes on the white stucco walls by the bed. She tries to push open the skylight but it won't budge.

The room tries to force its history on her. Shrink and sully her with its unhappy dust, its muted narrative of confinement and poverty.

Insolent excited male voices wake her up with a start. Her body registers the unfamiliar surroundings before memory returns to her. Feeling arrives quicker than thought. There is lots of bumping downstairs. Then heavy footsteps ascending the stairs. Her door swings violently open. She shields her eyes against the sudden wash of brightness.

"Come on!" says Signor Becchi. He's as if aglow, all in white - fedora and a linen suit. "There's work to do."

"What's the time?"

"Up you get." He grasps her by the hand and tugs. There is alcohol on his breath.

He makes her accompany him downstairs barefooted, in her nightdress. There are several crates in the hallway that weren't there when she went to bed. Four men in the sitting room, all in different uniforms. They have revolvers in holsters. Dance music on the wireless. She is told to rustle them up something to eat.

She boils some water for pasta in a large cast iron pan. Opens all the cupboards hunting for ingredients. She wants to spit in the food she makes but she also wants to show off her culinary skills. She wants to earn praise. She hates this vanity but is also its eager victim. While she chops garlic on the cutting board she can hear most of the conversation in the other room. It reaches her with disarming clarity as if these men are invisible presences in the kitchen.

"Could you be an informer, an infiltrator? I don't think I've got the nerve."

"Did Carità ask you?"

"No."

"He's asked me. And I'll probably do it. Why not? I enjoy telling lies. You know there's a priest who works for us as an informer?"

"Yes. The one who likes altar boys."

"He drives escaped British POWs to contacts further south."

"Except by some stroke of fortune the POWs never arrive?"

"Exactly. He delivers them straight into the hands of the Germans. He's done it twice now."

Before the pasta is ready she is forced to face the humiliation of re-entering the sitting room for further instructions.

The men all stop talking when she enters the room. Stare at her as though they have never before seen a barefooted woman in a nightgown.

"Hello beautiful," says one of the men. He has a gold tooth. It glitters with malevolence at her.

"Well?" says Signor Becchi.

"I wasn't sure if you wanted me to lay the dining room table or bring you the pasta here." As she speaks the man with the gold tooth walks up to her and puts his arm around her waist. His gun digs at her hipbone. Leaves a cold imprint on her skin through the flimsy material of her nightdress.

"Hands off my property, Attila," says Signor Becchi with a wide grin.

34 - November 1943

FREDDIE STANDS in church. Between his mother and his sister in the front row. The choir and congregation are singing *I Vow to Thee My Country*. Never has he heard the hymn sung with such heartfelt pathos. It is as if everyone is trying to sing themselves into being. It is the war that makes everyone sing out their hearts like this. The hymn expresses some imperative deep down in the blood. Like running fingers over the edge of things in pitch darkness.

I haste to thee my mother, a son among thy sons...

His eyes mist over. His skin prickles. His body is rocked by a mounting tide. He feels life is beautiful, that people are good. He doesn't want the hymn to finish. There should be more moments in life like this, he thinks.

Perhaps it is both the tragedy of life and the blessing of life that most moments only happen once.

His mother walks past the coffin to the lectern. He feels the unsteadiness in her legs in his own legs. She faces the congregation. Never has he seen her look so alone. But there is a stern determination about the set of her mouth. She clears her throat.

When he shall die,
Take him and cut him out in little stars,
And he will make the face of heaven so fine
That all the world will be in love with night,
And pay no worship to the garish sun.

How embarrassed his father would be if he heard these tributes. You wouldn't be able to find him if you looked into his eyes. He would be hiding. Waiting for all the attention to drift off somewhere else.

He pictures his father laying inside the coffin. Remembers him as he saw him in death. The stunned expression sculpted on his sallow face. He was barely able to look at him because of the overwhelming sense he had of him no longer being there.

"Nothing quite prepares you for the sight of your dead father. Nothing is more unbelievable than the sight of death on such a familiar face. His mouth was wide open. His eyes were open too. I think I had expected them to be closed. Those eyes had seen the shark appear – that's how I imagine the moment of death, like the beast that suddenly shimmies up from the depths, opens its mouth and shows its teeth."

Another screwed up letter to Isabella.

Everyone is kind to him after the service. Everywhere he goes he encounters kindness these days. Kindness and generosity. Because of his RAF uniform. Everywhere he goes he is treated as a saviour. Little boys look up at him as if he is a movie star. There are little boys now, pretending to be aeroplanes on the village green.

He leaves the wake. Takes the dog out for a walk by the sea. He has to find a way through the barbed wire entanglements and tank traps to reach the beach. Then he races the whippet over the sand. She shimmies past him like a rugby wing back avoiding a tackle. He needs to feel like a teenager again. Needs to reassert his pulse. Restore a connection with the ongoing continuity of his existence.

When he turns inland he sees two moving white columns in the sky. At first glance he thinks they are emissions of smoke. The two encroaching formations ripple into funnels and then spread out beneath the labyrinthine coral of clouds into fans. His vision blurs for a moment. Then he realises he is witnessing two perfectly synchronised flocks of birds. The abstract shapes they form are flawless. He stands with his hands in his pockets as the birds taper into a long undulating line, which gently vanishes behind the surface of things. The same thing has happened to his father. He has vanished behind the surface of things.

Tomorrow he has to return to base. He feels excluded that his crew will be flying without him. Jealous that another pilot will be sitting at V Victor's controls beside Reg. Stealing his role. Seeking to make his absence count for little. It is a bewildering feeling. To feel aggrieved that he is not being shot at. It occurs to him that if his crew are killed while he is on compassionate leave his father's death will have saved his life. There is a kind of celestial logic to this possibility that worries him. The war has taught him that an accident of timing for one person often turns out to be a miracle of timing for someone else.

He calls the station. It is late enough for the flight plans to no longer be a secret. He hears his crew has gone to Hanover. A diversionary raid to the main stream that has gone to Berlin. Due back in three hours. He pictures Davy with his cigarette and his tin mug of coffee and rum in the interrogation room. Tired and elated. The elation fading with the dawning knowledge that this or that crew are not coming back. He asks about the Australians. They have gone to Hanover as well.

Hanover, he remembers, is where Oskar is from. He has a photograph of himself and Oskar. Sitting together under a trellis of wisteria by the sea where Shelley died.

Part Two

1 - September 1943

THE WAVES BREAK over the bare feet of a man dancing on the beach. He is stripped to the waist. His ribs show through his pale skin. Over his shoulder the sun is sinking down into the sea. One solitary fishing boat rises and falls on the pink and gold water.

His feet kick up splashes of water. Kick up puffs of sand. He makes supplicating gestures with his hands, makes a windmill motion of his arms, makes sleeping gestures and gestures of defiance and sadness. His feet scuttle. His feet skip. His feet shuffle. It looks at times like he's having a heated argument with an invisible adversary.

A few people stand on the esplanade watching him. Behind them green-shuttered houses with chalky pink, red and yellow ochre façades cluster around the church in the piazza and totter up the incline of the hill in tiers of exhilarating disorder. This small fishing village cradled in the hills with its dark stairways smelling of cats and pine resin.

The dancer's daughter walks among the onlookers, holding out her father's hat.

When he stops dancing there is some applause and he bows.

His daughter walks down over the fine-grained sand to the edge of the sea. She holds his hat and its chink of coins with a solemn dutiful expression. He looks at the footprints she leaves behind. In these times when they must leave no footprints. They count the coins together, crouching down among the shells and seaweed. He is teaching her Italian. He writes down words in the sand.

The hills across the bay slowly recede into silhouettes of themselves.

Earlier he washed everything they owned in a stream and hung it on a fig tree to dry. The wet clothes had looked like tattered bits of cloth blown there by the wind that no one would ever come back for.

"People say children can't keep secrets," he says, thinking aloud.

"Is that what the bad people say?"

"Yes. The bad people."

Father and daughter fall silent as they watch a seagull feeding her chicks at the water's edge. Vomiting up the creamy mush. The mother pecks aggressively at one of the bright-eyed chicks that edges towards the gruel. Chases it away.

"Why is it being horrible?"

"Probably because that chick belongs to another mother seagull."

"Where is she?"

"I don't know. But don't worry, she will come back. Mothers always come back."

He sees she takes him at his word. Children don't expect words to be used to create false trails. Words to Esme are plain and simple with no hidden codes, no duplicitous underlife. He thinks of the conversations with his wife and how little of what they said was without encryption.

Tonight Oskar and his daughter are going to sleep in an abandoned wooden boat on the beach. He will try to make this seem normal. Every day he has to try to make what happens to them appear nothing out of the ordinary. As if he still has all the magician's tricks of a father. As if he still has the power to keep her from harm.

"Can you remember your new name?"

"Giulia," she says.

"And what's my name?"

"Can't remember," she says.

He takes the splintered bit of driftwood and writes his new name in the sand.

"Paolo Mazzoni," she says. "But I'm still Esme even if I have a different name, aren't I?"

"Yes. You're still Esme. But it becomes a secret name that only you and I must know about."

"Does Napoleon have to change his name too?"

Napoleon is her toy bear.

"He can be Napoleone. Say it after me. Napoleone."

"Napoleone."

"Are you hungry?"

She nods, but discreetly, without urgency, as if not wanting to make him feel bad.

"How hungry? From one to ten."

"Six."

"Liar! I reckon you're at least eight."

"No I'm not." She lets go of his hand. Kicks at a tendril of seaweed on the sand.

He walks with her past a fisherman repairing his net on the wharf. The man pauses in his work to greet them, smiles at the little girl in the ragged floral dress clutching a toy bear and the kindness of the man's smile makes Paolo, as Oskar now calls himself, feel more hopeful.

Along the seafront they crunch sand underfoot. Stepping over the tarred landing ropes and discarded fishing nets. Walking beneath the umbrella pines. He sees the pulse in a lizard's throat before his approach frightens it and it leaves a spin of green on the air and then disappears inside a crevice in the sea wall. Esme skips on ahead. Jumping from one foot to the other, as if she can see markings on the ground he can't. She is constantly jumping and skipping and twirling with the lightness of falling snow, looking up at him bright with questions, tugging on his hand, dashing off with all the speed her body is capable of and then skipping on the spot up ahead as if consecrating it for his arrival. It is so easy to make her happy that it seems like cheating at times. Cooking smells come from the shabby restaurants. He smells garlic and clams and baked bread. He pretends he is forking a clam into his mouth and in the imagined taste are memories of himself as a better man than the man he has become. This is his feeling, a feeling that is like a stone in his shoe.

They have enough money to share a bowl of soup in a trattoria. Except the woman there refuses to serve them because he doesn't have a ration coupon. One of the diners complains about the woman's zealous behaviour and there is a heated argument. He says it doesn't matter and leaves.

They go to another trattoria. Here they are given two bowls of pasta for the price of one. His daughter's lips glisten with the spiced oil in which the clams have been cooked.

They have travelled to Italy from Paris. Often on foot. When the roundup of the Jews took place in the early hours of the morning he was staying with his daughter at a friend's house in Saint Michel because it was past curfew when he realised the time. His wife had been arrested.

He practices his Italian accent as often as he can. Remembers Isabella telling him his accent made everything he said sound like text in an instruction manual. He listens carefully to the accents of the people he meets. Speaking to himself when his daughter is asleep. Talking nonsense to himself in a foreign tongue and sometimes smiling at the madness of it. He knows he needs to sound and act like the people he meets. That their continuing survival depends on his powers of imitation. It is dangerous to draw attention to himself by dancing in public but it is the only means of getting the money to eat so he dances.

"It's nice sleeping with the sound of the waves so close, isn't it?"

She lies with him beneath his coat in the hull of the wooden boat clasping her bear with its glass eyes and red jersey that her mother knitted for it. The waves embroider the darkness with a ragged silvered stitching. The percussive sigh they make as they withdraw over the pebbles seems to come from a distance in time as well as space.

"And with the stars," she says.

"I wish I knew the names of the stars so I could tell you what they're all called. Let's say that one up there is called Horatio."

"Do they have to change names sometimes too?"

"When you go to another country all names change."

"Why?"

"Because no one wants to be understood by the whole world," he says. "Not even stars. And because it's exciting to learn a new language."

"Dad?"

"Yes."

"Have you done something bad? Is that why we're not sleeping in our house anymore?"

"Everything's the wrong way round at the moment. If you're bad you're rewarded and if you're good you're punished."

"Why?"

"Because bad people have taken over the world. And for a while that's what we've got to get used to. Good people, like us, have to run and hide."

"How do you know if someone is good or bad?"

2 - October 1943

OSKAR PUSHES away the blanket. Lies looking down at his naked body. His naked body that will give the lie to any false identity papers he manages to procure. *Has anyone,* he wonders, *ever explained to me the significance of circumcision? Why I have had to sacrifice to God a piece of my sexual organ.*

He remembers an afternoon not long after his wife's arrest when he caught himself avoiding puddles of rainwater on the streets. When he realised what he was doing it struck him as ridiculous and even reprehensible that he was still prey to such petty concerns. He began deliberately splashing through all the biggest puddles, as if to show some higher power how little he cared about anything anymore. His daughter copied him. Skipping and dancing as if she and the rain shared a secret complicity.

He is now staying with his daughter in the bell tower of a pink church overlooking the sea. As if they were a pair of bats. He makes a joke of this to Esme, flaps his arms like wings. Teaches her the Italian word for bat. At night the push and pull of the sea makes itself felt in the groaning of mooring ropes and tackle.

The town has been built into the rock and is a maze of sloping arched alleys forking off at surprising angles, spiralling up to the church or down to the sea. No street is much wider than a corridor: people in opposite homes might almost lean out of their windows and join hands. The houses tumble crookedly, playfully into each other like drunken friends.

When they walk through the small town their footsteps echo up ahead of them. But there are no Germans here, no uniformed men with weapons.

One day he rows her out to sea in a boat. The waves, pungent with a salt seaweed smell, slap the wooden hull of the boat. Disperse in trickles of foam. The excitement on her face, the questions she asks and noises she makes make him feel like a good father. He has no other ambition for the time being.

She copies the way he peels an orange. Studies him discreetly, his method, while sitting opposite in the wooden boat out at sea. Makes the first incision into the peel with her thumb nail. Turns away her face as a spray of juice spatters her cheeks. Wipes her face with the back of her wrist. Later she will teach Napoleone, her bear, how to peel an orange.

Padre Enrico is their benefactor. There is a sculpted severity to his oversized features and a kind of mountainous vigour about his physical presence. His black robes, stained here and there by watermarks, seem part of his nature. It is impossible to imagine him in any other clothes.

"Before I became a dancer I went to a painting atelier in Florence. But I have little talent for painting. So this is what I do, this is what I have always done. I dance. Can you think of a more inappropriate talent to have at a time like this?"

They sit together around a long table lit by gas lamps with oak logs burning under the stove. There is a green bottle with a reflected flame on its glass on the windowsill. Esme has her bear on her lap and is feeding it with a spoon. He enjoys watching her climb up onto the high chair, slide herself into it. Every movement her young body makes is a vivid etching. How she trails her hand along walls as if they are water. How she skips on ahead, barely in control of her excitable limbs and then suddenly remembers him and returns and takes his hand, swinging it in wide arcs. The dances she does, of the purest spontaneity. He can think of nothing more incomprehensible than this fact of the jeopardy she is in. She is like a flame he is protecting. That he shields every day with tentative steps, with cupped hands.

The subject of conversation tonight is miracles. Padre Enrico tells them a story to highlight his belief in miracles.

"My friend Alessandro left his newspaper in the bar where he had gone for a coffee. On his way home he remembered it and at first was going to leave it there but he recalled there was an article about Etruscan sarcophagi and their funerary rites that he wanted to read and decided to go back for it. In the bar he met someone he had known at school. As a boy this man he met had once broken Alessandro's arm in a fight. Alessandro had always despised him. When he was half way out of the door the man apologised for what had happened all those years ago. Alessandro hesitated. The man offered to buy him a coffee. They were still chatting when the air raid sirens went off and the planes appeared in the sky. After the attack, Alessandro made his way home. The cloud of dust got thicker, the closer to his home he got. The inside of the building in which he lived was exposed. The floor of his apartment was no longer there. Some of his belongings he recognised amongst the smoking rubble scattered over the street. The man who had broken his arm had saved his life. In wartime everyone speaks of horror, yes, but they also speak of miracles. Almost everyone has experienced a miracle during this war."

"Esme here is my miracle," Oskar says.

He lifts her up onto a crate so she can see out of the window. The press of her fingers always feeds a current of health into his body. Out at sea the beam of the distant lighthouse licks at the vast horde of darkness and then expires as suddenly as it has appeared.

Esme finds a baby bird. Its left wing is damaged. She brings it to him, holding it to her chest. The bird becomes their patient for the rest of the day. He mixes up some slushy gruel with flour and water and she tries to feed the creature using a pair of tweezers.

"Why won't it open its mouth?" she asks.

"It doesn't trust you."

"Does it think I'm one of the bad people?"

"Probably."

"How can I tell it I'm not?"

"You'd have to learn bird language."

"Can you speak bird language?"

"Nope. It's even more difficult than Russian or Chinese."

He tries tickling it under its tiny golden beak.

Only once do they succeed in enticing it into opening its beak but they are too slow with the tweezers and the dollop of gruel looks like an ooze of pus on the bird's head.

She now has it in a box beside her bed in the bell tower. He fears the worst. Superstition in wartime takes a more powerful hold on the mind. One sees omens in everything. One is returned to a more primitive view of the world and its sign language.

3 - November 1943

ISABELLA RUNS her fingers tenderly over Pontormo's saint. Its mosaic of hairline cracks. She could prise off fragments like bark from a tree if she so wished. The texture of paint is uniform, the pigments evenly applied. There's a certain facility about the way the picture is painted. A clarity of purpose. She puts her face close to the framed image of St Anthony. Inspecting the painting's surface. Decides Pontormo used a less fluid elixir of sun-thickened oils than she does.

Probably he just used linseed oil, she thinks.

The head is under life-size. Pontormo's brushwork is more restrained on the whole than hers. It vanishes into the performance of his art. She will have to curb her natural instinct for flourishes and sweeping lines. For impasto. There is little colour in the painting. It is proudly austere. Though the flesh tones are of a rich burnished red with glowing highlights on the forehead and the bridge of the nose. The seized intensity of expression in the eyes, like the hearkening to a calling, might be difficult to achieve. One erroneous brush stroke could result in disaster there. And, she observes, the hands have been painted very cleverly. The most challenging detail of the painting to faithfully copy will be the wisps of hair of his right sideburn. These are the most flamboyant brush strokes in an otherwise soberly executed painting.

Ironic though, she imagines telling Pontormo, that you painted the patron saint of lost things and most of your paintings ended up lost.

And so she begins. Blocking in all the shapes with mathematical precision. She hears Maestro's voice in her head.

If you work out the form in terms of light and shade you'll see the big shape much better. Get your darkest darks in first. The key is to assign a destiny to every stroke of pigment you lay down on the canvas.

She measures the distances with her eyes. Lays down stroke after stroke with a soft sable brush. Striding with purpose up to the canvas. Then walking backwards. Examining the fidelity of the new mark. The amber-coloured resin in her paint fascinates her. The illicit chemical. Its seeded power to produce at a later date all the hairline cracks that will subtly corrugate the painted surface. She knows she will be able to copy this painting almost exactly. Most people in the world will not be able to tell the difference between Pontormo's picture and hers. Her picture though will not be a masterpiece. Because it wasn't her idea. Because the original inspiration wasn't hers.

And then the bell rings. She curses. If it's Captain Heinkel he's more than an hour early. She takes the Pontormo painting from the easel and hides it beneath two black drapes. Her copy she props facing the wall.

It isn't the SS officer. It is Fosco. Clean shaved, he looks as though he has spent half an hour in front of a mirror. Pinstripe suit, silk shirt with wide lapels over the jacket collar, polished leather shoes. He smells of the brilliantine he has lavished on his dark hair.

"Thought I'd take you up on your offer," he says.

"As long as you keep your Machiavellian eyebrow in check," she says.

"Who's this?" he says resting his palm on the skull of the yellow boned anatomy skeleton on its stand.

"I call him Pliny the Elder," she says. "Whom the sun has burned away."

Fosco's shoulders are always hunched, making him appear awkward. As if he is wary of straightening up to his full height, wary of the advantages his full height might grant him.

"How's the St Anthony coming along?"

"I've just started laying it in." She turns it round for him to see. "What's this all about?"

"I thought Maestro explained."

"Not really."

"It's quite simple. The Germans want to steal him; we're going to do our best to stop them."

He stands looking up at the framed paintings of hers that hang in profusion on the walls. The swarm of portraits and landscapes and nudes she barely notices any more. Now she sees them as if through Fosco's eyes. Flaws jump out at her, one after another. She remembers Maestro showing her Fosco's paintings when he needed to convince her Fosco wasn't sufficiently skilled to copy the Pontormo. She studied them with a critical eye. Not sure to begin with if she was eager to find fault or disposed to admire. Almost all of them had a sickly yellow hue, a jaundiced look. A fermentation in the sub-strata of paint and oil that seeped up onto the skin of the canvas. Cracks had appeared in most of the images, breaking up the glazed surface, like dried mud. The resin sealed behind the varnish and layers of paint still damp, still oozing to the surface, like pus. Fosco has not mastered his materials.

"May I?" he says picking up her portrait of Captain Heinkel and carrying it over to the less heavily shadowed part of the studio.

"Don't look at that. I hate it. I've been blackmailed into painting him."

"Oh?"

"You don't recognise him?"

"I don't fraternise with Nazis."

"I thought maybe you might have run into him while working on that committee of yours. Actually it's his job to find the two paintings we're forging. And he's coming to sit later. So you see what an uncomfortable position I'm in? One of the pictures he's looking for will be right under his nose."

"Why didn't you tell Maestro?"

"It's not something I want the world to know. A member of the SS visiting my studio. Half the neighbourhood has stopped talking to me as a result."

"They're all Communists around here," he says with a flicker of distaste. "What do you mean though, he blackmailed you?"

"He helped get me released when I was arrested."

He fiddles with his shirt collar. She notices the prominence of the knuckles on his long hands. "So you feel in his debt?"

"A little."

"Are you working for the anti-fascists?"

"No."

"In that case why were you arrested?"

"I was seeing someone who was working for the anti-fascists."

"Is Freddie dead then?"

She sucks in her lower lip. "Why do you say that?"

He stands by the skeleton with his hands in his pockets, juggling an unseen set of keys.

"I don't know. Women have instincts about these things, don't they? I suppose I never thought of you as an adulterous woman."

Now she can no longer hold the tears back. They are tears of anger at his insensitivity as much as tears of sadness for her missing husband.

Fosco removes his jacket, hangs it on the anatomy skeleton, and then takes her in his arms. He tries to kiss her when she has tears running down her cheeks. She places a hand over her mouth. Stiffens her shoulders.

She sees she has humiliated him. That he will have no sense of humour about this. He narrows his eyes when he looks at her.

"I couldn't betray Freddie. Not now. Even if I wanted to," she says.

He stands up. Cracks his knuckles. The form of his torso showing through the clinging cloth of his shirt. The bunched muscles in his forearms. "I did do it with mischievous glee," he says. "Because I knew Maestro would have to believe it was you. And this, what has happened today, is why I did it."

"What do you mean?"

"I always knew you'd lure me into your web if I dropped my guard. Maestro was right. You are a temptress. You summon and then you repel. This was a moment that was always going to happen. I sensed it almost the day I met you. Not even a world war could obstruct its inevitability."

She registers what he says, word for word, but still can't make any sense of his argument. "Why was this a moment that was always going to happen? It's happened because you made it happen. You can't hold me responsible for what you think or feel about me."

"Of course I can. You don't believe for one minute that anyone's innocent of what they make you feel, do you? Portrait painting would be nothing but a sham if your sitter were innocent of all your brushstrokes. And that's what you and I are. Portrait painters."

"I don't think I can follow your line of thought."

"That's because you're a woman with a woman's mind and there's always a self-serving quirk in the way a woman's mind works."

"Once a fascist, always a fascist? Has the war taught you nothing?"

"On the whole it's taught me that I was essentially right about the human race."

He takes his jacket brusquely from the skeleton, knocking it over in the process. Then he is gone.

She can't stop thinking about what he said. *Did I repel Freddie?* This now seems the charge of which she's accused. Her war crime. The gallery of painted faces on the walls become the jury.

4 - November 1943

OUTSIDE THE station of Santa Maria Novella Isabella has to stand aside while a line of prisoners are marched into the terminus by armed fascist guards. They pass within touching distance of her, carrying bags and bundles. There are old people and some children too. They all seem swamped by their clothes, disembodied by them somehow. Then she catches the eye of Ezra, a young Jewish man who once worked in the art materials shop where she buys most of her pigments and brushes. He is almost at the back of the line. The veins are high and urgent on his hand. His trousers are held up with a dirty piece of string. His cobalt blue eyes hold hers for the barest beat of a moment but some essence of his being conveys itself to her and her blood quickens in sympathy for him. She has the feeling of looking into the eyes of a ghost.

By her side a little girl asks her mother where all these people are being taken.

"A prison camp," the mother says.

"Why? Have they done something wrong?"

"No," the mother says. "They just didn't hide as well as they should have done."

The little girl seems to accept this as an explanation.

Isabella boards the blue Sita bus with her small bag. It is crowded, mostly with women. She sits next to an elderly man with a soft hat and moustache. He smells of cheese. Now and again she looks down at the newspaper he is reading. Outrage over the British bombing of churches and orphanages in Northern Italy. Notices urging men to apply for work in Germany.

The bus passes through the old city walls by the gate at Porta Romana where a makeshift market is underway. Isabella sees the woman from whom she sometimes buys vegetables and cheese. An elderly woman with crooked teeth and eyes bright with memories. The black market is in full swing. The trading of money for food has become an illicit moment, an act of suspense and wariness. It is another offence that means prison if you are caught. Meat and coffee and sugar cost as much as a factory worker earns in a month.

Last night she received a message from her father. Her mother is unwell. She is glad of the excuse to leave Florence for a few days. The hostility of the San Frediano neighbourhood towards her has got worse rather than better. And it is a relief to be rid of Captain Erich Heinkel, if only for a few days.

She looks out of the window as the bus shudders and wheezes down via Senese towards the open countryside. When the white walls of the Certosa of Galluzzo appear above the olive slopes and the world seems a place of peace she almost feels Freddie is by her side and they are on one of their weekend visits to see her parents.

She only realises she has been asleep when she is woken by shouts. The bus has been stopped at a roadblock. Two Italian fascist militia armed with guns are ordering everyone off the vehicle. However, they are not being obeyed. There is a great deal of complaining. One woman in particular, a small thickset woman with grey hair and blazing dark eyes, is shouting at the two guards and gesticulating furiously. She speaks in an abrasive dialect. She tells the guards they ought to be ashamed of themselves for persecuting a bus full of harmless old women whose only crime is to go in search of food for their families. The two uniformed men, neither of whom is much older than twenty, exchange sheepish glances. More women join in the remonstration. Soon the entire bus takes courage and a community of implacable resistance can be felt. The guards eventually allow the bus to continue on its way without any kind of search. The woman with the grey hair is applauded and there is a festive air on the bus for the rest of the journey.

Isabella walks through terraced olive groves and spindly woods. She cuts across unploughed fields of hardened earth. The yellow ochre house with the red tiled roof and irregular windows where she grew up is perched halfway up a hill. She can see it in the distance. When she nears the neighbouring farmhouse she sees Marcello who she played with as a child. She calls out to him.

"Hello stranger," he says. He is grasping a frantic pig in the courtyard by the hay barn.

As she joins him Marcello is deftly binding the front legs of the pig with two pieces of twine. The animal struggles. The animal makes pitiful noises. Piercing horrible noises.

"Murderer," she says.

"Yes, he knows he's about to enter pig heaven."

Marcello is wearing a blue roll neck sweater with frayed cuffs and has dirt beneath his long fingernails. He is two years younger than she is. The last time she saw him was back in July, the evening of Mussolini's fall when she joined the crowd in Piazza della Signoria to celebrate what was believed to be the end of the war.

He binds the back legs of the squirming animal and then lays it on its back. He snatches up the knife. He begins impersonating an imperious interrogator. He holds the twinkling knife with threatening malice. He demands of the pig the names of its accomplices.

"Tell us who your friends are and we will set you free," he says. "You only have to utter one name," he says. "One name and you can go home to your wife and piglets."

The face of Carità's henchman, the thug with the puckered scar beneath his eye, returns to haunt her for a moment.

"Can you hold back its front legs? So its throat is exposed."

"Do I have to?"

"Come on. It'll make his end swifter and less painful."

She does as she is told. The animal makes a new horrible piercing noise. The noise detonates deep down in her body. She looks down into the eyes of the squealing pig. She sees terror. She sees an appeal for help. She recalls the look of the Jewish boy Ezra outside the station. Marcello slits a neat gash from the animal's neck to its heart. A tremendous force shoots through her hands from the animal's brief struggle. She feels its life go out of it in the pulse of her own wrists. She watches the blood ooze out over the flagstones.

Marcello goes off to get some hay and heaps it over the dead animal. Bright red blood is still oozing out onto the flagstones. It bubbles and twinkles in the winter sunlight. Marcello heaps the hay over the slaughtered animal. A kind of carefree revelry in the actions of his boyish lithe body. Then he sets fire to the pyre. The singed fur makes a sickening stink. Isabella edges away.

"Word is, your old teacher is in trouble."

"Maestro? What do you mean?"

"Something I've heard."

"What have you heard?"

"You remember the Jewish women and children arrested at the convent in Piazza del Carmine?"

She nods.

"Well, it's thought the snitch was your teacher."

"That's absurd. Why on earth would he do that? And where would he get that kind of information from. He lives in an ivory tower."

"Love. To protect this pretty young boy who is either Jewish himself or pretends to be Jewish and is sharing Maestro's bed. He's struck a deal with the Nazis."

She releases a contemptuous snort of laughter. "Maestro has never shared his bed with anyone," she says.

"You sound almost jealous."

"I'm sorry but none of this makes any sense, Marcello."

"One thing I know for sure is your teacher is now on a hit list. You've heard of GAP? The Communist group in the city."

"Of course."

"Well, Guido del Monte, or Maestro as you call him, is on their list. Not very high up but he's there."

"Are you working for GAP? You are, aren't you?"

"The less you know the better."

"Well, tell them they've made a mistake. Maestro is an artist. A harmless artist."

"There's proof he's collaborating with the Nazis."

"What proof?"

"Two very valuable paintings were snatched away from the Germans and put into safe storage. Then they went missing. Apparently your old teacher has them."

She feels her body go clammy. The world around her recedes as though someone has turned the volume down.

"I don't understand."

"To be honest I don't fully understand either. But there's an informer working for the resistance who says your old teacher is making forgeries of the two paintings so the Germans can steal the real ones."

"Suppose I told you I know for a fact that the Germans don't know where those paintings are?"

"How could you know that?"

"Because I'm painting the German who is looking for these paintings and he hasn't a clue where they are. Unless he's playing some kind of twisted of game with me."

"Perhaps he is? But what on earth are you doing painting a Nazi?"

"I didn't have any choice. I was arrested and he got me released."

"Arrested?"

His show of surprise is pantomime acting. She is certain he knows about her arrest and is playing some kind of cat and mouse game with her. As if he no longer trusts her. It is painful not to be trusted by Marcello. She once climbed trees with Marcello, built snowmen with him and one time even shared a bath with him. When he was no taller than the cartwheel propped up next to the stack of firewood by the wall.

She stares hard at him.

"Doesn't the Third Reich approve of your painting style? Is that why you were arrested?" he says fanning the smoke away from his face.

"You know I was arrested. Why are you pretending not to?"

"Perhaps I did hear a rumour," he says.

She frowns at him and then walks away.

"Isabella."

"I'm going home."

5 - October 1943

THE BABY BIRD has died. Together they are burying it. In an olive grove within sight of the sea. Oskar digs out the small grave with his bare hands. Esme skips off, singing to herself, to collect ornaments - leaves, stones, flowers.

A bead of light glitters on the threads between the fork of two branches. The black spider pressed to the centre of its web.

Oskar can still hear the bells that wake him with a start every morning. He hears them all day inside his head.

"Will we die too?"

"Not for a long long time."

"Will we be buried underneath the ground?"

"Yes."

"Why?"

"So we won't be woken up."

"What happens if you wake up when you're dead?"

"You turn into a bat." He flaps his arms, does his bat imitation.

"No you don't."

"Let's go and see Maria. If you're lucky she might give you one of those horns with the cream inside."

That night the thin membrane of safety in the bell tower is shredded by metallic thunder in the sky. There is no window so he can't see what is happening but he guesses a large formation of planes are attacking the harbour at La Spezia, on the other side of the bay. The bell tower is rocked by explosions. One after another. In the dark he holds his daughter to his chest. Trying to make himself balm against the fear that makes her thin body heave and tremble.

The sun is shining the next day. Glittering on the sea. Transparent wings of light quiver over the flaking pink stucco of the church's façade. Inside the damp church the pews smell of cats. Padre Enrico has some news. They are alone in the church but he keeps his voice mistrustfully low.

"I've been in contact with someone who can get you forged identity papers and ration cards. You have to go to Pisa. Here's the address. The man's name is Claudio. Claudio Branimir. Strange name. And here's the money. You have to give it to this Claudio Branimir. He works at the police station. You will be given the identities of fictitious residents of one of the occupied cities in the south. That way no one can check up on you."

"And this Claudio is trustworthy?"

"I pray to God he is."

Oskar is tired and irritable. The air raid kept him awake most of the night. When Esme sulks on the station platform at Sarzana he gets angry with her. He is mortified afterwards. In the train compartment she refuses to look at him and he can't speak because he doesn't trust their fellow passengers and he has no papers, only a stamp sized photograph of himself and his daughter for the forged identity cards. So they sit, alienated from each other, while hilltop towns, the marble mountains of Carrara, fields of uncollected grain turning grey, slide pass the greasy windows.

"I'm sorry," he says the moment they are out of earshot of strangers. On the platform at Pisa station. "Daddy's tired because of all those explosions last night. I didn't mean to shout at you. Do you hate me now?"

"No. But I wish mummy was here."

He strokes her hair but succumbs to a sting of jealousy. A more inappropriate emotion would be hard to imagine but there it is, he is momentarily jealous of his wife, who was taken from her bed to the Velodrome in the middle of the night with thousands of other poor souls and then to an internment camp and is now apparently in a prison camp somewhere in Eastern Europe. He was always competitive with his wife for his daughter's affection. It was one of their unspoken battles. Sometimes now he thinks he's got what he always wanted, to be alone with Esme, as if this buried secret desire is to blame for what has befallen them as a family. He can't now think of his wife without guilt. Guilt that he never sought to see her when she was in the camp at Drancy.

But who would look after Esme if I were caught?

He hates Pisa station. Its bomb damage, the litter and rubble. Its pulse of deracination and exposure. The fear and hurry and cunning on drawn faces. The Nazi and fascist uniforms. The German military police in their tailored grey uniforms strolling about with their hands joined behind their backs. And the even more menacing solitary pasty-faced men in fedora hats and long raincoats.

She holds his hand as they enter the official building. He is directed towards a door with a frosted glass window. He pushes it open. Several people sit at desks. Officious and grim-faced. There is a little card on each desk – PS (Public Security). He has a bad feeling. Is about to leave when someone asks him what he wants.

"I'm looking for Claudio."

Claudio takes him aside. He is not in uniform. He has a moustache and a silk handkerchief in his top pocket. Sometimes with Esme he plays a game of spotting the bad people. He would identify Claudio as one of the bad people. Claudio denies any knowledge of forged identity cards until money is mentioned. A glitter of greed enters his eyes, which he tries to conceal.

"It'll be a thousand lire each."

A good meal in a trattoria costs five lire.

"My contact said 750. That's all I have."

"Who is your contact?"

"I'd rather not say."

"Okay, 750 each but you pay half now. Via la Pergola. Sixteen. Don't write down the address. Memorise it. And there's a code. Two long buzzes on the bell followed by one short one. Come tomorrow morning around eight."

Oskar hands over the bank notes and leaves. He takes Esme to see the Leaning Tower. The otherworldly white marble against the luminous green of the grass. Her curiosity returns. She asks questions he is able to answer. He picks her up and swings her round. They become friends again.

They go to see a friend of Padre Enrico. Don Giuseppe. He is reassured by the holy man's calm benevolence. Don Giuseppe walks them to the charterhouse, shows them to a room where they can stay the night. There is a wooden stove in the room.

"You're going to have another new name now."

"What name?"

"I don't know yet."

"Why can't I be Esme again?"

"Because we don't want the bad people to know who you really are. And when you've got a new name I'm going to take you to see a friend of mine in Florence. Isabella. She's a painter."

He rings on the bell of number 16, via la Pergola. Two sharp swift presses of the bell followed by a longer one. Behind the door he hears a dog bark. A vicious sickening bark. He takes Esme's hand and walks quickly away.

They are crossing the street when the imperious Germanic voice shatters all safety into shards of broken glass.

"Alt!"

6 - October 1943

THEY HAVE BEEN kept in a cell for four days. With half a dozen other people. They took his money. They didn't take her bear. She talks to it when he talks to the other prisoners. She pretends to feed it some of the soup they are given. Tepid water with a few peas at the bottom of the bowl.

More prisoners arrive every day.

The light is left on at night. It is brighter at night than by day. There are no windows. There are screams throughout the nights. From up above. Men screaming like children. Like wild animals.

He stands shielding her while she squats over the filthy bucket. The sound of her urine hitting the steaming filth inside. The hideous smell rising up stronger than ever.

They sit on the stone floor.

"You can be Esme again now," he tells her.

"Why did the bad men make you take down your trousers?"

"Because they're bad men," he says.

"When can we leave here?"

"We won't be here long."

On the fourth night they are called out of the cell. They are lined up in the tiled corridor outside. He can't hold her hand because they are told to keep their hands on their heads. The sight of her forced to keep her hands placed on her head, her bear in her hand. No language comes to civilise the primeval bloodrush of fury he feels. The fury he has to keep battened down. They are escorted outside by guards with dogs. It is dark outside. There are about a hundred prisoners. All looking frightened. All looking bewildered. There are a few other children. The dogs snarl and snap. They climb up on their hind legs and show their teeth.

He looks up at the stars. Breathes in the night air. Then he is shoved in the back. He would like to kill the man who shoves him in the back.

They are made to board a bus.

"Can we go back to the church now?"

"We're going on a journey first."

"Where?"

Every time he is unable to answer one of her questions he feels another theft of strength from his limbs.

They are driven to Pisa station. Shouted at in German. Shouted at in Italian. They are made to form an orderly line. Everything has to be done at the pace dictated by these soldiers. The instructions shouted into the beat of his heart. They are marched inside. One prisoner tries to escape. He suddenly begins running. The noise of the guns like a glass dome overhead shattering into splinters. His instinct is to run too. To run as fast as he can. In his mind he is hurtling across the road. A torrent of adrenalin. His muscles as tightly strung as springs. His heels pounding the flagstones. There are screams and shouts. A flock of birds rise up into the air from the station roof. Silhouetted against the crescent moon like a charcoal drawing. Then the noise of the guns dwindles to a sinister echo. The fugitive lies in the road. His body twisted in a grotesque otherworldly pose.

Esme looks up at him. Her eyes asking how frightened she should be. He takes her hand again. Tries to leech up some of her speechless bewilderment and terror.

Inside the station there are a few dimmed lights on. There are people sleeping on all the chairs. Curled up against walls. Other people whispering, trying to sell things. When these people see the Germans they stop what they're doing and try to become invisible. The dogs snarl and snap. They climb up on their hind legs and show their teeth.

They are marched onto a platform where a train waits. The people asleep on the platform are kicked awake by the guards and told to move away. He thinks for a moment of pretending to be a woken sleeper. He pictures himself leading Esme calmly away from the German and Italian guards. Pictures the sleepy innocent look he would sketch onto his face. Pictures arriving back in the ticket hall. Walking back out into the empty dark streets of Pisa. But it can't be done because there is a German soldier with a dog six feet away.

He tries to imagine the man who organised all this. The buses, the dogs, the train. Pictures his office. His desk. His secretary in a grey pleated skirt. A dab of perfume on her neck.

They are ordered to board the train. He lifts her up into the cattle truck. The door slides shut. A bolt goes down into place. He tries to position himself where he can see something of the world outside through the wooden slats.

An Italian railway guard opens the air vents. A German soldier closes them five minutes later. The train doesn't move. A fight breaks out. A woman is knocked over. She falls on Esme. Two men have to be separated. Everyone is nervous. Everyone is asking questions. To not know where you are going. To not know where you are being taken.

7 - December 1943

THE TARGET for tonight is again Berlin. The announcement brings a sick feeling to Freddie's stomach. When the curtain parts to reveal the mapped route to the German city he thinks of the Australians. Of all that boyish vitality and bluster. Three of them were seen baling out over Hanover when their aircraft was shot down. No one knows which three.

Take off has been delayed. He has a bad feeling about tonight. He has had it all day. Perhaps it is the death of his father that has weakened him in some way. His own face frightened him in the wash-room mirror earlier. Its mask-like impenetrability like some old childhood part of him dragged out of an attic chest.

He had a bad feeling about tonight even before he found out he was to pilot an unfamiliar aircraft. A Halifax. He doesn't like flying the battle weary old Hallibags. They possess little of the sleek vice-free grace of a Lancaster. He doesn't trust their rudders and he doesn't like their groaning inability to climb above 15,000 feet. Where they easily become the sacrificial victims of the stream.

The delayed take off has increased his tension. He is sitting inside the ground crew's hut. Pale and tense. His head screwed too tight to his shoulders. No flexibility in his neck.

He sees his crew through a ghost sheen of simmering dread. He feels no connection to them. Recognises no concourse of emotions in the meeting of his eyes with theirs. His deep uneasiness has smudged them to a painted transparency, a crackle of static. It has smudged everything he depends on for solace, for hope, for the orderly meshing together of one moment to another.

I can't go through with this tonight, he thinks.

He is convinced his crew are aware of something odd about him, some whip of distortion in the way he is experiencing the moment. He takes one of Isabella's old letters from his pocket. He stares down unseeingly at the faded script, presses his thumbs firmly against its pages as if seeking a current there that might chase away the fume of fear.

There's a rumour going round the station that one crew never fly to the target. That the pilot has lost his nerve. And now drops his cargo of bombs in the sea and flies in circles over the Channel until it's time to return to base. He considers suggesting this to his crew as an option for tonight. He fights through the shame of it. Imagines how he might phrase his foreboding to his fellow crew members.

I've not turned yellow. It's only that I have a really bad feeling about tonight. I'm sure I'll be fine tomorrow. But I don't think I can go through with the mission tonight. I feel we're all for the chop.

He is most ashamed of himself when he imagines saying these words to Davy. It's Davy he most wants to think well of him. He can't bear the prospect of disappointing Davy. He will have to climb into the Halifax with this spin of panic in his head. This high line of tension, this weakening sense of foreboding.

"You okay?"

He can't tell Reg he is not okay. That he feels they are all going to die tonight. At OTU a training instructor once told him, if your thoughts impede in any way your ability to perform your duty as an airman you have to stop thinking.

"Damn unsettling all this waiting around. That's all."

"I'll second that. I've got my fingers crossed we don't get off the ground tonight."

"Oh?"

"As my fiancé would sometimes say, not in the mood tonight."

"Your fiancé said that?"

"Didn't yours?"

"My wife's Italian."

"What's that supposed to mean?"

"She would say, *non ho molto voglia stasera.*"

"I like the sound of that."

"You wouldn't if your wife said it to you."

Freddie leaves the hut. Feels a lack of mastery over his limbs as he walks away. Like someone drunk pretending to be sober. He walks towards the perimeter track, the western margin of the field. The small grove of ash and elm trees beyond which are the still unploughed cornfields. The setting sun is reflected in the cockpit windows of the aircraft on the track. He lights a cigarette. Stands close to the trees. Breathing in the winter smell of the land. Feeling the presence of magnitude and then of being included in the intimacy all around him. As if a secret is about to be shared with him. The secret of whether or not this is to be his last night on earth. He blows out a column of smoke upwards towards the sky. Then feels he is being watched. He turns on his heels and is looking into the eyes of a fox cub. The animal remains stock still. A stroke of gold splashed over its fur by the setting sun. There is a heightened quality about the moment. It is a moment of import and eloquence. As if an oracle is speaking. A moment he knows he will never forget. But will never understand either. He and the fox make a connection. Then the fox cub turns and ambles leisurely away into the thickening shadows of the grove of elms and ash.

The order arrives to take off. The encounter with the fox has taken the edge off his anxiety. He still feels uneasy. Still feels it is a mistake to fly tonight. Perhaps he is just a little less frightened of death now?

In the cockpit he and Reg begin running through the starting sequence. Prepare to taxi the aircraft out to take its place in the queue on the perimeter track. One by one the propellers begin rotating. A huddle of WAAFs prepare to wave them off. Their shadows stretched long over the track, like monstrous puppet shadows. A long line of parallel lights tapers off into the darkness.

"You've got the green," says Reg.

The Halifax suddenly refuses to obey his commands. Something amiss with an engine. The port inner. Davy tells him the wireless is malfunctioning too. He and Reg exchange a questioning glance. He feels as though he has fed his foreboding into the aircraft's engines. Locked them up somehow. Reg hands him his parachute and his helmet. They unload the aircraft.

They are transferred in the crew bus to the reserve aircraft. Another Halifax. Bombed up, fuelled up and ready to go. Another half hour goes by. Bombers roaring up into the darkening sky. Circling overhead.

"I like late changeovers less than I like scratchy trousers," says Reg, packing the parachutes away.

Freddie opens the throttles. Doing his best to perform the act smoothly and firmly. Reg checks all the gauges. Again something is wrong.

"Someone doesn't want us up in the skies tonight."

They wait around for the engineers to fix the first Halifax. The CO and chief technical officer growing more flustered. Freddie plays cards by the stove in the ground crew's hut. The moon rises up over the base. The last of the bombers from their squadron are preparing to leave.

"If we don't get up in the air soon we'll never catch the stream up. Surely they don't expect us to fly solo over bloody Germany?"

Spike is the first to board the aircraft. He trips over the main spar. Davy tries to revive him. No luck. He has knocked himself unconscious.

"Spike, I love you," says Reg.

The deadline passes. It is too late now to find a replacement bomb aimer.

Reg thanks Spike but Freddie thanks the fox.

8 - December 1943

ISABELLA CLIMBS the wooden stairs to the small attic room
above her studio. She has Pontormo's framed painting in one
hand and her finished copy in the other that has been baked in
the oven and now shows a marvel of hairline cracks. The attic
room has a skylight that opens onto the sloping russet tiles of
the roof. Three storeys below, the river embankment and, to her
left, the arched gate of the old city wall. She climbs out onto the
roof with the two paintings. A tile slides beneath her feet and
for a moment she fears she is about to lose her balance. She
props the two paintings behind the chimneystack. Not wanting
them in her studio when Captain Heinkel arrives. Then she
stands looking across at the river and its bridges, the domes and
steeples. For a moment she feels like a ghost up on the rooftop,
above the city. As if she has broken all ties with the physical
world.

When there is a knock on the door she is expecting to see
Captain Heinkel in his SS uniform. Instead the door is shoved
violently open the moment she unfastens the catch.

"Where is it?"

The man with the puckered scar beneath his eye grabs her
hair and yanks her head down. Carità, Seagull Eyes and the huge
man called Piccolo are all glaring at her with contempt. Fear
opens a deep trench in her being. The men push past her. Her
painting of Captain Heinkel is on the easel.

"First the whore of that communist filth; now the whore of
Captain Heinkel," says Seagull Eyes with a cursory glance at her
painting of the German SS officer. "You swap partners as if this
war is a carnival ball."

Carità hands her a creased and pulped photograph of
Pontormo's St Anthony. She takes it from his cruel fleshy
hands. She is struck by how different the face of St Anthony

looks in the black and white reproduction. She steels herself to offer up her best mystified expression.

"We know you have it. If you don't want us to turn this place upside down I suggest you hand it over."

She feels herself recede under Carità's gaze. Major Mario Carità now. He has been promoted. She feels herself become less solid and distinct to herself. She has to take a breath to hold her shape. He is wearing a beret with a coy tassel, a black jersey, heavy boots.

"I don't know what you mean," she says. She glances up at her portrait in oils of Freddie. Freddie always told her she was a lousy actress.

Seagull Eyes is marching imperiously around her studio. He turns round the nude painting of Marina. Calls everyone's attention to it. Makes some appreciative lewd noises. He holds it up against himself and begins thrusting his groin into it. Scarface smiles but when he smiles there is no warmth or generosity in his eyes.

"So where is it?"

Seagull Eyes unhooks her portrait of Freddie from the wall. Freddie looking dashing and English in his fisherman's jersey. He studies it for a moment with an expression of distaste.

Don't you dare damage that!

"Another communist no doubt," he says and flings it across the studio as though it is a burnt piece of toast.

She delivers the slap to his face with a bloodrush of indignation that makes her perform the act before she realises what she is doing.

For a moment Seagull Eyes has the look of someone who has lost his place in the world, the dumbfounded self-consciousness of the child left standing in a game of musical chairs. Then he clasps her neck tightly in his fist and hisses at her. He raises his fist which remains suspended in mid-air because there is another knock on the door. Carità opens it. Captain Heinkel is holding a bouquet of flowers. He flushes with embarrassment when he sees the ring of coarse men staring expectantly at him and his gift.

"What's going on here?" he says.

She sees they are all a bit in awe of his authority.

"We've come to arrest this woman."

"I'll take care of this. You can all leave."

When Carità and his rabble of thugs have left she picks up the portrait of Freddie and restores it to its place on the wall.

Captain Heinkel arranges two chairs facing each other. He invites her to sit down.

"I can help you," he says, "but you need to be honest with me."

She lights a cigarette. She can't help but feel a swill of gratitude towards him. He is like a return to civilisation after the barbarity of Carità's secret police.

"I believe you know Guido del Monte?"

"He was my teacher."

"He has been arrested. I think you know why."

"What will happen to him?"

"He will probably be interned at the concentration camp at Fossoli as a political prisoner."

"But he's sixty-five years old."

"He was making a forgery of a painting that was to be a gift to our Führer. He is lucky not to be shot."

She is about to protest but checks herself. The set expression on his face reminds her how little sway rational argument now has.

"I believe you also know Fosco Scarafuggi."

"Yes."

"What kind of man would you say he is? Would he have any reason to bear your teacher a grudge?"

"I don't know."

"It would surprise you then if I told you it was him who informed the secret police of the whereabouts of the two paintings? That it's thanks to him that your former teacher is now in a cell."

Not in the slightest, she thinks. The only way Marcello's story makes any sense is if Fosco is somehow behind everything.

"Thanks to him too that Carità came here to your studio. I shouldn't be telling you this. However I feel we have built up an understanding during the course of my visits to your studio. I would hope we have even established a certain amount of mutual affection. Therefore I feel inclined to talk to you, not as a member of the Third Reich, but as a friend. Do you understand?"

"Thank you," she says.

"So you see you have both been betrayed by Fosco Scarafuggi."

"What will happen to him?"

"He will receive the reward for the paintings."

She tries to hide her expression of disgust.

"I want you to hand over the Pontormo and the copy you made to me. Are they here?"

"They're on the roof."

"I will do my utmost to ensure no further action is taken. Can I ask why you agreed to make the forgery?"

There is still a deep rooted resistance in her to making an ally and confidante of a German SS officer despite the blood thickening spite she now feels towards Fosco.

"What I don't understand is that it was Fosco who originally took those paintings," she says.

"That's as I thought. It was his idea to forge the paintings then?"

"Yes."

"And your loyalty to your teacher was taken advantage of."

"Something like that, yes."

9 - November 1943

EARLY MORNING. They are marched from the station through the small town. A German motorcyclist drives up and down the line. People on the streets engaged in daily chores look on, mostly with sympathy. There is a taunting smell of warm pastries when they pass a bakery.

"Are we going to get away from the bad people?"

"We'll have to think up a plan."

"Why don't they like us?"

"Because they're bad. Bad people don't like other people."

"Who do they like then?"

"Not even themselves probably."

They are marched out of the town, down a road in the middle of flat fields. Near a canal. The hard dry earth is chequered with cracks. Splits big enough to slide your hand inside. He points towards some sheep.

"Look," he says.

But she won't be so easily fooled.

They walk past the barbed wire, row upon row of it. The watchtowers on their long wooden legs. At the entrance to the camp a black flag hangs still. Washing hangs outside the windows of the brick huts. The inmates are in civilian clothes. They all turn to look at the new arrivals.

Inside the political prisoners are separated from the Jews. The men are separated from the women. He is separated from his daughter. A woman tells him not to worry, she will look after her.

"She can't speak Italian very well," he says.

"Don't worry."

He crouches down on the hard earth so he is her height. She is underdressed for the oncoming winter. He thinks of the small bundle of clothes they left behind in the bell tower of the pink church. Wonders what will happen to them. He looks into her frightened eyes. His whole being aches with protective love for her. He doesn't know how to explain to her what will happen next. How to explain to her that it is not his choosing that he has to abandon her. He knows she will feel he is failing her. And he can't help feeling she is right to blame him. It is the worst moment of his life.

"For a while this kind lady is going to take care of you."

"I don't want you to leave me," she says.

"I'm not going to leave you. I won't be far away. At the moment we have to do what the bad people say. I'd do anything to make this not true but at the moment the bad people have all the power and there's nothing I can do."

"I don't like it here."

"We won't be here long."

"Promise?"

"Yes, I promise." He looks up at the woman. "What is your name?"

"Elisa," says the woman.

"This is Elisa. She will look after you."

She refuses to look at the woman called Elisa. He talks to his daughter in French and to the woman called Elisa in Italian.

"I want you to look after me."

An Italian, a member of the fascist militia, shouts at Oskar. He would like to kill him. Kill him with his bare hands. He imagines his hands around the man's throat. Pushing the man's head into the dirt. He doesn't recognise himself in the satisfaction he gleans from this brief imaginary act.

The woman called Elisa takes Esme's hand. She leads his daughter and her bear over to the group of women. His daughter looks over her shoulder as she is tugged away. There is a look of reproach on her face when he turns to look at her.

Oskar stands in line. They are marshalled by two Italian militia with guns. He is given a number. It is sewn onto his shirt. 1717. He pictures the ugly number that will be sewn onto his daughter's ragged floral dress. He is given a yellow star. This too is sewn onto his shirt. By a woman with a yellow star on her cardigan. He can hear his daughter's voice. *Why have we got a yellow star?* This is what her voice asks. He wonders what answer the woman called Elisa will give.

He stands in another line. His head is shaved. A man wearing a yellow star shaves his head with an electric razor. Quickly, methodically, avoiding all eye contact, as if he is peeling a potato.

He stands in another line. He is given two blankets, a sheet, a bowl, a spoon and a tin mug. He is sent away. To another line. He is told to take off his clothes for a doctor. He stands naked while he is prodded. While a stethoscope is placed on his chest. He puts back on his clothes.

He stands in another line. Numbers are barked out. He is assigned a hut. He meets the man he will share a bunk with. A croupier from Siena. A large man with small shifty eyes. He speaks in a booming voice, resonating with nervous energy. Like a voice through a megaphone. And then laughs uproariously at his own jokes which are rarely funny.

In the showers he washes the dirt from his body. He is one of a dozen naked men gasping at the shock and violence of the scalding water.

In the barracks he meets a young man called Francesco. He is from Florence.

"I studied art in Florence," he says. "I wanted to return there. Got as far as Pisa. That's where we were arrested."

They go outside, sit on the steps of their hut. It is November but the sun is warm on their faces. They tell each other their story. How they were caught. The betrayals involved. Everyone here has been betrayed by someone. He learns that Francesco knows Isabella. He takes comfort from this news. The world shrinks. Acquires design, choreography. Francesco opens a balled sheet of newspaper. Inside are two plums. He hands him one of the plums. Oskar caresses it in his hand.

"Do they let us see the women?"

"Yes. All the Jews are allowed to mix with each other most of the day but not with the political prisoners in the other camp. My sister is here. And my father. Only my mother escaped capture. Except I expect to see her arrive here from one day to the next. There are quite a few children too. They run around like wild creatures. Generally speaking the guards treat the children well. Especially of course if they have children of their own. There's no need to worry about your daughter. At least not for the time being."

Francesco bites into the plum. The juice runs down over his bottom lip, glistens on his chin.

"Can I give this plum to my daughter?"

"Of course. I'm afraid plums aren't part of the rations here. A man who receives food parcels gave me these. Have you got any money?"

"No, they took it."

Later, after roll call and lunch, he gives his daughter the plum. She eats it without thinking, without savouring it. She has other things on her mind. He is happy she still has her bear. She shows him the yellow star and number sewn onto her dress. She is pleased with them.

"I asked for a number and a star for Napoleon but the man shouted at me."

She tells him she has made a friend. Looks around for him so she can point him out but he's nowhere to be seen. She makes him feel a little less needed, both a relief and a new source of hurt. They walk around the camp together. There is a group of people outside one hut, gazing in through the window. He lifts her up so she can see in through the window. Inside a man is having a tooth removed.

10 - December 1944

OSKAR SWINGS his feet over the bunk on the second tier. The secreted smell of a hundred men's sleep is like a sort of fog. It is difficult to think beyond it. The hut is astir with dazed men getting dressed. Fifteen minutes until roll call. The barrack leader shouts ugly commands.

For every three men in his hut there are only two straw billets. In the night his neighbour, the large comedian whose curly dark hair grows on the back on his neck and down under his shirt, presses up against him. They share each other's body heat. It irritated him at first but now he has got used to it. Has an intimate knowledge of the man's body odour, the noises he makes in his sleep. There is another man who cries out in his sleep. He keeps saying, I don't know anything. I swear I don't know anything. Sometimes someone else shouts at him to shut up. Petty arguments are always breaking out. The lights are turned out at half past eight every night. And then everyone talks in the dark. You have to guess who it is that is talking sometimes. They talk about what will happen to them. Over and over again. Planes often fly overhead. Sometimes the hut shakes underneath their thunder. Sometimes they hear explosions in the distance.

"You can get used to anything. Even start enjoying it," says Francesco who stands at the sink beside him in the latrine. Splashing the cold water up onto his pale unshaven face.

Oskar rubs at his teeth and gums with his forefinger. Pretending it is a toothbrush. "What do you mean?"

"This place. It provides moments every day that I'll miss. The sense of community, the evening meal outside when the sun's setting, the gossip and bartering. The colossal treat of eating. Even my longing to be home I'd probably miss if I were home."

"I thought they'd make us work here. Dig holes or something. Bit of a shock to find people playing cards and chess and listening to gramophone records and reading in the sun."

"I had to do something along those lines when Mussolini introduced the Mobilisation of Civilians Act. I was in a work party of Jewish men. Our first task was to dig irrigation channels for the farms in the countryside outside Sesto Fiorentino. My partner in the ditches was a man called Carlo. He muttered abuse under his breath almost all the time. He accused me of lacking idealism and the spirit of protest. He was right in a way. My only political concern back then was to go largely unnoticed. The ditch we were digging cut through the middle of an olive grove. Our supervisor gave us instructions to be careful not to damage the roots of the trees. The minute he was out of sight, overseeing work at another ditch, Carlo would take his pickaxe or shovel and hack at the uncovered roots with a satisfied malice and then mask the destruction he had achieved with a new layer of earth. At the time I thought it madness that someone could believe he was thwarting the fascist war effort by mutilating the roots of a few olive trees. But the world still seemed relatively sane to me in those days before the Nazis arrived in Florence."

During roll call a cat strolls around the parade ground. A ginger she cat. It is regarded with wonder and amusement. Often it stops and stares into space. Swinging its tail. All eyes are riveted on it. The cat behaves as though they are not there.

Oskar stamps his feet against the cold. He shouts out "Here" when his number is called. There is always a little skip in his heartbeat when his number is called out.

"Compliments on your daughter by the way. She's a ravishing little thing," says Francesco. "Hard to believe really..."

Oskar sits on the step of Hut 23 hugging his shoulders. Rocking gently back and forth. Insulating himself as best he can from the cold wind. "What's hard to believe?"

"This business of locking up children in internment camps. Sewing a number on their clothes. Sometimes I wonder what I would do if I was a guard in this camp. I think I'd rather be a prisoner."

Standing opposite is the man who is always publicly picking his nose. He picks his nose with a kind of feverish relish as if he is alone in a private place. Every time Oskar sees him he is picking his nose.

Perhaps that's his way of pretending he is in the privacy of his home, he thinks.

"I'm a bit worried about her. She was coping okay for a while. Happy to have other children to play with. Children are a kind of marvel. They can disappear inside their imagination. Often do. But she's caught a cold. And she's got so thin."

"We're all thin. I didn't recognise myself when I caught sight of my reflection the other day. My face – it looked so long and sunken."

A German soldier cycles past. Ringing the bell of his bicycle to warn of his approach.

"Except my bed companion. He's not thin. It's like sleeping with a horse. With two horses."

"My bedmate isn't much fun either. Farts the whole time. He's a zealous Zionist too. Talks about little else. I've never given much thought to the fact that I was born Jewish. It wasn't an issue at school or university. Until Mussolini signed the pact with Hitler and I was suddenly forced to stop attending all lectures. Now it's the most decisive component of who I am," Francesco says, picking at the yellow star on the breast of his jersey.

"Who were you writing to earlier?"

"Oh, a girl I like. She's called Marina."

"Jewish?"

"No."

Francesco tells him the story of Marina's diary.

"And there I was in only my shorts chasing after two fascist militia in the middle of the night. I went to see the secret police the next day because it was a less frightening option than telling Marina I had stolen and lost her diary. I can laugh about it now but I tell you it wasn't funny at the time."

"Hopefully you'll be able to laugh about it with her one day."

"Here comes breakfast."

The man walks towards them with the bucket. He and Francesco dip their mugs in, ladle up the bitter unsweetened lukewarm barley coffee.

"I've got half a cigarette I'll share with you."

After evening roll call he can see his daughter. She shuffles towards him. Still holding her bear. She is wearing the cardigan of an adult that the woman Elisa found for her. Its hem trails over the hardening ground. She sneezes. He wipes the snot away with the sleeve of his jersey.

"I don't feel well."

"Anything I can do to make you feel better?"

"Is this always going to be where we live now?"

"No. Are you mad? Live here! What kind of dad would I be if I made you live here forever?"

She copies his grin.

A woman is singing inside one of the huts. Her voice like wings rippling the surface of water.

He looks over towards the voice.

"The thing is," he says, "there are always difficult times in life. They are like tests we are put through. But the difficult times are always much shorter than the good times. The times when we are happy. And if we didn't have the difficult times, like this, we wouldn't enjoy the good times so much. But the good people are on their way and they will chase away the bad people."

"Soon?"

"They're coming as quickly as they can."

"And then we'll see mummy again?"

"Yes."

Oskar doesn't get jealous any more when she tells him she misses her mummy. He misses her too. His memories of her sustain him.

11 - December 1943

"HOW BIG A PART do you think skill plays in survival?"

"A pretty big part," says Freddie.

"More than luck?"

"You need luck, especially on your first few ops. But if you've got dozy gunners or a pilot with slow reflexes..."

"Or an incompetent navigator."

"You'll be fine."

"You more experienced chaps always look so calm."

Freddie watches Davy arrive on his bike. His characteristic way of swinging his right leg over the saddle while still in motion, standing both feet on the left pedal, jumping off and allowing the bike to run on and collapse against the other bikes propped up against the wall of the hut. The act a showcase of poise and readiness for the next moment of life.

"Just a mask," he says. "You'll have it soon."

Rickie Paine adjusts the reading lamp on the desk. His chart spread out on the table. Cyril is in bed with a fever. Rickie is the replacement navigator they have been assigned for tonight's trip to Berlin. Rickie is twenty and has only flown one mission.

"Can I tell you why I'm suddenly more frightened?"

Freddie nods. He feels okay today. He does not have a bad feeling about tonight's operation.

"Last night I met the woman of my life. I recognised her instantly. She's called Nancy. Do you know her? She's a WAAF here."

"Nancy who sometimes chalks us all in and out in the operations room?"

"Yes."

Nancy with the boyish body and the mouth that never closes on her teeth. Nancy who always looks as though tears are welling up behind her eyes, he thinks.

"Now I'm terrified I'll die without seeing her again. I wasn't too scared before I met Nancy. Now I just hope I don't let you down. That weather chart worries me a bit. All that expected heavy cloud."

Freddie rests his hand on the boy's shoulder. Anxious to impart reassurance. But he doesn't feel any older or wiser.

The ground crew close the rear door. Freddie seals it shut. Clambers along the dim interior of V Victor. The echo of his passage like an indistinct memory from long ago. It's another of his rituals to visit every area of the plane's interior before take-off. Like a priest exorcising a home. He always tries not to look at the stretcher propped near the dangling legs of Woodsy up in the mid upper turret. He raps his knuckles on one or two of the oxygen bottles in racks as he passes with bowed head through V Victor's belly, over her bomb bay.

They are on their way to Berlin again. Carrying a 4,000-pound "cookie" and fourteen 500-pound incendiary clusters. Rickie guides the aircraft to the target without problems.

"Turn starboard on to one-two-zero degrees."

Up ahead are a forest of searchlights. A thicket of long thin smoking beams pivoting back and forth. Stabbing at the darkness. Making of the sky a kind of dome as though V Victor is about to enter some supernatural cathedral of light. The Pathfinder flares have splashed a vivid carpet of red and green over the target area down below. Red candles drip down slowly in the shape of a tree through the clouds.

A Lancaster in front is picked out by the finger of the master searchlight. Almost immediately a dozen other slave beams converge on her. Silvered and silhouetted by the powerful lights she looks like a ghost of herself. A dead aircraft returned to haunt the battle scene. She dives down through the stream of bombers and turns sharply but she cannot escape the deathly grip of the beams. Bursting shells cluster around her. A dazzling mosaic of curving red lines flicker across Freddie's sight as he watches. For a moment he imagines he is inside that

Lancaster and not piloting V Victor. The sixty-degree turn at three hundred knots creating a chaos of falling equipment. The men in the gun turrets flung against the perspex roof. Ammunition belts jumping out of their cases. Twelve volt batteries and oxygen bottles tumbling through the air.

He watches the coned Lancaster fall out of the sky. Trailing fire and smoke. The searchlights scythe through the dark space twinkling with red stars ahead. Seeking out a new victim.

This is the bomb run. He can't weave or corkscrew V Victor. He has to keep her straight and steady. At 15,000 feet. The chewing gum becomes a bitter nugget in his mouth. Black clouds of smoke appear in the plane's path and are shaken and stretched into grotesque protean shapes by the wind. They thicken into what looks like a meteor storm.

"Ruddy hell," says Woodsy through his headset.

Menacing red dots snake up towards V Victor's snout. There is a sudden billowing of explosive orange light to the left. A shockwave that rocks the fuselage. That tilts the port wing towards the ground. From the cloud of black smoke flaming trails of red, green and orange debris drip down like candle wax. To port Freddie registers flames licking at the wing of another Lancaster. *The new recruits we played cricket with yesterday*, he realises. The aircraft drifts drunkenly across his flight path.

Another silver flash lights up a grid of miniature streets and houses below. Teases out of the night this unsettling glimpse of the hidden life of the city and the realisation that there are people down there. Mothers seeking to comfort their children.

Freddie looks at the photo of Isabella among the dials. The green glow of the compass by his knee reflecting up a green sheen that he pictures on his skin, like theatrical face paint. Reg next to him in his mask and helmet. The collars of his Irvin jacket upturned, as if he is showing off for a girl.

The drunken Lancaster on fire, silhouetted against the glowing sky, begins spewing out black smoke. Its nose down. Its starboard wing tilting at a grotesque angle. He looks for as long as possible. Willing live bodies to appear. Chutes to open. Then V Victor is tangled up in a skein of searchlights for a moment. There is a lightning flash of blue light in the cockpit. So bright he can see a smudge of cigarette ash on his trousers. The blue beam seems to fizz static inside his body. His skin shrinks beneath his clothes. He turns away his eyes. Lowers his seat. When the searchlight moves away he has glittering stars on his retina. A blue glow glazes over the cockpit window.

"Bomb doors open," says Spike over the intercom. Spike who is lying face down in the perspex nose of the aircraft staring down into his bomb-site.

The stink of all the explosions outside enters the cockpit along with an updraught of chill air. The smell of cordite stinging Freddie's eyes, bringing forth tears.

"Nice and steady, Skipper. Air speed at one-eighty."

V Victor leaps up into the air. As if hurdling a fence. Streams of red, orange and yellow tracer curve up towards her.

"Bombs gone."

"Okay. Another minute to get the photographs and then it's nose down and out of here. Navigator, confirm the course out of here."

The tension crackles with still more voltage as he waits for the camera light to go out on the instrument panel.

Two hours later, no matter whether he shepherds her upwards or downwards, Freddie can't free V Victor from the engulfing thicket of fog. He has tried every trick in the book. Every textbook manoeuvre he knows. But he can find no gallery of open sky. Frequently he glances up through the perspex canopy. Never catching sight of the glittering point of a star. The relentless tide of cloud muffles the sound of the engines. Feeds a lethargic rhythm into his blood. Like a sedative.

"Navigator. Any idea where we are? We should be close to the Dutch coast by now, shouldn't we?"

The words of the briefing officer keep coming back to him. "You've got eight hours fuel for a seven and half hour journey."

"By my reckoning we should be over the sea by now. Gee's still out though."

Freddie detects doubt in the new navigator's voice. A sheepishness, as though he feels at fault that makes him feel protective towards him.

"Not much hope of getting an Astro shot in this."

"I don't understand. I've double checked my chart. We haven't once veered off course. No dramatic changes in wind speed or direction. The compass is showing north-west. "

They have been in this vacuum of cloud cover for two hours. This polar waste bereft of landmarks. He has no sense of moving forward. Disbelieves the dials. Disbelieves in the presence of the earth below.

"Skip, searchlights ahead."

"Searchlights? Where the hell are we?"

"Perhaps they're ours?"

The floor of cloud is pierced by prongs of groping light. A spray of light flak rattles the length of the fuselage, each rap louder than the last. An explosion tilts the plane.

"Going into corkscrew. Starboard."

V Victor is suddenly like a galloping frightened horse. He heaves the control column fully to the left and dives down sideways 1000ft to starboard. Then soars with a wrenching of the controls into a climbing turn to port. Then dives again with all the rivets screaming as V Victor plunges at 300mph towards the ground. When he pulls her out of the final dive his breath comes heavy, his forearms ache and he is dizzy with a sick hollow feeling in his stomach as though he has just rowed a boat race.

"Well done, skip."

"The skipper. Nice man."

"Skipper here. Who's that?"

"He's probably a fairy. Has eyes only for pretty boy Davy. Good pilot. No doubt about that. Gooseberry tart. You're having a laugh..."

It's Spencer. And he's not mumbling. He's not muttering. He's delivering up his lines loud and clear.

Freddie feels violated and exposed. Over the airwaves he can feel the crew straining to hide their embarrassment on his behalf. Next to him Reg is pretending he didn't hear.

Freddie too has to pretend he didn't hear. Pretend this moment is seamlessly connected to all the other moments of this operation. Not a sudden glare of footlights picking him out alone and naked on a stage. "Spencer?" he says into his microphone.

"Roll out the barrel

Bring out the barrel

Don't bring out the barrel now..."

"Skipper to rear gunner."

"I'm cold, mum. Where's my hot water bottle?"

"Can someone go to the rear turret and find out what's wrong with Spencer."

"I'll go, sir."

It's Davy who has volunteered. The blush of embarrassment prickles Freddie's entire body. He doesn't want to speak to Davy.

He turns off his microphone. "Is that what everyone thinks? That I'm a fairy?" He has to shout at the top of his voice over the roar and rattle of V Victor.

"News to me," shouts Reg.

For the first time he sees how scared Reg is. His face above the oxygen mask translucently pale as though lit from beneath by a torch light.

"Skipper. Spencer's not getting oxygen. His pipe's frozen up."

Serves the fucker right, Freddie thinks.

12 - December 1943

OSKAR WALKS through the snow. He sinks into its crunching embrace. He slips and slides. He leaves his footprints on the world he is leaving behind. When his daughter talks he can see her breath on the air.

The snow, the effect of concealment and secrecy it creates, makes him think of the brutality of the wartime legislation to forbid and violently extract secrets. It is as if the hushed white landscape is showing how sacrosanct are our secrets, how much of our vitality is bound up in them. It is as if the snow has arrived to deliver a sermon.

The convoy of prisoners are marshalled by guards with dogs. The dogs are excited by the snow. They tug at their leashes.

"Look!" she says. His daughter, her nose bright red and streaming with snot that he keeps wiping away.

There are two boys making a snowman. Francesco, by his side, tosses his letter towards them. Flicks it through the air as though it is a slice of bread. His letter of love. His letter of farewell. Oskar tenses, waits for the bark of a guard. But there is only the crunch of the snow underfoot. His daughter looks back over her shoulder at the snowman. Reluctant to let it out of her sight.

At the station the train is waiting for them. A brown cattle train of about eight carriages. The high small windows crisscrossed with barbed wire. There are German SS soldiers with dogs on the platform. They shout instructions. In the midst of the quiet created by the snow.

He lifts up his daughter. Feels her breath on his cheek. They are herded onto the train. Up a wooden plank. About sixty in each carriage. Children are crying. People are arguing. Someone shouts at someone else to make the child stop screaming. An old man calls for calm. There is another old man who isn't wearing shoes. His feet are wrapped in rags but Oskar can see his filthy toes.

There is a thin covering of straw on the carriage floor. The door is pulled shut. The bolt is slotted into place. A stark harrowing noise that no child ought to hear. He doesn't know if the sudden surge of anxiety is his own emotion or a current conveyed to him by the other people in the crush of the carriage.

The whistle blows. The train shudders into motion. Billowing out its effacing smoke. The smoke oozes into the carriage through the barbed wired opening. Makes faces look even more spectral in the twilight gloom of the carriage.

"Why aren't there seats?" Esme asks him.

He lifts up his daughter. So she can see out of the window. He tells her to be careful of the wire.

"Tell me what you see," he says.

"Houses," she says. "With snow on the roofs."

He can see only the sky. Grey clouds patterned like fish scales.

The train stops and starts. He puts his daughter down. He pulls the sleeve of his jersey down over his hand. He raises his mittened hand to the wire at the high opening. He begins bending it. This way and that. It gives him something to do. This way and that. Bending it.

The train stops and starts. Outside Verona it stops for a long time. He stops working at the wire. He listens out for German voices.

He can see the crescent moon. Sneaking in and out of the clouds. Over the fields and hills. Fields and hills he cannot see but imagines. The train starts up again. It moves faster now. He works at the wire. Bending it. This way and that. He thinks of things he would like to do. So he sits on the terrace of a café in Montmartre with a cafe au lait. He walks barefoot over hot sand towards a sea glittering with thousands of points of light. He crosses Pont Notre Dame in the early hours of a spring morning. And all the time he works at the wire. Bending it this way and that. The first piece snaps off in his hand. All of a sudden there is hope. He feels it pulse in his arteries. It bodies forth pictures. He and his daughter out there, under the moon. Tearing off the yellow star. Tearing off the number stitched onto their clothes. He begins bending back and forth a new piece of wire. He makes calculations. Yes, he will be able to climb through the window. It will be awkward but he can do it. He imagines the leap from the moving train. Does he hold onto Esme when he jumps or does he make her jump first? Which is safest? The wire has to be torn free before they reach the border. The Austrian border, he imagines. He whispers to Francesco. Francesco copies him. He too begins working at the wire.

"What are you two doing?"

"We can get out of here. Look. I've prised away one piece of wire. We can get rid of the rest."

"You heard what that German soldier said. If anyone escapes they will kill ten of us."

"They want us to work and yet they give us no food or water."

"They'll give us food and water when we arrive. They want us to work."

"My daughter is six-years-old. What work can she do?"

"They can't separate children from their parents."

"And what about the old and sick? What work will they do?"

"I agree. We have to escape."

"Suppose there are sentries on top of the carriages? We'll be shot."

"Those who want to can try their luck. Those who don't or can't will have to face the music and they will be on my conscience. But I am sorry, I am not allowing these Nazi bastards to put my little girl in a work camp."

The argument continues. There is one man who says he will call the guards if anyone tries to escape. Oskar stops listening. He lets Francesco argue with the obstinate man.

The rhythm of the train rocks him back and forth on his heels. Esme leans against his leg. He has to concentrate to keep his balance. He continues working at the wire. Teasing it this way and that. Kneading it into compliance. It is cutting into his fingers. His hands are sticky with blood beneath his sleeve.

He pulls off the last piece of wire. Throws it out the window. The wire is all gone. His heart is racing. He takes a deep breath.

There are twenty-six people who want to take their chances. Who want to jump. He and his daughter will jump first. Followed by Francesco and his sister. Francesco's father will not jump. He is too old for such heroics, he says.

"Let's do it," Oskar says.

And Francesco lifts him up. He is a dancer. His body is supple. His body is trained to obey his will. He heaves himself up. Enjoying the feel of the muscles in his shoulders. It is easy for him to get his leg through the small opening. He sits at the window, his legs dangling down into the darkness outside. The night rushes by. The wind whips at his hair. No lights. Just darkness. Outlines. Thicker swells of shadow. He extends one leg experimentally. There is a narrow ledge. He tells Francesco there is a narrow ledge. He tells Francesco to pass him his daughter. He is standing on the narrow ledge with his daughter in his arms. The wind slaps at his face. Whips at his trousers.

"We're going to wait for the train to slow down a bit." He has to shout against the noise of the slipstream. "And then we're going to jump. I will count to three and then I'm going to throw you off the train. There is grass so it won't hurt too much though it might hurt a bit. But you mustn't cry out or make any noise. First though Napoleon will jump."

"Can't we jump together?"

"No. Because you both need free hands to help break your fall. We'll find him after we jump. Okay?"

"Okay."

The wind stings his cheeks. Blows his daughter's hair into his face. Her warmth reaches him through the chill air of the night. To throw his daughter off a moving train. It will be the hardest thing he has ever had to do. There is a resistance in his blood. An unwillingness in his body to perform the unnatural act.

The train jolts. There is a wrenching iron noise underneath the wheels. The train slows down. He tosses the toy bear into the darkness. He almost loses his balance on the narrow ledge.

"Okay," he says to his daughter. "Ready?"

"I'm scared."

"That's natural, sweetheart. But we must get off this train. Away from the bad people."

"Okay."

"Napoleon's done it. Now it's your turn. Then it's mine."

"Okay."

"One, two, three."

It is an agony to release his daughter from his embrace. To launch her out into the rushing void of darkness. But he does it. He lets her go. He is about to jump when the nature of the noise the train makes changes. Before he has time to fling himself down he is engulfed in a thicker darkness and deafened by a harsher noise. The wall of the tunnel is less than the length of his arm away.

13 - December 1943

ISABELLA STANDS in front of her mirror. She frowns at herself in the glass. At the inappropriateness of the long thin silver dress she wears. It is brighter than the moon.

She has already changed her clothes three times. Everything she puts on strikes her as either too flirtatious or too scruffy. Is it stupid to not want anyone to think she has made an effort to dress up for an SS officer? After all she's going out with him. The damage is done. Already she is anticipating the looks of contempt she will receive. The shame she will feel. The injustice of the silent accusations that will be levelled at her. In ten minutes the black staff car will pull up on the gravel forecourt outside her home and her neighbours will peer down through shutters to see her climb into the back of the ostentatious car with its Nazi pennants.

She steps out of the silver dress and takes a simple black dress from the wardrobe where some of Freddie's clothes still hang. She tries to remember if Freddie began buttoning his shirt from the top or the bottom. She tries to remember him tying his shoelaces. The images she sees of her husband nowadays are washed out and ghostly as if consisting predominantly of reflected light.

"I've spoken to your teacher. He's a very interesting man. I felt a good deal of sympathy for him."

She is sitting in the back of the black car with Captain Erich Heinkel.

"How is he?"

"He has a few bruises and a cut lip. Carità's men roughed him up a bit. At the moment he's still in their custody."

"How has that man Carità risen to such a position of power?"

"Yes, he brings out the snob in me too. His lack of culture. His lack of intellect. He used to be an assistant in an electronics store. He wheedled customers into admitting they listened to Radio London and then reported them to the secret police. That's how he made himself known. Ludicrous, isn't it? I didn't want to tell you before but I'm afraid he will be present at the dinner tonight."

"I wouldn't have come if I had known," she says. Her tone angry. Angry with herself because it is deceitful of her to presume she still has any high horse she might sit astride.

The curfew has been brought forward to eight because of the recent spate of attacks in the city by the communists. The streets are empty and dark. She is glad of the cover of darkness. No one about to see her engaged in civilised conversation with a top ranking Nazi official. The headlights of the car spray ghost light over Piazza della Signoria. She notices a shadowy figure by the Neptune fountain, caught for a moment in the beams. He holds himself as still as a cat, willing himself into invisibility. She can almost hear the thump of his heart in her own breast.

"I wonder what his secret is. I'm almost tempted to arrest him just to find out."

"You enjoy your work?" she asks.

"Sometimes I do. I find people interesting."

The air raid siren begins shrieking as the car leaves the suburbs of Florence and speeds along a winding uphill road flanked by tall pine trees. Three giant fingers of light skate around the sky, interlocking and then drifting apart again. She looks over her shoulder at the beauty of Florence cradled beneath the unearthly light down in the basin.

The car pulls up in a gravel drive outside a large villa up in the hills of Fiesole. The searchlights still create an ethereal dome of light over everything. Everything seems suspended in time as if caught in the flash of a camera. Two fascist guards stand to attention and salute. They are young boys, in new oversized uniforms, with guns. Drivers of the other cars parked outside the villa are standing about smoking.

The staff in white uniforms are obsequious. The very young waiters pale with stagefright. She takes a glass of spumante. Sees Carità. He sees her at the same moment and a current of antagonism passes between them.

A man in a pinstripe suit and black rollneck sweater takes Captain Heinkel's photograph. Then she is asked to move into the frame. She makes excuses but the man insists. *Photographed with Nazis*, she thinks. She exchanges pleasantries with an SS Untersturmführer called Dreisner. His blue eyes more insulated with cold than any winter she has ever known. He asks her what she does.

"I'm an artist," she says. It always costs her an effort to make this statement. As if she is handing over a false identity card.

Erich, she notices, drinks quickly and avidly. He downs three glasses of spumante before she is half way through her first glass. It's the first time she has allowed herself to call him Erich in her thoughts. There is a foreboding of guilt in her mind as if she has uttered a vulgar word in a church.

"Let's have a little bit of fun with Carità," he says.

"I'd rather not."

Once again she recoils from this heavy-footed man with the hooded lizard eyes and flabby jowls. His voice is resonant with volume, an advertisement of his virility and the steadiness of his hand.

"We've already met," she says.

"Yes. I arrested you. I apologise," he says. "We all make mistakes."

"You should commission Isabella to paint your portrait, Mario," says Erich. She has never seen this mischievous side to him. Is it the alcohol? "To immortalise you. To hand you down in all your virile splendour to posterity."

She would paint him as a troll. A Cyclops. A devil's henchman.

"I have a horror of seeing myself," he smiles. "I won't even let anyone take my photograph."

"Scared your soul might choose to migrate to the image, like primitive savages."

"I don't believe in souls, Erich."

"Just as well, eh?"

There are thirty or so people around the table. She is not sitting beside Erich. She is sitting between the imperious German SS officer Erich pointed out as his boss and a bullying little fascist official with numerous insignia and medals on his tunic, like a stamp collection. Carità's mistress sits opposite her. She is an attractive woman. Intelligent eyes, a cultured brow. Isabella wonders what she's doing with such a coarse uneducated brute. There is also a famous Italian comedy actor. A man who does propaganda work for the fascists. She watches him break open an ampoule of morphine. Allow the liquid to seep into the cigarette he holds. The religious devotion with which he performs the act. And the Fascist Party Secretary Alessandro Pavolini sitting next to the head of the Black Militia. She looks in turn at all the faces. Imagines painting each and every one of them. There is one man with a flattened misshapen nose and virtually no intelligence in his eyes. He does not speak. He holds his wine glass as if it is a mug, as if he is about to crush it in his huge hand. Another, this one in the black shirt uniform, with cunning watchdog eyes and comically jug ears. He is both victim and bully. She imagines painting them as a group composition. A Last Supper perhaps. With Erich as Judas. But in this case perhaps a laudable Judas. She sees the painting clearly in her mind's eye. It becomes a slight source of regret to her that she will never paint it. It takes its place in the graveyard of all the other paintings she has composed in imagination but will never paint. She suspects men have a similar graveyard of all the girls they might have kissed but did not. She is about to ask the German SS officer this when a man gets to his feet and knocks a fork against his wine glass.

Later she walks out onto the terrace with Erich. The searchlights are no longer active and a heaving tide of darkness waits beyond the semi-circle of pale light on the terrace. She can hear the plash of a fountain. So distinct it might be inside her.

"Can I ask you a personal question?"

She pulls her green shawl tighter over her shoulders. "As long as you don't expect me to answer it."

"Do you think your husband is still alive?"

"Do you mean would I sense it if he were to die?"

"Yes. That's exactly what I meant. Do you feel a psychic connection to him? I didn't sense that my wife and children were dead at all. It came as a complete shock. Clearly I'm not a man with psychic powers."

"Were you happy, you and your wife?"

"No. Not at all. I loved my children very much. But my wife went a bit crazy. She became an embarrassment to me. Deliberately became an embarrassment to me. One evening when I returned home she was entertaining an old Jew and his wife in our sitting room. They of course were terrified when I appeared in my SS uniform. My wife gave me this wild triumphant look. As if she had finally shown me the fact of who I am. Since her death I often think she was right about me. Why else do you think I'm willing to help you?"

"I remind you of your wife?"

He finds this idea amusing.

"No. I don't think you remind me of my wife at all."

"I don't know. I often feel I'm a bit crazy. When I was young I believed I was too sane for mad people and too mad for sane people."

"Yes, I have felt like that too. Do you know I wanted to be a motion picture actor when I was young?"

"You wanted to be recognised wherever you went?"

"No, it was more than that. I wanted someone else to script my character and actions. And my wish was granted. I got Adolf Hitler. The genie in the bottle."

Isabella says nothing.

"I have had an idea on how we might prevent your teacher from being detailed to a work camp in Germany or Poland. I'm a bit loathe to suggest it though as it might be a bit risky for you."

"Shouldn't I be the judge of that?"

"Very well. The prisoners are always escorted to the train station in large groups. It's official policy that we Germans don't get involved in anything that is likely to make the population see us in a bad light. So it is the Italian Republican guard or the carabinieri that escort the prisoners to the trains. As a result I would not be present. But in all likelihood I will be able to convince one or two of the guards on duty to turn a blind eye. If you were to wait at the station on the appointed day and at an opportune moment pull your teacher out of the line-"

14 - December 1943

OSKAR STANDS on the narrow ledge of the cattle carriage of the speeding train. His body is filmed in sweat. A spinning void sucks at his thoughts, overthrows his mind's familiar parameters, its laws of organisation. His heart begins beating in time to the pulsating iron noise of the train. The noise is violence in his ears. He is staring into what seems a blustering black place of origin.

The tunnel never seems to end. The roar and relentless stifling monotony of it. It is in his ears. On his skin. Trying to shake him off his perch. The train spews out a filth of fumes. He has to take the black smoke into his lungs. He splutters and chokes. He is dizzy and sick with the horror of what is happening. From inside the carriage Francesco is shouting at him but he can't hear what Francesco is saying. He is leaving his daughter behind. Already in his mind he is running back through this tunnel. He is pounding over the gravel. Through the thick darkness.

Then there is a taste of clean air again. The noise diminishes. The crescent moon appears. A halo in all the blackness. Oskar leaps. The slipstream takes hold of him for a split second. Lets him go. He is in mid-air. It's like when a cup slips from your hand and you try to catch it before it falls and smashes. Because he is tense, because he is wired with impatience he falls awkwardly on his left ankle. The pain makes him protest out loud. He rolls down an incline. Cushioned by grass. When he gets to his feet there is a sharp pain in his ankle. He grits his teeth. He casts one look at the back of the train. He ignores the pain in his ankle. He begins to run. Back towards the tunnel. He runs as fast as he can along the tracks. The sharp sliding stones underfoot. Feeling weak, feeling nauseous, because he hasn't eaten all day, because there is too much anxiety in his body. He is back in the tunnel. The darkness effaces even his outline. He is dizzy running in the clotted blackness. He trips and falls. The tunnel amplifies the urgency of his feet on the gravel. He can hear with what difficulty his breath comes. The sense he has of the ancient darkness and chemistry of the rock belittles him. This realm of prehistory. The tunnel makes him feel how old the earth is, how insignificant he and his daughter are.

"Esme," he calls out. Even though he knows he is still too far away for her to hear. His voice frightens him. He doesn't recognise it as his voice. It carries a threat of danger. Like all shouting voices. It echoes up ahead of him. His voice that isn't his voice.

"I'm coming," he calls out. He stumbles. He falls. He picks himself up. Begins running again. Fighting the darkness off. Pushing it aside. As if it is a physical force intent on obstructing him.

Perhaps she's hurt, he thinks.

He stumbles again. The darkness is suffocating. Like a weight on his chest. Pushing the air out of his lungs. He is not alone in the tunnel. There are sounds. Covert rustlings. He is disturbing other creatures. He pictures rats. He pictures bats. He runs. The sharp stones underfoot knocking against the iron rails.

Will the tunnel never end? These walls inside the ancient rock that he can barely see but which seem to graze the skin from his bones. Which seem to want to erase him. And then he sees the crescent moon. Then he breathes in clean air. Smells grass and moist earth. He stops running. He is suddenly frightened of what he will find.

"Esme," he calls out. Not loudly. There is no answer. The silence is vast. And in the comprehensive stillness there seems to be a purpose to things. A design. He thinks he sees a shape on the embankment up ahead. It doesn't move. But it is not her.

He knows now that if he calls out and she doesn't answer something bad has happened.

The crunch of the gravel beneath his ruined shoes. The pain in his ankle. The fear in his blood. Making his wrists ache.

"I thought you had left me here," she says when he finds her.

"There was a tunnel and I couldn't jump until the train came out of it. I'm sorry. Are you hurt?"

"My knee hurts."

"You've grazed it."

"Can we find Napoleon now?"

"Yes. Let's find Napoleon."

Her fingers locked in his. Her palm pressed against his palm. They walk beside the railway tracks. Beneath the moon. It's as if they are the only two people in the world. He and his daughter.

Finally he realises they are free. That there is no more barbed wire. Finally he is able to enjoy the chill cleansed air of the countryside he takes into his lungs.

"Did Elisa jump from the train too?"

"I hope so. And Francesco."

Please can we find the bear, he says to himself. The toy bear whose red waistcoat was knitted by his wife.

He walks with her along the side of the tracks. Peering into the shadows. Before long he finds the bear. He slides down the slope of the embankment. Tells her to slide down too. They make a game of it. He sits her in his lap and they slide down the slope of the embankment three times.

"Now where will we go?"

"Well, Daddy needs a hat," he says.

"Why?"

"Because of the funny streak in the middle of my hair."

At the camp a razor was frequently passed over the middle of every man's head. The shaven line was known as "the road". It means he is instantly recognisable as a prisoner.

He walks with her across frosted fields. She tells him she is thirsty. She tells him she is hungry. She tells him she is cold. She tells him she is tired.

"We'll try to find a house," he says.

"What happens if bad people live in the house?"

"Most of the bad people live in the cities," he says. He wonders if this is true.

When they sit down to rest in a vineyard he tears the yellow star from her oversized cardigan. Tears the number from her floral dress. He digs up clods of the hard earth with his bare hands. Buries the two yellow stars. Buries the two tags with the ugly numbers in black stitching.

The darkness is turning to mist. The moisture in the air soaks into his clothes. The dew seeps up through his shoes. He can see her breath on the air when she speaks.

They cross another field. Follow a dirt road. There is a house in the distance. It sways through the ground mist. It is a farmhouse. Of weathered white stone. Like the house in the fairy story.

"Who lives in that house?"

"I don't know. Yesterday we didn't even know this house existed. Now it's the most important house in the whole world."

"Will they let us sleep there?"

"If they are good people, yes, they will let us sleep there."

"Do you think they are good people?"

"I hope so."

There must be a woman in the house and surely no woman would turn Esme in to the Germans, he thinks.

He decides to wait until someone comes out of the house. So he can see a face.

15 - January 1944

THE WAAF DRIVER pulls up the truck outside V Victor's dispersal. Freddie jumps out the back onto the hard concrete. A taste in his mouth as though he has been chewing an elastic band. The usual pre-op tension.

"Thanks," he says to the driver. She is the pixie girl he surprised in the shower. The girl whose legs he complimented. The girl who pulled him away from Davy and made him jitterbug with her. Poppy.

"I've got something for you," she says, surprising him as he is about to get out his cigarettes.

"Oh?"

She hands him a red stringed pouch through the side window.

"For luck," she says.

He looks at the red bundle in her hand. Reluctant to touch it. Suspicious of its powers. He feels the eyes of his crew on him. The eyes of V Victor's mechanics too.

"What is it?" he asks.

"Quartz. Go on, take it." She smiles at him.

"Is quartz lucky?"

"It's never let me down."

He looks at her. Her knowing blue eyes. Her thin lips with a measure of mischief at the corners of her mouth. Her blonde hair sculpted up into whorls beneath her cap.

Is she a witch?

He takes the red pouch. Not because he wants it, but because it seems churlish and ungrateful not to.

"Be seeing you. When you get back," she says and starts up the truck.

"I'm not climbing aboard Vicky until you throw that thing away," says Woodsy. He puts down his bag and the caged homing pigeon and folds his arms over his chest. "I don't care if it's only the Eyeties we're visiting tonight."

It's ridiculous, he knows it's ridiculous but it is one of the most difficult decisions of his life. Does he take it with him or does he leave it behind? Either way there seems a curse attached.

"What do you think, Reg?"

"She's got very nice legs."

"And that makes this lucky?"

Woodsy is urinating over V Victor's rudder.

"I didn't say that. She's obviously taken a shine to you though."

"You're not helping me out here."

Davy and Spike are standing on the grass with some of the ground crew. He is still embarrassed around Davy. They have barely spoken since Spencer's outburst.

"What do you think, Cyril? Take it or leave it?"

"I had two letters from my girlfriend today. That's all the luck I need."

"And you're wearing your filthy shirt."

"And I'm wearing my filthy shirt."

He weighs the wrapped piece of quartz on his palm.

"Why don't you open it?"

He undoes the bow of the pouch and lets the pink sparkling chunk of rock slip onto his palm.

"Looks harmless enough."

He decides to take it. He puts it in the pocket of his flying jacket. The talisman or the curse. Woodsy kneels down on the grass and presses his palms together. But probably in jest.

They take off soon after dark. The reflection of the moon on the river and the funnel beacons of the aerodrome the only evidence of light down on the shrinking fields and villages of Lincolnshire below. Once again he has Italian banknotes in his pockets. Tonight's target is Turin.

There is a fly in the cockpit. Knocking against the perspex. Reg shakes his head as if to say, that's all we need.

Freddie plugs in his oxygen. Puts on his mask. Tells everyone to do the same. The fly, he knows, will soon pass out.

If it comes round again I'll see Isabella again, he tells himself.

When chalk scrawls of surf are visible 12,000 feet below he and Reg laugh about getting caught trying to skive off PT earlier. They were sent to the gymnasium, ordered into blue shorts and gym shoes and made to throw a medicine ball back and forth and climb up and down wall bars for half an hour.

"I don't think that corporal was very impressed with our levels of fitness."

"No. But he was impressed by Spike. Up and down those bars like a spider on its thread."

Spike clears his throat. The double cough. "I quite enjoy a bit of PT every now and again."

V Victor is flying at 19,000 feet over the French Alps when he notices Reg is asleep. His head in the helmet slumped down towards his shoulder. He wakes up with a start and then falls back asleep. Freddie is wondering whether to wake him when he sees the flickering of a light out of the corner of his eye. The starboard outer engine is wreathed in flame. He nudges Reg awake. Above his mask Reg's eyes show both indignation and bewilderment. He directs Reg's attention towards the wing. The skittish dance of the flames is highlighted in the moonshine reflected off the glaciers and peaks below. Reg snaps into action like a flicked on piece of machinery. He closes the throttle. Stabs the feathering button. Shuts down the fuel cock. The starboard propeller blades become visible in their whirring and then stop. Reg turns on the fire extinguisher.

"So much for the bloody quartz," he says.

Freddie watches the behaviour of the flames anxiously. The flames dwindle. He turns the trimming wheels to balance the drag of the dead engine. Tells Cyril what has happened.

"We'll lose about 10mph of our speed," he says. "And of course the hydraulics of Woodsy's turret are u/s."

Freddie remembers what they were told at briefing. Any trouble over Italy then make for the base at Blida in North Africa. He knows a crew who were forced to spend three weeks in Blida. They said it was a dump. Nothing to do. Dust everywhere. Nothing but spam to eat. Everyone living in tents. He wants to sleep in his own bed. Not in a tent. Once before they have had to turn back to base because of engine trouble before carrying out a mission. The Wingco made them feel like truant schoolboys. A thorough check was performed on the aircraft to make sure they were telling the truth.

"Skipper here. We've got one dead engine. But I say we press on. Even if it means spending a few days in Algeria."

V Victor is sick. He can feel her peevish reluctance to carry on in his own body. She slews away from his grasp. Veering from side to side. She loses her place in the stream. Other bombers glide past her. Trailing wakes of vapour behind that mist the perspex. She slips further and further back in the stream, like the fat kid in a cross country race.

He listens to Davy give Cyril the updated speed of the bombing wind over the intercom. Pictures him behind the curtain at his wireless set. Scribbling down messages in his small neat handwriting. Then he sees another image of him. Toothbrush between his teeth, towel draped over his shoulder.

V Victor has descended to 10,000 feet when she reaches the outskirts of Turin. A bizarre sight meets his eye. The columns of searchlights are not grasping up into the night sky. They are frozen, as if under a spell. Some point directly up at the stars, some towards the snow-clad mountains to the east, some lay almost horizontally over the rooftops. Lighting up the streets of Turin as if for a party. Looking down he can see individual buildings, gardens, statues in squares. If there were people walking about he would be able to see them too. But Turin looks like a city where time has stopped. He feels a disarming intimacy with the city below. That's his beloved Italy down there. One reason he became a pilot was to get through the war without firing a weapon. Not for the first time he wonders if what he's doing isn't much worse. A block of the city is already ablaze. The flames mirrored on the waters of the river Po. Their reflections flecking the snow clad mountains to the west. There is no flak. No guns at all.

"I love the Eyeties," says Reg. "If only the bloody Germans would take a leaf out of their book."

"Nav, give me a new course to base. I'm not flying her over the Alps with one dead engine."

"Will do, skipper."

"Skipper from bomb-aimer. Tracking in nicely."

He listens to the ever meticulous and unflappable Spike say steady a hundred times. He hears Spike say "Steady" in his mind while lying in bed. "Steady. Steady. Steady." The bombs are dropped. The photograph is taken. He tries not to look down at the damage. The white blasts turning red. A new course is set. West of Turin towards the French Riviera and the Spanish border.

Every star in the northern hemisphere is visible. V Victor is alone in the sky, above a tumbling canyon of cloud, when the starboard inner engine begins to play up. Flames flicking over the starboard wing. Reg pumps fuel from the tanks near the fire to those in the port wing. Freddie slips a Benzedrine tablet under his mask into his mouth. Has a problem swallowing the bitter pill because his throat is so dry.

"And then there were two," says Reg. "Have you ever landed on two engines?"

"No. But don't tell anyone," he says into the microphone.

"We have the faith, skipper."

"Better all keep your chutes close by. I'll at least try to get us as near to home as possible."

The cloud bank is at 15,000 feet. V Victor soon drops down below it.

He nurses the engines by reducing speed. They are off every planned chart now. Alone and wounded. Perhaps a solitary bleep on a radar screen somewhere down below or up above. If a night fighter appears there will be little he can do to evade its cannons.

The fly is buzzing around again. Starts bumping against the perspex. Freddie grins.

"Glad you find this funny," says Reg. But he grins too.

"Nav from bomb-aimer. To starboard there's a river with a castle thingy on a hill."

"A chateau," Reg corrects him.

"Okay, bomb-aimer. Bay of Biscay should be about ten minutes away."

V Victor is constantly losing height. Freddie is having to use all his strength to get her to hold course. His leg aching with the strain of holding on left rudder even with full trim applied.

"Start chucking things out?" says Reg.

"Skipper to bomb-aimer. Chuck out all your stuff, Spike."

A blast of chill air enters the cockpit as Spike opens the hatch in the snout.

Davy informs him they have been given the all-clear to land at a base in Cornwall. "St Eval. Cyril's checking his maps now."

V Victor is so low she is almost skimming the waves. She ploughs furrows over the surface of the sea. Her shadow gliding over the grey water like some leviathan beast.

"How are we doing for fuel?"

"I was hoping you wouldn't ask that."

The sun is rising over the fields of southern England. V Victor barely clears the uppermost branches of trees. She rattles houses, scatters cows and sheep in fields. A man out on his bicycle looks up in disbelief. He is so close Freddie can see individual hairs on the top of his head. As V Victor roars over him the man falls off his bicycle.

At the second attempt he bumps down V Victor's wheels onto the unfamiliar runway.

His crew give him a round of applause.

Davy waits for everyone else to leave the aircraft.

They have been in the air for eleven and half hours.

It's moments like this, Freddie thinks, but does not finish the thought.

16 - December 1943

FROM THE HIDING place among the vines Oskar watches the shutters of the house being thrown open. His nose stings with the cold. His hands are numb with the cold.

It's a man who first appears from the house. He wears only a white shirt and a leather waistcoat despite the chill morning air. He carries a bucket. Walks with a slight stoop. As if he has spent his entire life carrying things from one place to another. The man pays no attention to the red sun rising over the fields to his left.

Oskar has no strong feeling about this man. No guiding instinct. He might be trustworthy. He might not be.

He knows there is a big reward for the capture of prisoners of war. He knows the sentence for sheltering escaped prisoners of war is death.

"Good morning," he calls out. He knows he must look like a scarecrow.

The man shows no sign of alarm. He stops in his tracks. On the flagstones of the farmyard. Still holding the bucket.

Oskar walks towards the house. Through the rows of black vines that look like the charred remains of arrested dancers. Holding his daughter's hand. He and the man with the bucket are measuring each other up. In the early morning air with the sun rising above the fields and a cock crowing in the stillness beneath a vast sky.

"Apologies for intruding on your land. My daughter and I are lost. We need to get to Genoa."

"Genoa?"

The man with the bucket's voice is not unkind. He is wondering about the shaved track through the centre of his hair. Oskar can sense this. He is wondering what it signifies.

"It's a long way, I know. But my daughter here is very hungry and thirsty. Perhaps if you could spare us something to eat and drink? Then we'll be on our way."

"You've been out here all night?"

"Yes."

"I'll ask my wife to prepare you something. Come inside and warm yourselves up."

The woman of the house makes them a pancake each. She returns from the larder with a jar. Unscrews the lid and dips a knife inside. Oskar can't remember the last time he ate jam.

"And you jumped out of the train too?" says the woman when they are eating at the big oak table by an open fire.

"Yes. Didn't I, daddy?" She has red jam around her mouth.

"You did. It was exciting, wasn't it?"

"Napoleon jumped first."

It is a relief to be able to tell the truth. Like diving into a pool of clear water. Making a loud splash. He is Oskar, his daughter is Esme. They are Jews from Paris.

"What will you do in Genoa?"

"There is a Jewish organisation there. Funded by Americans. A man in the camp told me about it. I have to meet with the archbishop of Genoa. He is a good man, they said. He will help me contact someone in this organisation."

They spend eight days at the farmhouse. He is given a hat. Some shoes. He is reluctant to throw away his old shoes. Even though both soles have come loose and there are holes in the cheap leather. He thinks of them as his lucky shoes. He is a bit superstitious about throwing them away. He is given some money too. In return he helps out on the farm. He rises at dawn to clean out the cowshed. Esme helps him carry the dried chestnut leaves for the cows to sleep on. He climbs the ladder to the hayloft. Opens the trap door and drops hay down to Esme below. She bundles the hay into the feeding troughs. Then he brings buckets of water to the cows. He grows to love these cows. Their warm bosomy smell. Thinks this might be something he could do for the rest of his life. Even though he knows this isn't true.

The first train they catch is to Venice. He makes Esme look at Venice across the water as the train crosses the long railway bridge. He wants to create a memory of the moment for her. The sight of Venice across the water is a kind of miracle after the barbed wire and the cattle truck. There are a few gondolas on the water and it's these black boats that interest her.

They sit by the Grand Canal. On a wooden landing stage. It sways when the boats pass. Waves lap against the boards. Bringing with them a faint smell of the sea. The yellow ochre palazzo opposite with its green shutters is reflected in the water. The colours are beautiful wavering on the water. Now and again he forgets the danger they are still in. The anguish of hiding. Of being homeless. Of pretending to be someone he is not.

He queues for cigarettes in a tobacconists. Two blackshirt fascists jump the queue. Everyone stands aside passively. No one complains. The young fascists with their insolent swagger of privilege.

"That's why these young boys become fascists. So they don't have to stand in line," someone says when they have gone.

They are climbing the stairs to the station. She skips up them. Making some kind of private game of it. Singing quietly to herself. The church across the water is ringing its bells.

Inside the station Oskar catches the eye of a fascist guard. Often he can't help stealing a glance into these men's eyes. These men strutting about with their holstered revolvers and noses in the air. He quickly averts his eyes. But it is too late. He has aroused the man's suspicion.

"Papers," he says, the fascist guard. He is probably no more than nineteen years old.

"I don't have any. Everything I own was destroyed by the American bombers."

"Where?"

He has his story ready. He prepared it at the farmhouse after listening to the war bulletins on the radio. "Corsica," he says.

"You need to get some new papers then."

"Yes. We're on our way to Genoa. We have relations there."

"You don't have an Italian accent."

"They speak French in Corsica," says his companion. They are always in twos. The companion is a bit older. "Is this your daughter?" says the companion.

"Yes."

"Hello. What's your name?"

She hides her face behind her shoulder.

The older fascist produces a sweet in shiny red foil from his pocket. He hands it to Esme. She accepts it. Doesn't say anything but takes the sweet.

"Come on, Donato. Let's leave this man in peace."

Oskar recalls the kindness of this man more than once while he and Esme are on the train to Genoa.

When she stands up the momentum of the train throws her back down into her wooden seat. He sees she enjoys this game. Enjoys being knocked down by a force more powerful than her ability to withstand it.

In Genoa there are the shells and skeletons of buildings that have been hit in the air raids. Empty window frames revealing blackened interiors. Houses like crushed empty boxes.

The tram clanks and jerks alongside the harbour. There is a scurf of oil on the water, a broken tapestry of rainbow prisms. Abandoned fishing nets drape the sea walls on the quayside. The pastel coloured palazzos with reflections of the water on their walls.

They enter the cathedral. Esme wants to copy the woman who crosses herself with the holy water. He doesn't explain to her that this is not their religion. He lifts her up so she can reach the holy font. She dabs the holy water on her collarbone. As if it is perfume. And then she dabs some holy water on the bear too.

The archbishop is not to be found. He speaks with a priest. He trusts the priest.

"I'm a Jew. My daughter is a Jew. We have been told the archbishop can put us in contact with an organisation that helps our people."

The priest gives him an address.

17 - January 1944

MARINA SITS IN the back of the elegant black car. She is wearing her best dress. Her prettiest underwear. She feels more keenly the proximity of her nakedness beneath her clothes as an illicit pulse, a swirl of meeting currents.

The car speeds past the Baptistery. The Gates of Paradise, formerly hidden behind sandbags, now gone. Removed somewhere safe. Attila always drives too fast. Always has to show off. Whatever he is doing. Sometimes she catches his eye in the rear view mirror. His gold tooth glitters when he grins. The few people out on the streets look at the car. They are curious to see who is inside. She enjoys their curiosity. Reads it as envy. She cannot deny she enjoys feeling part of an elite group. The car splashes up rainwater as it passes these people. As if spitting with disdain.

Marina has been to the theatre. Now Angelo and Attila, in uniform, are taking her to a café. It is a relief to be out of that house. Away from the sick old woman. Signor Becchi dares not say no to Angelo. Signor Becchi is always deferential towards Angelo. It makes her wonder what Angelo does.

Attila accelerates into the large piazza. Slams his foot down on the brake. The car skids to a halt. Spraying up more rainwater. Angelo and Attila jostle for the privilege of sheltering her from the rain under an umbrella. They run across the piazza. To the muted coloured lights of the café.

They bring the smell of the rain with them into the café. Its dance music, its laughter, its clinking of glass, its denial of the hardships of war. The other women look her up and down. Stylish fashionable women with painted mouths. Mouths that hint at a memory of sexual pleasure. The men look her up and down too. The German soldiers. The fascist officials.

She sits down at a table with Angelo. Attila wanders off.

"Who's that Attila is talking to?"

"That's my boss. Mario Carità. Head of the secret police."

"The torturer?"

"That's just communist propaganda. Or idle gossip."

"So what exactly do you do?"

"Paperwork mostly. You wouldn't believe how much paperwork there is."

"I've never seen you with ink on your fingers."

"Try saying that with a German accent. The Gestapo would hire you in a flash. Now how am I going to wriggle out of that question? Let's say I'm a stickler for personal hygiene. I always wash after work."

"Who's that woman with all the pearls and jewels? The one with your boss?"

"That's Milly. His mistress. You don't want to get on the wrong side of her."

"I don't intend to. Do you know anything about the prison camps?"

"They're used to hold prisoners."

"Be serious."

"Why do you want to know about prison camps?"

"A friend of mine is in one. Or he was."

"Where?"

"Near Modena, he said."

"That will be Fossoli. Is this your boyfriend?" He makes his fleshy lips make a sulking shape. A piece of theatre. Making fun of her. Making fun of himself.

"I've already told you I don't have a boyfriend. He was a friend at university."

"So you were fraternising with insurgents? What was his crime?"

"He didn't commit any crime. He's a Jew. That's all."

"Well, the Nazis don't like Jews. We've got the Gestapo upstairs. They're more obsessed with rooting out Jews than tracking down the rebel fighters in the mountains. He'll be transported to a work camp. In Germany or the east. Ha ha. Look at Attila. Showing off again."

Attila is standing on a table. Opening a bottle of champagne with a sabre.

A young man Marina studied with at university comes over. He is in a fascist uniform. She is surprised he is a fascist. He was a good friend of Francesco. They played tennis together, she remembers.

"Good to see you're on the right side," he says to her.

"I'm not on anybody's side. I just want to go back to university and finish my education," she says.

"You and me both," he says.

"Have you heard about Francesco?"

"No. How is he?"

"He was arrested. He's being taken to a work camp."

"Might put some muscle on him. Perhaps when he gets back his serve will be a bit harder to return. I always beat him, you know. Anyway, see you around, Marina."

"See you around, Gianni."

She tells herself Gianni is not a bad person. Just as Angelo is not a bad person. They are still boys. She has to tell herself that Angelo is not a bad person often. Every time she accepts the benefits he offers. She thinks of Francesco. His letter is in her bag. She doesn't enjoy thinking of Francesco. It doesn't make her feel good about herself. She has been unable to warm to his mother. Her fallen circumstances force Francesco's mother to be kind. Force her to be humble. But there is no heart in her kindness, in her humility. She finds herself liking Francesco less every time she is in the company of his mother. She resents it that this woman who judged her not good enough for her son is now sleeping in her bed in her home. Worries about the risk her parents are taking. The penalty for sheltering Jews is enforced labour in a German camp or factory. The notices plastered to the walls. Always beginning, *Achtung!* She knows her parents are sheltering Francesco's mother as a supplication to God. To divine providence. "Look, they are saying to God, we are taking care of this homeless woman. In exchange we ask that someone is taking care of both our sons, wherever they are."

18 - January 1944

THE METALLIC VOICE over the tannoy system seems to prise open a chamber in her own mind. Her thoughts have the same hollow echo. She wills herself to stay calm. Wraps her arms around herself against the cold. A train to Venice is announced. For a moment Isabella is whisked back in memory to arrivals at Venice. She walks out of Santa Lucia station onto the steps and beholds and breathes in the Grand Canal. For the first time in her life she wonders if she will ever see Venice again.

At another platform a goods train prepares to depart. It starts up its grinding iron noise. Begins hissing and whistling out steam. Isabella is wearing a long fur-collared black coat and dark glasses. She is fearful of being recognised. The feeling reminds her of trying to dissolve into invisibility when a teacher at school asked the class a question she didn't know the answer to. Wehrmacht soldiers and fascist police wander around in the midst of all the weary disconsolate people with too much luggage. She looks at the clock yet again. Ten minutes late now.

She keeps mentally rehearsing the act she has to perform. She steps forward. She exchanges a glance with Maestro. She tugs him by the arm out of the line. She engages in idle chatter with him. She walks casually away with him, still chattering. Sometimes when she rehearses it she and Maestro leave the station unapprehended. Sometimes she hears an ugly shout or is confronted by a man with an unholstered weapon.

Another train arrives and with it a huff of steam and a fume of warmer air. Among its carriages is a flat car with an anti-aircraft gun. She looks with distaste at the two German flak gunners. Seeing murder on their set obedient faces.

Then her head spins, her legs sag. Fosco! She loses sight of him in the thicket of faces. Then there he is again. He is walking down the platform towards her. His familiar clumsy clenched gait. A black hat pulled down low over his eyes. He disappears in the crowd and then returns to view. She turns her profile to him. She covers her face with her gloved hand. Covertly she watches him stop to speak to the variety actor she met at the dinner party. The actor is soon recognised by a woman and he performs a charade of a tap dance for her. The woman smiles and other people stop to watch, smiling too. Fosco appears restless. She would like to slap him. For the first time today she isn't nervous. She is angry.

She lights a cigarette. When she looks up Fosco has vanished. She looks around for a sign of him. His disappearance seems an almost supernatural act.

She tells herself she will leave if there's no sign of the prisoner detail by three-thirty. But three-thirty arrives and she doesn't leave. She begins to feel still more conspicuous.

She has laid out a pair of Freddie's English pyjamas on the camp bed in Freddie's office for Maestro. Freddie's smell no longer on them. It is no longer on the vest of his she used to take to bed with her and inhale in the dark in the hope of keeping him alive. She will also give Maestro Freddie's toothbrush. And perhaps some of his clothes. She imagines Freddie laughing at the thought of Maestro wearing his clothes. A sure sign the world has gone crazy. She has bought some pecorino cheese and sun-dried tomatoes for a starter and will cook a rabbit stew for the main meal. She will open the bottle of Frescobaldi wine Erich brought her. She tries to make later feasible by picturing all the things she will do when Maestro is a guest in her home.

It is gone four o'clock when the first of the prisoners appear. She scans the line of faces. Some of the faces are bruised and cut. One or two have bandaged eyes. She sees Maestro towards the back of the line. Behind a woman carrying a suitcase and holding a child by the hand. She is shocked at the sight of him in unwashed clothes, unshaven with a scraggy beard. His usually pristine bald head has sprouted wisps of grey hair at the sides, like tangles of fluff in a neglected house. He has a dazed look, like someone wondering how long he has been asleep. There are bored looking guards at intervals on either side of the line of prisoners. They accompany the line of prisoners slowly towards her. Towards the platform where the cattle train waits and the blackshirt militia stand around smoking and laughing with boyish bravado.

You can do this, she says to herself. But she does not believe it. Her heart is thumping with reluctance.

19 - January 1944

A MAN IN BLACK robes walks with him and Esme across the cloisters. The grass in the quad has been recently cut. It gives off a good familiar smell. Oskar pictures the Jardin des Tuileries on a Sunday afternoon in springtime. The man in the black robes shows them to a small cell with a wooden stove in the corner. Here there is a smell of ants. This smells brings back memories of childhood. Of killing ants. The acid smell of dead ants. Almost a taste in your mouth. An irritation in your throat. He looks around for the ants he can smell. He sees a line of them close to a crack in the wooden door frame.

In the refractory they are given soup. There is a smell of onions, damp plaster, candle wax, old wood. There is a fresco of The Last Supper. Ugly Judas. Slyly fondling his purse of coins.

He paces himself to the gentler rhythms of the monks. As if there is suddenly more time. As if there is all eternity. The monks don't talk. She asks him why they don't talk and why they wear skirts. She speaks in a whisper. She is beginning to learn the rules of places without being told. She fidgets on the wooden bench. Her feet don't reach the ground. She watches him. Copies him. Wipes her mouth with the starched serviette like he does.

Afterwards they meet Francesco in an echoing corridor. He hugs them both.

"You made it! Thank heavens for that. That damned tunnel."

"We stayed with a very kind couple."

"Us too. We stumbled upon kind people as well. There were eight of us sleeping in a barn."

"How many jumped from the train? Do you know?"

"At least fifteen. There are eight of us here." He drops his voice. "Elisa didn't make it. She is dead. I didn't see what happened to her. They say she fell badly. Hit her head on a piece of concrete."

They both look at his daughter. She is trailing her hand over the wall. Abstracted in a world of her own.

"Your sister?"

"She's here. I did everything in my power to get my father to jump too. But he wouldn't. Said he was too old for such heroics. I keep thinking of him. In that damn train. Why wouldn't he jump?"

"It's not your fault," Oskar says. He lays his hand on Francesco's arm.

"My sister and I are both working for the American Jewish organisation now. The one I told you about in the camp. I'm to be their representative in Florence. The man who used to do the job has disappeared with lots of their money. The money arrives in Genoa from Switzerland. Don't ask me how. It will be my task to see to it that every Jew in Florence gets fake identity papers, a ration book and a monthly allowance. They give every one of our people 300 lire a month. Not much I know. Certainly not enough to buy anything on the black market. But it's something. They will give it to you. I will give it to you," he laughs. "And false documents. I go tomorrow to the police station to buy fifty blank ID cards and some rubber stamps. We're paying a huge sum of money for them. To a corrupt official. I'm going to learn how to make forged documents. I'm going to fight these Nazis every way I can. You and Esme must come to Florence with me. The padre priori at San Marco will help us to find a home. There are many good people in the Catholic Church. This I have learned in Genoa. They are hiding our people wherever they can. But you must be even more cautious than before. There are roundups almost every day now. Trucks arrive. Italian police. They force all able-bodied men not in uniform into them. These men are sent off to work camps and factories in Germany. Very few Italian soldiers have reported for duty. They refuse to fight for the Nazis. Many have fled to the countryside and are in hiding. They're forming into bands. The fascists call them bandits. They call themselves partisans. And our short hair makes us look like soldiers on the run."

"When are you going to Florence?"

"Perhaps tomorrow."

"You must be looking forward to seeing Marina."

"You remember her name."

"I could hardly forget it. You talked about her all the time at the camp."

"I am. I am looking forward to seeing her. I want you to meet her. Will you come to Florence with us? It's probably safer than here. Too many bombs are falling on Genoa. They won't bomb Florence. It is too beautiful to bomb."

He imagines Isabella's face when he turns up at her door.

"I always intended to return to Florence. I felt safe there."

There are German soldiers everywhere inside the station at Genoa. It is hard for Oskar to conceal the contempt he feels for what they represent. He talks constantly to Esme so he doesn't have to look at them. So they won't see his hatred of them. He doesn't like this hatred. He doesn't recognise it as an element of the person he used to be. It is like a germ he worries he might pass on to his daughter.

On the platform, while the train whistles, while the train pours out black smoke, he talks with Francesco.

Francesco says, "Hopefully this will be the last time you travel without documents. Let's keep our fingers crossed. I won't sit with you on the train. I have all these blank identity cards in my briefcase. If I am searched I am done for. When we arrive in Florence follow me out of the station. We'll go to San Marco. I think we're going to get through this war. I have met a lot of good people. I feel much better about everything. No harm must come to Esme. She is now my favourite person in the world."

"Except for Marina."

"Except for Marina."

20 - January 1944

MAESTRO IS ten feet away. Shuffling towards the deportation train in his filthy stained clothes with an absent glaze on his bruised face. She knows now she will never forgive herself if she doesn't act. He frowns at her when she catches his eye. Much as he often did while teaching her. He seems puzzled, almost alarmed by her presence at the station. Or perhaps it is the fear he reads on her face that unsettles him. Isabella looks across at the nearest guard. She wants some sign from him that he is expecting her to perform the act she is now nerving herself to perform. Nothing. He looks bored. A million miles away. Then the air raid siren starts up. It introduces a heightened mood of anxiety into the station. Sparks up a general agitation. Someone pushes into her from behind and then she is knocked by someone else. It won't be difficult to take hold of Maestro and merge in with the crowd. But there are two guards who cannot fail to see the act she still doubts she will be able to perform. She hasn't seen SS Hauptsturmführer Erich Heinkel for a week. But she has to trust him.

Maestro is still staring at her with a puzzled expression. She realises she has never seen him look so exposed before. He steps forward within reach. She takes hold of his wrist and tugs. He resists. Like a little boy in a sulk. She has time to glance back at the two guards. They are both pretending not to see her.

"Come on," she hisses.

He relents. She pulls him by the arm and pushes through the crowd towards the exit. She waits for the menacing shout of an angry man, her entire body is primed to hear the menacing shout of an angry man, but it does not arrive.

Maestro appears in the kitchen, aflame from the hot bath she ran him. She thinks back to when she was at the station and could find within herself no belief that this moment would ever arrive.

"I never thought I would find myself wearing someone else's clothes," he says.

"Freddie's clothes. They suit you." She thinks the bruising to his face, the cut lip and the fresh nick above his ear where he has cut himself while shaving, suit him too. They disarm him of some polished outer casing he has always had, give him a vulnerability, inspiring a tactile form of affection she has never felt towards him before.

"I've been thinking about what you said."

He had stubbornly refused to believe Fosco was responsible for his arrest. Became angry with her for even suggesting the idea. Shouting at her as they crossed the river by Ponte Santa Trinita. As if she had uttered a blasphemy.

He sits down at the kitchen table. At the place that was always Freddie's. He tucks a serviette inside the collar of Freddie's shirt. She puts the bottle of olive oil on the table that Captain Heinkel procured for her. "Did you know the English wouldn't dream of putting olive oil on food? They use it for ear infections. Freddie told me."

"Yes, I've heard their cuisine hasn't evolved since the Middle Ages."

She serves up the pecorino cheese and sun dried tomatoes and slices of toasted bread.

"I suppose I've always been a bit frightened of Fosco," he says. "Physically frightened of him, I mean. I'm a bit of a weakling. Easily intimidated by the threat of physical violence. Fosco was my bodyguard as well as my secretary. When that barbarian Carità started punching me and yelling abuse it was like something I always knew was going to happen the moment Fosco was no longer there to protect me."

"But Fosco made it happen."

"So you say. It's hard to believe. I know he's always hated you. But I thought he respected me. After all I've done for him. Does he really hate me so much? What have I ever done to incur this hatred?"

"You ruled with an iron fist," she says. It is perhaps the most audacious thing she has ever said to him.

He surprises her by smiling. "Yes, I did rule with an iron fist. You may not know this but there are very few people in the world still trying to paint like I do. Still trying to paint as I trained you to paint. Which means a great tradition is about to die out. Perhaps in many ways I am the custodian of a sacred chalice. Because I am passing on one of the world's most important traditions. What would have happened if I had allowed self-indulgence? Like you with the ultramarine blue on your palette. You might accuse me of being a tyrant, you might think me petty and mean spirited..."

"Were I to paint your face now I'd need ultramarine on my palette."

"The bruises? Do women always have to have the last word?"

"Perhaps we do. I hope so because then this war will end."

"What's happening in the war?"

"The British are bogged down outside Naples. The RAF is still bombing German cities. Berlin now."

"Good. I can't abide the dull-witted arrogance of these Germans. Who do they think they are? There were women and children they were going to load on that freight train. The best day of my life was when my father died; the second best day of my life will be when someone puts a noose around Hitler's neck."

She smiles, unsure if this is one of his witticisms or a confidence he is sharing with her.

21 - January 1944

FRANCESCO IS admitted to the house where he has been told Marina now lives and works. He is unprepared for the two fascists sitting with her in the drawing room. Marina stiffens when she sees him. Her mouth becomes smaller.

He has imagined telling her all about his adventures. This is what he did while walking to this house. Talked to her in his head. But because of the presence of the two fascists he can't even ask about his mother. His grip tightens on his briefcase. Inside are the blank ID cards. Are ten passport photographs of Jews in hiding, including Oskar and his daughter.

"This is Angelo," Marina says.

Angelo performs the fascist salute. With a undercurrent of irony. Of self-mockery. As if this business of wearing a uniform, carrying a firearm is a lark.

"And this is Attila."

Attila too, in his grey-green uniform with black leather accessories, performs the fascist salute. With a gold-toothed grin.

"How did you find me?" she says.

She is more beautiful than he remembers. He dislikes her beauty. As if it is another effect. Like a uniform. His experience in the prison camp seems to have exorcised all guilt for stealing and losing her diary. He looks at her with a clear conscience.

"I spoke with Isabella. There was no one in at your house."

"My mother is working now. She got a job at the paper mill in via Arnolfo."

"Your brothers?"

"Neither has come home still. No news of Marco in Russia. Leo is digging trenches in the south."

"You two haven't seen each other for a while?" says the fascist called Angelo. He is good-looking. About twenty-three.

Springy dark hair. Smooth tanned skin. A full sensual mouth. His uniform suits him.

"No. I've been away from Florence."

"Oh? Where?"

"In Genoa."

"Genoa. What's happening in Genoa?"

"It's been badly bombed."

"Poor Genoa," he says. "So what's your story, Francesco?"

"Francesco and I were at university together," Marina says.

"You intellectuals," says the fascist called Angelo. He makes an ironic gesture with his manicured hands. He lights a cigarette. "What do you do now, Francesco?"

"I keep my head down," he says.

"But you've seen some action? Russia? Greece? Albania?"

"No. I haven't seen any action."

"Oh?"

"I suffer from epilepsy," he says. He surprises himself with this lie. He has no idea from what corner of his archives it suggested itself.

He and the fascist called Angelo look each other in the eye.

"That must be terrible."

"It isn't much fun."

The fascist called Angelo turns to Marina. "By the way, you remember that friend of yours you asked me about? The Jew in the camp. What's his name?"

Marina's face shows some distress. "Why?"

"I could help find out what's happened to him."

"Vincenzo," she says.

"Vincenzo what?"

"Sangalli."

"Sangalli. Okay. I'll make some enquiries. Remind me, Attila to make some enquiries. You were never tempted to join the Fascist Party then, Francesco?"

"Says who?"

"I assumed..."

"Do you have to be a damn fascist all the time?" says Marina.

Francesco sees the power she has over the boy Angelo. The hurt she can cause him with criticism.

"Anyway, I just stopped by to say hello. I should be going now."

He looks closely at her. Looks for regret or some kind of protest in her that he is leaving.

"Come and see me again soon," she says.

When he kisses her on the cheek he is more conscious than ever of the breach between their bodies.

22 - January 1944

THE GIRL SITTING on his knees is called Jill. Or Joan. Freddie can't remember. She has short bleached blonde hair and her tie is crooked. He suspects she is what *Tit-Bits* magazine would call a Good-Time Girl. She spills another splash of cider over his battledress trousers every time she wriggles into a more comfortable position.

"You need fattening up," she says. "You're all skin and sharp bone."

"All skin and sharp bone," he chants, making a melody of the five words that he bashes out on the piano.

Jill or Joan asked him if she could blow his whistle and he said no but said she could sit on his knee while he played the piano.

"What are you going to play?"

"Schubert's piano trio in E major,"

"Sounds German to me. You're not a spy, are you?"

He plays the opening chords of the piano trio again. Teasing them out with a bit more feeling this time. Revolted a bit by the saccharin clamour of her scent.

"Is your name Jill or Joan?"

He feels her stiffen on his knee. Then relax again.

"Mary," she says. "And for that I'm going to call you Bert."

"Righty-ho. I shall enjoy being Bert for the night."

Furniture in the mess has been piled up into a tottering tower that almost reaches the ceiling. Half a dozen men have daubed Hitler moustaches on their faces with soot and are performing the fey salute of the German Führer every two minutes.

"Come on Freddie, play something wizard old chap. Enough of this high-minded stuff."

"His name is Bert. Not Freddie."

"All right, Bert. Play something we can sing along to."

He does as he's told. Begins the singing himself.

"I vow to thee, my country, all earthly things above.

Entire and whole and perfect, the service of my love..."

Gradually everyone stops what they're doing. Turns to face the baby grand piano and begins to sing. The entire mess surrenders itself to the singing of the song.

Even before his father died it surprised him how much he likes these moments when they all become one voice.

When the singing is finished he watches Davy remove his boots and socks. Roll up his trousers. His white legs as soft-skinned and shapely as a girl's. Then he looks around the room to see if anyone is watching him watch Davy.

Davy clambers up the mountain of chairs. Shoved up from below by several men whose caps and uniforms are askew. Davy perches on the summit of the wobbling scaffolding. An equipment officer holds the bucket of soot mixed with beer. Davy splashes both bare feet in the black muck. He lays on his back and lifts his feet. An upside down cyclist. Presses his black feet to the ceiling. The succession of black footprints is now half way across the ceiling.

"Your turn, Freddie," says Davy, from up on high. He jumps down. Lands on the pads of his toes and rolls back onto his heels in a crouching position and springs back up to his full height all in one lithe brushstroke.

Freddie begins his climb. His head is spinning a bit and he loses his footing half way up the teetering menagerie of chairs and furniture but manages to cling on.

"Don't tell me our pilot doesn't have a head for heights," shouts Cyril.

He settles himself on the top of the leaning tower. Removes his boots and socks to cheers. Dunks his feet in the bucket of black gruel. It slurps between his toes like river mud and the sensation has something of his childhood in it, like being lifted into the air by his father. He positions himself on his back and does the upside down bicycle walk on the ceiling.

"Raise your glasses. Here's to the dead already and here's to the next to die," someone says.

Outside, under the moon, Freddie lights a cigarette. His trousers are still rolled up just below the knee, his feet still naked and daubed in black muck but he is too drunk to feel the cold. He is half way through his cigarette when Davy joins him outside.

"It's not right what we're doing, is it?" Davy says.

"All this tomfoolery?"

"The bombing. Bombing cities I mean."

"They started it."

"What's the matter with the German people? Can't they think straight? Hitler's a bloody lunatic. Anyone can see that. Why can't they see it?"

"Beats me. Hell hath no fury like a nation scorned? They're still in a sulk about losing the last war."

"They're going to lose this one too. That's pretty damn obvious. They're just dragging out the inevitable now. Bloody pig headed bastards," he says, laughing.

He lights a cigarette for Davy. Cupping his hand around the straggling flame. It is Davy's job to decipher and transmit information into code. Sexual language is like that, Freddie thinks. Everything coded. Everything stripped down to elementary dots and dashes.

"Did I ever tell you I left school at fourteen?" says Davy.

He has told him. He remembers all his conversations with Davy. "You'd never guess," he says.

"It doesn't bother me. Well, it does a bit. The fact of not having had a decent education. But I like it here because there aren't so many class barriers. I don't feel looked down on. I suppose it's because we're all already dead so we're all on an equal footing. You see, I've never met people like you before."

"What kind of person am I?"

"Cultured. You play the piano, you read Tolstoy, you can speak three languages. You know all about painting."

"If you had lived my life you'd know those things too. My only significant accomplishment is that I can fly a plane. The one thing I can do that my father couldn't."

"I'm sorry about your father. I wanted to say so before."

"Thanks. Wonder how V Victor's getting on."

"I've been worrying about her all night."

A rookie crew have been given V Victor for tonight's sortie on Berlin because their assigned Lancaster failed to start. Rickie is navigating her.

"Awful how superstitious we've all become, isn't it? Scratch off a thin coating of acquired civilisation and there it still is, the primitive reverence for voodoo."

"Let's hope Rickie doesn't get lost again."

"It wasn't his fault we got a bit lost. Poor Spencer though, eh? He can't look me in the eye now. Someone must have told him he called me a fairy while he was drifting in and out of consciousness." Freddie has steeled himself to bring this out into the open. There is relief now he has done it, like removing a strand of hair caught in the mouth.

"I think we should cut off Spencer's oxygen during every homeward trip. Just to see what he comes out with next."

"He's an oddball, isn't he? I like him though. Reg chose him at crewing up because he said he looked like he saw everything through a magnifying glass. And Reg was right. He doesn't miss a thing."

"He hates losing. Cards, darts, billiards, drafts, chess, cricket…"

"Don't forget Monopoly. That's probably what makes him a good gunner. I've just remembered I left my photograph of my wife on the instrument panel of V Victor."

"You must miss your wife?"

"Yes, I do. What do you miss?"

Davy finishes off the beer in his tin tankard. "Looking forward to things. That feeling you have sometimes when you wake up and you're excited because today or tomorrow is the day. Here I always wake up with a feeling of dread."

He wants to rest his hand on Davy's shoulder. Feed some reassurance into his blood. Instead he makes a star shape of his right hand. "It's not all bad."

"No. Not at all. Like the sight of the Alps the other night. So near it felt like you could reach out and gather up some snow. I tried to describe it in a letter to my sister but words failed me."

Every operation yields up some new visual marvel. A gift of seeing the world anew. It might be the nose of the plane suddenly piercing swaddling cloud into a vast gallery of newly painted stars. It might be the ghost of a sunrise reflected up onto the cumulus below. Often it is the bomb site itself with its breathtaking pyrotechnic displays. Sometimes he feels that a mischievous god is constantly taunting him with visual representations of orgasm. And sometimes he feels it is just him, seeing orgasms everywhere.

He can't sleep. He puts on his Irvin jacket over his pyjamas and tiptoes past the sleeping Reg. Outside the three converging searchlights create a ghostly dome over the aerodrome. The blue taxiway lights, the red obstruction lights and the flarepath appear no less spectral through the early morning ground mist. He begins to feel like a ghost himself. Come back to reclaim a memory that is the lost part of a puzzle he has to solve. He walks across a lawn. The dew dampening the hems of his pyjama trousers.

He wanders over to the operations room when the sky begins to drone with the aircraft returning from Berlin. Nancy, Rickie's new girlfriend, is at the board. Chalking in the safe arrivals. Twenty planes from the base took part in tonight's operation. Rickie's, he sees, due back at 5.27 am. He greets Nancy with a casual smile. Careful not to allude in any way to the foreboding she must inwardly be fighting off. Her ears surely straining for the engine sound of another incoming bomber. She looks like she is fighting back an urge to shed tears. But she always looks like that. The telephone rings. She answers. Then chalks in the time, 5.38, by the name of Rogers. Rogers is not the pilot of V Victor. That leaves two more planes unaccounted for. One of which is V Victor.

23 - February 1944

"ESME?"

"I'm not coming out."

Isabella pauses as something in her body holds itself erect, then arches towards the voice of Oskar's little girl, like a flower tilting under the weight of its hoard of pollen. Esme has locked herself in the bathroom.

"Your dad will be back soon. I promise."

It's almost curfew and he should have been back an hour ago, she thinks.

"I'll come out when he comes home."

"I'm not that scary, am I?"

She is hurt though that she inspires no affection or confidence in this little girl. Esme's mistrust of her is like something she is forced to wear, a harsh fabric prickling her skin. "I'm going to sit down on the floor and we're going to have a chat. Is that okay?"

"Okay."

"I want you to come closer. You sit down on the floor too. By the door."

"Okay."

"How are you going to eat if you don't come out?"

"Not hungry."

"You will be. And I bet Napoleon's hungry."

"He isn't."

"I'm just going next door to get something."

"What?"

"Some photographs. I'm going to show you some photographs."

"Are you trying to trick me? I'm not coming out."

"I'll slip them under the door."

"Okay."

She returns to the bathroom door with the folder of photographs in her hand. She hasn't looked at these photographs for years. She is a bit frightened of them, excited by them too. She wonders how remote they will make her feel from the moments they have arrested.

She sits down outside the door, pushing her skirt between her raised knees. She looks down at the twenty-years-old Isabella sitting on the steps of the church of Santo Spirito and feels intimidated by her younger self. They are strangers to each other. There is a tug of mutual antagonism, of fearful resistance as they try to connect. The younger Isabella has no knowledge of the older Isabella but the older Isabella is made aware of all the interim damage done by the sight of the younger Isabella.

She slips the photograph under the crack at the foot of the door.

"That's your dad and my husband and me."

"Where's your husband now?"

"He flies airplanes."

"Is he one of the bad people?"

"No. He's one of the good people."

Isabella pushes the next photo under the door – Freddie and Oskar squinting into the sun on the bridge of Santa Trinita.

"There's your dad again. He studied at the same school as me."

"School?"

"We went to school together. To learn how to paint. If you come out I'll teach you how to paint. You could paint Napoleon. I'm sure he'd like that."

She has found an old sable brush and a large clean sheet of paper. She lets Esme squeeze out the colours from their tubes onto a plate. She sets Napoleon up into pose.

When Oskar returns his daughter has paint on her hands, on her clothes and on her face. He laughs. His infectious baritone laugh.

"Look at my painting, dad."

"It's brilliant. No wonder Napoleon's got a big smile on his face."

"And I did it all on my own."

"You can paint me next."

"Okay," she says, blasé now.

"Where's Maestro?"

"He's sleeping at my studio tonight."

"He's exhausting you, isn't he?"

"He is a bit."

"It's a bit absurd that we still have to call him Maestro."

"I tried calling him Guido once and he shot me a fierce disapproving look as if I had called him a fool."

"It's like a uniform he wears that he won't take off, isn't it? Uniforms conceal weakness but it's often our weaknesses that make us endearing. I've learned that from my daughter. In fact one thing the war has taught me is that it's probably our flaws rather than our qualities that plot out the maps of our lives."

She looks across at Esme who is kneeling on the floor, engrossed in her painting again.

Oskar has picked up the photographs she was showing to Esme.

"I had forgotten how fond I am of Freddie," he says. "Look at his face. It is one of my favourite faces. When those airplanes were crowding the sky earlier I couldn't help wondering if Freddie was in one of them."

"If he's still alive. I don't feel he's dead but then I'm such an unnatural woman."

Often of late she has accused herself of being a hard woman. As if she will not suffer her soil to be raw and tender, will not submit to the vulnerability of the new green shoot. She feels she is watching herself when she begins to cry. Then the tears push her down into her body, make her its prisoner. Oskar kneels down at her feet. Takes hold of both her hands.

"He isn't dead. And you're not an unnatural woman. Whatever that means. You're a fabulous woman to be around. Look how good you were with Esme. You create an atmosphere of intimacy around you. That's a real gift. I remember telling you that on the bridge of Santa Trinita. We were standing by the statue of Winter."

She wipes her eyes with the back of her hand. "Actually we were standing by the statue of Spring."

"No," he grins. "Definitely the statue of Winter. I have a clear image of it in my head. We were waiting for Freddie who had gone to the British Consulate for some reason."

"Exactly. And the statue of Spring is on the same side of the river as the British Consulate."

"No it isn't."

"Yes it is."

"How much do you want to bet?"

"You don't have any money. And even if you did I wouldn't take it from you."

"If I'm wrong I'll pose nude for you. For free."

"You are wrong."

"If I'm right you paint a portrait of Esme and give it to me. As a gift."

"Okay."

"Tomorrow morning we take a walk to Ponte Santa Trinita."

24 - January 1943

"BAD NEWS?" says Reg, spreading marmalade on his toast.

Freddie, still wearing his pyjamas underneath his Irvin jacket, has just finished reading a letter from the father of his best friend at OTU.

"Another friend of mine's got the chop. Over Schweinfurt. I went to his wedding three weeks ago. I think I knew then he wasn't going to make it."

"Odd how you can tell, isn't it? I often know in the locker room who won't be coming back. Look at that young sprog over there. The one writing a letter. He won't be coming back. That's why no one is talking to him."

Freddie looks over at the nameless young boy in his brand new peaked cap. Sitting alone with a pen in his hand but evidently no inspiration.

"If it's ever me, don't tell me, don't even drop me a hint."

"Only once did you worry me," says Reg. "That night we couldn't get off the ground and then Spike knocked himself out."

"I think he saved our lives by doing that."

Freddie has also received a statement from his bank. Though he tells himself he no longer expects to hear from Isabella a letter from her is always the first thing he looks for in the rack. The disappointment when it's not there never diminishes.

A crackling voice over the tannoy public address system tells the armourers to report to the bomb dump.

"Bugger," says Reg. "That's my plans for tonight scuppered."

"What were your plans?"

"Spike asked me if I wanted to see Abbot and Costello in *Pardon my Sarong.*"

"What did you say?"

"That I'd rather go to Berlin."

"Spike's girlfriend arrives the day after tomorrow. For the weekend."

"He needn't worry about me. Dumpy thing as I recall."

Freddie remembers Spike's girlfriend. A plump tidy young woman in a worn plaid skirt and flat walking shoes. "She was sweet though," he says. "She took me aside and shyly asked me to take care of Spike. I didn't tell her I feel about six years old around Spike."

The aircraft assigned to them tonight, now that V Victor is no more, is L Love.

On the way to the dispersal point to carry out the test flight in L Love he sees the pixie girl Poppy from the bench in the back of the lorry. She is pinning up a pair of knickers on a makeshift washing line among the trees where other bits of underwear hang near the WAAF ablutions hut. She turns around as if she can sense him looking at her. Waves the pair of navy blue passion killers as these underclothes are known at him.

"She likes you," says Reg. He is wearing sunglasses and a red and white polka dot scarf. "If I were you I'd ask her for the next rumba. It's a sign. L Love is already casting her spell."

At dispersal the ground crew and armourers are clambering over L Love. The tanker is in position and a fitter climbs onto the wings to place the fuel nozzles in the tanks.

"How much fuel you putting in?"

"Two thousand gallons, sir."

"Sod it. Bloody Berlin again."

Freddie watches Noel Barton at the next dispersal point throw a ball for his black sheepdog. The dog flinging up spray from the grass as it chases after the ball. Noel once took the dog to Germany with him. The dog barely stopped shaking for a week afterwards. Everyone jokes about the dog lacking moral fibre and calls it LMF now and likes it all the more for showing so nakedly how terrifying what they go through is. Freddie promises himself he will get a dog if he survives the war.

Spencer surprises everyone by producing a camera.

"For posterity?" says Woodsy.

"We should have done this with poor Vicky."

They all line up in front of L Love. Freddie with his hands in his pockets next to Reg and Davy. Then Spencer wants another shot with the groundcrew in it as well. Billy and Fats and Dim and Geordie and Tusk.

It's about time we invited them all out for dinner again, Freddie thinks.

He doesn't wonder if Isabella will ever see the photographs though there is something sad, almost elegiac about this business of standing in front of a camera. He is still thinking about the pixie girl. About Poppy.

He bumps into Poppy later. After listening to the wireless in the mess ante room - hungry for news of Italy, after sausages, cabbage and mash in the mess, two hours before the briefing for tonight's operation. He does not admit he was looking for her. He told Reg he simply felt like a bicycle ride. Except rather than cycle past the picket line and out into the country lanes, he cycled past the WAAF living quarters. She is standing by the makeshift washing line among the trees, as if the past three hours haven't happened.

"I knew I'd see you today," she says and then rests her tongue on her upper lip and stares at him with a smile that makes her blue eyes shine. "I had a dream you climbed in through my window. Connie, my friend, says a woman will always love a man who climbs in through her window, even though she can't help marrying a man who carries the shopping in through her front door."

"Is Connie the one who undresses behind a towel?"

"No. That's Joan. Why don't you help me bring in my washing? I think it's going to rain."

He looks at the array of brassieres, knickers, stockings and slips dangling from the piece of string tied between two trees. On the far side of the field the tractors are pulling strings of carts loaded with tonight's bombs.

"They're not mine," she says when he reaches up for a pair of pale blue silk knickers.

"We're only taking your stuff in? Is that charitable?"

"I'll get jealous if I see you holding someone else's knickers."

He grins. She has a knack of making him grin. A grin with a warm encompassing glow behind it.

"What about this?" he says, pointing to a thick padded pink cotton bra.

"Not my favourite but yes, it's mine."

"What's your favourite?"

"Those lace camiknickers and that white cotton camisole."

He unpegs these two items and then the others she indicates until he is holding with both hands the pile of her faintly damp underclothes. She smiles at the sight of him. Then leads him into the hut. He looks at her legs and her hips inside the tight skirt and the pins in her blonde hair under her pleated cap.

"Just plonk them down on the bed," she says.

"Aye aye skipper."

"Why are you married?" she says. She reaches out and touches his open shirt collar. For a moment the warmth of her fingers makes contact with his neck. Then she quickly withdraws her hand and there is a faint blush on her cheeks.

"Because I am, I suppose."

"Where is she, your wife?"

"Italy."

"What's she doing there?"

"She's Italian."

"I don't mind if you don't mind," she says and laughs at her own outlandishness.

"Suppose you had a husband in Italy?"

"I'm not sure I like Italian men. They have too high an opinion of themselves. Have you still got my quartz?"

He nods.

"I told you it would bring you luck. Since I gave that to you five of the crews I've driven to dispersal haven't come back. Five out of twelve."

He doesn't tell her his crew have forbidden him to take her quartz on board ever again.

"You don't seem like a married man."

"Why's that?"

"I don't know. Do you love your wife."

"Very much."

"Does she love you?"

"I hope so."

"But there's something missing?"

"I didn't say that."

"No. I did. I can't help speaking my thoughts aloud. My father always tells me off for it."

"What do you think is missing?"

"One of my friends, I'm not telling you who so don't ask, thinks you swing the other way."

"What way would that be?"

"You know. She thinks you like your wireless operator. She said it was obvious at that fancy dress party."

"My rear gunner thinks that too."

"You wouldn't be like that with me."

He joins in with her laughter.

"If you're not on ops Saturday night we could have dinner in Cambridge and get a hotel. I'll pay. My family are rich."

"Are you always this forward?"

"Of course not. I'll die of shame the minute you leave but why waste time with idle talk when there's a war on?"

"Idle talk costs lives."

"I know. But we've already seen each other without our clothes on anyway. You told me I have nice legs."

"You do have nice legs."

"Since that night I'm always terrified you won't come back. I lie awake in my bed counting the returning kites every time there's an op. And of course there's nearly always at least one missing. And I always have a horrible jumpy feeling the next morning when all the girls are talking about the crews that didn't make it back. And then I'm always so happy when it isn't you. I know that's awful. It's your fault I've got bags under my eyes."

"Sorry."

"That's all right. As long as you come to Cambridge with me."

"On Saturday?"

"On Saturday."

"Today's Wednesday. You're asking me to take an awful lot for granted."

"Another pilot I know told me he considered himself dead the moment he joined the squadron. That every new day is a bonus."

He's a bit jealous of this other pilot. "Which pilot?"

"Oh, he really is dead now. We don't have to, you know. Not if you don't want. We can just cuddle. You must need a cuddle. I know I do. But not with anyone else. It has to be with you."

He's got the silly grin on his face again, the glow in his loins.

"I have to go. I'm late for briefing."

"I'll be listening out for you when I'm in bed tonight."

"I'm flying L Love tonight."

He has an erection when he straddles his bicycle. Still has it when he is waved down by a Naval officer he does not know. A sour stiff-backed man with a pencil moustache.

"I'm looking for Flying Officer Moorcroft. Any idea where I might find him?"

"Tim? Tim went missing last night."

The awful strain on the man's face as he tries to keep his composure puts an end to Freddie's erection.

"Tim is my kid brother," he says.

"Four men were seen baling out of the kite before it crashed."

"Where? Where did it crash?"

"It was shot down over the target."

"Germany?"

"Yes. Berlin."

Twice in one day Freddie has been singled out to absorb a death.

Should I be worried about tonight?

When he passes the security guard and enters the briefing hut everyone twists round in their seats to look at him and LMF barks. He walks through the beam of the projector and his shadow is imprinted on tonight's weather chart for a moment. Then he takes his seat next to Reg.

"Glad you could make it, Hartson," says the CO.

Everyone laughs. LMF barks.

Tonight's target is not Berlin. It is Stuttgart. The proposed route takes them over France, better than flying over Holland and Germany and the heavy anti-aircraft defences and fighters of the bloody Kammhuber Line.

The fresh smell of the grass and soil is always a poignant sting before start up time. Because he knows it might be the last time he ever smells it. He can sense the dew on the land, feeding roots. It is a feeling on his skin, like rubbing a handful of earth between his palms.

L Love is approaching the French coast when the oxygen supply packs up. Searchlights in the distance pale silvery ghost fingers in the black sky. Freddie has to drop her down to 8000ft. He and Reg both swivel inside their harnesses to raise an eyebrow to each other. He explains the situation over the intercom.

"We could plough on seven thousand feet below our operational height or we could return to base. Cyril, what do you think?"

He pictures Poppy in bed, listening as L Love circles the airfield.

"Plough on. If chaps start looking at me as though I might have lost my nerve I'm worried I really might lose my nerve."

He can see the green orbs of the route marker flares up ahead. Looking like a giant Christmas tree suspended just above the clouds.

"Davy?"

"Plough on, sir."

"Spike?"

"You're wasting your breath asking Spike."

"Everyone agree? Woodsy and Spencer?"

"Press on, skip."

25 - February 1944

OSKAR STANDS on the model stand. Isabella looks at his naked long-limbed body through the gauze of smoky light. She is painting him life-size. She stands twelve paces from him. Scrutinising him. Willing the force of her scrutiny to channel a living pulse into her painting.

She lays on a swirl of flesh coloured pigment with her palette knife. Sculpts it into a semblance of the form of this strange thing, the male penis. She is embarrassed when she looks at Oskar's genitals. She steals covert glances. Always looking up at his face after to see if he senses where her eyes have been. She has never painted a circumcised penis before. It is not a sleeping thing as she is used to drawing and painting it. It has been awoken and looks a little vulnerable and a little angry. Like the neck and head of a tortoise poking out of its shell. The image makes her smile to herself.

"What's that secretive smile all about?"

"Just thinking."

"Good to see you breaking all Maestro's rules."

"I love painting with a palette knife. But I don't break all Maestro's rules." She smears a curlicue of flesh coloured paint on the canvas with her forefinger.

"Where is he today anyway?"

"He's gone to spy on Fosco again. He sits in the English cemetery where he can keep the studio under surveillance. He told me last night that he wants to procure himself a gun. So I asked him if he would be capable of shooting Fosco. And he let out this devilish laugh."

"Let's hope he doesn't get himself a gun then."

"Okay, I'm done for the day."

Oskar arches his back. Extends his arms. Fingertips straining to touch something just out of reach. His ribcage and musculature becoming a map on his skin. He places his palms at the base of his spine. Thrusts out his pelvis. She marvels at the ease with which he inhabits his naked body.

"You must miss dancing," she says. She wipes the paint from one of her brushes on the sleeve of her billowing smock. Studies her picture while she talks. Scrapes off some paint with a palette knife.

"I miss it very much. I worry I'll be too old when this war ends. I will be thirty-one in February."

He walks over to her side. They stand side by side looking at the image of his naked body.

"Put your clothes back on," she laughs.

He goes off to collect his daughter who is looked after by a woman with children of her own further down the street while he poses. She gives him her keys.

When the buzzer sounds she presumes he has forgotten she gave him the key. She opens the door with a light careless skip. Haupsturmführer Erich Heinkel stands there in his dove grey raincoat. His thin lips pressed together. He clicks his heels. She is not sure if this is an ironic pantomime or a sign he is displeased with her.

"May I come in?"

Her gaze fastens on the death's head symbol on his imperious cap. "Of course. I'm sorry I wasn't here for our last appointment. My mother needed me again."

"I was worried."

Oskar will see the car outside, surely there's a car outside, and will walk away, she hopes.

Captain Heinkel takes off his cap. Holds it against his thigh. She closes the door behind him. The windows are draped with black cloth and it suddenly becomes much darker as the sun disappears behind clouds.

"You might not be a Jew but he is." There is a sour twist to his smile. She feels uncomfortable with him in the dark. She switches on the light but nothing happens.

"No electricity again," she says.

"You know I could have you arrested for employing a Jew?" He walks up close to the painting on the easel. Peers closely at the textured layers of paint. Adopting the mien and posture of a connoisseur. "So you have replaced me with him?"

Is his vanity hurt?

"I can't imagine you would want to pose without your uniform on," she says.

"No. That would make me feel very awkward."

She hears the footsteps on the stairs. The excited chatter of Oskar's little girl. The key in the lock.

She wants to cry out her innocence at the injustice of the furious frightened look Oskar gives her when he sees the SS officer.

"Ah, here he is. The model. And this is your daughter?"

Oskar nods. There is, she sees, a struggle in him to hide the distaste he feels for his interrogator.

"So she too is a Jew." The stiffness with which he bows down to address Esme might be comical in other circumstances. "Hello. And what's your name?"

Esme looks up at her father. Her lips sealed.

"She doesn't talk? And you don't talk either. Say something. I want to hear your voice."

"This is my voice."

"German. I thought so. A German Jew. Where do you come from?"

"Hanover."

He turns to Isabella. "I want to talk to you in private. Come with me, please."

He remains silent as he leads her down the stairs. She is wearing her painting smock over a skirt and blouse.

Outside the black car is parked further down the street.

"I will forget I saw two Jews in your studio but you are putting me in a very difficult situation."

She looks askance at him. She is aware people across the street are watching.

"Oskar is my friend," she says.

"Not your lover?" It costs him an effort to say this.

"No," she says with a note of indignation.

"I would very much like for us to finish this painting of me. Before I am transferred."

"Where are you going?"

"I don't know yet. There is talk of Florence being made an open city. In which case most of the German military will be made to leave. How about I come on Friday at one o'clock?"

"Fine," she says.

26 - February 1944

THE SORTIE to Stuttgart turned out to be charmed after the oxygen packed up. Not once was L Love attacked by a fighter, not once held in the grip of a searchlight and not even a spattering of flak drummed on her skin. Only the sprog letter writer's crew failed to return. Proving Reg right.

Spike's girlfriend is somewhere in the darkness behind the wire perimeter fence. Waving him off. She has come to stay for three days but Spike hasn't seen her yet. Won't see her until tomorrow. When Freddie will see Poppy. Spike still has his familiar stilted way of walking, hands clenched behind his back. Still hums the opening bars of the same song intermittently throughout the day. But he looks a bit more tense tonight than usual.

Freddie counts the Italian banknotes he has been given as part of the escape kit. They are like a scent. The gift secreted in them to rustle up pictures from the past.

"First time I've seen Spike look nervous," he says.

Reg stands emptying his pockets on the desk. Separating his personal effects into the two numbered pouches – the things he wants forwarding on to his family in the event he doesn't return from tonight's operation he puts in the red pouch and the things he doesn't want them to see go in the green pouch. "It's because he can't wait to get back. That's the trouble with women. They give you something to look forward to."

"Well I wouldn't know about that," he says.

"You're not still smarting over Spencer's outburst?"

"Do you think he had a private giggle when he found out we'd be flying Q Queenie tonight?"

"I hope so. I did."

"So did I. Actually I've got something to look forward to as well."

"Oh?"

"Bumped into Poppy again."

"I knew you were going to look for her the other day, you sly fox."

"She wants to get a hotel in Cambridge tomorrow night. She'll pay. Because her family are rich."

"You jammy bugger."

Tonight Freddie is piloting Q Queenie to Milan. One of seventy or so heavy bombers in the stream flying in tight formation over occupied France, across the Rhone and within sight of the festive lights of Switzerland and the moonlit majesty of Mont Blanc. The stabbing scissor dance of the searchlights on the coast can't find her through the low level broken cloud. He alters course, height and speed every thirty seconds. The prescribed method for outfoxing the men below. The flak bursts in impotent angry puffs.

He calls Davy and Cyril into the cockpit once again when the wonder of the Alps, aglow with moonlight, is a vivid looming presence below. Mont Blanc seems to tower above them in the near distance. They all exchange glances that make him realise how fond of each other they are.

"Nav to skipper. Turn on to 124°."

The world below through the layer of very thin cloud sheet looks like a map, something ordered and pristine that can easily be made sense of. He looks down at an abbey on a hillside. A valley with a stream running through it. Tiny hilltop towns clustered around a church and surrounded by tiered olive groves. Italy, he thinks.

Half an hour from Milan the Boozer warning light on the instrument panel flashes on.

"Skipper here. We're being picked up by enemy radar. Eyes peeled everyone. Especially you, Spencer."

Spencer mumbles a reply into his microphone that is impossible to decipher.

"W/Op here. I've got a blimp on Fishpond. Eight o'clock."

Freddie's eyes burn into the starry darkness. Darting about like those of a hunted animal. He peers out through the granules of ice and moonscape reflections on the perspex, the thick vapour trails of the Lancasters in front. Then a star explodes. That's what it feels like. A shattering crescendo of light floods the cockpit. He lowers his seat. Screwing up his eyes against the glare. A string of flares have been parachuted down from above.

"Fighter. Low astern. Stand by to corkscrew port."

"Okay, Spike."

He sees the fighter out of the corner of his eye. A black speck with a pulse. Small like a mosquito against a white wall but quickly growing nightmarishly larger. Not sure if it is a 109, a 110 or a 98. He rolls the aircraft sharply to the left. Dipping her nose. She begins screaming. The log book and pencil fall from Reg's lap. Freddie waits for her to go through ten degrees before pulling to the right and up. Both hands on the column. Then sends her into a dive ten degrees to the right. The ground, lit up by the flares, tilts up towards Q Queenie, seems for a moment upside down as though every law of physics has been turned on its head. He is beginning to sweat. Remembers Isabella once asking him, don't you ever sweat? He can wear the same pair of socks for a week without them exuding anything but the faintest whiff of feet. He looks down for the photograph of Isabella on the control panel. Sees only the quivering needle of the altimeter.

"Another fighter. Three o'clock high. Eight hundred yards."

"Why are the bastards picking on us?" says Reg.

It's true. For some reason the two fighters have singled out Q Queenie as their prey from the seventy or so heavy bombers in the stream. As if they have picked up a scent of blood on Queenie's skin. He shoves the aircraft down into another diving twist. Sliding sidewards in his seat until the straps of his harness burn into his shoulders. The echoing roar of the four Merlin engines screaming out a more indignant protest. Tracer flickers above the canopy. He can taste blood in his mouth. He wipes his nose. There is blood on his glove. His nose is bleeding. Then there is a terrific crack. The noise startles him. As if someone is bashing the aircraft with a piece of lead piping.

"Woodsy, shoot that bastard down, will you."

"Here comes the other one again. Eight o'clock."

"Have we been hit? Feels like we've been hit in here."

This time he knows for a fact that cannon shells have hit Q Queenie. Splashes of bright light flicker before his eyes. She is lifted up into the air and the tip of the port wing tilts down towards the ground. A shower of perspex and fragments of shell casings zip through the cockpit. A bullet rips through the instrument panel. Tearing a hole in the oxygen regulator. A blast of chill air and white smoke rushes into the cockpit. Smoky red lights drilling up through the holes in the fuselage. The extinguisher is shaken loose and Reg's charts fill the cockpit with fluttering paper.

There is little grace or ease now in the momentum of the aircraft. It is bucking and making a guttural noise that gnaws up through his bones. She plunges 3,000 feet in a matter of seconds.

"Starboard fuel tank on fire."

The slipstream is peeling molten strips from the starboard wing. Freddie jabs the feathering button. Waits for the propeller to stop and then hits the fire extinguisher button. The flames continue to stream along the fuselage. Smoke smelling of petrol enters the cockpit and is sucked out by the slipstream. Reg is pumping fuel out of the hit engine into the port wing tanks. The wing is still burning and beginning to flap. Freddie thinks of all the bombs beneath his seat. All those incendiary clusters. He looks over at Reg. Reg shakes his head and reaches back for the parachutes.

"Bale out. Everyone bale out. Can you all hear? Spencer?"

No answer.

"Woodsy?"

"W/Op here. Cyril's been hit. I'm pretty sure he's dead. No pulse. He's not wearing his parachute harness. What shall I do?"

"Clip your parachute on and get out, Davy. Go to the rear hatch and see what's happened to Woodsy and Spencer. I'll hold her steady as long as I can. And remember, don't jump. Crouch down and topple out. Otherwise you'll hit the tailwing."

"Okay."

Reg clips his parachute on for him. Then clips his own on. Freddie can't really believe this is happening. That he won't be going home to eggs and bacon in the mess. That he is about to jump out into the sky. Can't believe he won't now be going to Cambridge with Poppy.

Spike down below in the nose turret is trying to kick open the front hatch.

The Ju88 is coming at them again. Head on. Freddie can make out the pilot's head but not see his face.

Out of the corner of his eye he sees Spike finally manage to get the front escape hatch open. He thinks of Spike's girlfriend waiting for him in the B&B. He remembers it's pay-day tomorrow. He pictures Poppy in her bed counting off the returning Lancasters. He watches Spike jump.

Freddie slips down as low as possible in his seat. He waits for the cannon shells to rip the cockpit to shreds. To gouge holes in his flesh. But the fighter pilot veers away without firing his guns. He waggles his aircraft's wings at Q Queenie.

"A compassionate Nazi?"

"He's done his job. Why rub it in? Your turn. Bugger off," he says to Reg.

"Why isn't Spike's chute opening?"

"Reg! Get the fuck out of here."

"W/Op to skipper. Rear gunner and mid gunner won't jump. Fear."

"Bloody push them out, Davy."

The only parachute training any of them have had is to practice forward rolls on a gym mat.

Reg crawls down the opening at his feet into the nose turret. He gives Freddie the thumbs up before he disappears out into the night sky. Freddie is alone now in the front of the plane. He has always sought out solitude. Moments when self speaks to self in intimate seclusion. Even as a little boy he liked best of all shutting himself away from the world in an empty room. It feels appropriate that he is now alone. For a moment he considers yielding to a perverse urge to go down with Q Queenie. Then he sees the leering face of death in the black smoke and flame trailing from the starboard wing and is suddenly very frightened.

Holding the stick until the last possible moment he slides down in his seat. Queenie sways backwards when he lets go as though someone cut one of the strings that holds her in the air. Her snout begins almost lazily lifting as if she is sniffing at something higher up. He crouches down by the opening. Feels the blustering icy slipstream whip at his bended knees and the side of his face. His muscles tighten as though squeezed in an angry fist. He attempts to roll out backwards but is blown back in by the slipstream. The G-force is so powerful he can't lift his arms. They are pinned to his side as if pinned there by a strait jacket. No matter how much effort he makes he cannot move. The roaring torrent of icy air in his face makes it difficult for him to breathe. Flames are melting away the metal spars of the wing as if they are wax. Revealing the flimsy framework beneath. Then Q Queenie's starboard wing falls off and she begins hurtling towards the ground at tremendous speed. He is thrown forward into the nose of the aircraft. Pinned against the Perspex blister. Held there as if in a clamp. The howling in his ears almost too much to bear. Still he cannot move.

I'm going to die.

The next thing he knows he is falling through a swirling white mist. A gusting freezing void. His body screams out in panic. There is a clotted and bursting sensation in his head as air rushes into his ears, floods his lungs. He flails and wavers like a puppet with a mad master. It's as if someone is trying to tug off his sheepskin boots. He digs his toes into the soles to keep them on. He is falling head over heels through clouds. He gropes frantically for his parachute but it's not there.

Did I leave it on the kite?

No I remember Reg clipped it on.

Then, as he does another somersault in the sky, he sees the pack hanging above his head. Still attached to the harness. He pulls it down and immediately tugs at the D-ring. Then a sudden jerk, an arresting shudder that pummels through his shoulders, burns his groin. He hears the agitated flutter of silk above his head and is cradled by a new sensation. Of silence and detachment.

Part Three

1 - February 1944

GIUSEPPE the gardener hands Isabella an envelope.

"Two carabinieri were looking for you earlier. They asked me to give you this."

The flimsy chit of paper with its official stamp informs her that she is required to be at a morgue in Modena the day after tomorrow. To identify the corpse of a man believed to be her husband.

Later she looks at the most recent photograph she has of Freddie. A photograph he sent her from Canada. How much it had alienated him from her, this photograph. First of all the shock of discovering he was in Canada. Never had they mentioned Canada to each other. Canada became to her like another woman. She felt only hostility towards this country that had never been part of the map they shared. As if by going there he had broken with some vow they shared. Then there was the photo itself. She hardly recognised him in his flying gear. It seemed like a fancy dress costume. For a party she wasn't invited to. She didn't recognise the man in the picture as her husband.

I don't believe you're dead.

She looks around. Fearing she said the words aloud. Feeling a bit like a mad woman. Someone who can no longer distinguish between sound and silence. Someone who has lost all sense of boundaries. But there is no one within hearing range. Only a scrawny black pigeon huddled inside its feathers on the river wall. A dishevelled thing with a wash of resignation.

There is a sundance of light on the water flowing towards the three arches of Ponte Santa Trinita. Detail on the distant wooded slopes beneath Fiesole is more defined today than usual. Her eye goes to a crenulated tower sheltered in the midst of cypresses and umbrella pines on the summit of a more distant hill. A cold wind gusts up her hair as she crosses the bridge. Steals inside her clothes. As if the natural world wants to share a more tactile intimacy with her this morning.

She doesn't feel on her skin that he is dead. Aren't women supposed to have instincts about these things? But she does not have much confidence in her instincts. Her biography is that of an unnatural woman. Childless. Living alone. Untouchable.

She passes a road sweeper who is quietly singing to himself. Two German soldiers in khaki who are sharing a joke. Everything she hears, except the echo her own heels make on the uneven paving stones, has a muffled quality as if she has her palms pressed to her ears. She can't believe Freddie is now unable to make any noise in the world.

She catches the train to Modena. There are no free seats. She leans on the handrail of the greasy windows in the corridor. The train moves at a snail's pace. Rattling and creaking through her joints. Black smoke and cinders come in through the open window that no one can close. Settling in her hair and on her clothes. Especially bad when the train passes through the innumerable tunnels between Florence and Bologna. At Bologna even more passengers board the train. People forced to sit on their luggage in the corridors. The train moves forward then comes to an abrupt halt. There is a crunching jolt as of thick ice cracking underfoot. The journey to Modena takes almost five hours.

Before entering the morgue she wonders if her clothes are inappropriate. The light lilac dress beneath her coat with its hint of transparency. Then realises with a stab of conscience that it's her state of mind that is inappropriate. She is about to see the corpse of her husband. She screws shut her eyes on a detailed vision of Freddie's lifeless body laid out on a slab of stone. A tiny charred hole in his cheek. In the exact spot where she had cut him with the fork.

She is led down some stone steps. A chill heavy reluctance in all her limbs. A panicky refusal in her mind to accept this descent. She feels as though her body has just been dragged from a freezing lake. She is cold and numb but deep within her body is the imminence of a violent convulsion. Of forces she will not be able to control.

When the man pulls out one of the metal trays to reveal the dead man's face she looks down at Freddie's features for a split second. Her throat tightening. Her legs sagging. Then she almost breaks out into laughter. She quickly converts the noise in her throat into a gasp of shock.

"Is this man your husband?"

"Yes," she says. She turns away.

The man pushes the metal tray with the unknown corpse back into the wall.

She isn't sure why she tells this lie. The man doesn't look anything like Freddie. He looks like a rogue. Even in all the thrift of death she can tell he was a rogue. Perhaps she might have lied even if the haunting grey face had been Freddie's. Because it is part of an unspoken pact between them not to make bald statements about each other to strangers.

She has to stay the night in Modena because of the curfew. On her way back to the hotel she stops by the river. Leans on the parapet smoking a cigarette. She notices a piece of driftwood being tugged by the tide towards the bend in the river. Follows its buffeted progress downriver. Feeling its fate is somehow bound up in her own. As if it is carrying the secret of what has happened to her husband with it.

2 - February 1944

FREDDIE IS sleeping among the trees with little idea where he is on any map when the man with the knife wakes him up. A man with dirt on his face, dirt under his nails, dressed in scarecrow clothes. He still has the hum of the aircraft's engines in his ears. Often when waking he initially believes himself to be strapped into his seat on a Lancaster and there is a moment of alarm as if he has fallen asleep at the controls. But today there are trees and a scarecrow man. The scarecrow man talks a foreign language. Or a language he has invented himself. A hissing gibberish. Spittle between his chapped lips. The scarecrow man menaces him with the knife, an old rusted kitchen knife meant for cutting bread or chopping garlic and onions. He motions to Freddie to remove his jacket. A frantic almost epileptic current twitching through his body. Freddie removes his Irvin jacket. In its pockets is his escape kit. The banknotes, the silk scarf with its map of Lombardy printed on it, the pen with the hidden compass, the shaving kit, the rubber water bottle. Everything he owns except the bar of chocolate in his trouser pocket. The scarecrow man leans forward. His breath a sewage stink. He claws at Freddie's white sweater. Rips off his two dog tags as if they are precious stones. Looks at them and stuffs them in his pocket. Then he points at his boots. Freddie takes off his boots. The scarecrow man snatches them up and walks away, muttering to himself.

Freddie goes back to sleep.

When he wakes he has to remind himself why he's not wearing boots. The ground is covered in crisping leaves curled like ancient scrolls. He stands up. Arching his back, stretching up his arms.

He has been unable to find the others. He spends the morning wandering about the countryside. Drinking from streams. Eating his chocolate ration. Fry's Crème. Doing his waste behind the trunks of trees. He has to keep moving to keep his feet warm. When the sun heats up a bit he sits in a vineyard inscribing characters in the dirt. It becomes a note he writes to his wife. There's a part of him, deep down beneath all the physical discomfort he is suffering, that is relieved he is not on his way to Cambridge with the pixie girl. With Poppy.

He finds a house he likes the look of. A yellow house with a red tiled roof. Hens pecking at the flagstones in the courtyard. A battered car parked at the end of the dirt track, beneath an awning of vines. He reminds himself the reward for information about prisoners of war is more than these country people earn in a month. Nevertheless he knocks on the door. A short irascible man with volatile eyebrows appears. And behind him a woman with thick masculine features and grey hair tied at the nape of her neck into a wiry bun. He feels the couple's hostility towards his uniform. It's highly unlikely they recognise it. He could easily pretend to be a German.

"You couldn't care less if I'm English or German, could you? You just want to be left in peace," he says in English. Making his voice louder and a bit more guttural than usual. To confuse the man. To make him think he might be German. Then he grunts and walks away. Because he has decided not to trust this man. He has walked about fifty yards when a voice calls out to him.

This man has weak eyes behind black-framed glasses. His coat is tailored. "Are you from the plane that crashed last night? I'm a doctor," this man says in English. "And I'm not a fascist. I can take you to safe place."

He looks at the doctor's mouth. Feels there is no deceit in its line. He holds out his hand. Introduces himself.

"You won't be safe in one place for long. You will have to be ferried around from one haven to another. And you need to get out of that uniform."

"I need to get to Florence," he says.

"You're a long way from Florence."

The doctor drives him to a remote house nestled in the folds of olive groves. The doctor is nervous. The doctor tells him the woman he will stay with tonight is a widow. That her husband was killed by the British in North Africa.

Freddie feels embarrassed to look her in the eye.

The woman fills a bath for him. There is no plumbing in the house. She heats the water on the kitchen range. She does everything in silence. He wonders if she has lost the power of speech.

She is a wiry blanched creature with no beauty. Her expression reminds him of a crumpled letter – there is both sadness and anger in it. She wears a dress with a faded flower pattern. A dress that has been scrubbed at too many times. It is easy to picture her hands in soapy dirty water. He offers to carry the pan of scalding water but she refuses. She holds the pan with a cloth in either hand. Cloths with charred black marks burnt into the fabric. When the tub is full she makes no gesture of leaving the room. He waits for her to leave but she does not leave. So he strips off his clothes in front of her. Stands before her naked. When he climbs into the tub she walks over to him, kneels down on the stone floor and begins washing him with her hands. She doesn't return his awkward smile.

She scrubs at the tidemark of dirt around his neck. Pokes soapy fingers in his ears. He isn't sure why he allows her to do this. Except that she seems to have some need to wash him and it would be churlish not to comply.

"I'm sorry about your husband," he says.

There is no change in the rhythm of her hand's ministrations. She soaps his hairless chest. The water has already clouded with his dissolving dirt. His thighs float like flotsam under the murky surface. He watches her hand, engaged in what visually looks like an act of love. Wonders if she is thinking of her husband. Wonders if it is her husband's wounds she imagines she is applying her woman's balm to.

"I've never been able to make love to my wife," he says, now in English. "It's my shameful secret. The prison I can't escape from."

She lathers up the soap and slides a hand under his armpit. The soap has a coarse smell. Not like the throaty whisper of Isabella's unguents and lotions.

"Of course you're right. We gain very little by talking. Perhaps that's why you don't talk? All the half-truths and downright fibs that come out."

Her fingers slide down into his lap. Beneath the surface of the water. Crawl into his pubic hair. Her wedding ring rubbing against his soft flesh. She lifts up his manhood at the base with her soapy fingers.

"With my wife I can't keep it up, with you I can't keep it down," he says. In English.

She slides the ring her fingers have made up and down along his erection. As if it is a chore she has no qualms about performing, like milking a cow or scrubbing grease from a pan. He stops fighting. He leans back with his arms resting on the sides of the tub. Looks down at his seed floating in globs and slicks on the surface of the water.

A few motions of a woman's hand, bereft of any intimate intent, and he has betrayed his wife.

"The absurdity of it," he says, as bewildered and ashamed as a schoolboy.

The woman brings him some clothes and shoes. Her dead husband's clothes, no doubt. He shows her how much slack there is in the trousers around the waist. She tries to smile for the first time. She brings him a black tie and he uses this as a belt to keep the trousers up.

He is not sorry to leave the woman. The doctor arrives in his car the following morning and drives him to a monastery. There are lots of orphaned children from Genoa staying here with the Franciscan monks.

At least I never did a bomb run over Genoa, he thinks, sitting at the table in the refractory, holding his spoon over a bowl of bread soup.

The next day he organises a game for the children. He steals a bible from the chapel, rips out some of its pages and hands each child a page.

"And for you, Psalms 22 and 23," he says handing the shyest child, a dark haired boy of about eight, his page. "Okay, now go out into the countryside, not too far, find something you like, wrap it up in your bible page and bury it. Bury it well, as though it is your secret that the world mustn't know about. Then draw a map of where it's buried because tomorrow you'll have to find it." He hands them each a piece of paper and a pencil. "It might be a stone or a flower or a fallen fruit. Anything you see that attracts you. And when you draw your map you need to draw landmarks and you need to measure out distances. And no cheating."

None of the children find their buried treasure the next day.

3 - February 1944

ISABELLA IS looking at the notice in the grocery store window. Working out what rations she is entitled to today. She is sharing her rations with Maestro and almost always gives him the lion's share of what she prepares in the kitchen. He either accepts this as his right or doesn't notice.

She returns to the studio with two tins of sardines, two grams of rice, a woebegone onion, a slab of leathery bread and some canned tomatoes. She almost bursts into tears when Signor Marcusi, the baker, doesn't say anything when she asks him how he is. Because she still has the reputation of fraternising with Nazis.

She is thinking of Freddie, puzzling over the mystery of the corpse, when she sees the dog again. It is the second time she has seen the dog. On the stretch of grass by the side of the old city wall. The appeal in its sad eyes moves her as it did the first time she saw it. A shaggy grey mongrel with a wet nose and a sad whippet tail. She remembers how fond Freddie was of his whippet. She leans down and beckons to it. It ambles up to her and allows itself to be stroked. "I know how you feel," she tells it.

She walks away from it with difficulty. A drag around her thighs like mud sucking at her shoes. Then is pleased to see the animal is following her.

She opens the front door to the building of her studio. The dog sits three feet away. Pretending not to look at her.

"Come on then," she says and the dog springs up, tail wagging, and follows her up the stairs. "Thank heavens you're a girl. I think I've had enough of men. We'll have to find a name for you."

A note has been slipped under the door of her studio. *Maestro has somehow got hold of a gun and he's gone to find Fosco.*

She curses Maestro. The dog has curled up on Freddie's tweed coat which Maestro must have thrown on the floor. She tells herself she will not get involved. The setting sun is beginning to filter gold onto the facades of the riverside palaces opposite. It will be dark soon. "If he thinks I'm going all the way to the English cemetery with curfew so close he's got another think coming," she tells the dog.

It is dark by the time she arrives on her bicycle at the English cemetery. Maestro is hiding behind a cypress tree near the grave of Elizabeth Barrett Browning.

"I'm glad you've come," he says.

"Oskar said you've got a gun." She realises before the words are out that Maestro would never have the audacity to risk being caught by fascist guards with a gun.

"Of course I don't have a gun. Where would I get a gun? I wish I did have a gun though. But I tricked Oskar. I knew you would come if you thought I had a gun. Now listen, I want you to confront Fosco. Tell him I want the keys to the studio. And I have a spare set of house keys in the studio. Tell him I want them back as well."

"Why me? Why don't you confront him?"

"Because you're a woman. He won't hit a woman. He does have a moral code of sorts."

It is pointless to argue. He has trained her too well to always obey his commands. Her heart is beating wildly in her throat as she walks down the gravel path of the cemetery. Fosco, the thought of his evasive yet probing eyes interrogating her, so terrifies her now that it is as if she has endowed him with supernatural properties. She is about to pass through the iron gate of the cemetery when an ambulance pulls up outside Maestro's building. She draws back into the shadow of the cypress trees. In the spray of the headlights she recognises Scarface. A phantom imprint of the slap he gave her makes her cheek burn. She watches him draw a revolver from his holster and fire off several shots into the air. Fosco, a silhouette, appears at the front door and she hears his laugh before he climbs into the front seat of the ambulance.

Maestro is crouched down behind Elizabeth Barrett Browning's tomb.

"He's gone," she says.

"Who was shooting?"

"A man did that instead of ringing the bell."

"And Fosco's gone?"

"Yes."

"You're sure you saw him leave?"

"Yes."

There is a moment's silence, then he whispers, "Now's our chance. We'll break in."

"Break in?"

"All my paintings. I'll go see Gianni who owns the hardwear store. He might lend us a ladder."

"It's only ten minutes until curfew."

"Let's be quick then."

Maestro treats Gianni like a servant. The little man with bushy eyebrows and a drooping moustache soon appears struggling with a ladder. He follows Maestro's instructions. Propping it up against the wall beneath the bathroom window of Maestro's studio.

"Thank you, Gianni. You can go now."

The look of anxious bewilderment with which he met Maestro's request has still not left Gianni's face. He complies and leaves.

"Up you go then," Maestro says to her.

She takes off her coat and hands it to him. Halfway up the ladder she is caught in the headlights of a passing car. She freezes. Half expecting to be yelled at in German.

"What are you waiting for?" Maestro hisses at her from down below.

There is a tremor in her legs as she steps up onto the top rung of the ladder.

"It's all right. I'm holding you steady," he whispers up.

She pushes the bathroom window open. Then there is a moment when her legs are dangling in mid-air. A shoe comes loose and falls to the ground. She is half in and half out of the small bathroom window. Her stomach pressed to the sill. She pushes herself forward and falls in a heap on the hard marble stone. It stinks of urine.

She enters Maestro's personal studio and then goes through to the second studio where she and Freddie used to draw and paint as students. Many of Maestro's paintings are lying face up on the floor. She has to carefully step round them. All Maestro's paintings have been replaced on the wall by Fosco's. There is a strong smell of turpentine.

When she lets Maestro in he is excited. Climbs the stairs with the urgency of a man half his age. Then he is dumbfounded. All his paintings now have Fosco's signature in the bottom right corner. He stares at them in disbelief.

"At least he hasn't destroyed them," she says. "But what on earth is he up to?"

"Isn't that obvious? He's going to claim all my paintings are his own work. He wants to go down in history as me."

She finds this hard to believe. "What about the war? Who is going to care who painted what pictures with this war going on?"

"What do you mean, what about the war? What's that got to do with anything? He's thinking about after the war. That's why he wanted me gone. He's going to steal the heritage I've left to mankind."

Maestro picks up a discarded blue satin shirt that she recognises as Fosco's. He douses it in turpentine. Down on his knees he begins erasing Fosco's signature on one after another of the pictures. He performs the act with a spiteful relish.

Isabella walks into the small room that was always forbidden to students. There is a bed on an elevated wooden platform with a ladder.

"Someone's been sleeping here," she calls out. She picks up an almost empty bottle of grappa. She is tempted to drink down what remains. There is an opened rucksack on the floor. Inside she finds several morphine ampoules. And an identity card. It has Fosco's photograph but is made out to someone called Ruggiero Perotto. She takes it with her into the next room. Shows it to Maestro.

"What do you think he's up to?"

"I want to get all my paintings out of here," he says. He isn't listening to her. "We can take them to Gianni."

"It's curfew," she says. "We can't leave here now."

There are stories of men being beaten to death, women raped and then shot during curfew when the streets are patrolled by the new breed of young fascist louts who get drunk and fire off their arms at will.

"Tomorrow morning then."

"Fosco might come back before then."

Maestro suddenly looks alarmed.

"But it's okay. You can shoot him," she says, showing him the gun she has found in the drawer.

Ten minutes later they both freeze as a car pulls up outside.

4 - February 1944

MORNING MIST soaks into Freddie's hair and slides down beneath his shirt collar. He stretches up his arms. Arches his back. Yawns with animal relish. He catches sight of the barest wisp of his own breath on the air. The air with its smell of wet bark, of crushed herbs, its muddy green smell of softened earth. He slides down the slope to the water. The shadows of fish passing over the stones on the riverbed. He splashes the cold water up onto his face. He stands listening to the morning.

People in villages are kind and give him food. But they also whisper warnings. There are fascist search parties in the district. Hunting down deserters from the Italian army, hunting down boys evading the draft, hunting down escaped POWs. Rewards are offered for snitches. He hears rumours of rebel fighters in the mountains. Outcasts forced from their homes. Other nomads constrained to move camp from one night to the next. No one knows exactly where they are hiding.

On the sixth day of his trek towards Tuscany he is swimming in a small icy lake when he notices a young man standing by his discarded clothes on the bank.

"Got any cigarettes?" the young man calls out.

"No," he says.

"Shame. You up here avoiding the military draft?"

"Not exactly," he says, his teeth beginning to chatter. Staying where he is in the water, making ripples on the surface with his arms because his feet don't touch the bed.

"Don't blame you for not trusting me. I'm not a fascist though if that's what you're thinking." He lifts a leg from the ground and stands comically balancing on one foot. "If I were a fascist I wouldn't have holes in my soles. And of course I'd have cigarettes."

"I'm not a fascist either."

"My name is Alfredo. You're not Italian, are you?"

He swims to shore, the ripples moving across the water on either side of him.

He rubs himself down with his shirt while the young man watches him. He decides Alfredo is trustworthy and tells him he is an English pilot.

"Trouble is I can no longer prove who I am. A man stole my identity tags. But I have an Italian wife. In Florence. How far is Florence?"

"Miles away. You're between Casello and Borgo San Lorenzo."

Neither of these names mean anything to him.

"You don't want to go to Florence at the moment. Not without papers. You'll be arrested before you enter the city gates. Why don't you speak to Gino? He might be able to get you some fake papers. Gino is head of our group. There are six of us in hiding. We have three guns and two grenades between us. One of the guns is a hunting rifle that's older than my grandfather. They'll suspect you of being a spy to begin with. You're not, are you?" he says, slapping Freddie on the back.

"No, I'm not a spy."

"Crazy times, eh? Even I could be a spy for all you know. You have to take everyone at his word. But people lie. They lie more now than they ever have. Often you have to tell lies to survive. And you tell so many lies that you begin to forget what the truth is. But I've made up my mind to trust you, Freddie."

They hike together through woods, clamber up slopes where dead leaves slide underfoot.

A squadron of planes fly high overhead. Silver streaks in the blue sky that make him feel small and alienated from his former life.

"More bombs on their way," says his companion.

Freddie says nothing. They walk on. Snapping dead wood, crunching scrolled leaves underfoot. Birds pecking at nuts, disturbing leaves up in the thickening trees. He can taste the damp earth in his mouth. Smell it on his clothes. Until his skin feels like bark, his hair like moss and grass. Then a hidden voice calls out.

"Password."

"Grana. It's only me, with a new recruit," Alfredo shouts back.

He has been with the band in the hills for a week. There are eight of them now. They all sleep in an abandoned shepherd's hut. On heaps of straw. It scratches at his cheek at night like a demanding pet. All the men nestle up close to steal warmth from each other. He finds the experience disconcerting at first.

Every day is the same. Except every day it seems a little bit colder. Down to the stream to wash. Using his shirt as a towel. Using his fingers as a toothbrush. Alfredo sings. The gnawing hunger only faintly appeased by the bitter barley coffee that is heated up on a fire.

There are political education classes between ten and twelve. He sits on the ground with the others while Gino, their self-appointed leader, talks about the necessity of creating a better fairer world. He doesn't listen to much of what Gino says. It all sounds naïve to him and makes him feel old and cynical. He misses Reg. He can picture the two of them together laughing about these political education classes.

After political education classes one of the young boys evading the draft arrives with the large saucepan from the trattoria down in the village. Vegetable soup. A little bread and a slice of goats cheese each. There is a demijohn of wine hidden behind a tree.

After lunch there is weapons training. This is conducted by Nero. Nero fought in Greece. He is the only one of the group who isn't impressed Freddie is English. He says he has no liking for the allies. That he only admires the Russians because they don't drop bombs on civilians in cities. Freddie feels uncomfortable around Nero. Nero is aware of his detachment from the political education classes and whenever he makes derogatory remarks about the ruling classes always look over at him. Freddie tells himself Nero's antagonism is probably the natural response to twenty years of Fascism, though he feels hard done by that Nero treats him as a fascist. Weapons training is conducted by Nero. Except they have so few bullets that no one is allowed to fire a gun. Freddie practices holding a gun. Taking aim with it from behind the trunk of a tree or a covering of scrub. It is like a childhood game.

Once a week a girl cycles all the way from Prato to the village. Prato is a name he knows. He has been to Prato with Isabella to see the cathedral and the frescoes of Filippo Lippi. The girl carries messages. Brings things they need. She brings him a pair of heavy boots. They are too big and his feet slide about inside. He fills them with dead leaves. Gino tells him he has arranged for him to have his photograph taken. The first step in procuring him a fake identity card. Then maybe he can return to Florence to see his wife.

One day Gino arrives at the camp out of breath. He tells everyone there is a fascist spy in the local trattoria. That they are going to ambush him because the man recognised him. Gino tucks the revolver into the waistband of his trousers. Following Gino they sprint down the steep slope, through the beech wood. It surprises Freddie how quickly Gino can run. He thinks of him as a man almost old enough to be his father. All eight of them running through the woods. Like a game. When they reach the road Gino orders them into battle positions. Freddie is lying down in a ditch. He hasn't been given a gun. His heart is beating a little more quickly than usual.

The man Gino says is a fascist cycles down the road towards them. It is a peaceful sight. A man in a dark suit cycling down a country road. The sun shining a transparency into the young leaves. Then Gino jumps out into the road. He points his revolver at the fascist on his bicycle. Orders him to stop. The man turns pale. Freddie can read his mind. The man thinks about making a dash for it on his bike. Weighs up his chances. Changes his mind. He stops.

"What do you want?" says the man. He tries to make his voice firm but there is a tremor in it. A slight wobble, like a tooth working itself loose.

"I want to know why you are snooping around. We both know who you are."

"Yes, I was a member of the old Fascist Party but I haven't sworn the oath of allegiance to the Republican Fascists. Enough is enough," he says.

"Enough is enough. But if enough's enough why have you got a weapon?"

Gino takes the revolver that is tucked inside the waistband of the fascist's trousers. The man's nose gets redder as his cheeks grow paler. Gino goes through the man's pockets.

"So you're not a member of the Republican Fascists?" he says, holding up the man's membership card to the Republican Fascist Party.

"Please. I've got a wife and family. It's my daughter's birthday today. She's twelve."

"So have I got a wife and family."

"I promise I won't say a word."

Gino thumbs through a small notebook he has found in the man's pocket.

Freddie feels sorry for the man. He is shaking with fear. He is so frightened he can hardly stand up. It all seemed like a game, like the war games he played as a child. It all seemed like a game until he felt the man's fear.

"Why have you written my name is this notebook?"

The man can't answer. His teeth are chattering. His knees trembling.

Gino orders him into the trees at the side of the road. The fascist is marched deeper into the woods. Freddie walks beside Alfredo.

"Do you think Gino is going to kill him?" Freddie whispers.

"Of course. What other choice does he have?"

Gino makes the man kneel down on the bracken. The man begins crying. Pleading for mercy. He looks up at them all in turn. He looks up at Freddie. Says *please* to him. Freddie averts his eyes. Gino shoots him in the back of the head. Birds take to the air. The spray of blood and brain tissue spatters over fallen leaves. Bright red drops on the soggy bracken. It is incomprehensible to Freddie that Gino has killed this man. This man who said please to him. He takes a dislike to Gino.

Gino sends Alfredo back to the village.

"Get a shovel," he says. "Two if you can manage it. And be discreet, Fredo. We don't want anyone seeing you walking into the woods with two shovels if it can be helped."

Freddie can still see the spray of blood exiting from the man's head as he eats his soup later that evening.

Freddie is asleep when the alarm is sounded. "Germans down in the valley," says the lookout. He joins the others outside the hut. There is a solitary moving light down in the valley. Then there are a string of lights, like flames burning in oil, sputtering in the darkness below. Slowly these lights edge towards the hideout. It is decided the Germans have come to rout their camp. Gino tells everyone to split up and retreat back down into the neighbouring valley.

The next day Freddie learns that the lights were the lamps of local farmers who joined together to assist in the difficult birth of a calf. Three of the band do not return to the hut.

5 - February 1944

WHEN THE door downstairs opens Isabella is prepared for the pitiless men in uniforms, the handcuffs, the abuse, the blows to the face, the descent down into the pit of hell.

The song the man sings as he climbs the stairs is out of tune. Isabella has never heard Fosco sing before and so is uncertain that it is him who is about to enter the room. The tension makes her shoulder muscles ache. Maestro is holding the gun. But without any conviction. As the song gets louder he puts it down on the floor.

She knows a moment's relief when Fosco enters the room alone. That Scarface isn't with him.

Fosco's face is puffy and unshaven. Her dislike of him crawls over her skin. She can taste it in her mouth.

"Come to give me a critique?" Fosco says, showing little surprise. He tosses the bag he is carrying to the floor.

Maestro turns sideways to him. As if offering as small a target to Fosco as possible. His lips quenched of colour. He looks up at Fosco from beneath his furrowed brows. "Get out of my studio." Maestro's voice is very quiet.

"Or what? You'll call the police? I'm done with taking orders from you, old man."

"Is there no end to your hubris? After all I've done for you."

Fosco undoes the buttons of his coat, tucks his shirt into his breeches, the braces hanging limp.

"I'm not your lackey anymore. We both know everything you did for me I had to pay for with one humiliation after another to my pride."

"Pride. That's always been your cardinal sin. You need humility to be an artist. To be a decent human being, no less. All those hours I wasted trying to train you. I should have known you would stab me in the back. Judas."

"You're not Jesus Christ."

"Get out of my studio."

"It's my studio now. I've got the paperwork. You're a war criminal. You've forfeited all rights to your property. I've heard a bombed-out family from Pisa are moving into your apartment next week."

Fosco negotiates his way between the canvases on the floor with difficulty, including Maestro's nude of her. For a moment she thinks it's the gun he's after but it isn't, it's the bottle of grappa. He takes a swig and then hands the bottle to Maestro. Maestro waves it away.

"Don't worry about your precious paintings. That was just my little joke. You took away my identity so I thought I'd get even. What do you want? Your house keys? Here they are. Fat lot of good they'll do you, unless you want to be arrested again." He takes the keys from his coat pocket and throws them down on a painting of an angel with folded silver wings. Maestro flinches. Takes the keys and runs a finger over the place on the picture where they fell.

"This war won't last forever. And when it's over, my friend, you will burn in hell."

"Maybe."

Fosco picks up his blue shirt doused in turpentine. "This was my favourite shirt," he says. He kneels down and wipes it over the painting by his side. She watches in horror as the face of a beautifully painted Madonna is smeared into a slick of washed out colour. "Anyway, all art is decadent now. The world has tired of the vanity of us artists. Don't you agree, Maestro?"

Maestro is staring down with disbelief at the ruined painting.

She feels giddy with rage like a spinning spool from which tape has just escaped.

"Do you think you could shoot me, Maestro? Let's put it to the test." Fosco picks up the pistol, unlocks the safety catch and hands it to him. "Go on, shoot me."

She snatches the gun from Maestro's limp hand and points it at Fosco. His unshaven face, as impassive as a mask. Her trigger finger itches with a mad impetus to cause him pain. There is a distant whistling in her ears, made by the excited thump of her heartbeats. She looks up at all Fosco's paintings hanging on the wall. His portraits with the sickly yellow hue, the jaundiced look. She takes aim at a picture of a man with slicked back dark hair and a pouting mouth. The retort of the gun, the sharp ferocity of its explosion, buckles her arm and almost knocks her over. The bullet rips through the canvas of another picture, not the one she was aiming at. Fosco laughs. Only the faintest lift of his stiff hunched shoulders. "An eye for an eye," he says. He walks over to the picture. Inspects it.

"You're insane. You know that, don't you?" she says, still holding the smoking gun.

"I've had enough of you now," he says. He takes the gun from her hand and then takes hold of her arm. "You're not staying here tonight," he says. "I want you to leave now. I want to talk alone with him for a bit. Then he's leaving as well."

She glares at him. "It's curfew," she says.

"You should have thought about that when you came barging in here. You ought to be more cautious. Nothing is easier at the moment than to denounce someone you don't like to the secret police. You've got an English husband. That's more than enough to arouse suspicion. You know she's become the whore of a Nazi? She's always preferred foreign men to us Italians. So are you going to leave or do I have to drag you out?"

The hatred with which they regard each other is an electric and powerful force. Feels more immediately consequential than love in its clamour for expression. Eventually she drops her gaze. She looks over at Maestro. He makes a motion for her to leave.

It's cold outside. The chill air is a relief after the malignant fumes Fosco has made her breathe. The blackout is in force and she can barely see three yards in front of her. The noise of her heels on the paving stones seems the only sound for miles around. She feels humiliated and angry and frightened. She sits down in a doorway further up the road. Folding herself up into the deep shadow.

Scuttling shreds of cloud are blown over the sickle moon.

It is eerily quiet. She wants to be reunited with her dog. It is her only wish at the moment. It is a wonder how much anticipated comfort the thought of the dog gives her. She sees it again curled up on Freddie's coat. Then she wonders what Freddie is doing at this precise moment. She is certain now he must be in Italy. How else did the dead man she identified as him get hold of his tags? She catches a glimpse of Freddie. The picture is startlingly vivid, like something torn out of the dark by the beam of a torch. Then she must have fallen asleep because Maestro is whispering to her.

"Are you awake? He's stacked up all my paintings outside on the street. He's lost his mind. That's what I think. He destroyed my painting of the Madonna. You know that painting was a masterpiece in its way. No one alive can paint like that anymore. And he destroyed it."

"What did he want to talk to you about?"

"He says, contrary to how it looks, he's working against the fascists. That things have become too dangerous for him in the city so he's joining up with the partisans in the mountains tomorrow. He also said I should stop associating with you."

"And why's that?"

"He says Carità hasn't forgotten about you and the first chance he gets…"

"That's who he's working for. The man who picked him up earlier was one of Carità's thugs."

"You think I'm going to believe anything he says? He's insane. I don't feel safe here. Let's go to the cemetery until it gets light."

She helps him carry his paintings to the English cemetery. They sit waiting for sunrise with their backs resting against the marble tomb of Elizabeth Barrett Browning.

6 - February 1944

HE IS DANCING on the grass quadrangle in the cloisters.
Dancing to imaginary music in his head. He is forever on the
point of losing his balance. This is the idea he is developing. He
stamps over the grass. Holds high his hands as though they are
pinioned to a cross. He flops. He swivels. He slaps his face with
his hands. Beats his thighs. He runs his hand over an imaginary
wall. Like he has seen his daughter do. He skips in circles. He
flops. Like a puppet whose strings have been lowered. Recovers
himself when he is on the verge of collapsing. He looks like a
mad man. But possessed by a primitive kind of grace. The
medley of shapes his body makes like ink forming letters into
words on paper. His daughter is watching him. He stops
dancing and smiles at her.

"What do you think?" he asks her.

"I like it when you slap your face. It's funny."

"It's supposed to be harrowing."

"I don't know what that is."

"It's what the bad people make us feel."

"There aren't any bad people here though, are there?"

"No. Just nuns."

"Why do the nuns wear funny hats?"

"Why don't you ask them?"

"Okay. I will," she says.

"I bet you don't. I think you're afraid of the nuns."

"I'm not afraid of the nuns."

"Ask them why they wear those hats then."

"I will."

"I bet you don't."

"I bet I do. What will you bet?"

"An ice cream."

"Any ice cream I want?"

"Any ice cream you want."

It is almost time to go to the printers. Francesco has asked him to pick up a package there. He debates whether or not to take his daughter. He is angry with Francesco. For forcing him to make these kinds of decisions. He wants nothing to do with the war. It is not an experience in which he can find any exalted idea of himself. Unlike Francesco who is becoming vain about the good he's doing. Who boasts about leaping from the moving train. Oskar likes being with the nuns. They do everything quietly. They move from place to place as though they are invisible. They do good deeds but they don't expect medals for them. He has come to realise how important is the company you keep. In these times of war. If the company you keep is not good at keeping themselves safe they will bring danger into your life too. He has little faith in Francesco's ability to keep himself safe. At times it's as if he wants to be caught. He is angry with Francesco. He feels less guilty about the attraction he feels for Marina. Until he thinks of his wife.

"Do you want to come to Florence with me?" he says. "On the train."

"I don't mind," she says.

The train from Prato is crowded. It wheezes forward very slowly. Several times it stops. It shunts onwards, shudders and stops again. There is a growing engine noise up in the sky. One rumbling bass note that increases its pitch until it fills the air. Everyone exchanges glances. Fidgets. Those by the window stare up at the sky. The noise in its menace is like a circling fin. Then there is a high pitched whistling rising to a screech that rips through the air and a shattering explosion and the entire carriage rocks and shakes.

For a moment he loses all sense of his body's equilibrium. It is as if all the air has been sucked out of the carriage. He can hear the beat of his own heart in his eardrums. Otherwise nothing but muffled sounds. He takes hold of his daughter. Sits her on his lap and wraps himself around her. There is another wave of explosions. The blast throws him forward as if all the weights in his body have dissolved. He is giddy with his own lightness of being. And then panic and everyone is clamouring to get out of the train. He too jumps down onto the tracks. Holding Esme to his chest. Several small fires are burning in other carriages. Stanchions and wires lie tangled. There is a cloud of grey and black smoke further up the line. A smoking carriage lies on its side towards the front of the train. There are people with streaks of blood and white dust in their hair, on their faces. Staggering about on the gravel.

An impenetrable hedge of dense prickly leaves runs alongside the tracks. There is no way through or over it. They are hemmed in. People scramble under the carriages of the train and lie flat on the grey slate. He stands by the hedge and looks up into the sky. The plane rears around elegantly and comes back towards them. He watches as another cargo of bombs comes swinging down through the sky directly overhead. He wrestles his daughter to the ground. Lies down over her. Waits. The explosions rip through the air one after another. The ground seems to heave up, slip and slide beneath him. Stones rain down. He feels for a moment that his chest has been crushed. He lifts his head. Watches the plane soar up into the higher sky. Watches it become smaller. Watches it become harmless.

A hot wind whips at his face. "Are you all right?" he asks her.

"I think so."

He is proud of her for not crying. For being so brave. He picks up the toy bear that is lying on the gravel a few feet away. Hands it to her.

"Napoleon's safe too."

"Was that the bad people again?"

He nods. Unable to formulate an explanation that a child could understand.

"They didn't get us, did they?"

7 - February 1944

"NO GAS UNTIL seven so I can't offer you anything warm to drink," says the lawyer over his shoulder. This man his friend from university Ciro has brought him to meet. He is standing at the kitchen sink. Soaking sheets of newspaper one by one under the tap and screwing them up into tight mushy balls. "Fuel," he explains. "You leave them to dry in the sun – if the sun ever returns - and then store them away for future use as fuel. They burn well, though not for long."

"I can't remember a winter colder than this one," says Francesco. He is wearing two thick sweaters and a woollen scarf. He tugs up his trousers that keep slipping down over his hips. He has had to improvise a new hole in his belt. He will now have to gauge out another.

"Soon we'll all have to start burning our books to keep warm. This is what fascism has led us to. Anyway," says the lawyer, moving away from the sink, drying his hands on a towel, "I know you studied at the university with Ciro here and he has vouched for you. I also know you were in the transit camp at Fossoli. That you've suffered under this regime. But we have to be extremely circumspect. How do we know we can trust you?"

Francesco takes off his coat. Pulls down his trousers and shorts. Lifts his shirt and two jerseys.

"I forgot to tell you. Francesco is Jewish," says Ciro, smiling.

"Unless of course the fascists, to allay suspicion, are now circumcising their infiltrators."

"That's beyond the call of duty even for a Republican Fascist."

"It's not that bad. Being circumcised."

"Sorry Francesco. I didn't mean to offend."

"No offence."

"Do you think you could kill a man, Francesco? In cold blood."

"If he was known without a shadow of a doubt to be zealously working for the Nazis, yes."

"And you have some experience with guns?"

"A little."

"Ciro will help you become more familiar with the weapons we use."

"Except the *bussolotto*. I'm not teaching you how to use that. I'm not going anywhere near those damn things."

"What's that?"

"The *bussolotto*. It's the name we've given a rather volatile handmade bomb we use. A couple have exploded prematurely. Anyway, we have a list of possible targets we're working on. We've been forbidden by high command to kill Germans because of their habit of carrying out reprisals on innocent civilians. But we can target prominent Republican Fascists. The Nazis don't seem to care about them. We operate in small cells of three or four fighters. You will have no contact with anyone outside your cell except for a *staffeta*. Usually a young girl on a bicycle who will pass messages back and forth. You will be assigned your own staffeta. No one knows how he or she will react to torture so the less you know the safer everyone else is. You will know me as Placato. My code name. You need to come up with a code name for yourself. Any ideas?"

"My father used to call me Rombo because I growled in my sleep."

"Okay, we will now all know you as Rombo. Here are some photos. This here is Mario Carità. You've probably heard of him. His ambition is to be Italy's Heinrich Himmler. He's the one we'd most like to get but he's clever. Always heavily guarded. Always changing his routines."

He looks at the photograph of Carità. An oafish looking man with hooded eyes in a heavy overcoat, uncomfortable at being photographed. He is standing between two men. One of whom is the fascist he met at Marina's.

"What about this man?" Francesco asks.

"Don't know him."

"I do. Or I met him once. His name is Angelo."

"He's not on my list but if he's one of Carità's torturers I can make room for him."

"I can probably find out more about him."

"Okay. But this isn't an organisation that allows personal vendettas of any nature. Everything we do has to be approved by the high command. This photo here is an Italian who is working for the Gestapo. Fosco Scarafuggi. It's believed he was the person who ratted on all the Jewish women and children hiding in the convent in Piazza del Carmine. He's to be your first date. I want you to gather as much information on his movements as possible. What time he leaves his house. Where he goes. Every day of the week. I want a map of his routines. Here's his address. Every written message you receive you memorise and quickly destroy."

Ciro, sitting at the kitchen table, pushes a newspaper page towards the man known as Placato. "Have you seen this article? The miracle of St Anthony. A painting of St Anthony by Pontormo was moved from the Uffizi to a villa in the country for safekeeping and a woman who works at the villa prayed to it for the return of her missing son. Two hours later her son returns home. St Anthony is the patron saint of lost things. Now women are flocking to the villa to pray underneath the painting."

"Until we Italians learn to be less gullible we'll always be in danger of succumbing to dictators, whether it's Mussolini or the Pope. Good things happen. Why does it always have to be thanks to divine intervention or state policies?"

He and Ciro leave the house. Its oppressive smell of soggy newsprint and onions. They walk under the aisle of huge oak trees along the viale below the church of San Miniato. He hitches up his trousers again. Ciro is talking to him when he sees Marina with Oskar and his daughter. Climbing up the steps towards the church. Her beautiful long black hair dishevelled by the wind. Her face in profile bright with some irresistible remark she is about to make.

"Francesco?"

"Sorry. I was miles away. Anyway shouldn't you be calling me Rombo now?"

8 - February 1944

HE CARRIES Esme on his shoulders. Up the never-ending steps which she is making him count. On either side is the terraced cemetery. Its stone memorials and marble angels with outstretched wings.

"Thirty-eight," he says.

She presses her small warm hands down on his skull. The bear she holds covers half his face.

"Thirty-nine."

Marina laughs. "It's worth it though," she says. "This is my favourite church in Florence."

They stand outside the church of San Miniato. On the gravel with its pleasing crunch underfoot. Looking down at the miniaturised city of Florence. The ribbon of river. The old city wall tilting up through the line of cypresses. The domes and spires. The orange tiled rooftops. The distant smoky hills and mountains.

Inside the church they stop to look at the marble zodiac on the floor by the entrance. The carved ancient symbols inside filigrees of stars and clovers and twisting vines.

"Do you believe in astrology?" she asks. "That it's the stars that are the divinity that shapes our ends, rough-hew them how they will."

In imagination he fits his palm to the inside of her naked thigh.

"Hamlet," he says.

"You haven't answered my question."

The acoustics of the church give her voice an echo. Her voice seems to come from both near and far. They exchange a moment of eye contact. Feeding current into each other.

How much astrology there can be in a glance, he thinks but does not say aloud.

"Maybe," he says. "What sign are you?"

"Libra," she says.

In imagination he sits behind her in a hot tub lathering up suds in her hair.

"There you are," he says, pointing down at the faceless woman holding a small set of scales in the marble.

"Where are you on this map, Esme?"

"You called me Esme."

"Sorry. Where are you on this map, Anna?"

"Anna is Cancer. This is you," Oskar tells her. Pointing down at the crab.

"No it's not," she says. She hits him. An open-palmed slap on the thigh.

They walk down the right transept. Heels clicking on the marble tombstones underfoot. They pass a confessional. In imagination he pulls down her knickers and presses his mouth to the inside of her thigh.

They go down into the crypt. The slender columns, the honeycomb vaulting and the bright vanishing frescoes with all the prayer candles flickering shadows over the walls. Two elderly women are praying before the altar. He and Marina sit down on wooden chairs while his daughter skips about in the vicinity of the candles. They can hear the chant of the Benedictine monks. His thoughts turn to his wife. In the dark crypt of marble tombstones, the liquid glow and strange shadows of the prayer candles, the ghostly echoing chant of the monks seems to be for his wife.

"Sooner or later one is always made to feel guilty in a church," he says.

"What do you have to feel guilty about?"

"The same petty sins as most people."

"You know you should try to find somewhere to stay in Florence. Prato has been bombed about three times already, hasn't it? It must be dangerous. Because of all the industry and factories. In terms of air raids, I mean."

"Yes. There are often two alarms a day now. We spend half of our time down in the vaults with the nuns. But the organisation Francesco works for is looking out for somewhere for us."

They are both awkward at the mention of Francesco. They both shift in their seats.

"Did Francesco tell you he came to see me?"

She re-crosses her legs. The rustle of her skirt brings him an image of satins and lace resettling against her skin. The scent of her perfume heightened for a moment. Then the smell of candle wax and damp stone returns.

"Yes. He said you were fraternising with the enemy."

"I hate living in that house. My father is in debt to the man I work for. He's called Signor Becchi and he's a crook. One of those men who benefit from the war. I think he gets first dibs on the valuables the fascists steal from the Jews before they're auctioned or sent to Germany. Often crates arrive at the house. Accompanied by lots of whispering. Did Francesco tell you about his mother's attitude towards me? When we were friends at university before the Jews were persecuted. His mother didn't think I was good enough for him. They were rich and my family are poor. I hate snobbery. Loathe it. And what is it if not an insane form of snobbery that drives the Nazis to persecute you Jews?"

"Ssssh," he says and smiles.

"Sorry. But that woman makes me so angry. And I've begun to see something of his mother in him. He's become so judgemental."

"We've all had that trait forced on us to some extent."

"Yes. But being civil to fascists doesn't make you a fascist."

Two SS officers enter the crypt. In full uniform. They look up at the honeycomb vaulting. They inspect the altar. They pace about with leisurely insolence.

His daughter is sitting down by the candles. Talking to her bear. One of the SS officers kneels down in front of her. His boots creak. He has sleek blonde hair. The innocent hair of a child.

Oskar gets up and walks over to his daughter, followed by Marina. In his mind he hears his own voice speaking Italian to another German. Knowing the secret of his origins will seep up into his voice. Betray him to his fellow countrymen.

"What's your name?" The Italian accent of the SS officer is that of an Italian actor playing a German for comic effect.

Is that what I sound like when I speak Italian?

Esme doesn't answer.

"What a beautiful child," he says.

"She's shy," says Marina.

"And you are her mother?"

"Yes," says Marina.

Oskar is not expecting her to say this. It gives him a glow of masculine pride that these Germans now believe he and she sleep in each other's arms. Despite his fear of them. Of their questions. This fear stiffening his muscles. Thickening his bloodflow.

But they do not ask any further questions. They walk away.

"I've never told a lie in a church before," she says.

"What a beautiful child," he says, imitating the SS officer. "But what would he have done if Esme had told him her name and told him she was Jewish? Would he have started barking and arrested her?"

"It's all insane, isn't it?"

9 - March 1944

FREDDIE TRAMPS through the aisles of trees in the early morning mist. The dew wetting his hair. Soaking into his clothes. His footfalls lift from the grass and earth smells that trigger many of his favourite memories of Italy so that Isabella is often a wan but poignant presence in his thoughts. He is returning from patrol duty with his companion. They don't speak, he and his companion. They make as little noise as possible. In case there is a German or fascist patrol combing the woods. He realises how much anxiety he is carrying in his body every time a branch snaps or there is a disturbance in the surrounding undergrowth.

He wears a grey-green cap with flaps, a long army coat and a good pair of army boots. All taken from an Italian soldier found shot in the woods. The coat is stained with blood. Stains no amount of scrubbing on the bank of the stream can remove. The boots too are stained. Sticky with congealed blood inside.

He has spent eight hours hiding in a ditch close to the roadside. Steeling himself to stay awake. His task was to count German vehicles heading south down the road. Jot down with a pencil each vehicle and the time of its arrival in a notebook. Important information, Justin tells him, that will be transmitted to the allied forces later tonight. But not a single vehicle appeared all night. He has a gun now. Tucked inside the waistband of his trousers.

Justin is some kind of British agent. He is cagey about releasing much information about his military status. After the scare in the night the small band led by Gino moved deeper into the mountains where they joined forces with a larger group of rebels. Freddie had intended making for Florence but Justin warned him against it and asked him to stay as a translator.

Justin is kindly, soft mannered, intelligent and yet it isn't difficult to imagine him slitting a man's throat. Freddie wonders how this paradox is possible. He inspires confidence. He is someone he would have chosen as a companion when crewing up in the hangar. He has thick straw coloured hair, confident blue eyes, thin wide lips that set in a surprisingly diffident line but open on a smile of warm generosity.

"It's good to be able to speak English again."

"I'll drink to that."

"I've had this craving to see myself in a mirror ever since I've been holed up in these hills. Just to reassure myself that I was still able to recognise myself. You're a bit like the mirror," says Freddie.

"Must be a bit of a shock then. I know what you mean though. Damn brave what you chaps do, by the way. I had a friend in 97 squadron at Coningsby. Wireless operator. He once described a sortie to Berlin. The bomb aimer was decapitated. They flew the plane back on three engines at a hundred feet. It had 140 holes in it. I don't think I could do that. I'd get claustrophobic."

"The bizarre thing is I miss it. I miss my crew. I miss the station. I even miss the ops. One night you'd be over Berlin, the next you'd all be piled in an old Morris Minor racing through the country lanes to a dancehall in Lincoln. I was hoping to get through the war without firing a gun. I'm not really cut out for this kind of fighting."

"To each his own." Justin is rolling a cigarette in his lap. "Still working on getting you some identity papers. No one would blame you if you hid out the rest of the war in Florence."

"That's not what I mean. I need to see my wife. Once I've assured myself she's well I'll probably try to get back to England and return to flying."

"If this drop is on tonight, I'd like you to come. Your Italian's so much better than mine and I have a job understanding these Italians when they're excited."

There are about thirty men now. Sleeping in a small abandoned farmhouse at the edge of a beech woods. There are no mattresses. The cement floor is heaped with straw and bracken.

It sticks to their damp mud caked clothes. Because it is so cold they all sleep in the same two rooms. Before going to bed they heat up stones, wrap them in cloth and use them as a hot water bottle. That moment when warmth flows up into his body from his feet is an event he looks forward to every night. In the middle of the night though he is woken up by the cold or by a nightmare and often finds Otto by his side has snuggled up close to keep warm. Otto reminds him of Davy. A rakish lock of dark hair falls over his left eye. A tall gaunt man who was training to be a chef before the war. He holds things, even a gun, with the delicacy of a refined woman. At a time when most men are keen to accentuate the more coarse and muscled side of their masculinity.

Many wear red neck scarves. Most have chapped lips and split skin on their hands and feet. They call each other comrade. They say this word dozens of times every day. They talk about guns more than they talk about anything. Most are still boys, only eighteen or nineteen. The older men fought in Russia, in Greece, in North Africa. There is a baker's apprentice, a mechanic, a jam salesman, two farm hands, a few students. Two Russian soldiers who the communists in the band are in awe of and treat like oracles. And they all talk about guns. They talk about guns while cleaning their guns. They talk about guns while eating their daily ration of soup. Revolvers are favoured over rifles. Perhaps because of the cowboy and gangster films they all grew up with. No one wants a hunting rifle. Your gun is your status. He has a Beretta. Better than the old 1899 revolver that lots of the boys have. But the most admired gun is the Frommer that a man called Paolo has. He took it from a German soldier at gunpoint. But what they all really want is a machine gun. They don't yet have a single machine gun among them. This will change when the drop arrives.

He sleeps most of the day. When he emerges from the house a boy is peeling back the skin of a freshly caught rabbit. The sight reminds him of Isabella unfurling her stockings. He cups his hands around the coffee heated for him on the fire. Looks around for Otto but can't see him. He walks away from the group of young men in red neck scarves playing cards. Sits down on a fallen trunk next to the blind boy. Aldo, or their guardian angel as he's known. His family was killed in a gas explosion at his home. It had nothing to do with the war. He was out buying bread at the time. He now lives with a family down in the valley but prefers spending his time at the camp.

"Hello Aldo. I thought Justino had banned you from coming to see us."

Freddie berates himself for his choice of verb. But realises he is being over sensitive on the blind boy's behalf. Aldo has a gentle expressive mouth and trust emanates from him like a smell. His thin frame in oversized clothes seems to sway unsteadily, as if there are no weights in his body. He uses his hands to mimic the action of every story he tells. He doesn't wear dark glasses. His eyes are like the sky at night. They give back to you nothing but an infinite black glitter.

"He has. But I get bored in the village."

"No Germans about last night. I had that damn fascist song going through my head all night. *Il tuo canto sqilla e va!*"

The blind boy joins in –

"*E per Benito Mussolini,*
Eja, eja, alalà…"

"Hey, you two! What's your game? You changing sides?"

"Never, comrade."

Behind them liquid copper streams over the bracken on the hillside. A grey green transparency floats all it touches in a sad withdrawn tide. The higher hills become a floating apparition. Beyond, the serrated mountain peaks harden into cut-out shapes of steely silver.

Later, when Justin returns from the village where he went to listen to the BBC messages, everyone is bristling with excitement.

"*The leaves fly*. We got the message. It's tonight. The drop is tonight."

"At last."

"Justino promises chocolate and cigarettes. Warm clothes."

"And more guns."

They set out for the drop zone after supper. Each armed with a revolver and a hand grenade. The thickening odour of leaf mould. The crunch of icy snow and bracken underfoot. The rustle of crisp leaves. The hooting of an owl. The movement of the clouds overhead.

They slide down icy slopes. Holding onto the trunks of trees for support. Climb steep inclines of mud with patches of snow gleaming between the tall trees under a big moon. Breath coming heavy. Heads tucked low against the bitter wind. Vigilant. Ears strained for any untoward noise in the surrounding landscape. Freddie still has the fascist song *Giovinezza* going through his head. He can't get rid of it.

The proposed drop zone is a flat field high up on a plateau of the mountains. A gleaming white rectangle of thick snow that seems all there is in the world that stands between him and the stars. He helps arrange one of the triangle of torches at intervals around the field. The moon is shifting in and out of view behind clouds.

They have almost given up hope when he hears a distant rumble and then a low buzzing up in the sky. The noise becomes gradually louder and by the thin light of the moon he sees the outline of the Dakota. Arriving from the south. Recognition signals are exchanged. The plane flashes a red light. He scurries off to light the torches. His huge shadow leaps across the ground when the little pyres of straw flare up into flame. There is a bewitching beauty about the isolated triangle of smoky illuminated darkness, as if it is some kind of stage on which a fairy story is about to take place. The plane circles back. Dips down lower. Sends its thunder down into the pit of his stomach. Black parachutes bearing gifts drift down out of the sky with a mesmerising grace. He counts them. He sees twelve. Clothes and boots fall down without parachutes and arrive first. A coat flails down close to him. A pair of boots tied together by the shoelaces almost hits Nero. Makes Freddie grin this surreal sight of clothes falling down from the sky in the moonlight. Eight of the heavy containers are easy to find. They land on the snow within easy reach. Then there is a kind of treasure hunt as they comb the area looking for the others.

They carry the heavy containers back to the camp. Everyone is excited by their contents. They are also excited by the capture of a suspicious stranger found down in the chestnut woods earlier.

"He says he wants to join up with us. He says he was sent by a man called Nocintini but none of us know anyone called Nocintini."

The man in question is a shadow against a tree trunk. A torch is shone on his face. Freddie can hardly believe his eyes. It is the sorcerer's apprentice. It is Fosco.

10 - March 1944

A FILIGREE OF LIGHT shimmers over the shadow on the ceiling like rippling water. Isabella watches the patterns. Almost inclined to look for meaning in them. She cannot sleep. It is so quiet she can hear a dead leaf scuttle over the stone steps outside her window when the wind blows. Zinnia is curled up at the foot of the bed. Or Zee as she always calls the dog. She is surprised by how much protective love she feels for the animal. How sensitive Zinnia is to her moods. How she seeks physical contact when Isabella most needs it, absorbing some of what is overflowing in her. They often exchange looks in which there is both admiration and empathy. Impossible now to imagine life without her.

Isabella hadn't realised how much she would like a child until Oskar's daughter entered her life. Esme has shown her how she might repair things in herself if she had a child of her own. Zinnia has become the next best thing.

She leaves the house before the sun has risen. Throwing a green embroidered shawl over her shoulders. She takes Zinnia with her.

On the brightening air drifts a scent of refreshed stone, moistened soil. She feels the earthy fingerprint of the cold morning air spread over her skin as if she is in the act of undressing. Her body has an early morning weightlessness about it. She might almost be a memory of herself. Conjured up by the sleeping city. Or perhaps by her husband.

There are already queues forming outside the tobacconist and butcher shops. Forlorn figures in heavy clothes stamping their feet and rubbing their hands together.

The German sentry on the bridge studies her appearance for a moment. Then he smiles at her. A kind smile that creates a troubling intimacy between them. She smiles back. The sky is a virginal blue translucence as though bereft for a fleeting moment of the effects of both light and darkness. A crimson streak smoulders over the outline of the hills, a simmering bloodline. There is a solitary canoe on the water. A cold white sheen rises from the water. She holds her breath. As if to stop any more time from passing, to stop the future happening. The peacefulness of the morning is almost heartbreaking in its fragility.

Zinnia is tugging her up the steep incline of Costa San Giorgio on her way home when she meets Marcello.

"You're still at liberty then?" he says, holding onto his hat as the wind gusts down from the Belvedere fort on the hill. A sign hanging outside an osteria creaks on its hinges.

"Am I under interrogation?" she says with a smile in her eyes.

"Aren't we all under interrogation at the moment? Has it ever been harder to live with oneself?"

"Come and have a coffee."

She leads Marcello down Costa Scarpuccia into the gravelled forecourt where there is a church and also a green door in an old stone wall laced in vines that leads to the building where she has an apartment. The dog stops to sniff at the steps outside the church. She almost wonders if the dog can smell her there. These steps are where she and Freddie often sat at the end of a night before they separated. In the days before they had kissed. They sat on the top step with their hips touching and she would smell her scent as it would smell to him and there was a dusting of arousal on her fingers as they talked in the dark, a softening of her body's resistance as if it were half persuaded to shape itself into an embrace.

She opens the door with its flaking green paint onto a small courtyard and the tiered emerald garden.

"Real coffee," calls out Marcello when she is at the stove in the kitchen. "I can smell it from here. It smells like the end of the war."

She brings the two small porcelain cups into the living room. The dog trots behind her. She blushes when she sees Marcello is standing in front of Maestro's painting of her naked nineteen-year-old self. As if when he turns round to face her he is looking at her without her clothes.

"You know you were the first love of my life," he says. He has pulled the sleeves of his pale blue jumper down over his hands. "When we were kids. That all seems like a different century now."

"It does, doesn't it?"

"I was so much in love with you I couldn't look you in the eye."

Marcello can never quite complete a smile. His smile is like a flag twisted in its own ropes, unable to unfurl.

"And then I disappointed you by encouraging that awful peacock Antonio," she says.

"Yes. Last anyone heard he was in Russia."

"I disappointed my first ever love too. She was my teacher at primary school. I adored her. And I know she secretly favoured me above all other girls in the class. Then one day I was reading aloud from some novel. I don't remember what novel it was. There was a word I didn't understand. Pregnant. I stopped reading and asked her what it meant. Pregnant. I suppose I was young for my age. There was lots of muffled giggling from my classmates and Miss Monaco, the object of all my ardour, blushed and then looked with fury at me. I saw immediately that she thought I was making fun of her. I became a kind of heroine among my classmates for my daring afterwards but Miss Monaco remained icy with me till the day she left. She was pregnant you see and everyone seemed to know except me. I had no idea."

"What about your Nazi? Have you disappointed him as well?" he says, finishing his coffee.

"Don't start on him again."

"Does he ever talk to you about his work?"

Marcello, she notices, has a habit of drawing in his underlip. It's like his way of retreating emotionally.

"Not really," she says.

"You said he told you about his investigations into the missing paintings."

"That's all."

"But you might be able to encourage him to talk more? Any information you can eke out of him might be invaluable."

"What kind of information?"

"Information about German artillery positions on the Gustav line, troop movements, the position of munitions warehouses, military command posts, factories, repair workshops, train times, road routes used by the Germans to send munitions, equipment and troops south. Planned raids on partisan camps or places Jewish people are hiding."

"He's hardly likely to discuss these things with me and it'd look damn strange if I suddenly took an interest in the Gustav line and troop movements."

"He might want to save his skin. Does he know you have an English husband?"

"Yes. And English bombs killed his wife and children."

"Serves him right."

"Does it?"

"I think so, yes. Aren't you angry? Isn't your blood boiling? These Nazi bastards and neo fascists poisoning the best days of our lives with their megalomania and re-education programmes. I saw a film the other night. A Nazi propaganda film about the Jews. I can't even begin to describe how vile it was. And when it was over most of the audience stood up and performed the Sieg Heil salute."

She calls Zinnia up onto the sofa beside her.

"Actually I'm glad I met you. You've given me an idea," he says.

Her pulse quickens, like a bird that tries in vain to fly away.

"We need a new courier for a couple of weeks. How would you like to redeem yourself?"

"I've done nothing wrong."

"But it doesn't look that way."

"And who isn't less innocent than they lead us to believe? That's one of the fundamental truths about human nature."

"But I know you are angry. How could you not be? Half the population starving. Our way of life destroyed. Children forced to wear uniforms and repeat slogans. We all have a moral duty to fight these bastards in any way we can."

She is huddled over the dog, stroking its back, its animal smell thick in her nostrils. "I'm a woman. What can I do?"

"There are lots of women involved in the struggle now. Precisely because you're a woman you have more freedom of movement. Do you know how many times a week I'm stopped and made to show my papers? You can't spend the entire war painting pictures. And you have the dog. We can use the dog instead of rolled up newspapers or carnations."

Footsteps can be heard clunking across the room in the apartment upstairs. Then the sound of coins or something metal falling to the stone floor.

"By the way, that matter we talked about last time we met."

"My teacher?"

"Yes. You still vouch for him?"

"Absolutely. You can interrogate him yourself if you want. He's in the bedroom there, sleeping."

Marcello winks at her.

"It isn't like that. God, what is it with everyone and this mania to see sex everywhere? Half the neighbourhood thinks I'm sleeping with a Nazi and now you have me sleeping with a sixty-five-year-old man."

"Just teasing. What about this stooge of his, this Fosco Scarafuggi? You vouch for him too?"

"No. There's nothing admirable about him. He's the one who's working for Carità's band."

"I know he is. But I wanted you to say it. We're watching Fosco. Or we were until we lost him. But his days are numbered."

Good, she thinks. But this is not quite her true feeling. Her true feeling is underneath. She has the impression her true feelings these days are a moving current beneath a crust of ice.

"Will you do it?"

"I don't see I have much choice now."

"Good. Next Friday at three pm you meet your contact by the Cellini statue on the Ponte Vecchio. He'll be carrying a red book. Ask him for a light. He will give you a box of matches. You keep the box. At six pm you meet the second contact outside the city gate at Porta Romana. This will be a young woman. She will approach you. You give her the matchbox. I'll tell her to keep her eye open for a woman with a dog. What might you wear?"

"A yellow coat?"

"Fine. I'll tell her you'll have a dog and be wearing a yellow coat. One thing you ought to know. If you get caught they'll torture you. The only person you know is me. You tell them you only know me by a codename. Corvo. Then tell them you have a meeting with me the next day. Make up any time and place. That way you'll both seem to be cooperating and you'll waste some of their time."

When Marcello leaves she sits down on the wall overlooking the garden. Looking down at the green shoe hanging off her arched foot in a precarious balancing act.

Giuseppe, the gardener, appears on the lawn from behind the magnolia trees. He is pushing a wheelbarrow heaped with dead branches and weeds. He looks as though he sleeps in a field at night. The furrows on his narrow clay-like face sculpted as if with an intricate tool. He wears a collarless white shirt and a greasy waistcoat. He puts down his wheelbarrow and gives her a spiky-chinned kiss on either cheek. Then he beckons her to follow him. He is a man of few words. He communicates his eagerness to show her something mostly with his hands and eyebrows. He leaves his wheelbarrow and leads her to a secluded fenced-in part of the garden, close to the medieval wall. The grass here is wild and overrun. In amongst this enclosure of seeded vitality there are dozens of tortoises, some so tiny they must have been newly born.

"The hibernation period is over," says Giuseppe.

11 - March 1944

"HAVE YOU seen Isabella?"

Fosco stands tapping a piece of brushwood against his thigh as if it is a horsewhip. The ashes of a fire smoulder and crackle in the darkness nearby.

"Yes. We bumped into each other a while back."

"And she's well?"

"Yes. I still can't believe you and I have crossed paths in such unlikely circumstances. Bizarre, isn't it? Thanks for speaking up for me by the way. Jumpy bunch here, aren't they? Though I suppose it's understandable. For all they know I could be a fascist infiltrator." Fosco smiles, as if at the absurdity of the idea. "But how did you end up here? I heard you were a pilot."

This is not the surly taciturn wary Fosco he remembers. When his face always seemed poised to clench into a scowl. He can't ever recall having seen in Fosco a bodily eagerness for the next moment of life. And yet tonight there is a twitch of withheld excitement about him.

"You're sure Isabella is well?"

"Last time I saw her, yes."

"What is it you're not telling me?"

Fosco takes a step back into a swell of shadow. "For your own good I don't think it's a good idea that you go and see her at the moment," he says, his face now a mask of darkness.

Freddie folds his arms over his chest. To still the pulse of agitation there. "Why's that?"

"There's something you should probably know. I just wish I wasn't the one who has to tell you."

"Fosco, just bloody tell me."

"She's taken a lover."

He takes a few steps away from Fosco. Wanting to hide the stab of pain this piece of information causes him. He arches his back and stands with his hands interlaced in his black hair.

"And worse than that."

"What do you mean?"

"He's a German SS officer. Not even particularly good-looking or cultured by all accounts."

"How do you know this?"

"Well this is the part that is difficult."

"I'd rather you told me."

"Well, she betrayed Maestro and me. I don't think she really meant to but obviously lovers have a tendency to share secrets. Even in wartime."

"She'd never betray Maestro."

"But she would betray me?"

"I didn't mean that."

"It's a long story. For a while I was working for the Ministry of Culture. In an unofficial guise. I was involved in the packing up of many of the paintings in the Uffizi. Word reached us that the Nazis intended stealing some of the paintings. I took it upon myself to try to save them. I sneaked out two paintings. Stupid now I come to think of it. Maestro was forging a Ghirlandaio Annunciation and I was forging a Pontormo saint. The idea was to give the Nazis the forgeries and keep the originals safe from harm. But Isabella told the SS officer and Maestro was arrested. By a huge stroke of luck I managed to evade capture. That's why I'm up here in this godforsaken place. But like I said I don't think Isabella really knew what she was doing. Just a bit of idle pillow talk probably. I understand you don't want to find fault with her. The more fault we find in people, the more power they acquire to hurt us."

Of course Freddie has asked himself a few times if Isabella might be capable of betraying him. Given his inability to love her, who could blame her? But somehow he has never been able to imagine her doing it. The idea is hostile to his knowledge of her. Which leaves him now with the belittling and shaming feeling that perhaps he doesn't know his wife very well.

"Listen, I'll do you a favour. But this has to be our secret. I've got to return to Florence at some point. I have this Jewish friend I've been sheltering. I need to find him a new hideout. I'll probably have to sneak out because some of these men are morbidly suspicious. But I'll go see Isabella and tell her you're here and set up a meeting for the two of you. It isn't safe for you to go to your apartment or the studio. The SS officer is always loitering around. But if I don't make it back here I'll try to send word via a courier."

The following morning Fosco has vanished.

"He said he had to go to the village."

"I said we should have kept him under guard."

"We should have shot the bastard. This is your fault," says Nero to Freddie. He shoves Freddie between the shoulder blades as he marches off, knocking the Bren gun out of his hands.

Justin bends down to pick up the gun. Hands it back to Freddie. "You think this Fosco will betray us?" he asks.

"I don't know. He told me my wife is having an affair with an SS officer." It is a test to say this aloud. Like the first act after acquiring a new identity. Also, it is the first time he has ever been embarrassed by Isabella in public. He succumbs to a backwash of guilt as he looks to Justin for a reaction, a verdict. Justin, he sees, accepts it as another small sad fact in the narrative of the war. "He also told me he had to return to Florence."

"Did he say why?"

"He said he has a Jewish friend he needs to help find a new hiding place."

"You believe him?"

"I don't want to, because if he's lying about that he's probably lying about the SS officer as well. He's always been a natural for the role of Iago."

"I'll double all the sentries for the next few days. Just in case. Okay, what say you we get back to weapon practice. How about you make believe you're taking aim at this SS officer?"

Justin is teaching Freddie to use a Bren machine gun. Birds scatter from the trees as Freddie fires off a round. The recoil shudders along the length of his arm. Knocks him back onto the grass.

"That's you dead," says Justin. "Your shoulders were too relaxed. And you held it too close to your face. This is not a rifle. You have to hold it lower. And you need to aim low to allow for the recoil. The recoil always lifts it up above your aiming point. Press it down on the side handle. Try again."

Freddie tries again. This time he stays on his feet.

"There you go. You're almost ready for a parachute regiment now."

"Don't talk to me about parachutes. I dream of the damn things nearly every night."

Later he is on sentry duty with Otto. The sun has not yet risen and there is a chill in the clean grey air.

"I noticed yesterday you have a tear in your shirt," says Otto. "Why don't I mend it for you? I've got a needle and thread in my bag."

Otto rummages about in his bag. Freddie watches him moisten the frayed tip of the cotton with his tongue and delicately thread it through the tiny needle. Otto holds out his hand with a smile. Freddie takes off his coat, heavy with dew. Unbuttons his shirt, slowly disclosing his thin tanned hairless torso. Self-conscious, for he is mistrustful of the effect of his nakedness, he hands over his shirt. Otto arranges it in his lap and Freddie watches him pass the needle and thread through the white cotton.

"Nero and his little gang give you a bit of a hard time, don't they?"

Shivering, Freddie wraps his coat around his bared torso. "You noticed?"

"Hard not to."

"I don't think Nero cares for the English much. He doesn't like Justin either."

"He's jealous. Because more often than not it's Justin who gives the orders. Communism, Fascism, it doesn't matter, there's always men who want to be in a position of telling other men what to do. Nero thinks he should be in charge."

"Now he blames me for Fosco's defection."

"If you hadn't have vouched for him Nero would have shot him."

"I sensed that."

"There was a warning from the Pannucci brigade that the fascists are sending up spies."

"One thing I didn't mention is that Fosco belonged to the Fascist Party when I knew him."

"So you've got your doubts as well?"

"I don't know. He's a bit of an oddball but essentially I'm sure he's harmless. I don't think he liked it up here. Everyone was pretty hostile towards him. Probably he'll just try to sit the war out."

He and Otto fall silent. A veil of virginal silence lays over the countryside. Foliage can be felt to stir with the aroused expectation of sunlight. A pale pink shimmer of light, followed by a more diffused yellow glow smudges the lower tract of grey sky. The hills to their left have turned an almost transparent dark blue. A cock crows. Birdsong and insect chatter starts up. Then the disc of the sun edges over the rim of the line of hills to the east. He remembers his farewell letter to Isabella. *Whenever life is beautiful you become part of the moment.* He wonders if his farewell letter was sent to her. If that is why she has taken a new lover.

That night he is woken up by another nightmare. His heart hammering. Otto, next to him, whispers that it is all right. Just a nightmare. He eases Freddie's head onto his shoulder. Stroking his hair. Some of the shadowy men in the room are snoring. The air is oppressive with thick male body odour.

"You keep having these nightmares."

"I'm fine," Freddie whispers back but he is still trying to calm down his heart. Otto continues to stroke his hair and forehead. Then he moves his hand down to Freddie's chest. At first Freddie takes no notice. He is wondering about smell. If his smell is like the sour masculine odour of these other men. He likes to think it isn't. That he still smells as he did when a boy with raw scrapes on his knees and his nose running in the cold. He thinks of Isabella because she is the only person in his world he would be able to ask for a description of his smell. Then he remembers and sees an image of her spreadeagled on a bed with a naked man between her thighs. A rush of anger flushes over his body. Otto, as if sensitive to this sudden inflammation of his blood, presses up closer to him. He can feel the pulsing dictatorship of Otto's desire. But it is not his desire. He changes position. Disentangles himself from Otto's greedy fingers and turns to face the other way. He can sense Otto feels betrayed. Just as he feels betrayed.

12 - March 1944

MARINA IS working as a secretary at Villa Triste. Until someone else is found to do her job. She is often alone in the small office on the second floor. Next door is one of the interrogation rooms. The last girl who did this job left because she couldn't bear the screams anymore. Marina too doesn't think she can bear the screams much longer. She takes them home with her and hears them again when she is in bed at night.

The oddest thing happened yesterday. She was sorting through some files in a cabinet - the names of informers all dutifully listed, sometimes relatives or neighbours of the person arrested - when she saw her journal. Just sitting there. The sight of it made her heart beat wildly in her throat. She was aglow with guilt when she slipped it inside her skirt. It unsettles her still that her journal turned up here. She can't move her thought beyond the mystery, as if some cog in her mind has ceased to turn.

Behind her desk, on the wall, is a huge map of Europe with coloured pins stuck in it. The coloured pins have not been moved since she arrived. Sometimes it is her job to receive the people who come to denounce a traitor. Usually women. Women who tell her there is a Jewish family hiding in a neighbour's house or a young boy evading the draft hiding on the roof of the building across the street. Women who cling tightly to their handbags. Lean towards her with stiff shoulders. Confidentially. As if she is part of their secret circle. Some of these women wear the steel band given by the state in exchange for the donation of gold and silver wedding rings. She has difficulty in concealing her distaste for these women. The curl of dislike on her lips.

She types up every denunciation. Types up every report. Every order. Sometimes, on her way to the bathroom or another office, she passes prisoners being dragged along the corridors. Sometimes they look at her with contempt. These faces haunt her in her bed at night too.

She had no choice but to accept the job. Signor Becchi reminded her again how much in debt her father was to him. "It's only temporary. Perhaps a couple of weeks. And you speak a bit of German," he reminded her. Within forty-eight hours of starting work in the house of terror a boy she knew at university stopped her in the street. Told her he was working for the resistance movement in the city. Asked her if she would be willing to collude with them. Pass on the occasional piece of information that might be of use to them.

"You have no idea how much good you would be doing," he said.

She couldn't say no. It is the plight of Oskar and his daughter, her intimate induction into the perils they daily face, that has made her see the Nazis and the fascists for the evil they are. Afterwards she felt a bit better about doing the job. At least now she is on the right side. Except her body now is knotted with fear and tension instead of being sickened with revulsion.

Every morning a car comes to pick her up at Signor Becchi's. And every evening the same car takes her home. For her own protection, they tell her. She realises that most people believe she is working for these monsters. In collusion with them. She wonders how many people know the truth. Few, she suspects. She also wonders if she is being watched. Every day she is tense. Her secret glowing hot and cold inside her. Setting aflame her cheeks. Seeping up sweat through her pores. When the information seems especially urgent she is required to take it over to Padre Enzo in the church further down the street. She copies out reports so quickly she isn't aware of what she is writing. She is too busy straining her ears for approaching footsteps. The incriminating pieces of paper on which she copies out documents she hides inside her knickers. Blushes when she then hands them over to the priest.

Angelo comes to see her at least once every day. He denies all involvement with the torturing. Says all his work is clerical. She doesn't want to believe he is capable of torturing anyone.

The telephone switchboard trills all day. Sometimes there is music from a gramophone. And sometimes someone plays the piano. Neapolitan songs. To cover the screams.

She is copying out an order without taking stock of the words until she sees a name that is familiar to her. The document is an order to raid the convent where Oskar is staying. She will have to deliver this to the priest immediately.

She stands by the door. Listening. All is quiet. Strange, she thinks, how vulnerable the back of your neck feels when you listen to silence. She sees herself slipping down the carpeted corridor. Guilt flaming in her cheeks. Guilt prickling underneath her armpits. She sees herself walking quickly and quietly down the stairs. Before she performs the act she rehearses it. Testing her courage. Warning her nervous system of the demands she is about to make of it.

She bends down to look through the keyhole. Can see nothing. Just blankness. She is troubled by this anomaly. Then she starts back. There is an eye looking at her through the keyhole. There is someone outside doing exactly what she is doing. Peering in through the keyhole. She flings open the door. Her fear making her angry. It is the huge man they all call Piccolo. His face flushes. He lowers his eyes. He is mortified with embarrassment. This is clear. She has never liked the way he looks at her. She pushes past him. No longer afraid of being intercepted. Too angry to care. She takes the stairs. Halfway down the wire cage of the elevator comes clattering up. Gives her a fright, as if its occupants are looking for her.

The guard at the iron gate says hello.

"Where you off to?"

"Need some air," she says.

The road is shadowed by towering pine and cedar trees. She has to push against the steep gradient of the road as though wading through water.

"Hey," calls out a voice. She hears it through the grind of the traffic. She turns round. Her heart a mad drum of fear in her chest. Angelo is standing on the other side of the road. Wearing his film star sunglasses. She waits for him to cross.

"I saw you sneaking off. Through the window upstairs. Where are you going?"

"To church."

"I didn't know you were religious."

"There's lots of things you don't know about me."

"Not my fault."

"Anyway I'm not religious. But I've promised my mother I will pray for my brother once a day. He's missing. In Russia."

"Mind if I come in with you?"

"Why?"

"I don't know."

"Prayer is private."

"Okay. Point taken. How about I wait for you here. And we go for a coffee after?"

She walks into the church. Her footsteps hollow sounding on the marble flagstones. One of the altar paintings is boarded up behind bricks and sandbags. A solitary old woman is kneeling before an icon of the Holy Virgin. The priest is talking to an altar boy. She catches his eye. Enters the confessional. Removes the piece of paper from her knickers. Quickly, before the priest arrives.

"This is very important, Father."

Angelo is waiting for her outside. In his pleated white trousers. In his black film-star sunglasses.

"Let's just sit in the sun for a bit," she says.

He smiles. Takes off his sunglasses. They sit on the wall. The wall follows the steep slant of the road. She feels as though she is sliding towards him. About to topple into his lap.

"Doesn't that place make you feel unclean?" She nods over towards the ugly grey building of grey marble and yellow sandstone. Four storeys high. It has something menacing about it even without the huge black banner hanging from its façade.

"I don't think about it."

"Perhaps you should? Most of the people you work with don't even seem capable of thinking."

"They're not the brightest bunch. Half of them are common criminals. They were let out of prison specifically to become torturers."

"Why are you a fascist, Angelo?"

"I don't know. Because I like the uniform?"

There are thistled weeds growing by her feet. Growing in clumps out of the stone. "You don't wear a uniform most of the time."

"When I was at school the subject that most bored me was the fascist education class. The teacher would drone on and on. I didn't listen to a word of it. All that chest-beating rhetoric. I wanted to be outside. Playing football. But the most exciting moment of my childhood was when I was chosen to be a musketeer. I loved that uniform. I drooled over it. I could not stop admiring myself in the mirror. I was so excited the night before the parade that I couldn't sleep. I felt I was twelve feet tall in that uniform. I see now that I probably chose the wrong uniform. But you can't just change sides because you're losing. Imagine if footballers did that. Your team is losing six nil so in the middle of the match you suddenly switch sides. You start playing for the other team. Can't be done. Your supporters would lynch you."

They are silent for a while. Watching the cars pass by.

"Do you know what I think?" he says. He is rubbing a small stone he has picked up between his thumb and forefinger. "Sometimes I think Italy is too much about the mother. The mother reigns. We all have to keep the mother happy. And it makes men a bit weak. So we feel a need to prove that we're not weak. We put on a uniform and wear a weapon. Perhaps all men secretly enjoy obeying orders. It gives you the sense of there being a structure. Fascism's just a strict father really. And if you please this strict father you get all kind of perks and advantages."

"Like a war? The thing that most irritates me about that building is everyone there is always accusing the prisoners of being cowards. But it's all you who are the cowards. Why aren't you fighting at the front if you're so brave?"

"For god sake don't let anyone else hear you talk like this."

He looks at his watch. She sees the veins are high on his wrist.

"I've got to meet Attila in the centre," he says.

13 - March 1944

JUST BEFORE sunrise a breathless sentry enters the room shouting.

"Everyone get up. Quick! Fascist militia are heading up through the woods."

"Have any shots been fired?" asks Justin, pulling on his trousers.

"No. We came straight here as soon as we saw them."

"Someone go and reconnoitre with the sentries behind the camp."

The man sent out has hardly left the building when he returns with the other two sentries. "The fascists are coming from that direction too. We're surrounded."

Freddie, carrying his rifle and ammunition, follows Justin upstairs.

"I guess this is your pal's doing," he says to Freddie.

"Sorry."

"Not your fault, old man. If we don't give the benefit of the doubt to friends who can we give it to? War can bring out the worst in the best of us."

Justin gives instructions. Freddie positions himself with his rifle at one of the two windows. The shutters are closed but some of the slats have been purposefully removed for this eventuality.

There is a stretch of grassland in front of the house with a few jutting rocks that slopes down steeply into the surrounding woodlands. To the rear is thick forest. Through the shutters he can see the fascists as smudges appear and disappear behind the trees on the slopes. They have fanned out into a line about 50 yards in diameter.

"Don't fire until they are within sixty or seventy yards of us," says Justin.

Freddie watches through the gap in the green slats the smudges of colour become distinct forms. They all come to a halt at the woodline. Two militia guards on the left flank begin setting up a machine gun. Justin gives the order to fire and immediately lets off a couple of eight-round bursts at the two guards in the act of setting up the machine gun. One falls and the other retreats into the woodlands. Everyone is firing. The fascists appeared unconcerned before the first hail of bullets arrived. There is now a seed of panic in their ranks. They are close enough for Freddie to make out faces. He chooses the face he least likes to aim at, a man with a sneering mouth who is firing his automatic weapon towards the window below. Bullets have begun ricocheting off the stone walls of the house. Shredding bits of wood from the shutters. Tracer flickers back and forth from the house to the trees. The noise rips deep down into Freddie's eardrums. Dulls the sharpness of his hearing which creates a medium of distance between himself and what is happening, as if his head is under water.

The fascists have retreated back into the cover of the beech wood. Three of the them are sprawled on the grass. One is wailing pitifully. Now and again someone tries to retrieve the machine gun that has still not been assembled and sits on the grass. Justin disables it with a rifle grenade. The intensity of the battle now subsides and the wailing of the wounded Italian fascist on the grass becomes the focal point of everything. He is calling out for his mother.

"It's a good sign none of his companions have the courage to go to his aid," Justin shouts. "I'm going to quickly see what's going on behind us."

Freddie looks round and sees Aldo has entered the room. He makes a motion for him to get down, forgetting he is blind. When Justin returns he leads Aldo over to the east wall of the room and makes him sit down on the floor.

"The situation is similar behind us, except there's better cover for the fascists there. One of our men has been wounded in the chest."

Freddie concentrates his fire on the Republican guard to whom he has taken a personal dislike. He is kneeling behind the trunk of a beech tree about fifty yards away. A huge splinter of wood is torn off the shutter by Freddie's left ear and then stucco and bits of stone explode from a jut in the wall by his side.

Justin says, "I've told four men in the other room to prepare to leave the house by the side door and make a foray towards the right flank while we provide covering fire. I'll fire off one of the rifle grenades and hopefully this will enable them to rush the carabinieri and take cover in the woodlands. The carabinieri are the weakest link out there. We'll then leave the house three or four at a time at quick intervals."

The explosion of the grenade among the carabinieri lifts a hail of smoke. The first four men make a run for it. There is another explosion, off to the right where Freddie's nemesis is. Three of the partisans now occupy the part of the woods where the carabinieri had been. Alfredo is writhing on the grass half way between the house and the woods. Then a red gash is ripped out of his jumper and Alfredo no longer moves.

The next four leave the house, repeating the procedure as before. This time all four make it to the edge of the woods, from where they keep up heavy fire, driving the fascists back into a more concentrated area. Freddie's nemesis in the peaked grey hat is still furiously shooting away but so far no one upstairs has been hit.

Otto is one of the four men next to go. Freddie feels bad about Otto. Several times he has tried to approach him but Otto always walks away. Otto has taken to sleeping in the other room with Nero's group.

The fascists have by now got wind of the trick and most of their fire is directed not at the house but at the four men running across the open space. A militia guard is shooting at the running men and in his excitement has drifted too far from the protection of a tree trunk. He is a relatively easy target and Freddie hits him in the upper body. He doesn't yet think about the man's family, about the empty place there will now forever be at the dinner table in his home; he feels the brief quick trill of pleasure you get when you serve an ace at tennis or hit a four at cricket.

When he looks down at the stretch of grass between the house and the trees to the left he sees the motionless body of Otto. It doesn't surprise him that Otto has been hit. There was always something overly passive and resigned about his expectations. But he feels a rush of anger as he fires off the next few rounds.

There are only six or seven of the fascists attacking out there who show signs of determination and courage. These are the Republican guards. For the first time Freddie feels a sense of superiority. It is beginning to seem probable that the fascists don't have the courage to launch an attack on the house. It no longer seems out of the question that he will still be alive to see another sunset, another sunrise, perhaps even see Isabella again.

The partisans among the trees are holding their own, though there is a worry about how much ammunition they have left. Justin therefore gives the order for everyone left in the house to make a run for it together.

"*Andiamo*," he says in his limp laissez-faire Italian accent that makes him sound like anything but a professional soldier.

They go to the back of the house to get the men there. Because the fascists behind were surprised they haven't been able to close the circle around the house. There appears to be no communication between the men out front and those out back.

Downstairs, machine gun fire is ripping into the window on the right side of the house. The boys stationed here stand flattened against the wall as bullets whistle into the room and tear clumps of smoking masonry off the walls. Justin prepares the last rifle grenade and gives the order to get to the side door. Everyone has forgotten about Aldo. Forgotten that he is blind.

Freddie ties a piece of rope to his belt. He hands the loose end to the boy. "Hold onto this when you run." It is the best solution he can think of. Aldo says thank you.

"How fast can you run?"

"I don't know. I've never really tried running before."

Freddie is suddenly less confident about his chances of seeing another sunset.

He picks up a Bren gun, clips on a new magazine and takes a deep breath. This is the adrenalin moment. When he hears the explosion of the rifle grenade he darts forth from the door. His body is clamouring to race at full speed but tugged back by Aldo's hold on the rope. Bullets whip through the air, rasping displaced air over his face. Now and again one cracks its menace in his ear. The smell of morning vanishes behind a stink of smoke and singed dust. An Italian boy sprints past him and Aldo shouting. Freddie fires off a couple of three-second bursts, shooting blindly towards the area where enemy fire seems to be at its most intense. He has the feeling that the spin of the Earth has slowed down, that it is revolving too slowly on its axis and as a result things have more time to happen.

He glances down at Otto as he runs past. He is lying face up in the grass with the radio transmitter on his back. There is no question he is dead. He feels a moment's sadness for Otto. Gratitude too, because Otto taught him something about himself and brought him back closer to his wife. Then, suddenly, he feels freer, like that moment when you're wading towards the shore and you can finally lift your feet out of the water. His body eases into a quicker pace before he realises the reason for its newfound agility. The loose end of the rope flicking at the backs of his legs. He dives down into the bracken amidst a thick clump of trees, gasping for breath, his lungs aching.

He looks up to see Aldo face down on the grass about fifteen yards away. Aldo has covered his head with his hands but isn't moving. Justin is running in zigzags towards him, followed by Nero and one of the Russians. Freddie watches Aldo tentatively lift himself to his feet. He shouts at him to stay down. Some of the fascists are still firing at the house. He feels another surge of adrenaline as he prepares to run back out into the nightmare clearing. Before he scrambles to his feet, Nero has taken Aldo by the arm and is dragging him towards safety.

Bullets rip off bark and leaves from branches. Fountains of earth rain down on the ground. Freddie's ears are ringing. He can taste the metal in the air. The length of his body is pressed hard against the ground, his cheek almost etched into the earth.

It is from this position that he notices a bee lazily settling itself inside the petals of a tall-stemmed violet flower. It is like something taking place in the past or the future. Yet at the same time it seems like an event meant for his eyes alone.

14 - April 1944

"THE GIANELLIS have been deported."

"Giorgio and Clara?"

"Yes," Francesco tells his mother. Every time he sees his mother she looks older, more sunken. They are sharing a small slice of chestnut cake at the marble-topped kitchen table. "And three of the children. Only the daughter Bia managed to escape. She wasn't in the house the night they came."

"Poor Clara. She is such a frail woman. She was always ill, even as a child."

"And the Modglianis. Augusto and Luisa. They were arrested last month. Sent to a camp in Germany or Poland. And they have been to the Bettini's house in via Pandolfini but they had already fled. Ransacked the house though. And the things they didn't take they threw out of the windows onto the street. Last week they arrested an eighty-six year old woman. Took her from the hospital. They say she probably would have died in the next two weeks. But the Nazis put her in a cattle truck. To comply with the paperwork, I suppose. It's pure madness but it's also systematic madness. They have us all on lists and they won't rest until they've caught every single one of us."

"Stop it, Francesco. You're frightening me."

"I'm just trying to make you see how careful you must be. There's a huge reward for giving information on the whereabouts of any Jews."

"But I'm no longer a Jew. That's what the new identity card you got me says."

"Yes and you've got to learn to be that woman. Why did the man in the bakery call you by your real name?"

"It slipped out."

"See. You've got to be much more careful. In fact I think you should stop going out altogether. Let Ivana do all the shopping."

"I feel like a prisoner as it is. Always cooped up in this cramped apartment."

"And I'm afraid you have to stop going to the shelter when the air raid siren sounds."

"Stop going to the shelter?"

"Yes. They put spies and informers in those shelters. That's how Mrs Salmon was caught. You have to become invisible, mother. It only takes one black-hearted person to view you with suspicion…"

"And what happens if a bomb falls on the house?"

"It won't. The allies won't bomb the centre of Florence. Just the railway stations."

"How can you know that? They've bombed Bologna and Pisa and now Rome."

"Most of the stuff in the newspapers isn't true. Unless you think it was Jewish bankers who instigated this war as a means of getting richer and that Jews constitutionally are far more likely to carry disease."

"There's no need to get aggressive."

"I'm sorry. My nerves are a bit frayed. "

"You don't look well. So pale and drawn. Are you eating, Francesco?"

"Yes, I'm eating. As much as anyone else. Soup without salt every day. Marina is seeing someone else," he says, surly. Eyes downcast. "A German. It's upset me."

"So I wasn't *completely* wrong about her."

"She helped us when none of your so-called friends would."

"Yes I know. Credit where credit is due. I wish I could like her but it's hard to like someone who despises you."

"She doesn't despise you."

"She'll never forgive me. I looked down on her. The same way the Nazis look down on us."

"Stop exaggerating."

"I've never met a Nazi. It's in *her* eyes that I see hatred."

"Whatever she feels about you, it's got nothing to do with you being Jewish. The German she's seeing is Jewish and she seems to like him all right."

"My poor boy."

He doesn't want her sympathy. It's humiliating. As if she wants to turn him back into a helpless child. He changes the tone of his voice. Makes it more perfunctory.

"His name is Oskar. I've just managed to get him out of a convent. He and his daughter are now being put up by a family of farmworkers near San Casciano. The Nazis have got wise to how much shelter the Catholic Church is providing. You can't fault them. The Catholic Church. They're providing lots of help. The cardinal here is a very good man."

He wants to keep talking. Because this time tomorrow he has to kill a man. And he doesn't think he can do it. Every time he imagines the critical moment his hand begins shaking. He points the gun and his hand is shaking. When he points the gun he sees a look of terror on the face of the man he has been tracking for the past two weeks. The man he feels he has come to know. Fosco Scarafuggi. He knows if he kills this man he will see his face every night before he goes to sleep. That his face will become more vivid to him than his own face. If he kills the man he will be forced to wear this man's face for the rest of his life. This is what he feels. But he can't tell his companions he hasn't the mettle to kill this man. He does not want to appear weak. So he will have to do it. Will have to wait outside the barbershop at 18.00 hours. With the gun tucked inside the waistband of his trousers. Will have to shoot to kill.

15 - April 1944

OSKAR WATCHES Esme play with the other children in the piazza. It is her turn in the game. She sits on the wall in front of the church. The other children wet the piece of rag in the fountain. One of the little girls holds the wet rag close to Esme's face while the others try to scare her or make her laugh. The children pull faces at her. They snarl at her. They simulate hysterical laughter. Esme keeps a straight face. As if they aren't there. He smiles. She resists all provocation. They can't trick her into laughing or changing her facial expression. He is proud of her. Of this further evidence of her ability to withstand interrogation without betraying herself. He has told her not to answer questions. Not even the questions of other children.

"Just say, I don't remember or I don't know. You can tell people you come from Isernia and that your house was bombed. Otherwise play dumb."

"What's dumb?"

"Pretending you don't know things that you do know."

He hates training her to be deceitful like this.

He watches as two boys arrive in the piazza with peashooters. All the girls scatter, shrieking. On the wall by the church there are posters. One announces a reward of fifteen thousand lire for the denouncement of any Jew. Threatens prosecution for anyone sheltering Jews.

They have been in their new home for three days now. Staying with a mechanic who works at the Todt factory and his wife. The man and his wife are by no means wealthy. And Oskar is paying little rent. Just what he can afford from the money he gets from the organisation Francesco works for. It is a marvel to him that these people are so kind. No less of a marvel than how evil other people can be. The ones hunting him and his daughter down. But no matter how kind they are he feels uncomfortable in their home. He tries to stay out of sight in the house. Feels always an intruder, a liability when he walks into the kitchen.

So he spends as much of the day as possible in the bedroom he shares with Esme. He gives her Italian lessons. He tells her stories. She uses her new coloured pencils to draw the things he describes and writes down their names underneath. He tries to tell stories that end with a homecoming. A happy reunion.

Now and again he catches her talking to her bear. She is always seeking to comfort it. Make a cosy ordered home for it.

One day they walk to a nearby farm to see a newly born calf. After the death of the baby bird he thinks it will be good for her to see a newly born life. When they arrive it has already been delivered and is lying on the straw, its naked black body webbed with slime and placenta. He holds her hand in the milky stink of the paddock. Its warm fertile earthy breath. Every now and again the otherwise inert calf shakes its head. He watches his daughter's eyes brighten with wonder. Bits of straw have stuck to its mouth. The mother is licking it clean. The calf tries to get to its feet. It staggers comically for a bit and then buckles back down onto the pungent straw. This routine is repeated over and over. Sometimes all four of its legs buckle and splay beneath it. The urgent pulse of life is poignant in its bright puzzled eyes, its brittle trembling legs. It is the most vulnerable thing he has ever seen. The war has made him feel the vulnerability of life but this is a moment of vulnerability he can give himself up to freely and exult in. When the calf manages to stay on its legs it staggers about drunkenly and makes blindly for Esme who runs off squealing, half with excitement and half with fear. Then it bumps into him and falls down again. She wants him to buy the animal for her. She makes him feel he is letting her down by not doing so. She sulks on the way back to the mechanic's house.

He stays up late drinking grappa with the husband. He doesn't want to but he feels obliged to. She tells him off when he returns to the bedroom. From beneath her heap of musty blankets. Says she doesn't like the smell of him when he comes to bed so late.

"Daddy feels a bit dizzy."

"Stop it!"

"Let's see if I can walk in a straight line."

He expects her to laugh at his comic attempt to walk in a straight line over the wooden floorboards, below the low wooden beams, but she doesn't.

"What's wrong?"

She holds her nose and pulls a face. "You stink."

"It's only a bit of grappa."

"I don't like it. And I don't like you when you're different."

"Okay. I promise I won't stink anymore."

The woman of the house teaches his daughter things. Tonight she is teaching her to fan the fire in the stove. She has given her a straw fan with a wooden handle. The woman and child are kneeling down on the flagstones beside the crackling glow of the furnace. He marvels at how little strength his daughter has in her hands.

The man and his wife have no children. They take pleasure in his child. The pleasure they take in his child makes him feel a little less unwelcome.

When they are half way through their meal a man comes to the house. A friend of the husband and wife.

"I have some bad news," he says. He stands at the centre of the large kitchen without taking off his hat or coat. "They're going to arrest you and your little girl tomorrow. The captain of the carabinieri told me to warn you. You have to leave here tonight."

"But where will they go in the middle of the night?" asks the wife.

"They can stay with my wife and me tonight. Unfortunately I can't put them up any longer because the man who lives below me is not to be trusted."

"They know we're Jewish?"

"Yes."

"How did they find out?"

"Your daughter didn't cross herself when some boys made her go into the church. That's what I heard."

"Just because of that? A child doesn't cross herself in a church and automatically she's considered Jewish?"

"It seems one of the women in the village was suspicious about you and made her son carry out this test. She's after the reward."

"Darling, did some boys make you go into the church?"

"Yes."

"Didn't I teach you to cross yourself when you go into a church?"

"I think I did."

"Never mind."

The air raid siren begins its howling while they are at the table. When they leave the house some of the inhabitants of the small town are running towards the woods. Carrying bags. They do this whenever the siren sounds. Take refuge in the woods. Everyone is looking up at the sky. There are about sixty planes. Rumbling with menace. Low enough for their four engines to be visible by the light of the moon.

He follows their new benefactor up the unsurfaced road that skirts the woods. Holding his daughter's hand. He carries what few possessions they now have. Up ahead against the skyline flares suspended by parachutes cast an otherworldly blue haze over the line of cypresses on the horizon. The explosions begin when they reach their sanctuary for the night. The hills in the near distance light up like volcanoes.

16 - April 1944

THE GUN IS inside his coat pocket. Francesco has cleaned and loaded it. Six rounds into the bastard's chest. *Are you sure you can do this?*

Why did he nod? He isn't sure he can do it at all.

He is about to leave the house when the woman who rents him his room tells him he has a telephone call. The loose wooden slat under which he has hidden the list of Jewish people the organisation is helping creaks as he walks over it.

His longing for the code words that signify the mission has been aborted is so intense that he thinks he hears them in the earpiece. But they never pass messages over the telephone. It is not the code word he hears in the earpiece. It is Oskar and he catches only a fragment of what he says.

"What did you say?"

"We're homeless again. The carabinieri were about to arrest us last night but we were warned beforehand. We managed to get out before they came."

"This is an awkward moment for me," he says.

"Everything okay, Francesco?"

"I can't do anything today. I'm tied up. Meet me tomorrow. Come to my apartment. Say at midday."

"You sure you're okay?"

"Don't worry about me. At least I've got a roof over my head."

"People say the war is going to end soon. Have you heard these rumours? That the Germans are going to pull out of Italy."

"The war isn't over. And people listen to telephone conversations."

"Sorry. Okay. Noon tomorrow. See you there."

I'll confront him about Marina tomorrow, he thinks. But it is hard for him to believe there will be a tomorrow. Before tomorrow can come he has to do something he doesn't believe he can do.

He looks at his face in the mirror while putting on his hat and coat. Trying to find in his features the face of a man who is able to kill another man in cold blood.

I can't do this, he imagines saying to his two companions. But he can't bear the impatience, the scorn with which they look at him. He keeps seeing the face of the man he is going to kill. Sees it animated with all the interest and expectation of being alive. Sees it in death.

Francesco cycles over Ponte Vecchio. Few of the jewellery shops are open. But lots of people are crossing the bridge. From all walks of life. None of whom know he is going to kill a man in less than half an hour. His knowledge makes all these people seem drab and meaningless. Makes them seem enviable too.

Perhaps it was innocent, he thinks, turning to look up at San Miniato on the hill as he waits for a horse and cart rattling with demijohns to pass before he can cross the road. *Perhaps they simply went for a walk together.*

But his mind will not let him think of anything else for long. Not even of the betrayal. His gloved hands grip the handlebars. There is no longer any tomorrow in his mind. He remembers when he broke a valuable vase as a child. Lived in dread of his crime being discovered. The empty place on the mantelpiece. How that empty place on the mantelpiece denied him all pleasurable expectation of time to come. How it became a vacuum in his own mind. An impediment to thinking himself into the future.

At the corner of Piazza San Firenze and via della Condotta he sees the first of his companions. The man keeps his newspaper rolled up. A sign that there are no problems. His heart sinks that there are no problems. There is a hollow sick feeling in his stomach. He feels as though he hasn't eaten for days. He leaves his bicycle outside a tailors in a nearby narrow street. Releases the safety catch of his gun. He walks past the barbershop. There inside, facing himself in the large mirror, is the man he is going to kill. The man who vanished for four days and then reappeared. Fosco Scarafuggi.

Francesco stops on the other side of the street. Plays the part of a man waiting for a woman to arrive. Looking at his watch every so often. He smokes the last cigarette in his packet. Takes the nicotine deep into his lungs. Watches the trail of smoke he blows out disappear on the cold air. He notices the cracks, the stains, the weeds and tiny bits of flaked stone on the pavement.

Aim the gun. Fire off six shots. Walk away. Down via dei Magazzini. Get on your bike and pedal like mad. To the safe house.

He rehearses it all continually in his mind.

A horse and cart, piled high with furniture and mattresses, clatters past. Two children sit on the heap of possessions in the back, swinging their legs over the side. The cart is followed by a lorry in which there are at least a dozen Wehrmacht soldiers. Then he sees two men he recognises. They are walking towards him. The fascist he met at Marina's. Angelo. And the man with the gold tooth. Another man his organisation wants dead. Neither is in uniform. They have seen him and are walking towards him.

Fuck, he thinks. He looks over towards his companion, the lookout. Catches his eye. Tries to alert him to the danger he is now in.

He walks away. As casually as possible. But in the wrong direction. Not back to where he has left his bicycle. He wants to be where lots of people are gathered. Thinks he'll be safer if there are lots of people around. He does not want to be followed down a narrow alley. He enters the wide sweep of Piazza della Signoria.

He needs to get rid of his gun. He looks around for somewhere he can dump it. He has the sense of being followed. But dares not look back over his shoulder. His legs are weak beneath him. He passes the Neptune fountain. He considers for a moment dropping his gun in the basin. But if they are following him they will see. He walks on, towards the Uffizi.

"Hey. Hold on."

He has almost reached the Loggia dei Lanzi. He has been waiting to hear this voice and now it arrives. Like a stone shattering a sheet of glass. He stops and turns around.

"I thought I recognised you. Aren't you Marina's friend? We met once."

"Yes. I remember you. Angelo, right?"

He has the feeling his features are sliding about on his face like smudged charcoal. He makes fists of his hands. To steady his nerves. To keep the fear from his features.

"That's right. You suffer from epilepsy I seem to remember."

"You look like you might be about to have a fit right now," says the man with the gold tooth. He beams an aggressive smile at him.

"Can we see your papers?"

He hears what they say to him as if through a thin wall. He sees them as if through several sheets of glass. He extracts his papers from the inside pocket of his coat. Hands Angelo his identity card. His hands are trembling. The two men notice. He knows they have registered the trembling of his hand.

"Guido Forti? From Palermo? I seem to remember your name was Francesco the last time we met."

"No. I've always been Guido Forti," he says. He attempts a smile.

"You don't have a Sicilian accent. You have a Florentine accent."

"So what?"

"What have you got in your pockets?"

The ground seems to shift beneath his feet, like ice breaking up into sliding slabs. Over Angelo's shoulder he sees his two companions. They have paused on their bikes in front of the steps of the Palazzo Vecchio. They are surveying the situation. Talking to each other. As if in the process of coming to a decision.

Shoot the bastards, he almost shouts out to them. He considers shooting them himself. He puts his hand back in his pocket. He thinks about running. And then he is running. Alongside the portico of the Uffizi. Past the niched statues of

Florence's most illustrious thinkers and artists. Pounding off towards the river. Clenched fists pumping the air. The stones underfoot jarring his ankles. The rabble of his thoughts pared down to one simple imperative. The rush of blood to and from his heart. He is being chased. He can feel the presence behind of someone quicker than he is. Gaining on him in the slipstream behind his sprinting limbs. There is a different choreography of light over the river. A promise of springtime. But he doesn't make it to within sight of the water. He is tripped from behind. Sprawls on the stones. His head smacking down on the paving stones. His elbows jarred and grazed by the stone coming up to meet his flailing body. His body that he no longer has control over.

"Look what we have here," says the man with the gold tooth. He is holding up the gun he has taken from Francesco's pocket.

Francesco looks around for his two companions.

17 - April 1944

WHEN ATTILA walks into the office with Francesco, whose hands are handcuffed behind his back and has a split lip, Marina is thrown back in her chair as if touched by a live electrical wire.

"I'm afraid your epileptic friend is in the doghouse. Caught him carrying a gun."

Francesco glares at her. They share no secret coded language. She cannot make him understand that she is not in the wrong.

"Aren't you going to take down his name? He says his name is Guido. Guido Forti from Palermo."

"Yes. Take down my name. Guido Forti from Palermo," Francesco says with a snarl that makes him ugly.

She threads a sheet of paper into the typewriter, aligns it and begins punching the keys.

"It was me who stole your diary. I used to feel bad about it but I don't anymore."

It is her turn to glare at him.

"Address?" she says.

"No address."

Attila sits down on a corner of the desk. Flashes his gold tooth in a smile. "Are you two having a private argument?"

"Date of birth?" she says.

When Francesco is taken away she breaks down. She is caught crying by the huge man Piccolo. He stands in the doorway looking at her. She tells him to leave her alone. She leaves the building. Never to return, she thinks. She is determined she will never set foot inside the ugly grey building again.

Late that night, when she is in bed at Signor Becchi's house, she is woken up by someone opening the door to her bedroom. A figure stands by her door in the dark. She lifts her head a fraction from the pillow.

"Who's there?"

"Is it you?" he asks.

"Who is it?"

"Angelo."

"What do you want?"

"The spy. Is it you?"

"What time is it?"

"About three in the morning. Are you listening to me?"

"You woke me up. How did you get in?"

He doesn't move from the door. She can make out his outline. But not his features.

"I've got a key. Listen to me. There's been lots of talk tonight in via Bolognese. Your name came up."

"What are you talking about?"

"A spy. There's a spy in the organisation. First someone warned the convent in Prato. Then someone tipped off the partisans in the hills. Yesterday they ambushed one of our patrols. Except it was supposed to be the other way round. They obviously knew the patrol was coming. You typed out the order. So you're under suspicion. I can help you but you have to be honest with me."

"Well, it isn't me," she says, surprised by how firm and convincing her voice is.

"Okay. Good. I didn't really think it was you."

"Yes you did. Now will you go and let me get some sleep?"

She cannot sleep though. She thinks of Francesco in a cell. She argues with his voice in her head. She thinks of him reading her diary. The one secret she has that he needs to know he doesn't know. She thinks of packing her things. Of running away. She feels like a little girl at the thought of running away.

And then they'll know I'm guilty, she thinks.

She is still awake when the sun rises. Standing by the window. In her white embroidered slip that her mother made for her.

The black car arrives to pick her up. She is attentive to the driver's attitude towards her. Mirko is jovial. A married man of about forty. He tries to make her laugh. As he always does. A task he sets himself every day. She uses the rear view mirror to check her make-up. The line of her eyebrows. She feels she is wearing a mask. And everyone will be able to see she is wearing a mask.

On the stairs she passes two guards. Skull and crossbones badge on their black berets. Daggers strapped to the chest of their tunics. They fall silent when they see her walking up towards them. Bristle with new curiosity about her. Or so she thinks. Her secret like a bubble of blood edging out of a new cut.

When she walks past the closed door of Carità's office she can hear her heart beating. Even though she knows it is far too early for Carità to be in his office. During the night she imagined him interrogating her. Imagined his huge ugly hands on her. Imagined this to test her body's powers to withstand intimidation. To sustain deception. To conceal all the repulsion she feels for this man in a situation where he would enjoy becoming repulsive to her.

She sits down at her typewriter. There are no messages for her on the desk. One of the switchboard operators comes in to talk to her. Doesn't mention anything about spying. Marina asks if Carità is in the building yet.

"Haven't seen him. Why?"

A prisoner is brought in by two guards. She has to type out his details. Name and address. Date of birth. He has a black eye and a cut lip. He is trying to act defiant but she can feel his fear. She wonders what his crime is. Knows it is nothing important by the bored expression on the faces of the two young guards.

After lunch she hears Carità's voice. Out in the corridor. She stiffens in her chair. She hears some laughter. A group of men joking among themselves. She can't hear what they are talking about. Then the voices fall silent.

Angelo comes to see her late in the afternoon.

"Sorry for waking you up like that."

He shuffles over to her desk. Looks down into the wastepaper basket. She waits. Can sense he has news. Something important to tell her.

"Well, they've found out who the spy is."

She pretends to be more interested in the piece of paper by the side of the typewriter.

"You'll never guess who it is."

"Probably not. Because I don't care."

"You must be a bit curious. That would only be natural."

"Who is it then? Carità?"

"I have to admit that would be even more shocking."

"Tell me then."

"Piccolo! Can you believe it? He barely ever says a word to anyone."

She remembers the eye at the keyhole. The surreal startling eye at the keyhole.

"Barely ever says a word to anyone but he's been passing classified information to the enemy."

"How do you know it was Piccolo?"

"He confessed. Everyone's talking about it. Some don't believe it. They say he must be shielding the real infiltrator. He's going to be tortured tonight. When the Four Saints get here."

"Those thugs."

He knew it was me and he is protecting me.

18 - April 1944

ISABELLA IS wearing her yellow coat. She is on her way to meet her contact on Ponte Vecchio. By the fountain in Borgo San Jacopo a German soldier leans down to stroke Zinnia. It is an awkward procedure for him to bend down because of his rifle and all the equipment strapped to his body. She can sense him feeding himself on the animal's warmth and affection. Zinnia is gratified, friendly. The soldier seems reluctant to leave. She lets him know she is required elsewhere by clearing her throat. He says something in German and smiles. She shrugs her shoulders and smiles back. It is churlish not to.

She reaches the middle of the bridge and lights a cigarette, forgetting she is supposed to have no matches. Two caped carabinieri in their black plumed hats and blue trousers with the broad red stripe pass by before the man carrying the red book arrives. He is wearing sunglasses. She hurriedly throws her cigarette away. Takes out a new one. If anyone is watching she knows suspicions will now be aroused.

"Have you got a light?"

The man hands her a box of matches. She lights a new cigarette and hands him back the matchbox. Realises her mistake and blushes with shame at her stupidity and incompetence. The man frowns when he hands back the matchbox.

"I've got a verbal message for you to pass on," he says under his breath after showily looking over his shoulder, like an actor in a vaudeville play. "The English pilot is to meet his wife next Tuesday at 3pm. The printers in via della Scala. Number sixty-two."

Her legs sag beneath her and her head is in a spin.

"Did you hear me?"

She looks at him open mouthed.

He repeats what he said before, word for word. She nods and he walks away.

19 - April 1944

"WHICH organisation are you working for?"

Francesco still can't believe it was Marina who was sitting behind the desk in this nightmare building. Typing out his details.

"I'm not working for any organisation."

The slack-jawed man with the greased back black hair looks at him as if he is vermin. He leans forward. His mouth almost touching Francesco's mouth. He places one boot on either of Francesco's bare feet. He is wearing boxing gloves. He steps back. Begins to weave and bob like a professional boxer. He aims a succession of jabs at Francesco's chin. Francesco's hands are handcuffed behind his back.

"Go on, hit me back," Carità says. All the men in the room laugh. Dutiful rather than heartfelt laughter as if this is an old familiar joke. A routine Carità goes through with all prisoners.

Francesco remembers as a child putting his hand in a candle flame. To test his power to withstand pain. It had not been a success. He had yelped. He had removed his hand almost immediately. The first arrival of the knowledge that he was not physically brave. Which no later experience has contradicted.

Carità punches him hard in the face. Points at his own chin, motioning Francesco to return the blow. He bobs and weaves. Francesco has never hated anyone so much in his life.

"By tomorrow morning you will wish you had never been born," Carità says. In a cordial voice as though offering a piece of useful advice. "Which organisation do you work for?"

He keeps asking the same question.

"I'm not working for any organisation."

They have already broken his nose. Loosened several of his teeth. Before asking him any questions they set on him. Six of them. They hit him with a rolling pin, a belt, a metal rod. Pulling him to his feet and hitting him again. Picking him up by his arms and legs and throwing him against a wall. His blood is smeared on the floor by his bare feet. His blood is drying on his face and on his scalp. There are six men in the room all staring at him with malevolent disgust. All shouting abuse at him. All showing off in front of Carità. There is a sort of competition among them as if Carità is a beautiful woman they want to impress.

"You're not working for any organisation and yet you carry a gun? That in itself is a capital offence."

"I found it on the bank of the river," he says. His legs are trembling. He can feel blood seeping into his hair. He wants to wipe his nose. He wants to press his palm to the back of his head. The cuffs are cutting into his wrists. He keeps thinking of the window. Of making a sudden dash for the window. Of throwing himself out of the second floor window. He pictures Marina looking down from her office window at his lifeless body.

Carità holds out his hands. Marina's friend Angelo approaches and unties the laces of the boxing gloves. "And you were about to hand it in, like a good Republican Fascist?"

"I didn't know what I was going to do with it."

"Which organisation do you work for?"

"I'm not working for any organisation."

"Attila."

The man with the gold tooth draws a knife. He grabs a handful of Francesco's hair at the top of his head. Cuts off this handful of hair. Presses the handful of hair onto Francesco's mouth. Trying to force it into Francesco's mouth. Francesco resists. Shakes his head. The man with the gold tooth punches him hard in the groin. Francesco splutters and chokes.

"Swallow it," he says. "Or do you need something to wash it down with?"

The man with the gold tooth picks up one of Francesco's shoes. Unbuttons his fly and urinates into the shoe. In full view of everyone. He pulls Francesco's head back by the hair and pours the urine over his face.

"What organisation are you working for?"

Carità marches imperiously back and forth asking the same question, one minute quietly, then with a bellowing insane fury.

"Why don't you ask me a different question?"

"Which organisation are you working for?"

"Which fucking organisation are you working for?"

Carità smiles. He enjoys this bit of cheek. This bit of fight. And then he grabs hold of Francesco's testicles and squeezes them with a sneer.

Francesco lets out another scream. Collapses in a heap on the floor. Rolls up into the foetal position. The man with the gold tooth hauls him up by the hair. Francesco screams again.

"You see those things over there on the table?"

Francesco has already taken stock of the torture implements on the table. They belong to a world he dares not think about.

"Look at them!" Carità slaps his face. "If you don't tell me what organisation you work for I'm going to ask Attila here to burn off all your body hair with that blowtorch. Crush your balls with those pliers. Take out your teeth. And then burn off the soles of your feet. And Attila will enjoy doing all this because he's the most sadistic bastard I've ever met. And he doesn't like traitors."

"I'm not a traitor."

"What organisation do you work for?"

"I'm Jewish. I don't work for any organisation."

"Pull down his trousers."

The man with the gold tooth unfastens Francesco's belt. Yanks down his trousers and shorts. Lifts up his penis with the blade of his knife.

"He is a Jew."

If I can count to ten before anyone hits me it means I'll get out of this hell alive. One. Two

"So Guido Forti from Palermo why does it not say you're a Jew on your identity card?"

Three. Four.

"It's fake. My name's not Guido Forti."

Five. Six.

"And who made you a fake identity card?"

Seven. Eight.

"A man in Genoa. I don't know his name."

Carità hits him with an open palm. Like a woman roused to fury.

"What's your real name?"

"Francesco Conte."

"Your address?"

He gives the address of his family's villa.

"That's not where you're living now though, is it? Where are you living now?"

"Fifty-six via Maggio."

"And those are the keys?" he says, nodding towards the table where all the things taken from his pockets are sitting.

"Yes."

Carità gives the keys to one of the men. "Send somewhere round there. Tell them to search the place and stay there for the next twenty-four hours. They are to arrest anyone who turns up. Even if it's a cleaning woman."

Oskar will go there tomorrow with his daughter and be arrested, he thinks.

He closes his eyes. Summons up an image of Oskar in his mind. *Don't go to my apartment,* he tells this image of Oskar in his mind.

The door of the room opens and the man he was supposed to kill walks in with a German SS officer. Francesco exchanges glances with the man he was supposed to kill. He sees the man is discomforted by the intimate intensity of his gaze. This is the face that has haunted him for a week. The face that replaced Marina's as the face he sees when he closes his eyes. It doesn't surprise him that it has come back to haunt him again.

"Look what we've got," says the man with the gold tooth. He turns Francesco round to face the SS officer. He lifts up Francesco's shirt.

"Which organisation do you work for?" bellows the man Carità. He shoves Francesco to the ground and kicks him between the legs. Another guard stamps on his feet.

Now they are all showing off for the German SS officer.

20 - April 1944

OSKAR AND his daughter are snuggled together against a wall in the waiting room of the station. Keeping each other warm. The journey into Florence has taken all day. No bus arrived for five hours. And then no train for another four hours. The train kept stopping. When they finally arrived curfew was in place so he was unable to go to Isabella's. Instead they have to stay the night in the station. There are lots of other people sleeping in the station too. People who have come from bombed cities in the north of Italy who believe Florence to be safe. There are other people with things to sell. Whispering down to all the bodies beneath blankets. Cigarettes. Chocolate. Eggs. A rabbit.

Then a strange man in a battered hat sits down next to them. The man is strange because there's a twist to his face. His head tilts at an odd angle on his neck. Twitches around in continuation. Esme stares at him with fascinated distaste. The man holds out a pack of grubby cards. He looks like a man who talks to himself. Who makes gestures while walking alone down a street. The man motions for Esme to pick one of his cards. She looks at her father. The same question in her eyes. *Is he a good person or a bad person?* Oskar can tell she thinks he is a bad person because there is something ugly about the way his face twists up. He tells her to pick one of the man's cards. She picks a card. The man can't get his words out. He stutters. His face contorts into an agonised choking expression.

"D-d-d-d-d-don't le-le-le-let me see it," he says.

She frowns at him. Wiping the sleeve of her coat over her mouth because he has spat at her. She doesn't like the man, his disability, his twisted agonised face. Oskar knows this.

"He wants you to remember the card you've chosen." Oskar wants her to be nice to this man. Wants her to know the man can't help making ugly faces when he talks. *Children can be like the Nazis*, he thinks.

"Ye-ye-ye-yes. D-d-d-d-don't te-te-tell me."

She does as she's told. Her eyes growing interested despite the aversion in her body for the man's contorted facial expressions. The man shuffles the cards. He shuffles them with flourishes and mesmerising sleights of hand. He shuffles the cards with the fluency he is unable to master for his voice.

"N-n-n-now you sh-sh-sh-shuffle the cards," he says.

She pulls back her head every time the man leans towards as if his breath smells of decayed teeth. "I don't know how."

"Yes you do," says Oskar. "Just mix them up. Change the order of them."

He watches his daughter's hands fumble with the cards. Her hands learning to do something they have never done before. The cards fall to the floor when she tries to mesh the wad in her right hand with the wad in her left hand.

Now who's stuttering? Is this man trying to teach my daughter not to be so judgemental?

The man motions to her to give him back the cards.

She hands him back the grubby cards.

"The ca-ca-card you ch-ch-ch-chose was this one."

He holds up the ten of hearts.

She shakes her head. Her expression solemn with a hint of apology in it for telling him he is wrong.

"Sure?"

She nods her head.

"Okay, this one."

He holds up the four of spades.

She shakes her head again. The ghost of a smile in her bright eyes now.

Oskar laughs.

"This one then."

"No," she says. She is giggling now. The man smiles and then shakes his head in disbelief and then stands up and walks away.

"Why did he talk funny?"

"He can't help it. It's like a cough."

"He kept getting my card wrong, didn't he?"

"I think he just wanted to make you laugh."

"Why?"

"Because you're beautiful when you laugh."

One or two trains have begun to arrive at the platforms now. He notices a train of brown cattle trucks. The windows are smaller now. No more than slits. There would be no climbing out of that train. They are told to move on by two fascist militia. She hides behind him when these two men approach and one of them smiles at her.

They walk along the river. She holds her bear by one of its ears. The sun is rising up over the skyline of hills. He takes her to the Boboli Gardens. They drink water from a fountain. In the middle of the amphitheatre he begins to dance. Encourages her to dance too. She twirls in front of the Neptune fountain. A gust of wind brings some of its spray to their hair.

"Look!" he says. "Winter will be over soon."

He is pointing up at an almond tree. At the flowers of white snow with tiny thumbprints of golden pollen on the anthers.

"Are we going to have a new house today?"

"I hope so. We're going to see Uncle Francesco."

"He's not my uncle."

They arrive early at Francesco's house. He hesitates a moment before ringing Francesco's bell. As if in anticipation of the clanging of the church bells. A black car with Nazi flags passes by. Speeding off towards the river.

A man in a long leather coat opens the door of Francesco's house. A short man with heavy-lidded eyes. Black hair swept back from his forehead.

Oskar has imagined this moment many times but never under these circumstances. In his imaginings they come to get him in the middle of the night. With violence and bluster. He doesn't walk into their arms in broad daylight.

"I was told there might be a room to rent here," he says. It is the best bluff he can think of. Then he spoils it by going into more detail. Providing a bogus history of his and his daughter's plight, their hardships. Showing his discomfort in this need to ingratiate himself and his daughter.

The man in the leather coat opens the door wider. "Do you know this man?" he says to a woman who is standing behind him. She is Francesco's landlady. Oskar has met her once before.

She is frightened. He can see this. She doesn't know what to say. She wants to help but she doesn't know what answer might help. "No," she finally says. But unconvincingly.

"You will have to come with us," says the man in the long black leather coat.

"Why?"

"Because I'm obeying orders. As we all must do."

"What about my little girl?"

He gives a faint shrug of his shoulders.

He kneels down in front of Esme. "I want you to go to Isabella's studio. Okay? Can you remember how to get to her studio? It's not far from here."

"I want to come with you."

"I'll be back soon. It's just a misunderstanding. Okay?"

21 - April 1944

FREDDIE IS sitting in the brook, splashing the chill water up onto his naked torso. Justin has finished washing and now stands on the bank. Towelling himself dry with a torn shirt.

A white butterfly spins up out of the long seeded grass. It settles on a white flower the shape of a star and then flits off over the water. Freddie tells himself the butterfly is a carrier of pollen and therefore is surely a good omen.

"So today's the big day. You must be excited?" says Justin.

"I still don't quite believe it's true."

"You're meeting her at home?"

"No. Apparently it's not safe. I'm meeting her in a printers near the station."

"Isn't that a bit odd?"

"Yes. Fosco set up this meeting." He hasn't told Justin this. For fear Justin would dissuade him from going. That he would hear from Justin's lips, in a more forthright tone, the warning he himself continues to stifle.

Justin stops towelling himself. "I suppose we don't know for sure he was the traitor."

"Doesn't bode well that he hasn't been back."

"No, it doesn't. One piece of advice in that case. Avoid the station. Teeming with Gestapo and Italian secret police. Arrive at the rendezvous by back streets if possible. And reccy the meeting place in advance. "

Freddie hikes several miles to the nearest town. He sits on the wall outside the small church. Near the newspaper stand. The village only has two shops and both are closed because they have nothing to sell. He watches an old woman cross the square. Three old men stand around chatting near the statue of Garibaldi.

On the bus he sits next to an old woman all in musty black. She holds her bag on her lap with both hands. As if wary of having it snatched from her. The bus snakes along the bumpy hillside roads. Cornfields rising up towards a ridge or dipping down towards a gully. Terraced vineyards. A Benedictine abbey high on a hill. He dozes off while listening to the two women in front discussing the hardships they face. The blast of the bus' horn startles him awake. With a joyful shout his body knows the city walls of Florence will appear at any moment.

He gets off the bus by the market at Porta Romana. Walks through the towering gate in the old city wall. A wonder that it is still there, that he is walking through it again after all these years. It seems like another life when he last walked down via Romana. His stomach tightens when he passes a pair of fascist guards standing by the entrance to the Boboli Gardens. He is unprepared for the high sweep of emotion when he arrives at the river. For a moment it is like standing transfixed at the centre of his world.

All the stories he now has to tell Isabella. He remembers his RAF medical. The task of blowing the mercury bubble up into a tube and sustaining it aloft with his breath for sixty seconds. He had wanted to tell her this story the moment he stepped out of the doctor's surgery. *At least I managed to keep that up*. Or the first time he piloted a Tiger Moth solo and how he saw a little boy looking up at him from the road below and felt as though he was more that little boy in his short trousers with his wide eyes than himself, the pilot of the plane. They always told each other about the parts of the day they had spent apart, sketching in detail so the other could see it, so it became a memory they seemed to share in common. They were good at talking. Sharing stories. Everything he did only seemed to take root when he told her about it. There were times when he arrived home as breathless as an inspired poet with the urgency to talk to her.

He turns into his street. There is no key inside the pocket of his coat. All the clothes he wears belong to someone else. They make him feel like he hasn't brushed his hair, hasn't shaved. He has a fake id card in his pocket. He is Paolo

Zamagni. Resident of Palermo. If he is stopped and questioned his accent will betray him. Because, like most of his countrymen, he can't erase the Englishness from his diction of the Italian language. The starch and ironed creases of his English voice.

Walking up his street is like reading an old letter. He sees everything as if from a distance in time. The familiar buildings seem to want to erase all that has happened to him since he last saw them. Want him to become again the man he was when he last saw them. He feels that man is walking by his side. He feels a blend of sadness and nostalgia for him. And yet he doesn't feel changed. It is everything else that has changed. Proof of this is the wall of bricks that hides the fresco of the Madonna in the tabernacle on the corner of the road. *To protect it from our bombs*, he thinks.

He is weightless, buffeted, rising and falling on fledgling wings with an urgent pulse in his blood when he rings on the bell. Or that's how he feels.

No one answers the door.

He sits down on the steps of the church. The door is closed. He remembers watching the rain slide down this old door one night after he and Isabella said goodnight, how its downward course was directed by the grain of the wood.

Then Giuseppe the gardener appears at the green door. His eyes widen. He puts down the box he is carrying and walks briskly over to Freddie and clasps him to his breast, knocking Freddie's hat off.

"What a joy to see you. But how are you here?"

"Long story, Giuseppe. It's good to see you are well."

"One survives, just."

"Is my wife here?"

"I don't think so. I saw her leave this morning. She goes to her studio every day. With her grandfather."

"Her grandfather?"

"I think he is her grandfather. A man has been staying here with her for a while."

The magnolia tree is still there by the gravel path. He caresses the bark of its trunk while looking out at the enclosed secret garden, the lawn where he read books while the sun trailed lover's fingers along his thighs and over his navel. Then he climbs the uneven steps up to the French windows. It feels wrong that he no longer has the key to open these doors. He peers through the glass, past his own glazed reflection, into the large sitting room. The furniture is the same but it has been arranged into a different pattern. He can see two plates smeared with red sauce and cigarette ash on the table. Two empty glasses with a crust of purple inside. One with an imprint of red lipstick around the rim. He feels betrayed by the secret narrative of these familiar objects. Then wonders if it might be his wife they are betraying. Manifesting a memory of some moment of intimacy he was never meant to know about. *With this SS officer.* Freddie stands there like a ghost, keenly aware of the betrayals that are perpetrated against the departed. He is tempted to smash the glass. Then he is tempted to stay in the garden. Sit down under one of the trees and wait for Isabella to come home.

Instead he decides to walk to her studio. He walks along the river. Past the Nazi banners hanging outside some of the riverside palaces. A seagull, swooping down low, races its reflection on the water towards the fairytale arches of Ponte Santa Trinita.

He sees from some distance the black staff car with the Nazi insignia parked outside Isabella's studio.

Signor Marcusi is more alarmed than pleased to see him.

"It's good to see you," says the baker, offering his hand.

"Do you know why there's a German staff car outside my wife's studio?"

"It's none of my business."

"Signor Marcusi, does my wife often receive visits from Nazi officers?"

"That's not for me to say. Like everyone else, I mind my own business these days."

"But it has happened more than once?"

Signor Marcusi nods gravely.

He sits down on a patch of grass by the river with his back resting against a lime tree. From here he can see the front door of Isabella's studio with an unlikelihood of being seen himself.

22 - April 1944

"I WAS PASSED a message for an English pilot telling him a meeting with his wife has been arranged. But no one has spoken to me about any meeting."

Maestro continues working up close on his canvas. "Perhaps it's a different English pilot," he says.

She is growing impatient with him and his refusal to leave the sanctuary of his painting. *I was like this*, she thinks. "You're telling me there are two English pilots married to women in Florence?"

"Stranger things have happened. As I've always said, strangeness is a necessary component of beauty."

"What does beauty have to do with it?"

"Without beauty, life is intolerable." He swirls the paint about on his palette, squinting at his picture. "What were you doing getting mixed up with the Communists anyway?"

"Not everyone sick to death of Fascism is a Communist."

"Even so."

"Of course it's Freddie. I identified his body two months ago."

Finally he stops fiddling with his painting and looks round at her with some emotion on his face.

"Except it wasn't him. It was a man wearing his dog tags. Which means Freddie is in Italy. Every time the buzzer goes my heart rises up in expectation of it being him at the door."

"Then why hasn't he come to see you?"

"How do I know? There's a war. People can't just do what they want to do. But if this meeting has been set up why has no one told me?"

"When is this meeting?"

"Today. At three o'clock."

"And you're going?"

"Of course I'm going."

"What if it's a trap?"

"That's what I keep thinking."

"Where's the meeting?"

"Via della Scala."

"Near the station. If Freddie were here in Florence he surely would have tried to contact you. Which means in all probability he's hiding somewhere in the countryside. So he'll have to get a bus or train to Florence. Wait for him at the train station."

She is about to leave the studio when the buzzer sounds. Her heart jumps up into her throat. She throws open the door and begins running down the stairs. Something in her tries desperately to impose Freddie's face on Captain Erich Heinkel. He is clearly disconcerted by the beseeching and then hostile look she launches at him.

"Forgive the intrusion, Isabella. I have something of importance to tell you."

"Yes?"

"Can we go up to your studio?"

"I'm in a rush. I have to go out."

"It won't take long." He motions his gloved hand towards the stairs. "I've brought you some cigarettes. English cigarettes. Kindly dropped to us by the British," he says following her up onto the landing where Marina's family live.

She stands by while he greets Maestro. Then becomes exasperated as the two men carry on a conversation about his painting.

"I really must leave," she says. She stumbles over Zinnia who is excited and circling around her feet. She shouts at the dog, for the first time. Zinnia cowers and looks up at her with mournful eyes.

"Of course," says Captain Heinkel. "Forgive me. Before you do may I see the nude painting of that girl you were working on?"

She throws back her shoulders in bewilderment.

"I'll explain," he says.

She turns round the large canvas that is facing the wall.

"I thought so. It's a fabulous likeness you've captured. Not of course that I have seen her without her clothes." He smiles at Maestro. "This girl is now working for Carità's secret police in via Bolognese. I thought I should tell you."

"Marina?"

"Yes. How is your Jewish model and the little girl?"

She is worried about Oskar. Has not seen or heard from him for too long. But it is absurd that Marina would betray Oskar. If that is what he is implying. She suspects Marina is in love with Oskar. Unless he has rebuffed her in some way…Hell hath no fury like a woman scorned.

"Why do you ask?"

"Word reached me the other day that a German Jewish man was arrested. I'm sorry."

She has sometimes felt guilty for not doing more for Oskar. She had intended to take him to her parents' house. He and Esme would have been safe there.

She stands on the street outside with Erich. Wearing a headscarf and dark glasses. He offers her a lift in his car. She declines. Aware once again that she is attracting disapproving looks. She says goodbye to him. Crosses the river by Ponte alla Carraia. Catches the eye of the soldier in the turret of the German tank. She feels distaste for him and probably shows it. Because she knows he would probably kill her husband if he got the chance. Before she knows it she is already entering Piazza Santa Maria Novella. The clip clop of horses drawing carriages. Women with elaborate hats and moneyed voices sitting outside the hotel. There are red and black banners hanging from a building under the loggia. This is a holding prison. Where the Jews and men rounded up for the work camps in Germany are kept. Two Blackshirt guards with faces like convicts and guns slung over their shoulders standing outside. There are posters for films. An illustration of a scantily clad woman with wet strawberry lipstick. A poster of a German soldier. *Germany is truly your friend*, it says.

She has decided she wants to see the printer. Evaluate what kind of man he is. She enters the premises imperiously. When she is nervous she always over-dramatises an idea of self-possession. She steps into a tide of lamp-lit smoke. A smell of rusting machinery and wet ink. The printer is an overalled man with thick spectacles. He is resting his hand tensely on a large metal wheel. A surly but private man. A lonely man. Or so she guesses him to be. His hands are blackened with dyes, inks.

"I'm lost," she says. "Do you know where via Palazzuolo is?"

He looks at her warily. An intense raking look that seeks out her secrets. Then, matter of factly, he tells her where via Palazzuolo is.

Is he a traitor? This private wary man with the inky fingers and thick spectacles. She has no idea. She turns her back on him and walks out.

The blue bus pulls up outside the station. She sees something of Freddie in every person who gets off. The images in her mind swimming over external detail like watery reflections. Then another crowded blue bus arrives. Fifty or so passengers file past her. She implores each and every one of them to be Freddie. But at the same time it seems like madness that she expects him to suddenly appear in Italy. She looks at her watch. Two forty. She walks back towards the printers. She sits down on the steps under the loggia. From here she can see the door of the printers. Her blood runs cold when she sees Scarface and Seagull Eyes. They are smoking cigarettes on the pavement opposite the printers.

Surely, if he comes, he will arrive from the direction of the station.

In which case she will be able to warn him before Scarface and Seagull Eyes see him.

23 - April 1944

FREDDIE WAKES up in a panic. The black car, he immediately sees, is no longer there. He looks down at his wrist before remembering he has no watch.

He rings the buzzer of the studio. No answer. He rings the buzzer of Marina's family below. The door opens. He looks up to see Signora Lozzio standing on the first floor landing. She too seems more alarmed than pleased to see him.

"I'm looking for Isabella."

"Isabella left about ten minutes ago but her teacher is still there."

"He didn't answer the door."

"Try again because he's definitely there. I heard him two minutes ago pacing back and forth above my kitchen."

He thumps on the door. A dog barks. Two sheepish barks then falls silent.

"Maestro, it's Freddie."

He hears a rustling noise behind the door but still the door does not open.

"Maestro? It's Freddie Hartson."

Finally the door opens. Maestro looks both aggrieved and sheepish.

"What are you doing here? Have you lost your senses? Isabella has gone to meet you."

He is taken aback by the fierce scorn of his old teacher's admonition. "Fosco told me…"

"You've seen Fosco? That devious little piece of shit."

Freddie has never heard Maestro swear before. Even in his agitated state he finds time to be shocked.

"Don't you see, it's Fosco who's the traitor. I was arrested because of him. Beaten by a band of common criminals because

of him. He betrayed me. He's stolen my studio and my home."
Maestro is shouting and refuses to make eye contact.

"Fosco told me Isabella's taken an SS officer as a lover. I
don't think I really believed it until I saw the Nazi car outside."

"She isn't his lover. You've been duped. Just as I was duped.
We've all been duped by signor Fosco Scarafuggi. I taught him
everything he knows. Do you have any idea how much time and
energy I've spent passing on my knowledge to him. And this is
how he repays me. Fosco lied. Don't you understand, Fosco is a
Judas."

"So Isabella might be walking into a trap."

"I told her. I tried to warn her. We thought you'd arrive at
the station. I told her to wait at the station."

Freddie is no longer listening. "What's the time?"

"You've got ten minutes."

He walks as quickly as he dares. Sensing he will appear
suspicious if there is too much urgency in his stride. The closer
to the rendezvous he gets the more the whole set-up seems like
a trap. He says Isabella over and over again in his mind as if she
might hear him, as if she might heed his warning. It is ridiculous
that they are going to meet at an unknown man's workshop.

A woman overhead is shaking a rug out of a window. She
stops when he walks directly underneath and he smiles up at her
to say thank you and it disheartens him that she doesn't smile
back. Then he steps off the kerb without looking and a man on
a bicycle with a metal basket over the front wheel swerves to
avoid him and, looking back over his shoulder, curses him. His
bad feeling worsens. His hands clenched into tight fists inside
his coat pockets.

In via della Scala there are long queues outside several
shops. A pile of rubbish stacked high and swarmed over by flies
on the kerb outside a padlocked metal gate. He watches a cat
wind its way in and out of railings outside a grim official
building on the other side of the road. There is a feeling in this
grey street that all the brightness is being drained out of the day.
An ambulance drives slowly past. He watches it pull up to a halt
about fifty yards away. He notices two men standing on the
pavement opposite. They both seem to be silently

communicating with the driver of the ambulance. Then both of these men are looking over at him. The current of their heightened interest producing a kind of time stopping static on the air. Behind them, about a hundred yards away, he suddenly becomes aware of Isabella. He recognises her by the tilt of her head, by the atmosphere around her. She is wearing dark glasses and a headscarf. She is waving at him. He freezes. His overwhelming instinct is to go to her but she is waving him away. The two men are now walking cautiously towards him.

Give myself up or run?

His feet slide about inside the oversized blood-stained boots stuffed with dead leaves as he turns on his heels and breaks into a sprint. A voice rings out. He hears it above the clatter of an approaching tram. Then the sound of a gunshot and a whistling crack close to his ear.

24 - April 1944

ISABELLA SEES Freddie just as she is about to light a cigarette. She holds the lighted match in mid-air until a draft of air extinguishes the flame. The ambulance obscures her view of him for a moment. She recognises Fosco at the wheel. Then Freddie reappears, a quintessence of himself, but too far away for her to make out much detail. She recognises him through the heartbreaking intimacy she feels tugging at her like a tide. Fosco stops the ambulance close to the printers. He hasn't seen her because he is attracting the attention of Scarface and Seagull Eyes and pointing with his thumb over his shoulder.

Freddie looks over at her. Finally he has seen her. Her body now a firebrand circuit of overloaded current. She shoos him away. As vigorously as she dares. It goes against everything in her nature to shoo him away. But he seems to understand. He turns and begins to walk away quickly. She is willing him in all her muscles to run to safety. Scarface shouts at him to stop. Unholsters his pistol and fires off a shot. Several pigeons scatter up from the russet roof tiles of the buildings. She sees Freddie fall to the ground. She sees Freddie sprawled on the pavement. She isn't sure if she releases the scream rising in her throat. Her mind suddenly emptied of all thought as if making space for the enormity of what is to come.

But Freddie levers himself up from the pavement. He turns around and raises his hands in surrender.

Her instinct is to run to him. The blood in her body is urgent with the desire to run to him. But she stays rooted to the spot. Freddie looks over at her while he is handcuffed. He is still looking at her when he is marched to the back of the ambulance. Her sense of powerlessness drains all the strength from her body. For an awful moment it occurs to her that he might think it is she who led him into this trap.

She remembers nothing of the walk back to the studio.

25 - April 1944

FRANCESCO WATCHES the man lift his little girl up into his arms. The tenderness with which the man holds the little girl reminds him of Oskar. Oskar and his little girl. It is a beautiful thing to watch.

Every day he expects Oskar and his daughter to arrive in one of the trucks that pass through the gate with their load of new prisoners. He is always relieved when Oskar and his daughter are not in one of the trucks.

Then, one morning, Oskar is standing to attention on the parade ground. Like a hallucination. Shaved and numbered and counted. He must have arrived in the middle of the night. When Francesco walks over to him he holds back his inclination to smile. He always now holds back any inclination to smile. After they knocked out his teeth.

"Forgive me," he says.

Oskar embraces him. "Don't worry."

"Your daughter is safe?"

"I hope so."

"It's stricter here now. A man was shot the other day for failing to obey a command. He was deaf. The SS man said, let's see if you can hear this and put the barrel of his pistol inside the man's ear."

"At least it's warmer this time."

"I saw you, you know."

"What do you mean?"

"With Marina. Up at San Miniato. I thought I minded but I don't think I do any more. You know she's now working for Carità? She typed out my details."

Oskar puts a hand on his arm. "Don't be too hard on her," he says. "We none of us can choose who we spend our time with any more."

"She was of no use to me while I was being tortured. The thought of her didn't help me bear the pain."

"Was it bad?"

"I wasn't thinking when I gave them my address. Then I remembered I told you to visit me the next day. But it was too late. They knocked out my teeth."

"I noticed."

"That's why I don't smile anymore," he says and smiles. The inside of his mouth looks like a charred and pillaged fortress. "Stupid, isn't it?"

"What's stupid?"

"Vanity. I don't smile because I'm vain about my missing teeth. I braved a look at myself the other night. In the window of the infirmary when no one was watching. It bothered me that I looked so ugly. Without teeth. It makes me feel I don't have long to live. Like an old man. But the fact that it bothers me, the fact that I want my teeth back means, I suppose, I still have hope of a normal life in the future. They didn't torture you?"

"No. Not really. Just made me drop my trousers."

"Do you know they go to convents and monasteries where evacuated children are sheltered and they make all the boys strip naked so they can take away the Jewish children? Grown men making children strip naked. There are rumours, you know. The Croatian Jews here say they are starving all the Jews to death in camps. Burying them alive in huge pits. That's what awaits us when our number is called."

Francesco's number is called the next day. His is one of twelve numbers called out at morning roll call. He is told to step forward. That is all he is told. Almost immediately, without being given the black water that passes as coffee, he is herded into the back of a truck that waits by the gate. At nine in the morning. The truck is followed out of the prison gates by an SS car. He sees it through an opening in the flap. Following close behind. He doesn't know any of the men on the benches facing each other in the back of the truck. The two German guards are glum and silent.

The journey only lasts ten minutes. Along roads riddled with potholes and bumps.

The tarpaulin is unfastened. The tailboard lowered. Francesco climbs down. He stands by the truck with the other prisoners waiting for the Germans to tell him what he must do next. The land is flat for miles around. He looks out into the distance, over a succession of cornfields. Wishing he was there. Tramping across fields with only sheep and birds for company.

They are given shovels. Told to dig a ditch at the far end of what he now sees is some kind of shooting range. Not deep but long and wide. Three metres by forty.

He listens to the talk while he digs.

"You think we're digging our own graves?"

"At least we'll die in Italy and not in Germany."

"With the end of the war so close."

"Says who?"

Out of the corner of his eye he watches two German soldiers set up a machine gun on a mound not far from the pit.

That's it then, he thinks.

Everyone is aware of the machine gun. Everyone slows down the pace of the shovelling. He is down in the trench, waist high. The smell of the fresh earth and grass hangs memories on the air. Memories he chooses not to acknowledge. He lets them drift by, be carried away on the currents of air like pollen from lime trees. The earth becomes more resistant to his shovel. His arms and shoulders ache.

Then the bark of a German voice. Telling them to stop. In German. The nervous glances exchanged by the men holding shovels in the ditch. Not understanding the German words except that there is anger and scorn in them.

"He's telling us to get out of the trench," someone says.

Francesco heaves himself up out of the pit. Trying not to look over at the German soldier manning the machine gun on the mound ten yards away. He sees him anyway. Sees he is smoking a cigarette. Watching them with a bored kind of expression.

Francesco stands on the edge of the trench. Breathing in the bosky clay smell of the overturned earth. Thinking of water. Thinking that if he had a glass of water now he wouldn't care about anything else. The veins in his wrist are high. He thinks of all the arteries in his body through which blood ingeniously performs its cycles.

The two German officers are talking among themselves. Laughing. He has the impression they are enjoying the suspense they are creating. That their talking and laughing is merely a pretence to prolong the mystery, the terror of what is going to happen next.

"If you're going to shoot us fucking shoot us. Get it over with," says someone under his breath.

But they are not shot. They are herded into a building with no windows near the entrance of the shooting range. Some kind of tool shed. They are given no water. Nothing to eat. They stand around waiting. There is a wand of sunlight beneath the door. It reminds him of tiptoeing past his parents' bedroom in the middle of the night. His heart loud with mischief.

His tongue looks for his missing teeth.

He listens to the sound of engines starting up. The car and the truck leave. Or so they speculate. Someone tries to open the door. Gently. With a delicate twist of the hand. But it won't open. He feels suddenly claustrophobic. As if the room is filling with water. As if soon his head will be under water. He has to take a number of deep breaths to calm himself down.

He can hear nothing outside. He never stops listening to the space behind the locked door. But the only noise he hears with clarity is a local bell tower ringing evening vespers. He listens to the talk while he sits crouched in a corner of this room that smells of rusted tools and damp stone and, before long, urine.

He curls up on the ground and falls asleep. He dreams of Marina. She is dressed in medieval clothes. Garish face paint. When he awakes there is no longer a wand of sunlight beneath the door. He thinks he hears the croaking of frogs. A sound that hangs another memory on the air.

He senses many of the men are asleep in the thick darkness around him. The stink of urine has got worse and there is also a smell of human shit.

The room stirs with rustles and fidgeting when the sound of a vehicle approaching is heard. He hears tyres raking through gravel with a pinpoint clarity. As if it is something happening inside his own body.

There is some shouting in German. Boots on the gravel, shifting the stones which make a light hissing noise.

"Can anyone hear what he's saying?"

"He's reading a death sentence. Whoever's out there is to be executed as a reprisal for a partisan attack on German soldiers."

He thinks of the men out there. The men about to be shot. Standing by the grave he helped dig. Standing beneath the night sky. Waiting to be shot. Every hair on his body anticipates the burst of machinegun fire that still does not arrive.

When it does arrive it is still a shock. He thought he had braced himself for the horror of it but it is as if a plate of glass shatters in his face. The howling, the moaning of men in agony is extinguished by a series of single gunshots that leave behind an echo.

An hour or so passes during which nothing happens. His craving for water increases. He talks with a man he doesn't know. They don't ask each other their names. They both think they are going to be killed but they don't say this aloud.

Then another truck arrives. German voices shouting orders. The death sentence is read out again. This time there is some shouting. A single gunshot. Then the machine gun fire again. But with more prolonged, less ordered bursts. There are cries of pain. Angry shouting. A light flickers back and forth under the door. There is a sense of chaos outside. Of the breakdown of law and order. It takes a long time for the noises to cease.

The door is opened. A torch shone into the shed. Tearing alarmed faces out of the darkness. The faces of men who think they are going to die in the next fifteen minutes. They are told that if they tell anyone what they see they will be shot. The shooting range is lit by one or two reflector lights held by German soldiers. Spectral and eerie. A place of ghosts and shadows. He is marched with the other men over to the trench they dug. The sky is full of stars. Shovels are still heaped nearby. He sees the machine gun is no longer mounted on the mound.

They are told to fill in the trench. The reflector lights show splashes of blood on the grass. There are about thirty bodies in the trench. It is heavily shadowed inside the trench but he thinks he recognises the back of Oskar's head among the corpses.

26 - April 1944

WHEN THE LIGHTS go out, at nine-thirty, there is a general discussion. Secretive talking in the dark. Oskar learns two hundred eggs have been stolen from the mess. Various prisoners are nominated as the most likely thief.

The searchlight rakes back and forth outside the windows. Cunning and inescapable. Like how he imagined the eye of God as a child. Oskar shares a thin straw mattress with a chemist from Bologna. A man with a kind tired face. Watery eyes. The man uses the pages of a book of Petrach's Sonnets as cigarette papers. Smokes anything he can find.

The next morning Francesco is one of the twelve Jews herded off in a truck. Everyone talks about this. Speculates on what it might mean. Plays the guessing game.

A German motorcyclist in goggles arrives at the camp after lunch. This too is discussed. The guessing game. There is another roll call in the afternoon. The vice commandant of the camp holds a sheet of paper. He begins reading out names. Not numbers.

Oskar continually expects his name to be next. He is listening out for his real name. He has forgotten that he does not go by that name any more. He has lost track of which of the many names he now goes under. The vice commandant has to read out his fake name three times before he realises it is him and he steps forward. His is the very last name on the list. He tells himself the order in which the names are read out is meaningless.

All the men on the list are Italian political prisoners. Wearing the red star. He too is a political prisoner. He too wears the red star. Because he joined the wrong line when he arrived and then thought it best not to point out his error. Was it best not to have pointed out his error? The guessing game again.

All the men whose names have been read out are told to prepare their bags and go to hut 17.

He has no bag. He is the first one to arrive at hut 17. Hut 17 is the closest hut to the gates of the camp. He stands by the door. On the roof of a farm building on the other side of the barbed wire perimeter fence he sees a male peacock. It fans out its pageantry of feathers as he looks at it. He asks himself what this might mean. If there is a connection between his fate and this impulse of the bird.

A young boy with a chalky face and wistful dark eyes is the next to arrive at the hut. He has no bags either. He feels immediately protective of this boy. It is good to have someone to be strong for. It's a feeling that brings his daughter closer.

"Do you think they're going to kill us?"

"No," Oskar says.

More men arrive at the hut. Oskar sits on a bunk with the chemist from Bologna and the young boy with the wistful dark eyes.

They are kept waiting in hut 17. Forbidden to leave. Their midday meal and their evening meal, the same soup, are both brought to them in the hut. They ask what this means. They are still in Hut 17 when it is dark.

"One thing about all this suspense, about waiting around after your name has been called out, you get to know yourself a little better," says the chemist from Bologna. "Except I'm not sure I want to know myself any better."

He looks over at a man who is praying. Threading his rosary beads through his gnarled fingers. Silently mouthing words he hopes to draw comfort from.

"Are you frightened of dying?" asks the chemist from Bologna.

"I've got a young daughter."

"She makes you frightened of dying?"

"She makes me want to live."

"I don't have any children. Where is she? Your daughter."

"In Florence. With a woman I hope. I think she'll be safer without me. With a woman."

"I hope so, my friend."

The voices of the Germans are raucous, angry. Like the voice of the vice commandant of the camp when he read out the names. This does not bode well, someone says. It usually means some unpleasant task is being demanded of them when the voices of these soldiers are so raucous.

"Your name is Berto, isn't it? Was it you who stole the eggs?"

Berto laughs. "You going to arrest me, are you?"

Berto is among the first group of men who are escorted out of the hut. Herded into the back of a truck. Oskar watches through the window.

"They're being made to leave their bags behind."

Thirty minutes later the truck returns. The bags are still piled up on the grass.

Oskar sits in the back of the truck between the chemist from Bologna and the young boy with the wistful eyes. The tailboard is raised. The tarpaulin is lashed down and secured. The journey only lasts ten minutes.

Oskar jumps down from the truck. He sees he is in a flat and desolate place. Over by a stone building there is the smoky white haze of a reflector light that highlights the individual bricks in the wall. He is marched with the other men to the far end of this barren compound. To a trench. Even in the darkness he can tell there are bodies in this trench. Dead bodies. He looks around. For somewhere to run to. The sight of the stars wrings out of him a sense of how vast and resourceful is his love of life still.

The vice commandant of the camp reads out from a piece of paper. Reads hurriedly. They are to be shot as a reprisal for the cowardly attack on a convoy of Wehrmacht soldiers outside Genoa. A soldier holds a reflector light so the vice commandant can read the typed words on the sheet of paper. Oskar wonders why they bother to read out this longwinded justification for their actions. He wonders this as if he is at liberty to think freely.

"*Jawoll. Jawoll.*"

It is the chemist from Bologna who interrupts the vice commandant with this impertinent ironic jeering. The vice commandant is shocked into silence.

"You're going to kill us. You bloody bastards."

The chemist from Bologna breaks rank. Charges towards the vice commandant. Strikes a blow.

Run, he thinks.

"Run," he shouts out. And all of a sudden everyone is running. Oskar pounds off sharply to the left. Towards the shadows. Bullets zip through the air. Lights reel around. He is caught in a spotlight. Bullets crack close to his head. He veers away sharply from the shaft of light.

27 - April 1944

ISABELLA HANDS Captain Erich Heinkel the finished portrait she has painted of him.

"You've had it framed," he says.

"The least I could do. Words can't express how grateful I am."

"All I need now is a home to hang it in."

She sits down at the desk opposite him.

He is wearing the swastika armband over the sleeve of his black uniform today.

"I spoke briefly with your husband."

She pauses in the act of applying lipstick.

"He was the pilot of a Lancaster bomber. I asked him if he had taken part in the raid that destroyed Hamburg."

"Did he?"

"He said he didn't but I think he was lying. Perhaps he thought I was trying to extract classified information from him. I felt I should have hated him. But I saw that he is a good man. Some men enjoy this war but he is not one of those men. He is like me."

"He is a good man."

"I'm sorry I can't do more."

"What will happen to him now?"

"He'll be deported to a prison camp, probably in Germany. One problem is he has no proof that he is an officer of the RAF. RAF officers have it a bit easier than most prisoners of the Reich. It's one of the oddities of this war. When you consider how much destruction and heartbreak the RAF cause to Germans and Germany."

"Does he know we're going to see each other?"

"No. I'm sticking my neck out here. I don't belong here. This is the headquarters of the Abwehr. Someone I know here has granted me this favour. This is strictly against regulations so I thought it best to keep it a secret between you and me. I'm afraid I won't be able to leave you alone."

The knuckle rap on the door startles her. She can't believe how nervous she is. She knocks over the chair when she stands up. Freddie stands between two guards. He has a cut on his lip and a bruised cheek. He is unshaved and his charcoal hair is matted and his clothes are filthy. She sees he quickly masks his shock at seeing her. She is hurt by this sudden extinction of emotion in him. The withdrawal of recognition from his eyes. As if she is a stranger.

Captain Erich Heinkel dismisses the two guards.

She takes a step towards Freddie but he is so bereft of every signal fire by which she recognises their intimacy that she has to stifle her urge to take him in her arms. She wonders if the war has changed him in some horrible desensitising way. Alienated him irreparably from the man he was, the man she loves.

"It's all right," says Erich, touching Freddie lightly on the shoulder. "This isn't a trap. I've arranged for you to have a chat with your wife."

Freddie appears mistrustful for a moment. Then recognition of her shines in his eyes. She embraces him and they stand clasped and swaying in each other's arms.

"I must stink."

"You still smell like you. Just." She wipes away the imprint of her painted lips over his mouth. "I've brought you some clothes."

"I liked the dog."

"Zinnia. I forgot you saw her. She followed me back to the studio one day. I felt if I looked after her, fate would look after you."

"My crew were all superstitious like that. I suppose I was too. Did you get any of my letters?"

"A few in the early days. Dinghy training in the local swimming pool. Your friend who leant down to pick up something he dropped and was decapitated by a propeller. One minute you had me laughing out loud, the next sick with heartache."

"That's me."

"You were at training school then. As if you had become a schoolboy again. All pranks and boyish camaraderie. Oh and I got a letter and a photograph from Canada. It made me feel like I was the victim of a practical joke."

She mirrors his wide smile.

"After that I heard nothing at all. I thought you had forgotten me."

"I wrote to you about three times a week. And I had to write you a farewell letter. Just in case. I enjoyed writing that. The clarity it gave me. I thought they have may sent it to you when I didn't make it back to base."

"No. But I was summoned to identify your dead body. Can you imagine what I felt on my way to that morgue? Of course it wasn't you at all. I had to stop myself from laughing out loud. Though of course I felt sorry for that poor unknown man."

"Hang on. What are you talking about?"

"A dead man wearing your salmon pink dog tags. They gave them to me."

"What did he look like?"

"A lost soul. Sort of grim and damned. But perhaps we all look like that when we're dead."

"Did he look like a scarecrow?"

"Yes, I suppose he did. It's awful how vivid his face still is to me."

"He stole my boots."

"I was never able to imagine what you were doing. I see now why. Because it all seems so farfetched."

"He woke me up the morning after I bailed out. Threatened me with a kitchen knife. I was so exhausted I barely took much notice of him. Poor wretch, eh?"

"I take it you didn't get my letters either?"

"A few, ages ago. There were whole sections crossed out. I wondered if it was you having second thoughts or the censor. You didn't really think that I had forgotten you, did you?"

"I didn't know what to think so I think I just stopped thinking altogether. You told me I think too much."

"I never did. You told me *I* think too much."

"Well that's true. Isn't it?"

"Beats me. Sometimes now I think I'll have to relearn from scratch what's true and what isn't. No, that isn't true. I have a much clearer idea now of what matters."

"And you saw Maestro."

"Seems like a hallucination now. I was so agitated I took his presence for granted. We spoke as if we saw each other every day. Then he started shouting at me about the near destruction of Leonardo's Last Supper. I didn't know it came within a whisker of being destroyed by our bombers. But he was jabbing his finger at me as if I had given the order. Giuseppe thinks he's your grandfather."

She smiles. "He'd be mortified if he knew that. Giuseppe said you'd been home."

"Except I couldn't get in."

"Oh Freddie. If only you had stayed there."

"I did think about it. I nearly broke the glass."

"I wish you had. It seems ridiculous we can't just go home now. Like the most unnatural thing in the world. Why does Fosco hate us all so much?"

"Is it true he's stolen Maestro's home and studio?"

"You don't think I'd be living with him otherwise," she smiles. "Oskar was here in Florence."

"I've thought about Oskar sometimes."

"He has a gorgeous daughter. I'm in love with his daughter."

"Good idea. Let's have a daughter when this war is over."

"I'd like that."

"I'd like it too."

"I miss the way you enjoy things," she says. "No one enjoys coffee and a cigarette like you. I think some people have to climb a mountain or swim with dolphins to find the joy you get from a coffee and a cigarette."

"Wish I had a cigarette. How am I going to manage back in that cell after this without a cigarette?"

There is a pause between them. She follows his gaze which is resting on Captain Erich Heinkel who has discreetly been sorting through paperwork he took from his briefcase but is now pointing to his watch.

"Time's up, I'm afraid. You will have to change into the clothes now. Can I trust you that there isn't a weapon concealed?"

She nods.

"Here's some cigarettes for you," he says. He puts them down on the desk.

"Thank you," Freddie says. "I've been smoking dried chestnut leaves for the past month."

She watches Freddie untie the piece of string that holds up his trousers. His bare feet filthy. His long toenails black. His shorts shredded. He gives her a shy smile when he stands naked in the middle of this office. His body thinner and dirtier than she has ever seen it, like the body of some feral creature.

"Come back to me," she says.

"I remember these," he says, referring to the trousers he is stepping into. "We bought them in Rome. I saw Maestro was wearing my clothes."

"Sorry."

"I think that was one reason he was so angry. He was embarrassed."

"Promise me you'll come back to me, Freddie."

28 - April 1944

"YOU WANT *me* to kill him?"

"Can't say that idea came up. Could you kill him?"

"No."

"Not even knowing that he's the most sadistic of Carità's torturers? We have information that he's about to do a runner. Get out of Florence. We'd like to get him before he does."

Across the street, beyond the tramlines, the fizz of the cables, there are at least thirty women queuing for bread outside a bakers. It's where Marina should be. In that queue with those women in their hats and the pinched expression of impatience on their faces. But she has been stopped in her tracks by this former university acquaintance of hers. A diffident fidgety young man with a sallow face who keeps sniffing. Someone she has never given a moment's thought to. Now announcing himself as a current in her destiny.

"Who exactly is this *we* you keep referring yourself to?"

"You've been working for us. We're the good guys, Marina. You should get out of that house you're in. Becchi is handling property stolen from the Jews. Did you know that? He's making a fortune out of this war. It's disgusting."

"I don't choose to work for him. My father owes him money. I work for him to help pay off this debt."

"I know. He'll be lucky if he's not hanged when this war is over. He'll certainly go to prison. Your father won't be in debt to him anymore. Not when the war's over. Go back to your family. Explain to your father. But first will you do us this favour?"

"What do you want me to do exactly?"

"Our friend Attila is elusive. He doesn't have any set patterns. It's our patterns that condemn us or keep us safe. And he knows this. He sleeps at the Savoy hotel. Like his boss,

Carità. We can't get either of them there. Piazza Vittorio is swarming with Germans and fascists."

"There's no set pattern to when he turns up at the house either. He hasn't been there for a while."

"I know. That's why we need your help. The next time he comes we want you to let us know."

"How?"

"Here's a telephone number. Memorise it and destroy this piece of paper before you get home."

She takes the ragged minuscule slip of paper. The numbers scrawled on it seem to jump about as she seeks to commit them to memory.

"The next time he arrives at the house call that number as soon as you can. As soon as he arrives if possible."

"Who will I be calling?"

"It doesn't matter. When that someone answers say, *pronto*. Nothing else. Just *pronto*. Then say goodbye. Is that clear?"

"I say *pronto* and then I say goodbye. Then what happens?"

"We kill him."

"Not in the house?"

"Outside the house. The moment he leaves the house."

"But he won't be alone. He's never alone."

"He'll be with another of Carità's henchmen. Angelo dell' Innocenti. He's got it coming to him as well."

"Angelo? He wouldn't hurt anyone."

"Angelo, as you so affectionately call him, burnt off the soles of one of our comrades with a blowtorch. He's a piece of shit. We'd have no problem doing away with him too. I've got some news about Francesco. I know you two were friends. He was put on a train yesterday for Auschwitz."

"Where's that?"

"Poland. It's a labour camp. It's not good news I'm afraid."

29 - April 1944

SIGNOR BECCHI and Attila arrive, each carrying a crate into the hallway. Marina stands aside to let them pass. Attila winks at her. Feigning ease under the heavy load he carries.

"I hope you haven't made any plans for tonight," he says, over his shoulder.

"Why?"

"You always answer everything with a question. Like our boss," says Attila. He disappears into the sitting room behind Signor Becchi.

She looks at the telephone.

It's not me who's killing him, she thinks.

She creeps closer to the sitting room. Listening. They have closed the door behind them.

She picks up the receiver. Half hoping the numbers she has memorised will elude her. But she listens to herself reciting the number to the operator.

"*Pronto,*" she says into the receiver. She waits for some word back, some acknowledgement of her presence. Nothing.

When she replaces the receiver she flinches because Attila is at the end of the hallway. Looking at her.

"You gave me a start. Creeping around like a cat."

He lights a cigarette. His face a spotlit mask of concentration for a moment in the lurid leap of the flame. "Who was that you were calling?" he says, the flame still glowing on his cheeks.

"None of your business. You see, this is the world you've created. A world in which you can't even make a telephone call without falling under suspicion."

"Suspicion? Who said anything about suspicion?"

"Do you ever relax? I can't imagine you in any kind of state of relaxation. Ever."

"Ha ha. You're right. I do like to throw myself around. Too much nervous energy. So you think we'd be better off under the communists?"

"There are more than two choices in life."

"Not always. Not at decisive moments."

"So it's fascism or communism for you? And there are no other options. What about England? What about America?"

"You mean our enemies?" His lips part in a boyish smile.

"*Your* enemies."

"You could be sent to a German prison camp for saying things like that."

"Exactly my point. We can't even say what we think in Italy. We all have to repeat the same formulas. Obedience. That's the fascists' favourite word, isn't it?"

"What is?" asks Signor Becchi, coming out into the hallway.

"Marina and I were having a political debate. But it's okay. We don't have to arrest her. At least not yet."

The front door opens and Angelo steps into the hallway. Carrying another crate.

"What are you doing here?" she says. He is stopped in his tracks by the fierce blaze of anger in her eyes.

"Has he told you?" asks Angelo. There is a new shyness in him. More accentuated every time she sees him.

"Told me what?"

"No need to snap his head off," says Attila, flashing his gold tooth.

"That we're taking you out to dinner tonight."

"Tonight?"

"Don't look so scared. You look like you've seen a ghost. Whooooo," says Attila, pulling a macabre face and flapping his hands in front of her face like a pantomime ghost. "We're not going to eat you. You're coming to the birthday dinner of our boss with Angelo and me. You've got half an hour to get ready."

30 - April 1944

FRANCESCO RUNS down the dusty road. He is one of about five hundred prisoners running down this dusty road. There is a barbed wire fence on either side. SS guards with dogs line the road. Shouting orders. Always the same orders. Faster. Faster. Stragglers are hit with whips and truncheons. The dogs tug at the leashes. Snarling and barking. The sky is silvery grey. The sun a ghostly imminence on the horizon.

Never has he been grated down to less of himself. He can think of nothing else but water. His entire being is screaming out for water. His fellow prisoners hold no interest for him. There has been no trading of stories. No seeking after intimacy. Three days in the cattle truck without water. His missing teeth remaining a secret behind lips that neither parted to talk or to smile. He runs down the dusty road. Towards a red brick building with two chimneys. Thinking of water.

He runs through an iron gate into a large yard. He is allowed to stop running now. His heart racing. Dizzy and sick with hunger. His tongue feels swollen, like some foreign growth on the roof of his mouth. The tongue that still searches for his missing teeth. It is the inside of his mouth that reminds him without mercy that a severance has taken place. That his old life has gone forever. The life when he could smile without feeling ugly.

The yard is lit by arc lights even though daylight is beginning to return to the sky. Some prisoners in filthy striped pyjamas are carrying large logs across the yard. They behave as though the five-hundred prisoners in the yard are no more interesting than a flock of pigeons. He can hear an electric saw in the near distance, behind the crying of children. The people behind press against him as the crowd swells in the yard. He catches a blast of a woman's perfume. In the midst of the stink of sweat and urine and body bacteria. The woman is ugly but her perfume holds a promise of beauty. For a fleeting moment it prises him open to the expectation of youthful wellbeing and desire. He glimpses again all the things he no longer dares to hope for.

An SS Lagerführer stands on a box. His thighs bulge against the cloth of his trousers. He has an obstinate face with a pulse of vanity in the eyes. "Now then, you Jews," he says. "We know you're not used to working but I am sorry to say this is not a holiday camp and here you will be forced to work. Think yourselves lucky that you are not fighting at the front. You will be working for the new Europe of the thousand year Reich. But you will be paid and fed well. First of all we're going to get you cleaned up and disinfected. Afterwards there will be soup and coffee for everyone. So I want you to get undressed as quickly as possible. Leave your clothes by one of the numbered pegs you will see. And memorise your number so you can retrieve your clothes quickly after the shower. The quicker you are, the sooner you will be served your bread and soup."

They are marched towards the sound of music. Towards the red brick building. Black smoke bellowing out of its two chimneys. The orchestra of male prisoners in the grubby striped outfits playing an upbeat folk song. There are a dozen sprinklers spraying arcs of glistening water over a well-kept lawn. He parts and licks his lips at the sight of this abundance of water. He quickens his step a little. In time to the music. Impatient to get to the showers despite a foreboding at the back of his mind, in the pit of his stomach that he does not allow himself to look at. There is a red-cross ambulance parked near the red brick building. Another puzzling detail. Like the band. Like the sprinklers. No interest was shown in the four people who died in the cattle truck during the long journey from Italy - the whiff of decomposition is still in his nostrils - and yet now an ambulance has been laid on. He has a feeling there is something purposeful in the trail of details the Nazis leave for their prisoners. Each one a clue as to what lies in store. He puzzles over these clues while he drags his feet over the gravel path where the crowd advance three or four abreast.

The movement of the long line of prisoners slows down to a restless shuffle. He kicks up a spume of dust from the gravel. A woman behind rams her baby carriage into the back of his foot. She apologises. As though this is a normal situation where normal rules of courtesy apply. The orchestra is positioned on a grass verge above wide concrete steps that descend down into an underground realm. There is a desire in his body to keep in step with the lively tempo of the music and because he can't his restlessness to press on increases. Becomes a sort of irritation with the people in front who obstruct his way. He knows this is an irrational desire because he doesn't want to go down those steps. To disappear from the daylight world. He follows a man with a rolled up mattress strapped to his back. When he stepped down from the train into the brutalising glare of the searchlights in the marshalling yard he noticed two SS soldiers pointing at this man and laughing.

A gust of wind blows the smoke from the chimney towards him just as he reaches the ten or so concrete stairs that descend underground. He looks across at the copse of trees to his left before lowering his head beneath the entrance to the long narrow columned room beneath the ground. It has a musty odour and a low oppressive ceiling. Wooden benches along the concrete walls. Whitewashed walls. Numbered clothes pegs and signs in a variety of different languages. *To the baths and disinfecting rooms. Cleanliness brings freedom. One louse may kill you. Hurry while the water is still warm.*

Some prisoners in the filthy striped pyjamas walk among them. Acting as ushers. Speaking in Yiddish which Francesco doesn't understand. Deadpan voices bereft of emotional history. There is also a German shouting out in Italian. Telling everyone to hurry up. To get undressed. To find themselves a numbered hook and hang their clothes there.

He undoes two buttons of his shirt. Standing by hook number 3371. In front of hook number 3372 a woman is kneeling in front of a little boy. She is trying to untie his shoelaces but the little boy resists.

He undoes the other buttons of his shirt, working down from the collar.

"Look at that whore."

It is a middle-aged woman in a black headscarf by peg 3370 who says this to him. She points at a girl across the room who reminds him immediately of Marina. The same physique. The same long blue-black hair. Once again he becomes momentarily who he was, who he will never be again. He watches the girl who looks like Marina slide up her skirt to reveal a suspender and a glimpse of naked thigh. He sees she has the attention of two of the SS guards. That they have forgotten about the whips they hold in their hands. She peels down her right stocking with a kind of slow swaying indolence. She doesn't look at the two SS guards but she lets them know she is enacting a ritual for their pleasure. She moves a few steps towards them, unbuttoning her blouse. She leans against a column and bends down to remove a shoe. Every act of her hand is a lingering caress. Conveys an arousal of the blood. Then, in the blink of an eye, she is ramming the heel of her shoe into the face of the uglier of the two SS guards. He drops his whip and yells out in pain. Her hand goes to his holster. It is a marvel how lightning-fast her reflexes are. She is holding his gun. Pointing it at the other SS guard. The freckled younger one with a mole on his chin. The shot from the gun explodes into the low-ceilinged room. The cap of the SS guard lifts up into the air. His strawberry blonde hair is flustered up into comic disarray. He spins backwards and is dumped down onto the floor. Trying to free his weapon when the second bullet rips into his chest. Sticky thick blood seeping through the grey cloth of his uniform.

Francesco watches the woman push through the crowd of naked and half-dressed prisoners. Attempting to hide. There is another shot. He catches a glimpse of another grey uniform stained with blood. The SS guards are all backing off towards the steps and the door while opening the flaps of their holsters. A cymbal crash of alarm on their faces. There is a moment's satisfaction in seeing the smug sneer of command wiped off their faces. But he is angry with the Marina woman. For delaying the moment when he will be able to lift up his face to water. One of the SS guards fires off some shots into the crowd before disappearing behind the door. Everyone tries to hide behind the columns or drops to the concrete floor. Children crying. Women screaming. The door closes. There are no longer any SS guards in the changing room. Only some of the prisoners in striped pyjamas who are acting as ushers. People begin shouting at the woman who reminds him of Marina. There is a scuffle. Another shot goes off. Francesco stands on his toes to see what is happening. Two men have pinned the woman's arms behind her back. Another man holds the gun. A naked woman walks forward and slaps her face. For putting the lives of her children at risk, she says.

"You fools. Don't you understand? We're all already dead," the woman who reminds him of Marina says.

The small bald man holding the gun glares at her. "Dead? If they were going to kill us they would have done it in Italy. Why waste trains and guards to bring us all the way here to do something they could easily have done there? It doesn't make any sense. They want us to work."

He too feels indignation at this woman who reminds him of Marina. For slowing down the process of getting out of this sordid underground world.

"Hey you," says the small bald man turning to one of the ushers in striped pyjamas. "You know the drill here. What will happen to us?"

"You have a shower. You get some food. You're assigned to a barracks and then you work."

"See! What did I tell you?" The small bald man raises his voice. He wants the entire room to hear what he says. "He says we have a shower, we get some food and then we have to work."

A gust of relief sweeps through the low-ceilinged room, like a sea breeze. As if everyone has finally been allowed to drop a heavy bag they were made to carry. It is not by any means a spirit of acquiescence that prevails but there is a slackening of tension, an increase of hope. Until the lights go out. Women begin screaming again. Children crying. People push at him in the dark. Muttering and crying. Some people are praying. The stench of sweat returns. Then the door at the top of the steps opens. An SS officer peers in. He is silhouetted against a brutal light behind him. He calls out for all the members of the Sonderkommando to leave the undressing room.

"It's okay. We've got her. We've got the gun," the small bald man who has appointed himself as a leader calls out. He holds the Marina woman by her arm. She offers no resistance. The small bald man marches her forward. Towards the door. Accompanied by the half a dozen members of the Sonderkommando who are also walking towards the concrete steps. The door is flung open on a blinding glare of searchlights. There are SS men in steel helmets. Some with dogs. Two machine guns have been set up. The Jewish man holds out the pistol by the barrel. The SS officer strides down the steps into the pillared changing room. He unholsters his pistol. Shoots the Marina woman in the face.

Francesco's body contracts as it absorbs the retort of the gun. His throat tight, like when you swallow a boiled sweet in its entirety by accident before it has dissolved on the tongue. He looks down at the emptied eyes of the woman who reminded him of Marina. The frayed blue-grey circle on her forehead.

The SS begin shouting at the top of their voices. Blowing whistles. He undresses quickly. Everyone undresses with more urgency. When he is naked he watches the mother untie the laces of her little boy's shoes at peg 3372.

Francesco is shoved towards the shower room. In the corridor he is pressed against the people in front. His naked body parts making contact with the naked body parts of strangers. Some people hold a bar of soap and have a towel slung over their shoulder. He has no soap, no towel. The shower room is dimly lit. Its low ceiling supported by concrete columns and hollow iron stanchions. As more and more people enter it becomes difficult not to make physical contact with his neighbours. Still more people enter and he is pressed up against other bodies. Everyone is scared now. There are too many people inside. Everyone is trying to push their way towards the exit. The door is bolted shut. He counts three heavy metal bolts slotting into place outside.

He knows before the first woman screams, before the sweet sickly taste enters his toothless mouth, that the woman who reminded him of Marina was right. He was too quick to judge her. He was unfair on Marina.

31 - April 1944

ATTILA IS DOWN on his hands and knees by the sofa. He has hold of one of the cat's paws. The black and white cat with the mournful eyes. The cat is struggling to free itself. Attila hisses at the cat. Makes clawing motions at it with his free hand.

Marina stands by the door. Dressed in a black satin dress, a few dabs of perfume on her exposed neck and shoulders.

"You do look like you've seen a ghost," says Angelo.

"You're supposed to tell her she looks beautiful," says Attila.

"She does look beautiful. But she also looks like she's seen a ghost. Have you finished tormenting that cat? We'll be late if we don't leave soon."

"We won't be late. I'll drive like the wind."

"He ran over three hens yesterday," says Signor Becchi. "Accelerated at them all of a sudden. The farmer was furious. He was shouting at us and waving his fist. So Attila got out of the car and shot another hen. Told the farmer that if he didn't shut up he'd shoot all his hens. And then his wife. The farmer said he was more than welcome to shoot his wife but not his hens."

"Come on, cat. Hiss one more time. I want to see your fur go up again. What's her name anyway, this cat?"

Signor Becchi blows out another funnel of cigar smoke before answering. "Miccia," he says. "And he's a male."

"Dino, get your camera," says Attila, finally letting the cat go.

"Why? What mischief have you got up your sleeve now?"

"I want to take a picture of Angelo and Marina together. Let's commemorate this evening."

"I don't like having my photograph taken," says Marina.

"One photograph won't hurt you. You don't even have to see it if you don't want to."

Signor Becchi returns to the sitting room with his camera.

"How does this thing work?"

"Much like a gun. Take aim and shoot," laughs Signor Becchi.

"Okay. Stand closer together. Come on, Marina. Show us some enthusiasm. Dino, make Marina smile."

"How do I do that?"

"I don't know. Drop your breeches and wiggle your arse at her."

Marina forces herself to smile. Attila takes the photograph. The benign explosion of white light makes her flinch.

"And another one for luck," Attila says. "Put your arm around her waist, Angelo."

She feels Angelo's hand on her waist. Pressing gently through the satin. The warmth of his palm. The sensitivity of his fingertips. His hand leaves an imprint of heat on her skin after he takes it away. A memory of itself.

"See you tomorrow," Angelo says to Signor Becchi. "And don't forget what I told you."

"Votive candles," he says and winks. He doesn't accompany them out into the hall.

"Do you think old Becchi is offended he wasn't invited?"

"No, he's probably glad. Everyone at this dinner will probably be hanged before the year's out."

"Except the women of course," says Attila, for Marina's benefit.

Marina isn't listening. Her eyes are fixed on the front door. Her ears straining for any noise behind it. She can still feel the press of satin on her waist from Angelo's hand. She thinks she is going to tell him. Prepares the words in her mind. Feels them making the mysterious journey towards her tongue.

Angelo unlatches the door. Holds it open for her.

"You do look beautiful tonight," he says.

She looks at him with irritation before stepping out into the street. There's a car parked directly outside the house. She can see her reflection in its side windows. And the reflection of

Angelo and Attila behind her. Like two phantoms. There is another, more battered car on the other side of the road. It's from behind this car that the two young men appear. She hears the metallic tremor of a weapon being cocked.

"Marina, get the hell out of the way!"

Angelo looks round at her as the first bullet rips through his jacket. Lifts the hat from his head. Their eyes meet for an instant. She sees the knowledge in them. He looks at her instead of going for his gun. The next bullet flecks some moist matter onto her face. She doesn't know the man who has used her name. Has never seen him before. She wants to tell Angelo this. As if it is proof of her innocence.

She isn't aware that Attila has hold of her by the arm and is trying to pull her in front of him. As a shield. She feels she has sidestepped time and might never rejoin the ongoing storyline of her life. There are more harsh sharp echoing cracks. A taste of burning metal in the air. A smell of burning powder. Attila lies sprawled at her feet. Blood seeping through his jacket from the region of his heart.

"Look out!" screams one of the assassins.

She looks round. Sees Signor Becchi has opened the front door to investigate. Is still holding his cigar. Then he is knocked backwards off his feet. His body twists while his feet are off the ground. It is the most graceful movement she has ever seen his body perform.

The assassins shout something at her before running away. Steel-plated boots raising a menacing echo in the empty street. She is aware of faces at windows. Looking down at her. She glances down once at the body of Angelo. He still has a surprised betrayed look about him. Or so she feels. She gives a moment's thought to those two photographs secreted inside Signor Becchi's camera. As yet unborn. Angelo smiling, his eyes bright with expectation, his hand resting on the satin of her dress.

32 - April 1944

"I'VE COME to say goodbye."

Captain Erich Heinkel holds out his hand to Zinnia who sniffs his boots and then his fingers.

"What's happened?"

"I suspect I've been demoted. Probably I have made a few enemies here who want to see the back of me."

"Where are you going?"

"Ravensbruck. A labour camp not far from Berlin. Perhaps it won't be so bad. With any luck I can closet myself in my office and limit myself to my clerical duties. I leave Florence tomorrow. I shall greatly miss it here. And of course I will miss our friendship."

She lowers her eyes, feeling awkward, a little bit mean, for her inability to reciprocate his emotion.

"Your husband was on a transport yesterday. He's being taken to Mauthausen. A work camp in Germany."

Isabella fingers Freddie's dog tags which today she wears around her neck. She is in love again, like an eighteen year old. She knows if she had a glass he had drunk from she would not wash it. Sometimes she holds a fork or closes her hand over a door handle and realises his fingerprints are still there. His smell is still faintly on his clothes in the wardrobe. Or so she likes to think. She can't stop thinking about him. Can't stop sending herself and all her protective instincts out to him. There is a constant pulse of longing to touch him again in her fingers. His atmosphere clings to her skin as if she is wearing him under her clothes.

"He'll be safe there, won't he?"

"No one is safe anywhere anymore. And this is what I want to talk to you about. The SD and the Italian secret police both have a file on you. You need to be very careful. If it is possible I would advise you to leave Florence. Otherwise we might be seeing each other again."

"What do you mean?"

"The camp I'm being posted to is mainly for women. It's not out of the question that you are being watched. You're not involved in any resistance activity, are you?"

She has another appointment with the red book man and then the young woman at Porta Romana this afternoon.

"No," she says.

"Good. Word is the Allies will liberate Florence before too long. Perhaps by the autumn at the latest. You just have to hold out until then."

She is more nervous as a result of Erich's warnings (she still recoils from calling him Erich in her mind) when she prepares to leave for her appointment. She wonders if it might appear suspicious that she is wearing a coat because finally, after the interminable winter, there is a whisper of spring in the air.

Today's first appointment is outside the Brancacci Chapel. She then has to pick up a British wireless set at Porta Romana and hide it in her studio until Marcello comes to pick it up. The most dangerous thing she has had to do to date.

Zinnia stops and sniffs at walls every ten yards or so and Isabella is able to casually look around and assure herself she is not being followed. There are some nuns in Piazza del Carmine. Returning to the convent with brown paper parcels. Jewish women and children were hidden in this convent and the Nazis arrived in the middle of the night. It was said the Mother Superior refused to allow any men on the premises and there was a scuffle. She imagines how terrified these nuns must have been. She is watching the nuns disappear into the yellow ochre building when the man with the red book arrives. He is wearing the large sunglasses again. His thin lips stretched tight over his teeth. This time she remembers to keep the matchbox he hands her when she asks for a light. She watches him walk away and then heads off towards Porta Romana holding onto the matchbox inside the pocket of her yellow coat.

The same girl waits for her by the market stalls outside the gate at Porta Romana. The beautiful girl as thin and graceful in her movements as a dancer. Were Isabella a man she would fall in love with this girl. She has long black hair and a breeze gusts the scent of her hair to Isabella. The girl puts down the suitcase and kneels to stroke Zinnia. Pleasantries are exchanged about the dog. Isabella tries to think of something else to say. To detain her a little longer. In the hope another gust of wind will arrive. They say goodbye. Isabella picks up the weathered brown suitcase. She is taken aback by how heavy it is and grimaces. Zinnia tugs at the leash and it is difficult for her to walk at Zinnia's pace with the weight of the suitcase straining the muscles in her arms and shoulders. She does her best to appear nonchalant but the physical exertion of carrying this weight makes her feel conspicuous.

When Zinnia is squatting down beside a lamppost near the gate to the Boboli gardens, a middle-aged man with an officious moustache hiding the edges of his mouth suddenly appears. He is wearing the Republican Guard uniform. His ballooning trousers tucked inside black boots. He stops and sidles down onto his haunches beside Zinnia. "What's her name?"

"Zinnia."

"How old?"

"I don't know. She was a stray. Followed me home one day."

"Why don't I give you a hand with that?"

"It's no problem. I'm nearly home."

"I insist." He takes the suitcase almost by force. "Mamma mia, this is heavy. What's inside? Gold bullion?"

The smile she gives him is so strained she sees it in her mind's eye as more of a gargoyle grimace.

They begin walking side by side on the narrow pavement. Many of the shops are closed. Iron grills pulled down. Green shutters fastened in the apartments overhead. As if everyone is hiding.

"I see you're married. Happily?"

"Yes. What about you?"

"No one will have me. What does your husband do?"

"He's missing."

"Sorry to hear that. Whereabouts?"

"I don't know."

"Which regiment was he in?"

She claws about in her mind for the memory of a regiment someone might have once mentioned to her. "Is it the 41st Infantry Division? I'm a bit of a scatterbrain when it comes to this kind of thing."

"They fought in France, Greece, Yugoslavia and Albania."

This man is making her feel more uncomfortable by the minute. And either she is letting her nerves get to her or he is becoming more and more suspicious of her.

"Yes, I received one or two letters from Greece and then nothing more."

She assumes he is going to the militia barracks in via Maggio.

"I'm going this way now," she says, pointing in the opposite direction, towards the huddle of people outside the communal baths.

"No problem. It's bad form to jump ship half way through a commitment. That's what disgusts me about the King and Badoglio. How much further?"

"Lungarno Soderini," she says just as she sees Marcello approaching from Piazza Santo Spirito. She watches Marcello's eyes momentarily narrow and his features stiffen when he sees the fascist and watches him grip what she is sure is a gun inside the pocket of his light beige jacket.

"Hello Isabella," he says kissing her on either cheek. "Marcello Santucci," he says, holding out his hand to the fascist.

The fascist salutes. "Sergeant Favara."

"Are you off to your studio?" Marcello asks her.

"Yes."

"I'm going that way so I'll walk with you."

"Marcello can take the suitcase now," she says. "Thank you so much for your kindness."

She sees the fascist does not like this turn of events. As if he feels cheated or tricked. She tilts her head to one side, offers him her most coquettish smile. With an undertow of reluctance he hands the suitcase to Marcello.

They have taken a few steps away when her legs sag beneath her. The damn man has called out to her. She looks at Marcello before turning round. His face is strained and his hand is gripping whatever it is in his pocket.

"I hope your husband gets home safely," the man calls out when she turns to face him.

33 - April 1944

THE SCREECH and hiss of the train braking yet again. The iron grinding. This time there are German guards with dogs waiting on the platform of a station. Rain falls through the nimbus of the station lights from the dark sky. The sign says Mauthausen.

The pitiless German voices. Always shouting.

Freddie has been in the cattle truck for three nights. Without food or water. *Give us this day our daily bread.* The slop pail stinking and overflowing in the corner of the carriage. Every time someone tried to empty it out of the narrow wired window the slipstream of the moving train gusted its contents back into the carriage.

It is the middle of the night. They are marched from the train station. The guards shout *Los Los*. There is murder in their voices. They tramp through a small town. No sign of life in the ghostly streets. No face at a window. No lights. The rain arrows down in a smoky mist. As if to hide what will happen next. He lifts up his face to lick at the drops.

They are marched up a hill. *Los. Los.* They move slowly towards the lights in the distance. The rain on his face makes him feel he is crying. The heavy reluctance in his legs. As if he is wading through heavy snow.

They arrive at the gate of a sinister fortress. Lights blazing. Soldiers with dogs. A bronze eagle on the gate. *Arbeit Macht Frei* says the black iron latticework.

They are kept waiting in line on a large parade ground between the huts and the perimeter fence. There is another group of prisoners here. All standing in line. Looking cold and forlorn and frightened. The beam of the searchlight up in the tower frisks the parade ground. He sees his breath for a moment in the aisle of light. Mixed in with the swirling rain. The searchlight throws large grotesque shadows over the walls of the barracks. Fingers its way along the overhanging double barbed wire perimeter fence.

It's as if a rip has appeared in the fabric of his life and he has been pushed through to the far side, an alternative reality, utterly severed from and obeying different laws to life as he has always known it.

An SS officer stands on a wooden box. He has a disdainful air. He wears an Iron Cross. Begins talking in German. About rules and the necessity of work. "No harm will come to you if you work hard," he says. "Work is freedom." His speech is translated into Italian and Russian over a tannoy system. The voice over the loudspeaker is broken up by metallic crackles and high-pitched demonic hissing.

Shaven-headed men in blue and white striped pyjamas and berets pass along the lines demanding all valuables and telling everyone to strip naked. They speak in German. They have a green star sewn onto their shirts and carry a truncheon. The SS officer tells everyone that these men are kapos and that they are in charge of discipline. The kapo allocated to his group has a scar from his ear to the corner of his mouth. He looks like a common criminal. A man capable of murder.

He hands over the ring Isabella gave him. He feels immediately weaker without his ring as if it was a part of his body strength.

He takes off his coat. Pulls his jumper off over his head. He looks along the line. At all the other men taking off their clothes. He looks for someone whose friend he might be. Someone whose appearance offers a grain of reassurance. An ally. In the rain which is still falling. Picturesque against the halo of the spotlights and the revolving searchlights. He steps out of his trousers. Pulls down his shorts. He has always been shy of his naked body. Even at school. Everything here is against his will. He stands naked. His hands covering his genitalia. Barely convinced this is really happening to him.

He is ushered down some concrete stairs into a vast whitewashed bunker. The kapo with the scar shouting at them to run. *Schnell. Schnell.* They jog to the far end of the chilling room. Its hollow echoes. Its harsh white flood of light. Here they are shaved. By prominenten, privileged prisoners. One man shaves his head. With disdain. With hurried brutality. Then he is moved onto the next man who shaves his armpits and his pubic hair. A third man slops some kind of disinfectant over him with a brush. His skin screams out. As though he has been stung by a hive of bees. His skin is still stinging when he is marched back outside onto the parade ground. The absence of hair on his head makes him feel a stranger to himself. He keeps running his hand over his shaved skull. More intimate now with the skeleton beneath his flesh. His naked head leaves a texture of bereavement on his palm. One part of his body estranged from another part. He urges himself to calm down. To steel himself against this rising surge of panic.

A few prisoners in threadbare stripy pyjamas walk past. Across a rubbled part of the parade ground. Escorted by a soldier with a dog. They all have red stars on the breast of their jackets. They walk with an odd lurching gait. Arms held stiffly at their sides. Heads bowed. Eyes on the ground. Like puppets on strings. He looks down at their feet. At the cumbersome clogs they wear. They all remove their caps when they pass by the SS officer. He doesn't acknowledge them. Not even with a glance.

Freddie and his group are marched into the shower room. *Schnell. Schnell.* He stands with forty or so other naked men in the large sordid tiled room. There is a rasping stench. Some kind of industrial chemical that catches in his throat. Makes him feel nauseous. No water emerges from the shower attachments above their heads. He realises he is avoiding eye contact with everyone. This policy of concealment, of silence is shared by all and sundry. No one wants to be acknowledged. No one wants to be seen or heard in this place. No one wants acknowledgement that they are here. Then the water arrives. Splashes down on his shivering body. It is scalding hot. It makes him gasp and catch his breath. His heart thumps in his chest at the shock of it. His blood fizzing like a belligerent current. All the other naked men disappear behind a cloud of steam. Crying out with the shock of the scalding water. Then the water is suddenly icy cold. Again he gasps at the shock of it. Clenches his fists and grits his teeth against the pummelling of the freezing water. He drinks as much of the cold water as he can. To get rid of the awful taste in his mouth. But it doesn't taste like water.

Back on the parade ground they are kept waiting again. Perhaps another hour passes. He stands naked in the rain. His teeth chattering. He struggles to recognise himself in the thoughts passing through his mind. As if he is dissolving back into an unknown realm of his being. A primitive place of ice and floods and screams and panic.

The kapo with the scar hands him a piece of cloth with a number on it. 57.774. The SS officer steps back onto the wooden platform. He explains the roll call procedure. Everything he says is translated over the tannoy into Italian and Russian. He reads out a number. This is not translated into Italian or Russian. No one answers. Then the number is translated into Italian and Russian. An Italian man answers. He is immediately set upon by three kapos. They drag him from the line and beat him with truncheons. They knock him to the ground and continue beating him until he is coughing up blood. The SS officer tells them that this is what they can expect if they don't obey orders.

They are told to run past a huge pile of clothes. *Schnell. Schnell.* Pick up a pair of trousers. Pick up a jacket. Pick up a beret. At random. If they don't fit they must exchange them afterwards among themselves.

The trousers he has picked up fall down. They are at least three sizes too big for him. They are also too short in the leg. Discipline is lax for the first time. They are allowed to mingle and talk. He is reminded of the day all the newly graduated recruits were left to crew up among themselves in the hangar. He approaches the man whose friend he wants to be. He knows he will not survive here without a friend. He needs to hear the sound of his own voice again. *And forgive those who trespass against us.* To confirm he is still the man he was yesterday and the day before. The man he has chosen to be his friend is in the act of stepping into his stripy pyjama bottoms. He is a good-looking man with high cheekbones. Dark sensual eyes. And an air of self-possession. Except there is a blankness in his eyes, as if he has suspended time within himself.

He can think of nothing appropriate to say. So he quotes Dante. "Abandon hope all ye who enter here," he says. Then he offers up a smile of sorts.

"Yes, someone had to imagine this before it could come into being. We're to be treated like circus animals it appears." The man has a loose effeminate way of making gestures with his hands. He has no fear of exhibiting the delicacy in his nature. A bit like Otto.

"My name's Freddie," he says.

"If I were you I'd lose that look in your eyes. It makes you look like an intellectual. The Nazis don't like intellectuals."

Freddie's hand clasps the waistband of his baggy trousers. If he lets go they will fall down. "The look in my eyes?"

"Try to look less intelligent. Like you're not thinking about Dante. Like you're thinking of a bowl of pasta or a woman's thighs."

He thinks of a bowl of pasta and Isabella's thighs. "Is that better?" he asks.

"No."

For the first time in this nightmare place he manages to smile.

"You're English, aren't you? Why have they branded you as Italian?"

"Don't know. I didn't have any proof of my identity. Or perhaps it was a clerical error?"

"Didn't know the Germans made clerical errors. I don't think they do. My name's Mirko."

"Why are you here?"

"I was in the wrong place at the wrong time. I sat down in a bar. Should have just carried on walking. Old habits though die hard. Next thing I knew there was a roundup. The street closed off at either end. Trucks. The Germans hate us Italians. We betrayed them. Everyone hates us Italians. The Russians, the French. With reason, I suppose. You should try that guy with the bulging buttocks over there. To swap pyjamas with, I mean."

He exchanges trousers with the fat man. This new pair are a better fit but still too large in the waist. He has to hold these up too.

The SS officer is back on his platform. Explaining the drill. A smile twitches at the corners of his mouth. "At the command, *mutzen ab* everyone takes off his beret. At the command *mutzen auf* everyone puts his beret back on his head. And if you don't all do this in harmony I will make you do it again and again until discipline is established."

All this is translated in Italian and Russian over the crackle and hum of the loudspeaker.

He imagines breaking ranks. Rushing forward. Snatching the revolver from the holster of the SS officer. Shooting him in the face. He imagines it so vividly that he begins to frighten himself. As if he might actually perform this act.

Any guilt he feels for bombing the cities of these men is gone.

Half a dozen times they are ordered to go through the pantomime of taking off and putting back on their berets.

They are marched into another building. Here he has to pick up a pair of clogs from a colossal pile. *Schnell. Schnell.* He picks up a pair at random, like everyone else. They are different sizes. One too big. One too small. Now he understands why the prisoners he saw earlier walk with the strange lurching gait. Like puppets on strings. He has to grip hard with his toes to keep the clogs from sliding beneath him. He too is forced to shuffle over the parade ground. Like a puppet on strings.

They are marched into a hut. Hut 11. They are four to every bunk. The fat man with whom he swapped trousers has taken a liking to him. He is called Andrea. A social worker. Arrested for sheltering two Jewish children in his home. Freddie likes him. So he will share a bunk with Andrea and Mirko and a wiry man with a mean mouth whose name he still does not know. They are talking when two kapos drag the man who was beaten for not answering to his number into the hut. Another kapo carries a wooden stool and a length of rope. He makes a noose in the rope. Ties it to the rafters. It is like a piece of well-rehearsed theatre. It is evident they have done this before. The noose is put round the man's neck. But the stool is not kicked away. The man with the noose around his neck can touch the stool with the tips of his bare toes.

Freddie stares at the man's feet. At all the struggle in them to gain a foothold on the stool. His urge to go to the man's aid strains in all his muscles, twitches all his nerves. But he knows that if he makes any move towards the hanging man he will be strung up next to him. Everyone in the hut knows this. So they sit still, in silence. Helpless. Waiting for the man to die. Hating the three kapos. And beginning to dislike the hanged man for taking so long to die.

It takes more than an hour for the man to die.

He does not sleep. He tries to slow down his quickened breathing. As if there is only a limited supply of oxygen, like there was in the cockpit. He feels for a moment the discomfort on his skin caused by the rubber mask. Then remembers he is not wearing a mask. That he cannot remove any of the things that cause him discomfort here. The fat social worker Andrea, whose feet are by the side of his face, is sobbing. He has delicate childish feet with a deposit of dirt on the heels. Now and again there is a splashing noise from the corner of the hut where the slop pail is. Outside the searchlight rakes back and forth across the windows. The dead man's face in all its stricken detail made explicit for an instant.

He is woken by a shrill whistle and guttural shouts. "*Aufstehen. Aufstehen.*"

He was dreaming about Isabella. When his hand touched hers it was a marvel how much restorative intimacy there was in the contact. As if they were wired into the mystery of each other. How much sorrow too. For all the waste and missing shared time. The replenishing touch of her hand. The blood memories plunging him down into depths, heartening him with achievements, shaming him with his inadequacies. When he wakes he feels what it means to have her close again. The way she fitted his body to his in bed before sleep. Her absence is a hollow tunnelling ache in his being. Until he remembers where he is. The dead man still hanging from the wooden beam. The smell of urine and excrement. The imminence of humiliation and terror in the crowded hut.

Like everyone else, he is given a bowl and spoon. The bowl is called *Miski*. He joins the queue outside the hut. Dips *Miski* into the pan of black water. It has a bitter taste but it is hot and for this he is thankful. He collects his piece of black bread. Is about to turn away when someone behind punches his elbow. He drops the bread. Looks down at the ground where he sees a hand snatching up his piece of black bread.

34 - June 1944

ISABELLA IS painting Freddie's portrait from memory. She is trying to create an image of him that she can look at without feeling she has failed him. Tonight there is no electricity. Tonight she is painting by candlelight. Her shadow huge and macabre over the walls and ceiling. Maestro has gone back to the apartment. She is alone with Zinnia.

She hears a vehicle pull up outside the building. She stops mid-stride. Her paint brush with its dab of burnt ochre poised in mid-air. She listens to doors slamming. Steel-plated boots ringing out menace on the sidewalk. An imperious thumping on her building's green door. The steel-plated boots carrying their menace ever closer to the door of her studio. She opens the door before the footsteps reach her floor. Stands out on the landing. Zinnia beside her. She shields her eyes from the beam of a flashlight shining up into her face. Two uniformed fascist militia are climbing the stairs towards her.

"Isabella Hartson?"

"Yes."

The wireless set is no longer here, she reminds herself.

"You're to come with us."

"Why?"

"Shut up and do as you're told."

The boy slaps her in the face. The unprovoked impertinence of the act stuns her. Her instinct is to slap him back. But she remembers that the rules have changed now. This boy has the right to do whatever he pleases. Even in her studio. Even in her sanctuary he can slap her face if he pleases.

"Shall we search the place?"

"No. They'll do that later."

The young boy pushes past her. He has an ungainly way of walking. Stamps down heavily on his heels. As if to make as much noise as possible. As if the world isn't paying him enough attention. He sweeps all her brushes from the table to the floor. Flings her palette against a wall as if it is a stale piece of bread he is chucking away. He picks up a jar of honey-coloured medium. Sniffs it. "What's this?"

It is a humiliation to have to answer his questions.

"It's my elixir," she says.

He grunts with scorn. He turns round the paintings facing the wall. He picks up the nude study of Marina. Shows it to his colleague with a lewd grin. For a moment she thinks he is going to damage it. Vandalise it.

"Are these paintings valuable?" he asks with a note of marked contempt.

"They're valuable to me."

They're all I have now, she thinks.

"Leave the paintings alone, Mario," says the older guard.

She feels thankful towards this older guard. Turns towards him hoping for an exchange of kindness, of sympathy. But he lowers his eyes. Zinnia is sniffing at his boots. He flicks his foot at the dog with a fastidious warning. She watches Mario step on her palette. He doesn't do it on purpose. He lifts a leg to inspect the heels of his boots. Curses. Sneers at her. He now leaves footprints on the wooden boards. Naples yellow, alizarin crimson and lead white footmarks.

She is made to lead the way down the dark stairs. Zinnia follows her, wagging her tail. Isabella tries to send her back. Out on the sidewalk the older guard shuts the front door.

"What about my dog?"

The young boy draws his revolver.

"Don't you dare shoot my dog," she snaps, her voice shrill and unfamiliar to her.

He unfastens the safety catch.

"No need for that," says the older guard.

The boy fires off three bullets anyway. Isabella screams. She launches herself at the grinning boy but the older guard holds her back. Zinnia, tail down, has withdrawn several paces. A cowering silhouette beneath the crescent moon. The boy is either a rotten shot or deliberately aimed to miss.

Isabella is shoved into the back of the white car. She twists back her head but she can't see Zinnia in the darkness. The older guard drives the car. They cross the river by Ponte Santa Trinita after papers have been shown to the German sentry. She watches the shafts of the car's headlights make tunnels through the dark and empty streets.

The car passes the building in via Bolognese where she met with Freddie. Pulls into a courtyard behind the building. She is led up the cold grey stairs. Before they reach the first floor she hears screams. Barking German voices. Dull thuds. More yells. Cries for help. Pleas for mercy. She is led into a large ante-room. There are four men and a woman facing the wall. Standing on tiptoes. Hands held high above their heads. Carità is in the room. Together with a dozen or so other men. Some of these men she recognises. Scarface and Seagull Eyes are both here. Also the German with the ice-cold eyes. They are all excited. Pleased with themselves. They are standing over a man who is curled up on the floor. There is blood in his hair. Blood on his clothes.

Carità looks at her without surprise. A faint flicker of dislike twitching over his fat lips. He is wearing spectacles tonight. He has a white streak in his black hair. Brushed back from his small forehead. She hasn't noticed this before.

"You again," he says in an almost jovial tone of voice. "Give me your bag."

He empties the contents of her bag on the table.

"There's a loft with a window onto the rooftops. Perfect for a radio transmitter," says the older guard who arrested her.

She is suddenly much more frightened without her bag. Without her keys. Her fear makes her feel she is cold. Carità hands her a crumpled greasy bank note. A smug expression on his face. She looks at the banknote and then she looks at him. Perplexed. Until she turns it over and sees the address of her studio is written on it. In her own handwriting. It's the banknote she gave to Fosco.

"You've arrested me because I wrote my address on a twenty lire note?"

Scarface grabs hold of her chin. Grips it in the vice of his hand. She slaps him on the cheek. Hard. It gives her pleasure to slap him. He recoils with the shock of it. He draws back his fist. She thinks it's merely a threat. But he punches her in the face. Holds back none of his strength. As if she is a man. The blow knocks her to the ground. Her body sprawled in a shape that is new to her. The man who punched her grinds the heel of his boot on her hand. Scarface.

Not my hand, she thinks. *I have to paint Freddie tomorrow.*

Scarface pulls her up by the hair. He shoves her across to Seagull Eyes. Seagull Eyes puts his hands on her breasts. Then he shoves her back and Scarface pushes her back to Seagull Eyes. They play this game for two minutes or so. Shoving her back and forth with ever more violent force as if playing some kind of children's game.

"Your address was found in this man's wallet. You know this man?" Carità points down to the man on the floor. The man's body twitches every now and again. Otherwise he is as inert as a sack of corn.

Someone lifts the man's face. Pulls it up by the hair. Blood is seeping out of his nose and mouth. Out of his ears too, she notices. There is so much grotesque alteration to his face that he might have returned from a period of decomposition in a grave. His hands are cuffed behind his back.

She feels a reluctance to disassociate herself from this man. As if to do so is to align herself with these thugs. She wishes she did know him. She is tempted to say yes, I do know him. She has the crazy idea that they might send her to the place they have sent Freddie.

"I doubt if his own mother could recognise him. The state you've reduced him to," she says.

"This, as you very well know, is Enrico Bocchi. Codename, Placido. Except his placid days are over."

Some of the men make noises in their throats which might be laughter.

"He and his band of communist terrorists have been sending messages to our enemies. Messages responsible for the deaths of thousands of our Italian comrades. And they've been sending these messages from your studio."

Seagull Eyes kicks the man in the midriff. His name is Luigi, she remembers. As if one day she might be given the chance to testify against him in a court of law.

"There's never been a radio transmitter in my studio."

Carità sweeps back his hair. "You deny knowing Marina Lozzio as well no doubt."

"No. She lives in the apartment beneath my studio."

"Exactly. And she's a traitor. No doubt the two of you were working with these scum together. Put her in a cell," says Carità. "We'll interrogate her later. And send two men to search her studio."

She watches Carità hand Scarface her keys.

She is led beneath ground. The temperature drops. A guard sits on a stool in the narrow damp corridor. Cleaning his weapon with a rag soaked in kerosene. There is also a smell of coal dust. It tickles her throat. Makes her cough. She is shoved into a cell. There are three women and a young boy inside. The women look up at her with suspicion. She is made to feel she is not trusted. Because she has no blood on her clothes. She sees they are all disfigured. The boy's face is so swollen up that his eyes are barely visible. One of his ears has been mutilated and all the fingers on his right hand are lacerated and broken. He holds his hands in front of him. Brittle lifeless-looking things like curled up dead leaves. His head rests on the shoulder of one of the women. Her face too is bruised and cut. Though not so bad.

She sits down on the cold stone floor. It is smeared with dark blood as are parts of the bare wall against which she leans.

"Bad luck," says one of the women. Her Italian accent is similar to Freddie's.

"Are you English?"

"You'll have to talk louder than that. They've ruptured both her eardrums," says the youngest of the three women. Her bottom lip has been sliced open and there are burns on her cheeks. "She is English though. She was arrested for concealing Aaron here in her apartment. He's Jewish. One of her neighbours ratted on her. The Germans torture Aaron every night and they make her watch. She slapped one of them and he beat her black and blue. Why did you ask if she's English?"

"Because my husband is English."

Isabella looks up at the narrow window high in the wall. Through the metal bars. A yellow light burns an imperfect circle on the black glass.

35 - June 1944

OSKAR EATS the bread and cheese a girl gave him. Eats it under an almost full moon on the uppermost terrace of an olive grove. The air smells of earth root and crushed herbs. The only noise is the piercing chant of mating cicadas. The figs the girl also gave him he saves. As something to look forward to. Every time he thinks of them he can taste the juice as a sweet wetness on his lips. He told the girl what happened to him. "One bullet was this close to my head. I heard it crack in my ear. Then I tripped and landed flat on my face. I think the man shooting at me thought he had hit me and so he started shooting at someone else. When I got up no one was shooting at me anymore."

"You've heard the news?" the girl said. "That Rome has been liberated."

"When?"

"Four or five days ago," the girl said.

He told the girl about his daughter. That he had to get to Florence to see his young daughter. The girl returned with a rusty old bicycle. Her kindness brought tears to his eyes.

Oskar has to keep telling himself the urgency he feels to hold Esme in his arms again is not a matter of life or death.

She will be safe with Isabella, he thinks.

He is not sure he is on the right road. He has to trust his instincts. When he arrives at a fork in the country lane he stops. The sun is hot on the back of his neck. There are some poppies among the roadside grass. And a pleasant baked smell rising up from the earth. The signposts bear the names of places he has no knowledge of.

Left or right?

Both roads look innocent. Peaceful. It is hard to imagine either might lead him to harm. He takes the turning to the left. Skirting an untended vineyard. Within an hour he sees a military lorry appear in the near distance. Behind it a long column of vehicles. On either side of the road is flat countryside. There is nowhere to hide. The road begins to shake as if something monstrous is moving underneath the earth's surface. The handlebars of his bicycle shudder. A breeze blows up across the flatlands. He worries it will sweep off his hat. Reveal him as an escaped prisoner. He clamps the hat down looking over at the driver of the lorry as he cycles past. The driver ignores him as do his two companions in the front seat. He enters the torrent of dust and black smoke thundered up by the lorries and panzers of the endless procession of ugly metal vehicles. The countryside has now lost its innocence for him.

He is excited when he sees the twisted and rusting sign. Florence 6km. The conjuring act of signposts. He momentarily sees Florence glitter before his eyes like a mirage in the desert. He pictures the big toothless smile on his daughter's face. The rush of delight in her young body when she sees him again. Can feel the warm beating presence of her little body in his arms.

Hello, my darling.

Florence looks like home as he cycles alongside the river. He looks across at the succession of bridges, up at the tiers of cypresses, the façade of San Miniato on the hill. Not even the red and black swastika banners draped outside some of the riverside palaces spoils his sense of homecoming. There is a mirage of translucence on the water in which a swan looks etherealised, a divine creature. He wishes his daughter were there by his side to see the magical swan too. He wonders where she is at this very moment. Pictures her in one of Florence's shops. Standing on tiptoes to peer over the counter.

He leaves his bicycle propped up against the wall of Isabella's building. The main door is open. He follows a trail of faded painted marks up the stairs. Higher up the ugly marks resolve themselves into footprints. Footprints descending the stairs. He reaches the door to Isabella's studio with a sense of foreboding. He knocks on the door. It edges open under the contact.

"Isabella?"

The studio has been ransacked. A foxtrot of painted footprints crisscross the wooden boards. Like a representation of madness. Splinters of glass crunch beneath his shoes. Turpentine has been spilled and the smell of it is almost overwhelming. As if the place is about to go up in flames. All her paintings have gone. There is something final about the air of dispossession. It seems as though a year of grief has passed since he was last here.

He knocks on the door below. A woman opens the door a fraction. Peers at him around the narrow gap. She is wearing a dressing gown. Smells of milk and medicine. A woman who has stopped looking at herself in mirrors.

"Do you know what happened to Isabella?"

"She was arrested. A few days ago. Then they came back and started breaking things. They woke us up in the middle of the night. We watched them leave through the window. They took away all her paintings."

"What about the little girl?"

"What little girl? Isabella didn't have any children."

"She was looking after my little girl."

"I haven't seen any little girl here. I spoke to Isabella the day she was arrested. There was no little girl and she didn't mention any little girl."

"You're Marina's mother, aren't you?"

She looks at him with suspicion.

He takes off his hat. Shows her his convict brand. Proof that he too is one of the persecuted. "I've been with Francesco in a prison camp. You know Francesco, right?"

"Poor Francesco," she says.

"Do you know where Marina is? She might know where my daughter is, you see."

"Marina's in hiding. There was some trouble at the house where she worked. The secret police have been here looking for her. They arrested her father."

"Can you give me her address? I promise..."

"She's staying with Francesco's mother. In Piazza Santa Croce. Number 17."

He cycles across the river to Santa Croce. Passing the queues outside the grocery stores, butchers and bakers. There seem to be more Germans in the city. More fascist militia too.

Marina looks pale and tired. There is no longer the blooded female challenge in her eyes. The rustle of arousal her body sent across to his body. She leads him into the kitchen. Introduces him to Francesco's mother who sits like an effigy of herself at the table.

Marina tells him she has not seen Isabella for a long time. She is very attentive to the older woman, he notices. When Francesco's mother says she will go and lie down Marina hugs her.

"You two have made the peace then?"

"Yes."

"I have to go. I must find Esme."

"Oskar, do you think I'm a bad person?"

She stands in front of him in her print skirt. Her hair loose on her shoulders.

He brushes the hair back from her forehead. "Of course not."

"Two men have died because of me. Three if you count Francesco."

"I saw Francesco in the camp. He isn't dead."

"But I've done things I'll have to answer to."

"So have we all. There's a war. It's not your fault."

"I hope you find Esme. I hope that more than anything."

"I'll bring her round to see you. She likes you."

He cycles to Francesco's apartment building. Rings on the bell. No answer. Knocks on the door. No answer. He climbs back on his bicycle. He has no plan now. He scans all the children out walking on the streets as he pedals. Once or twice he thinks he sees her but is disappointed again. He cycles between the Duomo and the Baptistery. Across Piazza Vittorio with its hotels and outdoor cafés. It is while cycling towards the loggia of the market that he catches sight of her. He sees her bear before he sees her. Swinging from her fist. As he cycles past he snatches the bear from her hand. Stops, turns round and grins across at her. He lets the bicycle fall to the ground and opens his arms. When he holds her up to his face she accidentally knocks his hat off. He forgets the significance of this for an instant. Then he remembers. He looks around. Two carabinieri are chatting by the bronze boar. But they take no notice of him. He puts her down and retrieves his hat.

He says hello to Francesco's landlady.

"She refuses to talk to anyone except her bear. She chatters away to him for ages though. Whenever she thinks I'm out of earshot. Always reassuring him that they will get home soon."

"Is that true? You stopped talking?"

She nods. With a solemnity he has not seen in her before.

"But you're going to talk to me, I hope."

She nods again. Parting her lips in a grin.

36 - July 1944

THE WHIRRING drone, the low prowling rumble. Arriving from the south. Setting up a vibration in the walls of the barn that tremors up through his body. Up in the sky the tight formation of glinting planes. Every day now they pass by overhead.

Oskar has to interrupt the story he is telling her. Frequently he is not allowed to finish the stories he begins to tell her. She doesn't seem to notice. As if she expects stories to remain unfinished.

"Come on!" he says. "We have to go to the shelter. And don't forget Napoleon."

"Napoleone," she corrects him.

He climbs down a few of the rungs of the wooden ladder from the hay loft. Beckoning for her to follow him. His arms open to receive her.

Across the yard people are leaving the old stone house built on a slope at the side of the road. Looking up at the sky as they walk or jog towards the cornfields. Some are carrying suitcases.

Esme skips and twirls in her orange dress. Bits of straw clinging to the fabric and her hair.

"Look, there's Aldo with Anna," he says pointing to the blind boy.

She runs over to the other children. The children whose house in Bologna was bombed. They all flutter around the blind boy who smiles. All the children. Fascinated by the blankness in his eyes.

"Suits you," says Anna. She wears the same black dress every day. The same mother-of-pearl clip in her wiry grey hair. She means the white shirt she has given him. One of her husband's shirts. Her husband who was shot by the Germans for no reason. Oskar is ashamed to be German around Anna and these people. It is Anna's home he and Esme are staying in. The stone house that balances awkwardly on the sloping ground. As if about to topple and slide down the hill. Up on this high ground above the long graceful sweep of the valley. Its chequered curves of earth colours with cypresses like sentinels on the surrounding hills.

There are more people in the fields. Arriving from the nearby farms. All making for the concealed wooden hatch between two fields with steps leading down to an underground vault. The shelter the local farmworkers built. Where he and his daughter now spend at least two hours every day with twenty or so other people. While the planes drop their bombs on the nearby bridges and roads.

Down beneath the ground it is more intimate. As if everyone is half undressed. They have to sit in close proximity. Squashed together like things packed into storage.

The man who tells everyone he is an Hungarian aristocrat tweaks his daughter's nose. Esme doesn't like him and turns her face away.

"You're attached to that bear, aren't you? What's its name?"

"Napoleone," she says, mumbling the name with reluctance.

"I won't bite," he says and tweaks her nose again. His lank greasy hair. His half-closed left eye.

"Keep your hands to yourself," says Anna. Still wearing thick home-made stockings despite the heat.

"Excuse me for breathing," he says in his foreign accent. He holds his sharp thin nose between thumb and forefinger. Dirt underneath his long nails.

The first series of muffled thuds silences everyone. The bombs seem to detonate inside Oskar's ribcage. Amplify the beat of his heart in his ears. A relentless barrage. Anna squeezes her hands together. He watches at the same time as realising that he is doing the same. Thoughts are drawn out of him that he does not want. There is an explosion that seems much nearer. He imagines dirt fountaining up from the earth. Branches falling from trees. The woman sitting opposite mutters a prayer. Fondling her rosary beads. Two old men play cards by the light of the acetylene lamp. Sitting on the ground. Indifferent to the cacophony.

"Sounds like Pontassieve is getting it again," someone says.

"If you ask me they're worse than the bloody Germans," says the man no one quite trusts. The man whose left eye is partially closed. As if he is in the act of winking.

"No one did ask you."

"I've heard the Allies have reached Arezzo. They'll be heading towards Val D'Ambra now. We'll be in the middle of it soon."

"The Germans have mined all the roads leading in and out of Pontassieve."

Oskar has taken his daughter to the Tuscan countryside. Made the decision that they would be safer away from the city. He wonders now if this was the wrong decision. The front coming ever nearer. German patrols obsessively combing the area. Looking for deserters. Looking for partisans. Looking for men to dig trenches for them. Mining the roads. Stealing food and livestock. Raping young girls. Or so they say.

The wavering light of the kerosene lamp makes everyone look like ghosts. Emitting a fume of black smoke.

At least they are too busy to hunt for us Jews now, he thinks.

The daily bread ration is now the size of his daughter's hand. He no longer has his ration card. Is dependent on the charity of Anna. She makes them watery soup every day. Feeds all the eleven people she is giving shelter to in her house. She gives his daughter little treats. Cherries. Figs. A peach. A slice of rice or chestnut cake.

They are eating outside on the long wooden table later that evening. The moon is full. The sound of crickets all around. One or two fireflies with their flashing green fairy light that Esme always chases after. Then there is a scuffling noise. And the man who no one quite trusts appears out of the darkness. He is wearing a straw hat no one has ever seen him wear before. He acts as though he is expected. Offers no greeting. The expression on his face, cadaverous in the thin light, suggests he is secretly amused.

"Sit down," Anna tells him.

He touches Esme's hair as he walks round the table. Not with affection but deliberately to annoy her, it seems. She flinches and turns away. A look of revulsion on her face.

Anna brings the man a bowl of soup. He accepts it ungraciously. Pours himself a full glass of wine.

"Don't let me interrupt," he says. Showing a mesh of chewed bread between his gums.

"It seems we've all forgotten what we were talking about before you arrived," says the mother of two of the other children.

"Probably the kind of stuff that would get you into trouble with our German cousins."

"They're no cousins of mine. So you're Hungarian, you say?"

"You don't believe me?"

"I didn't say that."

"The look in your eyes. How much are the Germans offering for Jews these days. Any idea?"

"I'll give you soup but I won't listen to that kind of talk at my table."

"Just curious. No need to snap my head off."

"They've got more pressing things on their minds at the moment anyway. Like the imminence of being routed."

"They've got a secret weapon. Haven't you heard? They destroyed London and the whole of the south coast of England yesterday. It was on the radio. It's a bomb that flattens everything within a twenty mile radius." He makes an unpleasant noise. Lifts up his hands. Enacting a sweeping explosion.

"On German radio."

"Swiss actually."

He pours himself another full glass of wine. It splashes over the rim of the glass onto the table.

The women take their children off to bed. Oskar lifts his daughter up into his arms and carries her across the yard towards the hayloft.

"What is it you don't like about that man?"

"You don't like him either," she says.

"It's okay. You're probably right not to like him."

He recites another story for her. Another story that will have a happy ending. About woodland fairies. Except she falls asleep before he gets to the end. He creeps back down the ladder. Returns to the table. Anna and the mother of the other children are still sitting there.

"Where's our dubious Hungarian friend gone?"

"Wandered off. No thank you. No nothing."

Heads tilt up in unison at the sky as the metallic insect drone of a solitary plane becomes a louder noise than the chant of the crickets. Across the valley two prongs of light sweep in arcs across the sky. Pencil strokes of smoky light that cross and recross. Like some kind of mating dance. A flare lights up the whole sweep of countryside. A beautiful etching in silver and black. The plane passes overhead. The glasses on the table vibrate.

"Look!"

"Hey!" Oskar calls out. He gets to his feet. The Hungarian man stops in his tracks in the shadow of the barn.

Oskar walks over towards him. Stops within ten yards of him. The man is holding his daughter's bear by the ear. At first it is like an hallucination. The sight of this man holding his daughter's bear by the ear. In his right hand the man holds a serrated knife. He brandishes it. Snarls. Unsteady on his feet.

"Esme!" he calls out. "Have you hurt my daughter?" Anger makes him feel he is standing on mattress springs. The muscles in his legs clenched tight. He is about to charge at the man, his blood roused, when he hears his daughter call out from inside the barn. She appears at the entrance. Her nightshirt gleaming white against the thick shadow.

"He's stolen Napoleone," she says. A sob in her voice.

"Are you mad? Stealing a toy bear."

"Your daughter doesn't like me. Who does she think she is?"

"She's a child."

"You're just a pair of dirty Jews anyway."

He throws the bear to the ground. Walks away.

He lets the man walk away. He picks up Napoleone and hands him to Esme. Lifts her up in his arms, as if to touch her is to stop her vanishing.

There is a popping sound in the distance. Streams of flickering red and orange light shooting up into the sky across the valley. They follow a graceful curve. Breaking up finally into fiery red dots. Then there is a fountain of golden rain showering down towards the white smoke on the ground.

37 - July 1944

ISABELLA SHARES a cell with two other women. Flaking white walls stained with ugly brown damp patches. Covered with inscriptions. Doodles and names and dates. In the women's prison of Santa Verdiana. The prison is run by nuns. The nuns bring the prisoners food in tin bowls. The nuns turn out the lights at night. The Mother Superior is called Ermelinda. Ermelinda was hard to like at first. So severe. So curt. But Ermelinda has revealed herself to be an admirable and kind woman. Isabella likes her very much.

It is usually quiet in the women's prison. There are none of the piercing screams and shrieks of that other place. No one is tortured here. Sometimes there is a fight. Two women yelling insults at each other. But the nuns always break up fights quickly.

Isabella often holds her chewed and blackened wooden spoon. Because she is used to holding a paintbrush all day and this wooden spoon is the only thing she owns in the cell. The only thing she can hold and twirl in her hand. She is still wearing her blue painting smock.

The map of cracks on the wall becomes as familiar to her as the lines on her palm. At times she thinks maybe the mystery of her fate is encrypted into them.

Amelia, one of her cellmates, is nineteen. She is not very pretty. But she is radiant with young life. Isabella often studies her face. Wondering how she might paint it to capture the girl's lovely ebullience.

"I was arrested by an old classmate of mine," Amelia told her. "A girl my age. Neither of us could quite believe what was happening. It didn't seem that long ago that we were sitting in the same classroom gossiping about boys. She took pity on me afterwards and tried to put in a good word to Carità for me.

Didn't do any good. I was beaten every day for over a week. My crime was to have incited a boy to hang a red flag from a tree. Which wasn't even true. This boy is a bit touched in the head. I knew him vaguely. Then when they brought him in and he saw me all beaten and bloodied he denied it. Said he had mixed me up with someone else. But that didn't make any difference. They accused me of all sorts of other things. Of running messages for the communists. Distributing illegal newssheets. They kept showing me photographs and asking if I recognised any of the people. There was one fascist brute. Ugly beast with a scar and cruel lines around his mouth. I wish I knew his name. He and this young boy stripped me naked. I thought he was going to rape me. I'm still a virgin, you know. But he didn't rape me. Do you know what he did? He started burning my pubic hair with his cigarette. Until some German SS officer came in. One of those elegant cruel Germans. And barked at him to stop."

For an hour every day they are allowed to walk in the large courtyard. Isabella holds up her face to the warm sun. It is a moment she looks forward to. Sometimes the scent of the flowering lime trees reaches the yard. Here in the yard Amelia has pointed out to her the famous inmates.

"That's Tosca. She tried to kill Carità in one of the cafés by planting a bomb under a table. Except the bomb was spotted and she was arrested. They beat her so badly she was in intensive care for a while."

There is also a Jewish woman with small two children. The two children are great favourites with all the women. With the nuns too. Everyone wants to hold them. Wants to be the focal point of their innocent happy gaze. Then one day two SS officers arrive and take away the woman and her children. Everyone is depressed that night. Not least of all the Mother Superior.

There are rumours they are all to be transported to Germany.

The Mother Superior gives her a pencil stub. She draws Amelia's portrait on the wall of the cell. Draws Amelia in several different poses. Draws her while the air raid siren howls. Until she exhausts the lead in the pencil.

She tells Amelia about her life. About her early childhood in the Tuscan countryside. About Maestro and Fosco. About Max. Finally about Freddie. In the dark of the cell after lights out. Tells her the detail of her marriage that most perplexes and pains her. That her husband wasn't able to make love to her.

"I thought all men were ravenous for sex. Wanted it all the time."

"Not my husband. Our marriage is still a work in progress."

"Did you ask him why?"

"No. I never quite had the courage. I always pretended not to mind. Pretended I hadn't noticed anything was wrong. Then I began to feel it was my fault. Sometimes when I was out, perhaps on a tram or a train, I used to look at people and imagine them naked. It seemed so odd that everyone had genitalia under their clothes."

"I think that sometimes."

"Do you? Thank heavens for that! I thought I was a bit mad. Most of the time we do everything possible to hide this fact and yet there it is, with us all the time."

They both burst out laughing.

"The cannons sounded nearer today."

"I know."

Then, one night, the beautiful girl Isabella would fall in love with were she a man arrives in the cell. Her contact at Porta Romana. Her clothes are filthy, her hair is matted and there are cuts and bruises on her face. But she is still beautiful. Her name is Giuliana. She and Giuliana talk all the next day. They promise to be friends when the war is over.

"I've never had a really good female friend," Isabella says, out of earshot of Amelia, feeling a bit guilty. "It's always bothered me."

"Now you've got me."

A few days later Giuliana is taken for more questioning at the building in via Bolognese where the torturing takes place. She doesn't return.

Isabella begins to think she might be losing her will to live.

She is bitten by mosquitoes at night. For the first time in her life she envies mosquitoes. She envies them their wings.

Then, one night, she is startled by shouts. She sits up on her thin straw mattress. A fascist official in uniform stands on the other side of the bars. Ordering Ermelinda to unlock the door. Isabella instinctively retreats to the far corner of the cell. These night-time intrusions usually mean a spell back in the ugly building in via Bolognese where the torturing takes place. Women are often taken back there. And then return with new marks on their faces and bodies. Except Giuliana. Giuliana did not return.

"It's all right," says the large figure of Ermelinda. "He's not a fascist. He's a partisan in disguise. They've organised your escape. Quickly. Everyone out."

At the entrance the two real fascist guards stand with their hands on their heads. Watched closely by a man in a German uniform with a revolver. No one is who they pretend to be. Isabella passes through the gate. Together with twenty or so other women. Out into the dark deserted street. Dusted with a sheen of moonlight. Free again.

"You're all on your own now," says the man dressed as a fascist. "And don't go home. That's the first place they'll come looking for you. And split up too."

She walks away. Feeling the absence of any bag slung over her shoulder. The absence of any keys in her possession. She walks until she is standing opposite the English cemetery. High on its walled island of cypresses. She has the world to herself. There is a sense in the early morning stillness that everything might be begun from scratch. It is another of nature's deceptions.

38 - August 1944

THE GERMAN soldier jabs his rifle towards him. The German soldier in his khaki uniform. His scrimmed helmet.

"Communist? Bandit?"

Oskar shakes his head. "Father," he says. Resting his palm on Esme's head.

"Ah. Beautiful little girl. I take with me. For the luck."

He wonders what he would do if this German soldier really did try to take Esme away. He shifts his weight from one foot to the other.

"Just I joke."

The other German soldiers are carrying things out of the house. Mattresses, blankets, linen, towels, crockery, tools, food. Everything they find, it appears. Behind them the sun is setting over the receding hills. The Germans load everything into the back of the lorry. Now and again looking up anxiously at the sky where planes have been circling all day. Dropping bombs. Swooping down to machine gun the roads. These other German soldiers are not like the joking German soldier who stands guard over the inhabitants of the house. These other Germans are jumpy and pale and dirty. They smell of sweat. They shout orders with hoarse voices.

"No good here. Too high. You go down," says the joking German. "Leave house. Good luck." He gives Esme a dented tube he takes out of his lapel pocket. "Cheese," he says. "No chocolate. Sorry."

The lorry drives off down the road. Oskar watches it disappear around the bend.

"Was he a good bad person?" says his daughter.

"Yes. Try the cheese. Unfasten the cap and squeeze out some onto your fingers."

She does what he tells her. Screws up her face when she licks up a dab of the pale yellow paste on her fingers. Adding some theatre to the act of expressing dislike. "Yuk. It's disgusting."

"That's what the bad people eat."

"I'm glad we're not bad people."

The arrival of the German soldiers took everyone in the house by surprise. Even though they knew the local village was looted earlier today. A farmer shot for arguing over the theft of his cow. Five men hung. From olive trees near the church. In retaliation for the murder of a German soldier by the local band of partisans. One of the hanged men was the man no one quite trusted. The man who wanted to steal his daughter's bear.

All the adults return to the house when the Germans leave. To pack their bags. It has been decided to move down into the valley until the shelling stops. To sleep out in the open. In the woods.

"I don't like all these bangs."

"That's why we're leaving," he tells his daughter. "To get away from the bangs."

There have been explosions all day. Even more than yesterday. The Germans mining the bridges, railway viaducts and tunnels before retreating. So it was speculated. Today shells are screaming over the valley. Over the stone house sitting awkwardly on its slope. One shell landed in a neighbouring field. Hollowing out a crater amongst the corn. Dust was shaken down from the beams of the barn. The air above their heads is whistling with hot flying metal. He has a sensation of crouching down inside himself all day. Making himself smaller. He tries to make a game of the dull boom and thud of cannons. Making her count how many seconds pass between the firing of the cannon and the explosion of its shell.

"Twelve," she says, triumphantly. Then she looks up at him. Confused. Not sure what this means. Expecting him to tell her. To reveal the secret of another of life's mysteries.

They have also counted the planes in the sky together.

"Thirty-seven. Thirty-eight."

The smaller ones swoop down low. In the near distance. Accompanied always by a higher pitched noise. And then the rat-a-tat-tat. Like glass marbles shaken in a box close to one's ear. And small puffs of white smoke which quickly turn black. Like a magician's trick.

Anna emerges from the house. Anna looks like she is wearing unfamiliar shoes. Her body has none of its usual poise. He sees she is crying. All her jewellery has been stolen. The children stare at her. Solemn faced. Unaccustomed to seeing tears slide down Anna's cheeks. Oskar offers to carry the suitcase she holds. Her deeply-tanned round face without its usual jovial crinkling of folds. He takes the case. It isn't at all heavy. He wonders what's inside. Then he pictures his apartment in Paris. The things he would take if he thought his home might no longer be there the next day.

Eleven people walk in a straggling line across the fields. Towards the woods lower down in the valley where they will spend the night. The children are excited. Skipping and twirling. Running ahead. Doubling back. Pushing and shoving each other. The noise of the cannons and the planes is of no more importance to them now than the noise of a threshing machine or the barking of a dog.

They traipse deeper along a track through the undergrowth of the forest. As the trees thicken other people start appearing. Anxious expressions on their faces. Everyone talks of what has been stolen from them. Of who has been killed. Everyone wants to know what will happen next. They arrive at a clearing around a stream. There must be about a hundred people gathered there. The children grow still more excited. It is dark now. The croaking of frogs is louder than the bangs. Some of the people Oskar recognises. There is the couple whose house further along the road was destroyed by a shell. The wizened little man who made the partisans bread. A family has even brought their livestock with them. Some children are splashing each other in the water. He sends Esme off to play with them.

He sits down by the water. Takes off his shoes that have flapping soles. There are holes in his socks. He has been wearing the same pair of socks for at least two months now.

When he looks up he sees Aldo, the blind boy. Three women form a ring around him. Touching him as if he is the image of a saint. Brushing bracken from his hair and sleeves, stroking his cheek, straightening his shirt.

Sitting by the stream while the water moves the moon this way and that, never very far, he imagines telling his wife about this. Imagines they are lying together in the dark.

"The overwhelming feeling there by the stream was one of virtue. People were pared down to what was generous, selfless and clean in their natures. When we were staying in a church by the sea the priest there spoke about war bringing forth miracles. About war not just as horror and deprivation. But of it creating moments, unrepeatable in peacetime, when it spurs an intimacy of fellowship that makes you feel proud of the human race. That's what I felt in the woods, by the stream. That there's a deep compulsion in the human spirit to overcome the selfish antics of the I in us. War, grindingly, shifts one's perspective from I to we. Never again will many of us feel our lives so interdependently entwined as we do in these times of war. Never again will someone else's loss or gain become such an integral part of our own store of resources. It seems to me that it is one elusive and expensive emotion that makes this reciprocity of care possible. An emotion that is difficult to find when one feels in control of one's destiny. It's the emotion in the Bible that no one can quite find the right word for. *And now abideth faith, hope, charity, these three; but the greatest of these is charity.*"

He throws a small stone into the water. Watching the ripples gently tug at the moon on the water. Laughing at himself a bit for his pompous silent outburst. He looks up as more planes fly low overhead. He lies on his back. Looking up at the night sky. The sky lights up with coloured smoke. A breathtakingly beautiful colour. Somewhere between orange and red. All of a sudden he and all his companions by the stream are singled out in the startling revelation of this bright coloured light. He looks over at Esme. Esme sits wrapped up in her own arms, as if miming loneliness, but not to him, to the stars above the bright coloured smoke.

The next morning he wanders off with Esme. To look for

peaches. After twenty minutes or so there is an orchard. He has to climb up into the tree to pick the peaches. Stands in the fork between two branches. She stands beneath him. Marvelling at him. He leans down. Takes hold of her wrists and swings her gently back and forth. Almost losing his balance. Then he stops swinging her. He can hear bells. A mad clanging of bells.

"Can you hear the bells?" he asks. "The bells are saying that the bad people have gone away."

39 - August 1944

THERE ARE numbers and arrows painted in different coloured paint on roads and walls. As if there's some kind of game going on in the city. A treasure hunt. There are notices on the city's walls. Ordering all residents in certain areas near the river to evacuate their homes. Within twenty-four hours. There is a gathering of people around each of these notices. The people debate and speculate. The bridges have been mined, people say. They're going to blow up the whole city, people say. Isabella walks away. Not knowing what to think. There is no electricity. No one can listen to the radio. There are no newspapers. No one knows what's happening. Even though the war is now happening on their doorstep. The explosions of cannon and mortar fire beyond the city's cradle of hills growing ever louder.

And then it starts snowing. In August. She looks up with an almost fearful disbelief. White flakes fluttering down from a clear blue sky. She realises it is paper. Thousands of pieces of cascading paper. A plane is dropping leaflets on the city. They fall down on the roads. On the roofs. On the piles of rubbish already heaped on street corners. She picks up one of these leaflets. It is a message from the English. Telling the Florentines to do everything in their power to stop the Germans from blowing up the city. *It is vital for the Allied troops to cross Florence without delay to complete the destruction of the German forces in their retreat northwards.*

"If the Germans didn't intend blowing up the bridges they sure as hell will now," an old man says.

Her studio is near but not in one of the areas designated for evacuation.

She was told not to return to any addresses known to the Italian secret police. But after one night sleeping in the English cemetery and another in the station with thousands of refugees and no change of clothes and no toothbrush and no money she decided to throw caution to the wind. It was incomprehensible to her that the authorities would give importance to her whereabouts.

So she crept back into the building like a child playing hide-n-seek. The lock on the door was broken. She could hardly believe her luck. She only had to give a gentle shove for the door to open. Her door.

Inside it was as if a battle has been fought. Her inner sanctuary vandalised. The flash of broken glass on the wooden boards. Crunching beneath her feet. Her sketchbooks lying open on the floor. Her drawings smudged and stained. The red, yellow and white bootprints. All her paintings gone. She picked up Pliny the Elder, the skeleton, and stood him upright again. The rattle of his bones making her aware of her own bones, the hidden structure of her body. *As I am so you will be.* She stood in the middle of her studio. Accustoming herself to what she saw. Trying to make it credible as if only then will she become credible to herself again. It was like looking in a mirror and seeing no trace of her own reflection in the glass.

Afterwards she spent the day searching for Zinnia. Asking in all the shops and workshops. The baker was friendly with her again. He now gives her a few slices of the black bread on credit when he has any. All the shopkeepers and neighbours are friendly to her now. Everyone in the neighbourhood of her studio seems to know of her imprisonment. The prevailing idea seems to be that she was some kind of glamorous double agent. Fraternising with Nazis so as to pass information over to the resistance.

On the streets she passes families pulling handcarts heaped with possessions. Pushing baby prams heaped with possessions. Carrying trunks and boxes. Twenty thousand people on the move. So they say. She tells herself she is fortunate compared to some.

She has to ring on her own bell. It doesn't work because there's no electricity. She raps on the green door with her knuckles. Giuseppe is more embarrassed than pleased to see her. He looks even more like he spends the nights sleeping in a field. He takes her aside and tells her there is a family living in her apartment. She realises it is difficult for him to tell her this. This is why he is embarrassed to see her. As if he feels in some way to blame. He keeps saying there was nothing he could do.

"They are evacuees whose house near the train station was destroyed in the air raid back in May."

She raps on the glass door overlooking the garden. The woman is embarrassed and then aggressive when she learns she is living in Isabella's home.

"Don't worry. You can stay. I'd just like to pick up some things. If that's all right?"

The woman nods. Wispy dry hair, hollowed cheeks, stains on her dress. Three children are gathered around her. Looking up at Isabella with a hint of antagonism. She packs a suitcase. Returns to her studio. She puts on a summer print dress without looking at herself in the mirror. The dull thud of cannon fire can be heard in the distance. Flashes of light flaring up on the skyline. Beyond the line of hills. Now and again she stands at the window to watch.

She goes out again and meets Marcello by the river, opposite the chalk white church of Ognisanti.

"How was prison?"

She makes a face.

"At least now no one thinks you're a traitor. Thanks for not giving me away."

"I did."

He grins.

"I did what you told me," she says. "Made up an imaginary meeting. I told them I was meeting Corvo outside the church of San Lorenzo. They got quite excited when I said your nom de guerre."

"I'm flattered. What happened?"

"They drove me there and I had to sit on the steps while they all hid among the market stalls. We waited for you for two hours."

"Ha ha. All be over soon. Can you believe it? No more fascism. Of course there might not be any more Florence either. There's a rumour the Nazis are going to blow the city to bits."

"Did you find Fosco?"

"No. He's vanished along with Carità and most of the other fascist scum. Your old teacher is back in his studio though."

"That makes me happy," she says. "I was worried about him."

"I'm worried about you. Are you eating?"

"Not much, no. I've got no ration coupons and no money."

He takes out his wallet and hands her two fifty lire notes. "You earned it. Not that it's much use."

When she returns to her studio Zinnia is waiting for her at the foot of the tabernacle to the Virgin Mary. She wants to shout out loud with joy.

"Did you pick up my smell?"

Zinnia is all skin and bones. She wags her tail for a second or two then the effort seems to exhaust her. Isabella lifts her up and carries her up the stairs.

The next morning she turns on the tap. To wash her face. No water comes out.

Later she goes outside. There are women out in the streets with saucepans and demijohns. Some kneel on the pavement. Getting water from underground hydrants. She goes home to get a saucepan. Copies all the other women.

She had planned to visit Maestro today. But there are new notices. Severely forbidding everyone to leave their homes or even open their windows. Anyone seen outside or at a window, the notices say, will be shot.

Nobody is allowed to leave their house or open a window for three days. She lives behind closed shutters. The temperature is up in the nineties. The heat suffocating. Mosquitoes buzzing in her ears. Stealing her blood. There is no water. No gas. No electricity. The guns continue to pound in the distance. Perhaps coming a little closer. She and Zinnia eat nothing but a watery pea soup for three successive days. Given to her by Marina's mother downstairs. She barely recognised Marina's father the first time she saw him after her imprisonment. So pale and speechless. He too held by Carità's thugs. She learned Marina is in hiding. Somewhere in the country.

The first of the mine blasts lifts her bed into the air. Brings all the books crashing down around her from their shelves. The explosion is like a volcanic eruption, like something emanating from deep below the earth's crust. She feels she has been moved to a different centre of gravity inside her body. Her body a stranger to her. She gets out of bed. Zinnia is cowering under the bed. She refuses to come out. Isabella walks barefoot over the wooden boards of the attic room above her studio. She has to feel her way forward, as though moving down the carriage of a speeding train. She is half way down the ladder when the next explosion arrives. It throws her to the floor. Seeming to detonate deep down inside her. Jolting her heart. Shattering her eardrums. A warm blast of air hits her in the face. In the chest. Plaster falls down from the ceiling. A window flies open. The glass shattering. The whole building rocks on its axis. She crouches down on the floor. Wraps her arms over her head. There is dust in her hair. The stink of rubble dust. Of acrid black smoke. When the reverberations die down she can hear children crying. Dogs whimpering. She wants to open the shutters. Wants to see. It is more frightening not to know what is happening.

Every new explosion makes her scream. There are so many explosions she soon loses count. Each one is the most primordial and sundering noise she has ever had to endure. Each one makes her skin go raw. As if splinters of glass are being rubbed into her bare flesh. It is almost a miracle when silence returns to the world, like the end of excruciating physical pain.

She wakes up to hear voices. The taste of dust in her mouth. Grey powder on her hands and arms. She turns on the tap. No water. She peers through the slats in the shutters. Outside women are talking to each other from one window to another.

"I thought it was the end of the world."

"Are the British here?"

"I don't know. Have the Germans gone?"

She and Marina's mother go out together. Each carrying a saucepan. They walk along the river. A ghostly stillness over the city. A stench of rotting garbage. Of rubble dust. Glass crunches beneath her feet. Breaking up into smaller splinters. She and Marina's mother don't talk. They are speechless at the sight of the devastation of the blown up bridges. The debris of broken white stones and bits of metal that lay across the river. The beautiful bridge is no longer there. Ponte Santa Trinita no longer spans the river. Only two piers and abutments still intact. She can't stop looking at the space where the honey-coloured arches of the bridge used to be. The city has been cut in half. The broken bridge gives her a feeling of horror. Freddie loved that bridge. It was what brought him to Florence, he told her once.

He would know what to say now, she thinks.

But she doesn't believe it is true. She feels sure the bridges will be back as soon as the war is over. That this is merely another effect of the war. Like the absence of coffee and meat. The bridges too will return when the war is over. Like coffee. Like meat. Like her husband.

There are mainly only women and children out on the streets. The children are solemn, grimy, like creatures who live underground.

Many of the buildings by the river have gone. New vistas have appeared. There are mountains of smoking rubble where they once stood. Blackened beams and bricks. One or two walls still stand. Looking exposed, as if caught in the act of undressing. Nothing recognisable except as rubble. The road and pavement are sheeted in white and red dust. On the other side of the road is the body of a dead woman. Lying twisted on the pavement. Covered in the red and white dust.

The queue at the fountain winds down the street for three hundred yards. There are arguments and fights outside the bakery which is closed. The stink of dust and plaster and rotting garbage. Shells begin whistling overhead. One explodes two streets away. She and Marina's mother join the queue for the fountain. Then she notices Scarface in the queue. He sees her at the same moment she sees him as if they share some kind of psychic connection. He looks away quickly but she sees the terror her presence has induced in him. Four men with beards and red neck scarves and rifles have entered the piazza. She knows if she tells them who Scarface is they will shoot him. She remembers when he punched her in the face. When he grinded his heel down on her hand. She is about to walk over to the partisans but something stops her. It is the longing for Freddie's safety that stops her. As if a charitable deed on her part might trigger a reciprocal deed in another distant part of the world.

40 - November 1944

FREDDIE STANDS naked on the dirty ice and snow. Hollow with
hunger. Teeth chattering. Nose streaming. Blisters on his lips.
Black specks dancing in his eyes. His blue and grey body a map
of raw red sores. There is a piercing stab in his lungs. It is as if
there is a pause between one breath and another. A moment of
suspense as if this time maybe the next breath will not arrive.
His feet are black and swollen. Numb. He jogs on the spot. An
idiot dance. His heart knocking at his chest. And so he fears the
worst. Like the others in the line he has watched Poborsky sent
to the group on the right. Poborsky the silversmith. Poborsky
can barely stand up. He looks like he has been disinterred from
a grave. Barely a flicker of light in his swollen red eyes. Hunger
stretching his lips over his blackened teeth in a grimacing
grotesque grin. Poborsky is sent to the right. Poborsky who can
barely stand up. Poborsky who is already decomposing. To be
sent to the right therefore is to be sent to the crematorium. The
chimney vomits out its acrid black smoke without break now.
This is the deduction they have all made. Everyone in the line
waiting to be inspected by the Nazi in the white coat.

A guard is on hand with a Doberman. The dogs trained to
go for the calves. Bring the man down. Then go for the jugular.
He has seen how well trained these dogs are more than once.

It is his turn to approach the man in the white coat at the
table. The man who represents the order they are all forced to
live under. An order which dictates that even if a prisoner is
dead he must still be brought to roll call and counted. Freddie
summons his strength. He has to trick the man in the white
coat. He has to induce the man in the white coat to believe his
life is worth saving. He sees in his mind's eye an image of how
he would like to appear. Sees the man he was when courting
Isabella. Sees the portrait in oils she painted of him. A

handsome young man on the verge of smiling in a fisherman's jumper. He sees in the other prisoners how comic all effort is to look healthy. The slapping and pinching of cheeks to bring some blood up into faces. The biting of lips. It is another source of amusement, of light entertainment to this man in the white coat and the order he represents.

He approaches the table with his head bowed. Fighting the drag of exhaustion in his limbs, the expression of impotence on his face. It is vile, something he wants to spit out of his mouth, that this sordid encounter in the black snow is the most important moment of his life. That if his life is to continue he needs a quirk of benevolence from a man who could not be more hateful to him. He is forbidden to catch the eye of these men. But he risks a fugitive moment's eye contact with the man in the white coat. This man who has the power of a god. He wants to convey that he is a likeable man. A man of intelligence and wit. Though he realises he must appear fawning and despicable. He is tempted to speak in German to him. To show him how well educated he is. To tell him he performs important functions at the camp. It is he who has the numbers of the work force every day and has to check them in and out at the quarries. He who has to go to the chief kapo of each of the six blocks and ask which members of his block are working today. He has learned to do the roll call in Russian and Polish too.

He walks up to the Nazi in the white coat. Stepping forward with a hobbling gait as if there are sharp stones in his shoes. The Nazi in the white coat barely looks at him. He points to the right. Where Poborsky stands, gasping for breath. As if he has a fish bone caught in his throat.

Freddie stands with the condemned men. Looking up at the wide sky. At the grey confetti of ash swirling about above the rooftops of the camp.

Part four

1 - 1946

ISABELLA HAS read about the shadows of people remaining on surfaces after the explosion of the atom bomb. It doesn't perplex her the way it does many people. Freddie's shadow is on her bedroom wall at night. She can sense it in the darkness.

She tacks up a photograph of him on the board. With all the other photographs. Row upon row. Hundreds of them. The faces of people sent to the Nazi camps. The faces of people who haven't come back. She looks carefully at all the faces. The portraits of these missing people. None of them look like they will return. They all have a faded haunted look. Imprisoned forever in that pose. Already ghosts. Even the faces that are smiling. Some of the photographs have a black X pencilled over the face. She recognises Francesco in one of the photos. The photo of Francesco has a black X scrawled over it. It seems a callous way to quash people's hopes.

She talks to the other wives of missing men. They become her best friends. The only people she feels she has anything in common with. They talk about their husbands. Share stories. Often of their husbands in their most fallible and unguarded moments. They all agree that it is usually inadvertently that their husbands arouse the most tenderness. When they can't help themselves.

They don't discuss the things they have heard about these camps. The unspeakable horrors of them.

Every time a train arrives from Germany Isabella goes to the station. They all do. All these women whose husbands or sons have not come home. She stands on the platform. Trying to impose Freddie's face on the faces of the men walking towards her. Gaunt grey faces with bloodshot disbelieving eyes.

One day she goes to the office in via San Gallo and there is a black X over Freddie's face. The photograph of him in his flying kit in Canada. She asks the woman at the desk about it. The woman refers to a sheet of paper. Gives her the name and telephone number of the person who reported her husband dead. The telephone number doesn't work. The tone goes dead in her ear. She tells the woman in the office. But there is still the black X over Freddie's face. She takes that photograph down and puts up a new one. A photograph of Freddie in his tweed coat standing outside the church door in Costa Scarpuccia.

When she goes back to the building the woman calls her over. Gives her the address of the man who says he was with her husband in the camp. The man who is responsible for the black X over Freddie's face.

She goes to see the man that same day. His cadaverous face. His unnaturally large eyes. His odd tentative way of walking. As if feeling his way forward with two invisible walking sticks. She has never seen such a thin brittle man. She could pick him up and carry him in her arms. The man who is responsible for the X over Freddie's face. She feels hostility towards him. She can't help herself.

How dare you disfigure the photograph of my husband.

He invites her to sit down in his kitchen. She can't look at him directly. Because she can feel aversion in him to any form of intimacy. An aversion that she brings to the fore by looking at him. She steals glances at him. Like a child intimidated by an adult stranger. She imagines the entire structure of his bones on display under his clothes. The perfect anatomy model. If Freddie looks like this it's possible he has passed her on the station platform without her recognising him. She stores this thought away as another possibility.

"You say my husband is dead," she says with what must sound like cold abruptness. "That he died in the camp."

"I didn't say that for a fact," he says. Only intermittently does he raise his eyes from the ground. His stiff fingers are fattened at the base with purple swelling. "I told them at the centre that I thought I recognised the man in the photograph. An English man whose name I never learned who was with me at the camp in Mauthausen. We were never in the same hut though. Or on the same work detail. I never exchanged a word with him in fact."

Mauthausen. She has formed a picture of Mauthausen. It has become a place she knows well in her imagination. The place in her imagination she most often visits. It is like somewhere she has seen vividly in a vanished dream. She conjures up this dream image time and time again. Tries to locate Freddie there. Tries to visualise and feel his presence behind the high voltage wire, beneath the sentry towers, among the long stone huts, the stinking latrines. It is one of the hardest things she has ever had to imagine. Freddie surrounded by squalor, stench. Freddie forced to obey orders. It makes her realise how strong willed he was. Despite his dandyish air. His self-deprecating smile.

"So you don't know for sure that my husband is no longer alive?"

"Not for sure. No. Your husband spoke German. Am I right?"

"A little, yes."

"Then he is the man I think he is. Because he spoke German he was on roster duty. He was spared the worst jobs. The work in the quarries. He was still alive in January or February of 1945."

"Then what happened?"

"To the best of my knowledge he didn't make it through one of the last selections."

"Selections?"

"When they decided if you were still fit for work or not. You stripped naked and stood before SS men in white coats. They looked you up and down. For about two seconds. They either sent you to the left or the right. It was usually clear which side was which. You'd watch which side the most sickly looking man was sent to and then you'd pray you weren't sent to join him. Though sometimes the SS amused themselves by playing games. They'd send someone obviously on his last legs to what we all thought was the gas chamber line but turned out to be the reprieved group. I was in the infirmary during this selection. But I never saw your husband after that. So I presume he didn't make it through. I was then moved to another camp."

"But didn't you say he had it easy? Why would he be pronounced unfit for roster duty?"

"Relatively speaking, he had it easy. Easier than most. But the SS played games. We were their entertainment. All of us hobbling about on clogs that didn't fit, like village idiots. They took great pleasure in making us look stupid. That was the beginning of the show for them. They made sure we looked ridiculous. And because we looked so ridiculous they could do anything they liked to us. They were the school bullies and we were the weak deformed kid. No one had it easy. We were all virtually starved. We were half-naked in sub-zero temperatures."

"So you think he was sent to the gas chamber?"

She has read about the gas chambers. She has formed a picture of them. She has forced herself to imagine Freddie and these gas chambers in the same frame. But he always refuses to disappear inside. He always refuses to be killed.

"Maybe he caught typhus or scarlet fever or pneumonia. Maybe he just gave up. Do you know what the only consolation was in that camp? That at least if you couldn't stand it anymore you knew you could take your own life by touching the electric wire."

She winces at an image of Freddie doing this. Feeding deadly current into his body.

2

"HE LOOKED like he had come back from Dante's Inferno."

"Those camps were Dante's Inferno," Maestro says. "I've seen the newsreels. If Botticelli had seen those newsreels he might have painted a more convincing Inferno. But you know what I think about Botticelli."

Maestro has returned to a softer, more grandfatherly version of his old self. Still brings every conversation back round to himself but does now appear to listen to what she says. Isabella is climbing the main stairway of the Pitti Palace with him. Before Florence was liberated Palazzo Pitti had become a refugee camp. Florence's homeless, its dispossessed and deracinated, thousands upon thousands of starving filthy wretches were living in its most prestigious palace. It was yet another sign that the world had been turned inside out.

"This man made it seem as though the lucky ones had been killed. As if I should feel myself lucky that Freddie hasn't come back. He didn't seem at all thankful to have survived. And that can only be because of what he went though. And I keep thinking that Freddie must have been through the same thing. And so might be unrecognisable to me now."

"We've all been in the grip of evil. You realise that? Pure unadulterated evil. Evil has always baffled me. Is it a force in its own right or is it merely the good gone bad? Why did Fosco suddenly become a foe? Was he always evil without my realising it? I was cuckolded. Maestro was cuckolded by his assistant. He was like some little demon always flattering me. Sometimes I think it was like we were re-enacting the temptation of Christ with Satan in the wilderness. What was the war if not a wilderness?"

They enter the Palatine gallery. All the masterpieces returned to its bold red walls.

"There it is," he says, pointing to the portrait of St Anthony on the far wall.

"That's mine. That is the fake."

"Yes, I can see that."

Maestro goes up close. Becomes critical of her brush strokes, her fusing of the flesh tones.

"How come no one else has realised?" she asks.

"Because this is the world we're now living in. No one can any longer tell the difference between the fake and the authentic. That's why my talent will go unrecognised. Because no one any more knows what they're talking about. There's your explanation for the death camps. When people cease to be able to recognise truth and beauty nothing in life is sacred."

"It's the only one of my paintings left. The only one of my paintings to survive the war. Did I tell you they think my paintings got mixed up with the really valuable stuff Carità's band took north with them. To think he might have used my paintings to barter for his freedom with. It's almost comical."

"Didn't do him much good, did it? Dead now and good riddance. I haven't told you this but I've decided to go and see Fosco. I've made up my mind. I want to know why he did what he did."

Last month Isabella was called upon to give evidence at the trial of various members of Carità's band. Scarface was one of the accused. Looking at him in the dock it was a wonder to her that he ever had the power to inspire such terror and hatred. He appeared now a weak servile man, a street beggar, unable to look anyone directly in the eye even when pleading for charity. She had to take the stand and recount the details of the night she was arrested with Max. She blushed with shame when telling the court the details of the humiliation they had forced her to participate in. She steeled herself to look Scarface in the eye. He kept his eyes lowered. Three other people gave evidence against Scarface, real name, she finally discovered, Osvaldo Corradeschi. She listened to the testimony of a mother whose son was beaten by Corradeschi. Learning that the son later died in Mauthausen. Her heart raced when she heard the name of that place. Wondering if he and Freddie had ever set eyes on each other, spoken even.

A woman took the stand and told how she was taken from her home wearing only her nightclothes and slippers, forced to leave her five-year-old son alone in the house. She told the court how she was verbally abused and then how the accused made her strip and bend over a desk and stubbed out cigarettes on her genitals. Osvaldo Corradeschi kept his head bowed. Even when the woman began sobbing and shouting at him. Osvaldo Corradeschi was sentenced to twelve years imprisonment.

Isabella was about to leave the courtroom when she had the impression someone was looking at her. She turned round to see Fosco being led to the dock. He was accused of murdering a woman prisoner of Carità's. Giuliana Arditi. Giuliana who was to be Isabella's friend after the war.

A man called Ascanio Falaschi was called upon to give evidence.

"At dawn on July 18th, Giuliana Arditi and myself were dragged from our cells at Villa Triste and forced into the back of a car. There was a fascist guard in the car, Enzo Bernasconi and the informer Fosco Scarafuggi. The car sped off, up via Bolognese. The two men had been drinking and were laughing among themselves while taunting Giuliana and myself. They told us we were being taken to a prison and from there would be deported to a German concentration camp.

Between Pian di Mugnone and Caldine there is a small bridge known as the Ponte delle Tre Stelle. It was here the car stopped. We were ordered out of the vehicle. In a moment of confusion I made a run for it, darting down the bank and across the stream and up into the copse of beeches and poplars. The two fascists opened up machine gun fire and wounded me in the side. However, I managed to escape. I heard further rounds of machine gun fire as I staggered deeper into the woods. I eventually made it to a local church and was hidden there."

Isabella struggled with a sick feeling through the autopsy report of the damage done to the body and face of Giuliana. The biography of harm instigated by each bullet was catalogued in clinical detail. She was made to visualise an eye missing most of its orb, the shattered bone structure of the once beautiful face, exit wounds at the back of the head through which brain tissue - her memories, her secrets, her wishes - had vanished.

In all, Giuliana Arditi had suffered eleven bullet wounds: the three shots in the face were fired at point blank range, the others at an indeterminable range.

She heard that Giuliana had been wearing *a cardigan of black wool smeared with blood at the back and with some traces of blood on the front with several perforations caused by bullets passing through the spinal and right side of the chest areas. A skirt of grey and black cloth soaked in blood at the back and with bloodstains also on the front in the pelvic region. A black silk blouse with patterns of red flowers soaked in blood at the back and on the left frontal part of the chest with various perforations made by bullets including four in the back, three in the middle of the chest and two in the front stomach wall. A white chemise with black stitching perforated in numerous places and displaying several bloodstains. Black satin knickers with a bloodstain at the front. Black leather boots with rubber soles.*

Isabella saw Giuliana more clearly for being reminded of what she had been wearing. She remembered the sensation on her fingers of the crumpled silk when she embraced Giuliana in the cell they shared. Remembered the white chemise Giuliana wore when she rose from sleep in the mornings and stretched out her arms. The black leather boots with the rubber soles lying on the floor by the side of the filthy mattress.

The prosecution counsel maintained the two men had gone on shooting at the woman long after she was dead. There was madness involved in the slaughter. This was not a political act.

Fosco denied shooting the woman. He blamed it all on the guard who had not been found. He maintained he had no weapon. The witness, Ascanio Falaschi, contradicted this. Swore on oath that Fosco Scarafuggi was armed with a machine gun.

Fosco glanced round at her after he was sentenced to death. There was an overabundance of meaning in his eyes but still now she has no idea what, if anything, he was trying to tell her. Except she knows he was not saying he was sorry.

3

HE MET Piero in Linz where the remaining prisoners were taken from Mauthausen when the Russian cannons could be heard. In the camp at Linz they were virtually left to themselves. Then one day there were gunshots all through the afternoon. He, Piero and about twenty other prisoners were marched to a tunnel by two German soldiers. He thought the end had come. He was going to die in a tunnel. But then he realised the German soldiers were no longer there. Someone said the Germans had run out of bullets. Then the Russians arrived.

He and Piero were shuttled from one transit camp to another. Camps run by Russians. Waiting for trains that never arrived. Sick with one ailment after another. Gums bleeding from malnutrition. He was frightened every time he saw his reflection in glass. Unable to recognise himself in the image staring back at him. Another winter arrived. He and Piero were put on trains that went through Hungary, Rumania, Russia and Germany before finally returning to a cattle truck that took them back to Italy. He wasn't as impatient as Piero to get home. He didn't want Isabella to see him like this. His hands trembling, his eyes as shy and nervous as a frightened child. He wanted to stay behind a fence of sorts. Piero is now his fence.

So he has accepted Piero's offer. To stay for a while in his house in Modena. He and Piero know little about each other. Only that they share this desire to hide from the world and talk as little as possible. His most frequent longing is to be back up in the night sky. Hidden from the earth below by canyons of cloud. Stars pulsing in an eternal black night. Sitting at the controls of V Victor with Reg by his side. He thinks he would like to be up in the night sky for the rest of his life.

He is sitting in the back seat of a car. Piero is in the front passenger seat. And an uncle of his is driving. Freddie is finally back in Italy.

The road reflects up a nimbus of heat as the car dips down into another tunnel. Piero's uncle uses one hand to lightly nudge the steering wheel to left and right. Enjoying his nonchalance. Exhibiting it as an accomplishment. The precarious control. Keeping his foot firmly down on the accelerator.

Up on a hill a small medieval town attracts Freddie's attention. It defies him to look away, like a zealous beggar. He thinks that this is the kind of place he would like to live in now. A private town of hardy old stones sheltered from the world below. Somewhere he need talk to no one. Somewhere only one word answers would be required of him.

When he turns his attention back to the road he hears himself shout out in alarm. It shocks him that he still worries for his safety. Fifty yards away there is a white car that has unaccountably stopped in the middle of the road. Piero's uncle slams his foot down on the brake but the nightmare white obstacle is fast occupying the whole frame of his vision like a curtain coming down on a shrinking stage. Freddie's body braces itself for violence. For the twisting and crumpling of pitiless metal. When the collision comes he lets out a gasp before being thrown forward at the seat in front. After a heartbeat he puts his hand to his chest and takes a deep breath. He has survived again.

The car won't start. He sits down on the grass verge at the side of the road. Poppies glowing among the thirsty spikes of grass. The driver of the white car, a wiry-haired man with no physique, is shouting at Piero's uncle.

"Don't you shout at me, you piece of shit." Piero's uncle marches menacingly forward and the frightened old man steps back. Stupid to think men might stop shouting at each other for a while now.

An hour passes before a tow truck arrives. Piero and his uncle sit in the towed car. Freddie sits between the two men in greasy overalls in the truck. He expects them to comment on his appearance but they don't. They are silent.

And so he enters the medieval hilltop town which attracted him but he never thought he would know.

He leaves his two companions. He strolls down a cobbled street in whose cracks lime blossom has collected in drifts. The green shuttered houses look as though their façades would flake off on his hands were he to press his palms to them. He walks down a steep road with shops. He has no money in his pockets. The pockets of clothes that once belonged to someone else. Someone, no doubt, dead now. Then he sees something that knocks all the breath out of his body. It is himself in the window of an antique store. But not the face he now recoils from. It is the face he used to have. He rests his hand on the glass to stop himself from toppling over. He presses his nose to the glass. There he is. Taking shape as himself behind the glass. In his fisherman's jersey. Signed by his wife in the bottom left corner. Isabella Hartson. He shakes his head. He smiles to himself.

4

SHE ADDS medium to the colour she has mixed on her palette. Her palette with its pageantry of firebrand earth colours. She holds a bundle of brushes. Fans them out like a pack of cards and selects one. She squints along the length of her arm. At the choreography of lights and darks on Esme's face. The shadow shapes and submerged order of half tones.

"Bravo for keeping so still," Isabella says.

Esme doesn't reply or move. She sits like a sculpture of herself. This precision of fidelity to the dictates of the moment is part of her character now. She wonders if it was the war that has made Esme so conscientious, so determined to hold her shape. She adds another touch of cadmium red to the colour she has made on her palette, which makes it glisten pink like the fruit of a newly spliced open watermelon. She holds out the long-haired sable brush as she strides forward. She is about to lay down the brushstroke when the phone rings. She frowns. She curses. *Why can't people leave me alone?*

"Stretch your legs," she says to Esme.

"Yes?" she says into the receiver.

"Hello."

"Freddie?"

"Yes."

"Freddie."

"Yes. Freddie."

"Freddie! My darling. You're alive."

"Alive. Yes."

"I knew it was a sign. Where are you?"

"Italy. What was a sign?"

"Where in Italy?"

"What was a sign?"

"Are you not well? You sound strange. What have they done to you?"

"Shaking a bit. I don't know why."

"I'm shaking so much I can barely hold the receiver."

"What happened to your paintings?"

"My paintings? All gone. Stolen. But what do you mean, what happened to my paintings?"

"I've found one of them."

"You've found one of them?"

"Yes. Your portrait of me. In my fisherman's jersey."

"What were you doing looking for my paintings? I don't understand. How did you even know they were missing?"

"I didn't."

"Are you all right?"

"I was in a car crash."

"You're hurt?"

"No. But the car was broken. So I was taken in a truck to this small town. And one of your paintings was in the window of a shop."

"Freddie?"

"So I went inside. I wanted to buy it back but I didn't have any money. What was a sign?"

"You had a visitor two weeks ago. A lovely man called Reg."

"Reg was in Florence?"

"Yes."

"Reg?"

"Yes. He told me lots of stories. He told me what a brilliant pilot you were. He told me lots of stories about you and your crew. He said it was unforgivable of Winston Churchill not to have mentioned the aircrews of Bomber Command in his victory speech. That you've all been made to feel like social pariahs. Freddie?"

"Sorry."

"It's okay. I'm crying too."

The line goes dead.

When Oskar arrives she is still shaking.

"Freddie just called. At least I think he did. Unless I am going mad. Then the line went dead."

"Freddie's alive?"

"He's been in a car crash. What shall we do?" She watches Oskar's hand go to the new wedding ring on his finger.

"What else did he say? Where is he?"

"I don't know. In Italy. I told him about Reg and he started crying. I don't understand why he hung up."

"Probably the line went dead," says Oskar, taking her in his arms. "These things happen. If he called once, he'll call again."

5

FREDDIE SITS down on the warm stone of the top step. Leaning back on the closed door of the church. Wisteria froths over the wall behind which is his home. Its scent brings tears to his eyes. He can see fragments of the tower of Palazzo Vecchio down through the lime trees. So many times was he unable to imagine this moment when in the camp that it seems only an act of intense concentration on his part that now holds it together.

A little boy walking down the slope with his mother turns to look at him. Twists his head to keep him in sight for as long as possible. He sees what he looks like in the eyes of the little boy. A scarecrow. But with tears flooding down his face. He remembers the scarecrow man who stole his identity tags. The man whose corpse Isabella identified as his own corpse. It's all like a prophecy he can't quite make sense of.

When Isabella enters the forecourt he doesn't stand up. She is with a man and a little girl holding a toy bear. He turns round the portrait of himself in his fisherman's jersey. So she can see it. Then a dog is padding over towards him. The dog pushes its nose into his lap. Isabella says nothing. Just stands stock-still on the gravel. Staring wide-eyed as if frozen in time. With her new family.

"The man in the shop recognised me," he says, his voice surprising him. How casual it sounds. How remote from his thumping heart it is. "He recognised me from your painting. So he gave it to me."

Isabella is crying now. She stands on the gravel by the side of the man, crying. He looks from her to the man. Recognises the man now as Oskar.

"Hello Freddie. You remember me, I hope. And this is my daughter. Esme."

Freddie is stroking the dog.

Oskar walks towards him, holding the little girl by the hand.

"I think I know what you're thinking but it's not how it looks. I married Marina. You know Marina. She talks about you. She told me you gave her rides on the handlebars of your bicycle."

"You married Marina?"

"Yes."

"Esme, this is Isabella's husband, Freddie."

"Hello."

"Hello Esme."

"Listen, we're going to leave you and Isabella alone now. But I can't say how wonderful it is to see you well, Freddie."

About the author

Glenn Haybittle is a translator and freelance writer from London who lives in Florence. He currently translates academic books for the Florence University and Italian history books for a Florentine publisher.

The Way Back to Florence is his first novel.

Printed in Great Britain
by Amazon.co.uk, Ltd.,
Marston Gate.